Every seductive, commitment-wary,
rugged and independent cowboy nee
woman to come home to – he ju
not have realised it

CATTL
WOM

Three incredible, popular and prolific
bestselling authors deliver three exciting,
sexy tales of passion.

We're proud to present

MILLS & BOON

Spotlight

a chance to buy collections of bestselling novels by favourite authors every month – they're back by popular demand!

December 2008

Romancing the Crown: Kate & Lucas

Featuring

Under the King's Command by Ingrid Weaver
The Prince's Wedding by Justine Davis

Cattleman's Woman

Featuring

Cattleman's Pride by Diana Palmer
Kiss me, Cowboy! by Maureen Child
A Cowboy's Pursuit by Anne McAllister

January 2009

The Danforths: Reid, Kimberly & Jake

Featuring

The Cinderella Scandal by Barbara McCauley
Man Beneath the Uniform by Maureen Child
Sin City Wedding by Katherine Garbera

Ready for Marriage?

Featuring

The Marriage Ultimatum by Anne Marie Winston
Laying his Claim by Beverly Barton
The Bride Tamer by Ann Major

CATTLEMAN'S WOMAN

Cattleman's Pride
DIANA PALMER

Kiss Me, Cowboy!
MAUREEN CHILD

A Cowboy's Pursuit
ANNE McALLISTER

MILLS & BOON®
Pure reading pleasure™

This collection is first published in Great Britain 2008.
Harlequin Mills & Boon Limited,
Eton House, 18-24 Paradise Road, Richmond, Surrey TW9 1SR

ISBN: 978 0 263 86115 0

064-1208

Printed and bound in Spain
by Litografia Rosés S.A., Barcelona

Cattleman's Pride

DIANA PALMER

To Amy in Alabama

Chapter One

Libby Collins couldn't figure out why her stepmother, Janet, had called a real estate agent out to the house. Her father had only been dead for a few weeks. The funeral was so fresh in her mind that she cried herself to sleep at night. Her brother, Curt, was equally devastated. Riddle Collins had been a strong, happy, intelligent man who'd never had a serious illness. He had no history of heart trouble. So his death of a massive heart attack had been a real shock. In fact, the Collinses' nearest neighbor, rancher Jordan Powell, said it was suspicious. But then, Jordan thought everything was suspicious. He thought the government was building cloned soldiers in some underground lab.

Libby ran a small hand through her wavy black hair, her light-green eyes scanning the horizon for a sight of her brother. But Curt was probably up to his ears in watching over the births of early spring cattle, far in the northern pasture of the Powell ranch. It was just barely April and the heifers, the two-year-old first-time mothers, were beginning to drop their calves right on schedule. There was little hope that Curt would show up before the real estate agent left.

Around the corner of the house, Libby heard the real estate agent speaking. She moved closer, careful to keep out of sight, to see what was going on. Her father had loved his small ranch, as his children did. It had been in their family almost as long as Jordan Powell's family had owned the Bar P.

"How long will it take to find a buyer?" Janet was asking.

"I can't really say, Mrs. Collins," the man replied. "But Jacobsville is growing by leaps and bounds. There are plenty of new families looking for reasonable housing. I think a subdivision here would be perfectly situated and I can guarantee you that any developer would pay top dollar for it."

Subdivision?! Surely she must be hearing things!

But Janet's next statement put an end to any such suspicion. "I want to sell it as soon as possible," Janet continued firmly. "I have the insurance money in hand. As soon as this sale is made, I'm moving out of the country."

Another shattering revelation! Why was her stepmother in such a hurry? Her husband of barely nine months had just died, for heaven's sake!

"I'll do what I can, Mrs. Collins," the real estate agent assured her. "But you must understand that the housing market is depressed right now and I can't guarantee a sale—as much as I'd like to."

"Very well," Janet said curtly. "But keep me informed of your progress, please."

"Certainly."

Libby ran for it, careful not to let herself be seen. Her heart was beating her half to death. She'd wondered at Janet's lack of emotion when her father died. Now her mind was forming unpleasant associations.

She stood in the shadows of the front porch until she

heard the real estate agent drive away. Janet left immediately thereafter in her Mercedes.

Libby's mind was whirling. She needed help. Fortunately, she knew exactly where to go to get it.

She walked down the road toward Jordan Powell's big Spanish-style ranch house. The only transportation Libby had was a pickup truck, which was in the shop today having a water pump replaced. It was a long walk to the Powell ranch, but Libby needed fortifying to tackle her stepmother. Jordan was just the person to put steel in her backbone.

It took ten minutes to walk to the paved driveway that led through white fences to the ranch house. But it took another ten minutes to walk from the end of the driveway to the house. On either side of the fence were dark red-coated Santa Gertrudis cattle, purebred seed stock, which were the only cattle Jordan kept. One of his bulls was worth over a million dollars. He had a whole separate division that involved artificial insemination and the care of a special unit where sperm were kept. Libby had been fascinated to know that a single straw of bull semen could sell for a thousand dollars, or much more if it came from a prize bull who was dead. Jordan sold those straws to cattle ranchers all over the world. He frequently had visitors from other countries who came to tour his mammoth cattle operation. Like the Tremayne brothers, Cy Parks, and a number of other local ranchers, he was heavily into organic ranching. He used no hormones or dangerous pesticides or unnecessary antibiotics on his seed stock, even though they were never sold for beef. The herd sires he kept on the ranch lived in a huge breeding barn—as luxurious as a modern hotel—that was on property just adjacent to the Collinses' land. It was so close that they could hear the bulls bellowing from time to time.

Jordan was a local success story, the sort men liked to tell their young sons about. He started out as a cowboy long before he ever had cattle of his own. He'd grown up the only child of a former debutante and a hobby farmer.

His father had married the only child of wealthy parents, who cut her off immediately when she announced her marriage. They left her only the property that Jordan now owned. His father's drinking cost him almost everything. When he wasn't drinking, he made a modest living with a few head of cattle, but after the sudden death of Jordan's mother, he withdrew from the world. Jordan was left with a hard decision to make. He took a job as a ranch hand on Duke Wright's palatial ranch and in his free time he went the rounds of the professional rodeo circuit. He was a champion bull rider, with the belt buckles and the cash to prove it.

But instead of spending that cash on good times, he'd paid off the mortgage that his father had taken on the ranch. Over the years he'd added a purebred Santa Gertrudis bull and a barn, followed by purebred heifers. He'd studied genetics with the help of a nearby retired rancher and he'd learned how to buy straws of bull semen and have his heifers artificially inseminated. His breeding program gave him the opportunity to enter his progeny in competition, which he did. Awards starting coming his way and so did stud fees for his bull. It had been a long road to prosperity, but he'd managed it, despite having to cope with an alcoholic father who eventually got behind the wheel of a truck and plowed it into a telephone pole. Jordan was left alone in the world. Well, except for women. He sure seemed to have plenty of those, to hear her brother Curt talk.

Libby loved the big dusty-yellow adobe ranch house Jordan had built two years ago, with its graceful arches and black wrought-iron grillwork. There was a big fountain in the front courtyard, where Jordan kept goldfish and huge koi that came right up out of the water to look at visitors. It even had a pond heater, to keep the fish alive all winter. It was a dream of a place. It would have been just right for a family. But everybody said that Jordan Powell would never get married. He liked his freedom too much.

She went up to the front door and rang the doorbell. She

knew how she must look in her mud-stained jeans and faded T-shirt, her boots caked in mud, like her denim jacket. She'd been helping the lone part-time worker on their small property pull a calf. It was a dirty business, something her pristine stepmother would never have done. Libby still missed her father. His unexpected death had been a horrible blow to Curt and Libby, who were only just getting used to Riddle Collins's new wife.

No sooner was Riddle buried than Janet fought to get her hands on the quarter-of-a-million-dollar insurance policy he'd left behind, of which she alone was listed as beneficiary. She'd started spending money the day the check had arrived, with no thought for unpaid bills and Riddle's children. They were healthy and able to work, she reasoned. Besides, they had a roof over their heads. Temporarily, at least. Janet's long talk with the real estate agent today was disquieting. Riddle's new will, which his children knew nothing about, had given Janet complete and sole ownership of the house as well as Riddle's comfortable but not excessive savings account. Or so Janet said. Curt was furious. Libby hadn't said anything. She missed her father so much. She felt as if she were still walking around in a daze and it was almost March. A windy, cold almost-March, at that, she thought, feeling the chill.

She was frowning when the door opened. She jumped involuntarily when instead of the maid, Jordan Powell himself opened it.

"What the hell do you want?" he asked coldly. "Your brother's not here. He's supervising some new fencing up on the north property.

"Well?" he asked impatiently when she didn't speak immediately. "I've got things to do and I'm late already!"

He was so dashing, she thought privately. He was thirty-two, very tall, lean and muscular, with liquid black eyes and dark, wavy hair. He had a strong, masculine face that was dark from exposure to the sun and big ears and big feet. But he was handsome. Too handsome.

"Are you mute?" he persisted, scowling.

She shook her head, sighing. "I'm just speechless. You really are a dish, Jordan," she drawled.

"Will you please tell me what you want?" he grumbled. "And if it's a date, you can go right back home. I don't like being chased by women. I know you can't keep your eyes off me, but that's no excuse to come sashaying up to my front door looking for attention."

"Fat chance," she drawled, her green eyes twinkling up at him. "If I want a man, I'll try someone accessible, like a movie star or a billionaire…."

"I said I'm in a hurry," he prompted.

"Okay. If you don't want to talk to me…" she began.

He let out an impatient sigh. "Come in, then," he muttered, looking past her. "Hurry, before you get trampled by the other hopeful women chasing me."

"That would be a short list," she told him as she went in and waited until he closed the door behind him. "You're famous for your bad manners. You aren't even housebroken."

"I beg your pardon?" he said curtly.

She grinned at him. "Your boots are full of red mud and so's that fabulously expensive wool rug you brought back from Morocco," she pointed out. "Amie's going to kill you when she sees that."

"My aunt only lives here when she hasn't got someplace else to go," he pointed out.

"Translated, that means that she's in hiding. Why are you mad at her *this* time?" she asked.

He gave her a long-suffering stare and sighed. "Well, she wanted to redo my bedroom. Put yellow curtains at the windows. With ruffles." He spat out the word. "She thinks it's too depressing because I like dark wood and beige curtains."

She lifted both eyebrows over laughing eyes. "You could paint the room red…."

He glared down at her. "I said women chased me, not that I brought them home in buckets," he replied.

"My mistake. Who was it last week, Senator Merrill's daughter, and before her, the current Miss Jacobs County...?"

"That wasn't my fault," he said haughtily. "She stood in the middle of the parking lot at that new Japanese place and refused to move unless I let her come home with me." Then he grinned.

She shook her head. "You're impossible."

"Come on, come on, what do you want?" He looked at his watch. "I've got to meet your brother at the old line cabin in thirty minutes to help look over those pregnant heifers." He lifted an eyebrow and his eyes began to shimmer. They ran up and down her slender figure. "Maybe I could do you justice in fifteen minutes...."

She struck a pose. "Nobody's sticking me in between roundup and supper," she informed him. "Besides, I'm abstaining indefinitely."

He put a hand over his heart. "As God is my witness, I never asked your brother to tell you that Bill Paine had a social disease..."

"I am not sweet on Bill Paine!" she retorted.

"You were going to Houston with him to a concert that wasn't being given that night and I knew that Bill had an apartment and a bad reputation with women," he replied with clenched lips. "So I just happened to mention to one of my cowhands, who was standing beside your brother, that Bill Paine had a social disease."

She was aghast, just standing there gaping at his insolence. Curt had been very angry about her accepting a date with rich, blond Bill, who was far above them in social rank. Bill had been a client of Blake Kemp's, where he noticed Libby and started flirting with her. After Curt had told her what he overheard about Bill, she'd cancelled the date. She was glad she did. Later she'd learned that Bill had made a bet with one of his pals that he could get Libby any time he wanted her, despite her standoffish pose.

"Of course, I don't have any social diseases," Jordan said, his deep voice dropping an octave. He checked his watch again. "Now it's down to ten minutes, if we hurry."

She threw up her hands. "Listen, I can't possibly be seduced today, I've got to go to the grocery store. What I came to tell you is that Janet's selling the property to a developer. He wants to put a subdivision on it," she added miserably.

"A what?" he exploded. "A subdivision? Next door to my breeding barn?!" His eyes began to burn. "Like hell she will!"

"Great. You want to stop her, too. Do you have some strong rope?"

"This is serious," he replied gravely. "What the hell is she doing, selling your home out from under you? Surely Riddle didn't leave her the works! What about you and Curt?"

"She says we're young and can support ourselves," she said, fighting back frustration and fury.

He didn't say anything. His silence was as eloquent as shouting. "She's not evicting you. You go talk to Kemp."

"I work for Mr. Kemp," she reminded him.

He frowned. "Which begs the question, why aren't you at work?"

She sighed. "Mr. Kemp's gone to a bar association conference in Florida," she explained. "He said I could have two vacation days while he's gone, since Mabel and Violet were going to be there in case the attorney covering his practice needed anything." She glowered at him. "I don't get much time off."

"Indeed you don't," he agreed. "Blake Kemp is a busy attorney, for a town the size of Jacobsville. You do a lot of legwork for him, don't you?"

She nodded. "It's part of a paralegal's job. I've learned a lot."

"Enough to tempt you to go to law school?"

She laughed. "No. Not that much. A history degree is enough, not to mention the paralegal training. I've had all the education I want." She frowned thoughtfully. "You know, I did think about teaching adult education classes at night...."

"Your father was well-to-do," he pointed out. "He had coin collections worth half a million, didn't he?"

"We thought so, but we couldn't find them. I suppose he sold them to buy that Mercedes Janet is driving," she said somberly.

"He loved you and Curt."

She had to fight tears. "He wrote a new will just after he married her, leaving everything to her," she said simply. "She said she had it all in his safe-deposit box, along with the passbook to his big savings account, which her name was on as well as his. The way it was set up, that account belonged to her, so there was no legal problem with it," she had to admit. "Daddy didn't leave us a penny."

"There's something fishy going on here," he said, thinking out loud.

"It sounds like it, I guess. But Daddy gave everything to her. That was his decision to make, not ours. He was crazy about her."

Jordan looked murderous. "Has the will gone through probate yet?"

She shook her head. "She said she's given it to an attorney. It's pending."

"You know the law, even better than I do. This isn't right. You should get a lawyer," he repeated. "Get Kemp, in fact, and have him investigate her. There's something not right about this, Libby. Your father was the healthiest man I ever knew. He never had any symptoms of heart trouble."

"Well, I thought that, too, and so did Curt." She sighed, glancing down at the elegant blue and rose carpet, and her eyes grew misty. "He was really crazy about her, though.

Maybe he just didn't think we'd need much. I know he loved us...." She choked back a sob. It was still fresh, the grief.

Jordan sighed and pulled her close against his tall, powerful body. His arms were warm and comforting as they enfolded her. "Why don't you just cry, Libby?" he asked gently. "It does help."

She sniffed into his shoulder. It smelled nice. His shirt had a pleasant detergent smell to it. "Do you ever cry?"

"Bite your tongue, woman," he said at her temple. "What would happen to the ranch if I sat down and bawled every time something went wrong? Tears won't come out of Persian carpet, you just ask my aunt!"

She laughed softly, even through the tears. He was a comforting sort of man and it was surprising, because he had a quick temper and an arrogance that put most people's backs up at first meeting.

"So that's why you yell at your cowboys? So you won't cry?"

"Works for me," he chuckled. He patted her shoulder. "Feel better?"

She nodded, smiling through tears. She wiped them away with a paper towel she'd tucked into her jeans. "Thanks."

"What are prospective lovers for?" he asked, smiling wickedly, and laughing out loud when she flushed.

"You stop corrupting me, you bad influence!"

"I said nothing corrupting, I just gave advance notice of bad intentions." He laughed at her expression. "At least it stopped the cascading waterfalls," he added, tongue in cheek, as he glanced at the tear tracks down her cheeks.

"Those weren't tears," she mumbled. "It was dew." She held up a hand. "I feel it falling again!"

"Talk to Kemp," he reiterated, not adding that he was going to do the same. "If she's got a new will and a codicil, signed, make her prove it. Don't let her shove you off your own land without a fight."

''I guess I could ask to see it,'' she agreed. Then she winced. ''I hate arguments. I hate fights.''

''I'll remember that the next time you come chasing after me,'' he promised.

She shook her head impotently, turning to go.

''Hey.''

She glanced at him over her shoulder.

''Let me know what you find out,'' he said. ''I'm in this, too. I can't manage a subdivision right near my barn. I can't have a lot of commotion around those beautiful Santa Gerts, it stresses them out too much. It would cost a fortune to tear down that barn and stick it closer to the house. A lawsuit would be cheaper.''

''There's an idea,'' she said brightly. ''Take her to court.''

''For what, trying to sell property? That's rich.''

''Just trying to help us both out,'' she said.

He glanced at his watch again. ''Five minutes left and even I'm not that good,'' he added. ''Pity. If you hadn't kept running your mouth, by now we could have…''

''You hush, Jordan Powell!'' she shot at him. ''Honestly, of all the blatant, arrogant, sex-crazed ranchers in Texas…!''

She was still mumbling as she went out the door. But when she was out of sight, she grinned. He was a tonic.

That night, Janet didn't say a word about any real estate deals. She ate a light supper that Libby had prepared, as usual without any compliments about it.

''When are you going back to work?'' she asked Libby irritably, her dyed blond hair in an expensive hairdo, her trendy silk shell and embroidered jeans marking her new wealth. ''It can't be good for you to lie around here all day.''

Curt, who was almost the mirror image of his sister, except for his height and powerful frame, glared at the woman. ''Excuse me, since when did you do any housework or cooking around here? Libby's done both since she turned thirteen!"

"Don't you speak to me that way," Janet said haughtily. "I can throw you out any time I like. I own everything!"

"You don't own the property until that will goes through probate," Libby replied sweetly, shocked at her own boldness. She'd never talked that way to the woman before. "You can produce it, I hope, because you're going to have to. You don't get the property yet. Maybe not even later, if everything isn't in perfect order."

"You've been talking to that rancher again, haven't you?" Janet demanded. "That damned Powell man! He's so suspicious about everything! Your father had a heart attack. He's dead. He left everything to me. What else do you want?" she raged, standing.

Libby stood, too, her face flushed. "Proof. I want proof. And you'd better have it before you start making any deals with developers about selling Daddy's land!"

Janet started. "De…developers?"

"I heard you this afternoon with that real estate agent," Libby said, with an apologetic glance at her brother, who looked shocked. She hadn't told him. "You're trying to sell our ranch and Daddy hasn't even been dead a month!"

Curt stood up. He looked even more formidable than Libby. "Before you make any attempt to sell this land, you're going to need a lawyer, Janet," he said in that slow, cold drawl that made cowhands move faster.

"How are you going to afford one, Curt, dear?" she asked sarcastically. "You just work for wages."

"Oh, Jordan will loan us the money," Libby said confidently.

Janet's haughty expression fluttered. She threw down her napkin. "You need cooking lessons," she said spitefully. "This food is terrible! I've got to make some phone calls."

She stormed out of the room.

Libby and Curt sat back down, both angry. Libby explained about the real estate agent's visit and what she'd overheard. Curt had only just come in when Libby had put the spaghetti and garlic bread on the table. It was Curt's favorite food and his sister made it very well, he thought, despite Janet's snippy comment.

"She's not selling this place while there's a breath left in my body," he told his sister. "Anyway, she can't do that until the will is probated. And she'd better have a legitimate will."

"Jordan said we needed to get Mr. Kemp to take a look at it," she said. "And I think we're going to need a handwriting expert to take a look, too."

He nodded.

"But what are we going to do about money to file suit?" she asked. "I was bluffing about Jordan loaning us the money. I don't know if he would."

"He's not going to want a subdivision on his doorstep, I'll tell you that," Curt said. "I'll talk to him."

"I already did," she said, surprising him. "He thinks there's something fishy going on, too."

"You can't get much past Jordan," he agreed. "I've been working myself to death trying not to think about losing Dad. I should have paid more attention to what was going on here."

"I've been grieving, too." She sighed and folded her small hands on the tablecloth. "Isn't it amazing how snippy she is, now that Daddy's not here? She was all over us like poison ivy before he died."

"She married him for what he had, Libby," he said bitterly.

"She seemed to love him…."

"She came on to me the night they came back from that Cancun honeymoon," he said bitterly.

Libby whistled. Her brother was a very attractive man. Their father, a sweet and charming man, had been overweight and balding. She could understand why Janet might have preferred Curt to his father.

"I slapped her down hard and Dad never knew." He

shook his head. "How could he marry something like that?"

"He was flattered by all the attention she gave him, I guess," Libby said miserably. "And now here we are. I'll bet she sweet-talked him into changing that will. He would have done anything for her, you know that—he was crazy in love with her. He might have actually written us out of it, Curt. We have to accept that."

"Not until they can prove to me that it wasn't forged," he said stubbornly. "I'm not giving up our inheritance without a fight. Neither are you," he asserted.

She sighed. "Okay, big brother. What do you want to do?"

"When do you go back to work?"

"Monday. Mr. Kemp's out of town."

"Okay. Monday, you make an appointment for both of us to sit down with him and hash this out."

She felt better already. "Okay," she said brightly. "I'll do that very thing. Maybe we do have a chance of keeping Daddy's ranch."

He nodded. "There's always hope." He leaned back in his chair. "So you went to see Jordan." He smiled indulgently. "I can remember a time not so long ago when you ran and hid from him."

"He always seemed to be yelling at somebody," she recalled. "I was intimidated by him. Especially when I graduated from high school. I had a sort of crush on him. I was scared to death he'd notice. Not that he was ever around here that much," she added, laughing. "He and Daddy had a fight a week over water rights."

"Dad usually lost, too," Curt recalled. He studied his sister with affection. "You know, I thought maybe Jordan was sweet on you himself—he's only eight years older than you."

"He's never been sweet on me!" she flashed at him, blushing furiously. "He's hardly even smiled at me, in all the years we've lived here, until the past few months! If anything, he usually treats me like a contagious virus!"

Curt only smiled. He looked very much like her, with the same dark wavy hair and the same green eyes. "He picks at you. Teases you. Makes you laugh. You do the same thing to him. People besides me have noticed. He bristles if anyone says anything unkind about you."

Her eyes widened. "Who's been saying unkind things about me?" she asked.

"That assistant store manager over at Lord's Department Store."

"Oh. Sherry King." She leaned back in her chair. "She can't help it, you know. She was crazy about Duke Wright and he wanted to take me to the Cattleman's Ball. I wouldn't go and he didn't ask anybody else. I feel sorry for her."

"Duke's not your sort of man," he replied. "He's a mixer. Nobody in Jacobsville has been in more brawls," he said, pausing. "Well, maybe Leo Hart has."

"Leo Hart got married, he won't be brawling out at Shea's Roadhouse and Bar anymore."

"Duke's not likely to get married again. His wife took their five-year-old son to New York City, where her new job is. He says she doesn't even look after the little boy. She's too busy trying to get a promotion. The child stays with her sister while she jets all over the world closing real estate deals."

"It's a new world," Libby pointed out. "Women are competing with men for the choice jobs now. They have to move around to get a promotion."

Curt's eyes narrowed. "Maybe they should get promotion before they get pregnant," he said impatiently.

She shrugged. "Accidents happen."

"No child of mine is ever going to be an accident," Curt said firmly.

"Nice to be so superior," she teased, eyes twinkling. "Never to make mistakes..."

He swiped at her with a napkin. "You don't even stick your toes in the water, so don't lecture me about drowning."

She chuckled. "I'm sensible, I am," she retorted. "None of this angst for me. I'll just do my routine job and keep my nose out of emotional entanglements."

He studied her curiously. "You go through life avoiding any sort of risk, don't you, honey?" he mused.

She moved one shoulder restlessly. "Daddy and Mama fought all the time, remember?" she said. "I swore I'd never get myself into a fix like that. She told me that she and Daddy were so happy when they first met, when they first married. Then, six months later, she was pregnant with you and they couldn't manage one pleasant meal together without shouting." She shook her head. "That means you can't trust emotions. It's better to use your brain when you think about marrying somebody. Love is...sticky," she concluded. "And it causes insanity, I'm sure of it."

"Why don't you ask Kemp if that's why he's stayed single so long? He's in his middle thirties, isn't he, and never even been engaged."

"Who'd put up with him?" she asked honestly. "Now there's a mixer for you," she said enthusiastically. "He actually *threw* another lawyer out the front door and onto the sidewalk last month. Good thing there was a welcome mat there, it sort of broke the guy's fall."

"What did he want?" Curt asked.

She shook her head. "I have no idea. But I don't expect him to be a repeat client."

Curt chuckled. "I see what you mean."

Libby went to bed early that night, without another word to Janet. She knew that anything she said would be too much. But she did miss her father and she couldn't believe that he wouldn't have mentioned Libby and Curt in his will. He did love them. She knew he did.

She thought about Jordan Powell, too, and about Curt's

remark that he thought Jordan was sweet on her. She tingled all over at the thought. But that wasn't going to happen, she assured herself. Jordan was gorgeous and he could have his pick of pretty women. Libby Collins would be his last resort. The world wasn't ending yet, so she was out of the running.

She rolled over, closed her eyes, and went to sleep.

Chapter Two

Janet wasn't at breakfast the next morning. Her new gold Mercedes was gone and she hadn't left a note. Libby saw it as a bad omen.

The weekend passed with nothing remarkable except for Janet's continued absence. The truck was ready Saturday and Curt picked it up in town, catching a lift with one of Jordan's cowboys. It wasn't as luxurious as a Mercedes, but it had a good engine and it was handy for hauling things like salt blocks and bales of hay. Libby tried to picture hauling hay in Janet's Mercedes and almost went hysterical with laughter.

Libby went back to work at Blake Kemp's office early Monday morning, dropped off by Curt on his way to the feed store for Jordan. She felt as if she hadn't really had a vacation at all.

Violet Hardy, Mr. Kemp's secretary, who was dark-haired, blue-eyed, pretty and somewhat overweight, smiled at her as she came in the door. "Hi! Did you have a nice vacation?"

"I spent it working," Libby confessed. "How did things go here?"

Violet groaned. "Don't even ask."

"That bad, huh?" Libby remarked.

Mabel, the blond grandmother who worked at reception, turned in her chair after transferring a call into Mr. Kemp's office. "Bad isn't the word, Libby," she said in a whisper, glancing down the hall to make sure the doors were all closed. "That lawyer Mr. Kemp got to fill in for him got two cases confused and sent the clients to the wrong courtrooms in different counties."

"Yes," Violet nodded, "and one of them came in here and tried to punch Mr. Kemp."

Libby pursed her lips. "No. Did he have insurance?"

All three women chuckled.

"For an attorney who handles so many assault cases," Violet whispered, "he doesn't practice what he preaches. Mr. Kemp punched the guy back and they wound up out on the street. Our police chief, Cash Grier, broke it up and almost arrested Mr. Kemp."

"What about the other guy? Didn't he start it?" Libby exclaimed.

"The other guy was Duke Wright," Violet confessed, watching Libby color. "And Chief Grier said that instead of blaming Mr. Kemp for handling Mrs. Wright's divorce, he should thank him for not bankrupting Mr. Wright in the process!"

"Then what?" Libby asked.

All three women glanced quickly down the hall.

"Mr. Wright threw a punch at Chief Grier."

"Well, that was smart thinking. Duke's in the hospital, then?" Libby asked facetiously.

"Nope," Violet said, her blue eyes twinkling. "But he was in jail briefly until he made bail." She shook her head. "I don't expect he'll try that twice."

"Crime has fallen about fifty percent since we got Cash Grier as chief," Violet sighed, smiling.

"And Judd Dunn as assistant chief," Libby reminded her.

"Poor Mr. Wright," Mabel said. "He does have the worst luck. Remember that Jack Clark who worked for him, who was convicted of murdering that woman in Victoria? Mr. Wright sure hated the publicity. It came just when he was trying to get custody of his son."

"Mr. Wright would have a lot less trouble if he didn't spend so much time out looking for it," came a deep, gruff voice from behind them.

They all jumped. Blake Kemp was standing just at the entrance to the hallway with a brief in one hand and a coffee cup in the other. He was as much a dish as Jordan Powell. He had wavy dark hair and blue eyes and the most placid, friendly face—until he got in front of a jury. Nobody wanted to be across the courtroom from Kemp when a trial began. There was some yellow and purple discoloration on one high cheekbone, where a fist had apparently landed a blow. Duke Wright, Libby theorized silently.

"Libby, before you do anything else, would you make a pot of coffee, please?" he asked in a long-suffering tone. He impaled a wincing Violet with his pale blue eyes. "I don't give a damn what some study says is best for me, I want caffeine. C-A-F-F-E-I-N-E," he added, spelling it letter by letter for Violet's benefit.

Violet lifted her chin and her own blue eyes glared right back at him. "Mr. Kemp, if you drank less of it, you might not be so bad-tempered. I mean, really, that's the second person you've thrown out of our office in a month! Chief Grier said that was a new city record...."

Kemp's eyes were blazing now, narrow and intent. "Miss Hardy, do you want to still be employed here tomorrow?"

Violet looked as if she was giving that question a lot of deliberation. "But, sir..." she began.

"I like caffeine. I'm not giving it up," Kemp said curtly. "You don't change my routine in this office. Is that clear?"

"But, Mr. Kemp—!" she argued.

"I don't remember suggesting anything so personal to you, Miss Hardy," he shot back, clearly angry. "I could, however," he added, and his cold blue eyes made insinuations about her figure, which was at least two dress sizes beyond what it should have been.

All three women gasped at the outrageous insinuation and then glared at their boss.

Violet flushed and stood up, as angry as he was, but not intimidated one bit by the stare. "My...my father always said that a woman should look like a woman and not a skeleton encased in skin. I may be a little overweight, Mr. Kemp, but at least I'm doing something about it!"

He glanced pointedly at a cake in a box on her desk.

She colored. "I live out near the Hart Ranch. I promised Tess Hart I'd pick that up at the bakery for her before I came to work and drop it by her house when I go home for lunch. It's for a charity tea party this afternoon." She was fuming. "I do not eat cake! Not anymore."

He stared at her until she went red and sat back down. She averted her eyes and went back to work. Her hands on the computer keyboard were trembling.

"You fire me if you want to, Mr. Kemp, but nothing I said to you was as mean as what you were insinuating to me with that look," Violet choked. "I know I weigh too much. You don't have to rub it in. I was only trying to help you."

Mabel and Libby were still glaring at him. He shifted uncomfortably and put the brief down on Violet's desk with a slap. "There are six spelling errors in that. You'll have to redo it. You can buzz me when the coffee's ready," he added shortly. He turned on his heel and took his coffee cup back into his office. As an afterthought, he slammed the door.

"Oh, and like anybody short of a druggist could read those chicken scratches on paper that you call *handwriting!*" Violet muttered, staring daggers after him.

Libby let out the breath she'd been holding and gaped at sweet, biddable Violet, who'd never talked back to Mr. Kemp in the eight months she'd worked for him. So did Mabel.

"Well, it's about time!" Mabel said, laughing delightedly. "Good for you, Violet. It's no good, letting a man walk all over you, no matter how crazy you are about him!"

"Hush!" Violet exclaimed, glancing quickly down the hall. "He'll hear you!"

"He doesn't know," Libby said comfortingly, putting an arm around Violet. "And we'll never tell. I'm proud of you, Violet."

"Me, too," Mabel grinned.

Violet sighed. "I guess he'll fire me. It might not be a bad thing. I spend too much time trying to take care of him and he hates it." Her blue eyes were wistful under their long, thick lashes. "You know, I've lost fifteen pounds," she murmured. "And I'm down a dress size."

"A new diet?" Libby asked absently as she checked her "in" tray.

"A new gym, just for women," Violet confessed with a grin. "I love it!"

Libby looked at the other woman with admiration. "You're really serious about this, aren't you?"

Violet's shoulder moved gently. She was wearing a purple dress with a high collar and lots of frills on the bodice and a very straight skirt that clung to her hips. It was the worst sort of dress for a woman who had a big bust and wide hips, but nobody had the heart to tell Violet. "I had to do something. I mean, look at me! I'm so big!"

"You're not that big. But I think it's great that you're trying so hard, Violet," Libby said gently. "And to keep you on track, Mabel and I are giving up dessert when you eat lunch with us."

"I have to go home and see about Mother most every day at lunchtime," Violet confessed. "She hates that. She said I was wasting my whole life worrying about her, when I should be out having fun. But she's already had two light strokes in the past year since Daddy died. I can't leave her alone."

"Honey, people like you are why there's a heaven," Mabel murmured softly. "You're one in a million."

Violet waved her away. "Everybody's got problems," she laughed. "For all we know, Mr. Kemp has much bigger ones than we do. He's such a good person. When Mother had that last stroke, the bad one, he even drove me to the hospital after I got the call."

"He is a good person," Libby agreed. "But so are you."

"You'd better make that coffee, I guess," Violet said wistfully. "I really thought I could make it half and half and he wouldn't be able to taste the difference. He's so uptight lately. He's always in a hurry, always under pressure. He drinks caffeine like water and it's so bad for his heart. I know about hearts. My dad died of a heart attack last year. I was just trying to help."

"It's hard to help a rattlesnake across the road, Violet," Mabel said, tongue-in-cheek.

Libby was curious about the coincidence of Violet's father dying of a heart attack, like her father, such a short time ago. "Violet could find one nice thing to say about a serial killer," Libby agreed affectionately. "Even worse, she could find one nice thing to say about my stepmother."

"Ouch," Mabel groaned. "Now there's a hard case if I ever saw one." She shook her head. "People in Branntville are still talking about her and old man Darby."

Libby, who'd just finished filling the coffeepot, started it brewing and turned jerkily. "Excuse me?"

"Didn't I ever tell you?" Mabel asked absently. "Just a sec. Good morning, Kemp Law Offices," she said. "Yes, sir, I'll connect you." She started to push the intercom button when she saw with shock that it was already depressed. The light was on the switch. She and Libby, who'd also seen it, exchanged agonized glances. Quickly, without telling Violet, she pushed it off and then on again. ''Mr. Kemp, it's Mrs. Lawson for you on line two.'' She waited, hung up, and swung her chair around. She didn't dare tell poor Violet that Mr. Kemp had probably heard every single word she'd said about him.

''Your stepmother, Janet,'' Mabel told Libby, ''was working at a nursing home over in Branntville. She sweet-talked an old man who was a patient there into leaving everything he had to her.'' She shook her head. ''They said that Janet didn't even give him a proper funeral. She had him cremated and put in an urn and there was a graveside service. They said she bought a designer suit to wear to it.''

Libby was getting cold chills. There were too many similarities there to be a coincidence. Janet had wanted to have Riddle Collins cremated, too, but Curt and Libby had talked to the funeral director and threatened a lawsuit if he complied with Janet's request. They went home and told Janet the same thing and also insisted on a church funeral at the Presbyterian church where Riddle had been a member since childhood. Janet had been furious, but in the end, she reluctantly agreed.

Violet wasn't saying anything, but she had a funny look on her face and she seemed pale. She turned away before the others saw. But Libby's expression was thought-provoking.

''You're thinking something. What?'' Mabel asked Libby.

Fortunately, the phone rang again while Libby was deciding if it was wise to share her thoughts.

Violet got up from her desk and went close to Libby. ''She wanted to cremate your father, too, didn't she?''

Libby nodded.

''You should go talk to Mr. Kemp.''

Libby smiled. ''You know, Violet, I think you're right.'' She hugged the other girl and went back to Mabel. ''When he gets off the phone, I need to talk to him.''

Mabel grinned. ''Now you're talking.'' She checked the board. ''He's free. Just a sec.'' She pushed a button. ''Mr. Kemp, Libby needs to speak to you, if it's convenient.''

''Send her in, Mrs. Jones.''

''Good luck,'' Mabel said, crossing her fingers.

Libby grinned back.

''Come in,'' Kemp said, opening the door for Libby and closing it behind her. ''Have a seat. I don't need ESP to know what's on your mind. I had a call from Jordan Powell at home last night.''

Her eyebrows arched. ''Well, he jumped the gun!''

''He's concerned. Probably with good reason,'' he added. ''I went ahead on my own and had a private detective I know run a check on Janet's background. This isn't the first time she's become a widow.''

''I know,'' Libby said. ''Mabel says an elderly man in a nursing home left her everything he had. She had him sent off to be cremated immediately after they got him to the funeral home.''

He nodded. ''And I understand from Don Hedgely at our funeral home here that she tried to have the same thing done with your father, but you and your brother threatened a lawsuit.''

''We did,'' Libby said. ''Daddy didn't believe in cremation. He would have been horrified.''

Kemp leaned back in his desk chair and crossed his long legs, with his hands behind his head. He pursed his lips and narrowed his blue eyes, deep in thought. ''There's another thing,'' he said. ''Janet was fired from that nursing home for being too friendly with their wealthiest patients. One of whom—the one you know about—was an elderly widower with no children. He died of suspicious causes and left her his estate.''

Libby folded her arms. She felt chilled all over now. ''Wasn't it enough for her?'' she wondered out loud.

''Actually, it took the entire estate to settle his gambling debts,'' he murmured. ''Apparently, he liked the horses a little too much.''

''Then there was our father.'' She anticipated his next thought.

He shook his head. ''That was after Mr. Hardy in San Antonio.''

Libby actually gasped. It couldn't be!

Kemp leaned forward quickly. ''Do you think Violet is happy having to live in a rented firetrap with her invalid mother? Her parents were wealthy. But a waitress at Mr. Hardy's favorite restaurant apparently began a hot affair with him and talked him into making her a loan of a quarter of a million dollars to save her parents from bankruptcy and her father from suicide. He gave her a check and had a heart attack before he could stop payment on it—which he planned to do. He told his wife and begged forgiveness of her and his daughter before he died.'' His eyes narrowed. ''He died shortly after he was seen with a pretty blonde at a San Antonio motel downtown.''

''You think it was Janet? That it wasn't a heart attack at all—that she killed him?''

''I think there are too many coincidences for comfort in her past,'' Kemp said flatly. ''But the one eyewitness who saw her with Hardy at that motel was unable to pick her out of a lineup. She'd had her hair color changed just the day before the lineup. She remained a brunette for about a week and then changed back to blond.''

Libby's face tightened. ''She might have killed my father,'' she bit off.

''That is a possibility,'' Kemp agreed. ''It's early days yet, Libby. I can't promise you anything. But if she's guilty and I can get her on a witness stand, in a court of law, I can break her,'' he said with frightening confidence. ''She'll tell me everything she knows.''

She swallowed. ''I don't want her to get away with it,'' she began. ''But Curt and I work for wages…''

He flapped his hand in her direction. ''Every lawyer

takes a pro bono case occasionally. I haven't done it in months. You and Curt can be my public service for the year,'' he added, and he actually smiled. It made him look younger, much less dangerous than he really was.

''I don't know what to say,'' she said, shaking her head in disbelief.

He leaned forward. ''Say you'll be careful,'' he replied. ''I can't find any suspicion that she ever helped a young person have a heart attack, but I don't doubt for a minute that she knows how. I'm working with Micah Steele on that aspect of it. There isn't much he doesn't know about the darker side of medicine, even if he is a doctor. And what he doesn't know about black ops and untimely death, Cash Grier does.''

''I thought Daddy died of a heart condition nobody knew he had.'' She took a deep breath. ''When I tell Curt, he'll go crazy.''

''Let me tell him,'' Kemp said quietly. ''It will be easier.''

''Okay.''

''Meanwhile, you have to go back home and pretend that nothing's wrong, that your stepmother is innocent of any foul play. That's imperative. If you give her a reason to think she's being suspected of anything, she'll bolt, and we may never find her.''

''We'd get our place back without a fight,'' Libby commented wistfully.

''And a woman who may have murdered your father, among others, would go free,'' Kemp replied. ''Is that really what you want?''

Libby shook her head. ''Of course not. I'll do whatever you say.''

''We'll be working in the background. The most important thing is to keep the pressure on, a little at a time, so that she doesn't get suspicious. Tell her you've spoken to an attorney about the will, but nothing more.''

''Okay,'' she agreed.

He got up. "And don't tell Violet I said anything to you about her father," he added. His broad shoulders moved restlessly under his expensive beige suit, as if he were carrying some difficult burden. "She's...sensitive."

What a surprising comment from such an insensitive man, she thought, but she didn't dare say it. She only smiled. "Certainly."

She was reaching for the doorknob when he called her back. "Yes, sir?"

"When you make another pot of coffee," he said hesitantly, "I guess we could use some of that half and half."

Her dropped jaw told its own story.

"She means well," he said abruptly, and turned back to his desk. "But for now, I want it strong and black and straight up. Call me when it's made and I'll bring my cup."

"It should be ready right now," she faltered. Even in modern times, few bosses went to get their own coffee. But Mr. Kemp was something of a puzzle. Perhaps, Libby thought wickedly as she followed him down the hall, even to himself.

He glanced at Violet strangely, but he didn't make any more comments. Violet sat with her eyes glued to her computer screen until he poured his coffee and went back to his office.

Libby wanted so badly to say something to her, but she didn't know what. In the end, she just smiled and made a list of the legal precedents she would have to look up for Mr. Kemp at the law library in the county courthouse. Thank God, she thought, for computers.

She was on her way home in the pickup truck after a long day when she saw Jordan on horseback, watching several men drive the pregnant heifers into pastures close to the barn. He had a lot of money invested in those purebred calves and he wasn't risking them to predators or difficult births. He looked so good on horseback, she thought dreamily. He was arrow-straight and his head, covered by that wide-brimmed creamy Stetson he favored, was tilted in a way that was particularly his. She could have picked him out of any crowd at a distance just by the way he carried himself.

He turned his head when he heard the truck coming down the long dirt road and he motioned Libby over to the side.

She parked the truck, cut off the engine, and stood on the running board to talk to him over the top of the old vehicle. ''I wish I had a camera,'' she called. ''Mama Powell, protecting his babies...''

''You watch it!'' he retorted, shaking a finger at her.

She laughed. ''What are you going to do, jump the fence and run me down?''

''Poor old George here couldn't jump a fence. He's twenty-four,'' he added, patting the old horse's withers. ''He hates his corral. I thought I'd give him a change of scenery, since I wasn't going far.''

''Everything gets old, I guess. Most everything, anyway,'' she added with a faraway, wistful look in her eyes. She had an elderly horse of her own, that she might yet have to give away because it was hard to feed and keep him on her salary.

He dismounted and left George's reins on the ground to jump the fence and talk to her. ''Did you see Kemp?'' he asked.

''Yes. He said you phoned him.''

''I asked a few questions and got some uncomfortable answers,'' he said, coming around the truck to stand beside her. His big lean hands went to her waist and he lifted her down close to him. Too close. She could smell his shaving lotion and feel the heat off his body under the Western cut long-sleeved shirt. In her simple, jacketed suit, she felt overly dressed.

''You don't look too bad when you fix up,'' he commented, approving her light makeup and the gray suit that made her eyes look greener than they were.

"You don't look too bad when you don't," she replied. "What uncomfortable answers are you getting?"

His eyes were solemn. "I think you can guess. I don't like the idea of you and Curt alone in that house with her."

"We have a shotgun somewhere. I'll make a point of buying some shells for it."

He shook her by the waist gently. "I'm not teasing. Can you lock your bedroom door? Can Curt?"

"It's an old house, Jordan," she faltered. "None of the bedroom doors have locks."

"Tell Curt I said to get bolts and put them on. Do it when she's not home. In the meantime, put a chair under the doorknob."

"But why?" she asked uncertainly.

He drew a long breath. His eyes went to her soft bow of a mouth and he studied it for several seconds before he spoke. "There's one very simple way to cause a heart attack. You can do it with a hypodermic syringe filled with nothing but air."

She couldn't speak for a moment. "Could they…tell that if they did an autopsy on my father?"

"I'm not a forensic specialist, despite the fact that there are half a dozen shows on TV that can teach you how to think you are. I'll ask somebody who knows," he added.

She hated the thought of disinterring her father. But it would be terrible if he'd met with foul play and it never came out.

He tilted her face up to his narrow dark eyes. "You're worrying. Don't. I'm as close as your phone, night or day."

She smiled gently. "Thanks, Jordan."

His thumbs moved on her waist while he looked down at her. His face hardened. His eyes were suddenly on her soft mouth, with real hunger.

The world stopped. It seemed like that. She met his searching gaze and couldn't breathe. Her body felt achy. Hungry. Feverish. She swallowed, hoping it didn't show.

"If you play your cards right, I might let you kiss me," he murmured.

Her heart skipped. "Excuse me?"

One big shoulder lifted and fell. "Where else are you going to get any practical experience?" he asked. "Duke Wright is a candidate for the local nursing home, after all..."

"He's thirty-six!" she exclaimed. "That isn't old!"

"I'm thirty-two," he pointed out. "I have all my own teeth." He grinned to display them. "And I can still outrun at least two of my horses."

"That's an incentive to kiss you?" she asked blankly.

"Think of the advantages if you kiss me during a stampede," he pointed out.

She laughed. He was a case. Her eyes adored him. "I'll keep you in mind," she promised. "But you mustn't get your hopes up. This town is full of lonely bachelors who can't get women to kiss them. You'll have to take a number and wait."

"Wait until what?" he asked, tweaking her waist with his thumbs.

"I don't know. Christmas? I could kiss you as part of your present."

His eyebrows arched. "What's the other part?"

"It's not Christmas. Listen, I have to get home and make supper."

"I'll send Curt on down," he said.

She was seeing a new pattern. "To make sure I'm not left alone with Janet, is that right?"

"For my peace of mind," he corrected. "I've gotten... used to you," he added slowly. "As a neighbor," he added deliberately. "Think how hard it would be to break in another one, at my age."

"You just said you weren't old," she reminded him.

"Maybe I am, just a little," he confessed. He drew her up until she was standing completely against him, so close that she could feel the hard press of his muscular legs against her own. ''Come on,'' he taunted, bending his head with a mischievous little smile. ''You know you're dying to kiss me.''

''I am?'' she whispered dreamily as she studied the long, wide, firm curve of his lips.

''Desperately.''

She felt his nose brushing against hers. Somewhere, a horse was neighing. A jet flew over. The wind ruffled leaves in a small tree nearby. She was deaf to any sound other than the throb of her own heartbeat. There was nothing in the world except Jordan's mouth, a scant inch from her own. He'd never kissed her. She wanted him to. She ached for him to.

His hands tightened on her waist, lifting her closer. ''Come on, chicken. Give it all you've got.''

Her hands were flat against his chest, feeling the warm muscles under his cotton shirt. She tasted his breath. Her arms slid up to his shoulders. He had her hypnotized. She wanted nothing more than to drown in him.

''That's it,'' he whispered.

She closed her eyes and lifted up on her tiptoes as she felt the slow, soft press of her own lips against his for the first time.

Her knees were weak. She didn't think they were going to support her. And still Jordan didn't move, didn't respond.

Frustrated, she tried to lift up higher, her arms circled his neck and pulled, trying to make his mouth firm and deepen above hers. But she couldn't budge him.

''Oh, you arro...!''

It was the opening he'd been waiting for. His mouth crushed down against her open lips and his arms contracted hungrily. Libby moaned sharply at the rush of sensation it caused in her body. It had never been like this in her life. She was burning alive. She ached. She longed. She couldn't get close enough....

''Hey, Jordan!''

The distant shout broke the spell. Jordan jerked his head around to see one of his men waving a wide-brimmed hat and gesturing toward a pickup truck that was driving right out into the pasture where Jordan was putting those pregnant heifers.

"It's the feed supplement I ordered," he murmured, letting her go slowly. "Damn his timing."

He didn't smile when he said that. She couldn't manage even a word.

He touched her softly swollen mouth with his fingertips. "Maybe you could take me on a date and we could get lost on some deserted country road," he suggested.

She took a breath and shook her head to clear it. "I do not seduce men in parked cars," she pointed out.

He snapped his fingers. "Damn!"

"He's waving at you again," she noted, looking over his shoulder.

"All right, I'll go to work. But I'll send Curt on home." He touched her cheek. "Be careful, okay?"

She managed a weak smile. "Okay."

He turned and vaulted the fence, mounting George with the ease of years of practice as a horseman. "See you."

She nodded and watched him ride away. Her life had just changed course, in the most unexpected way.

Chapter Three

But all Jordan's worry—and Libby's unease—was for nothing. When she got home, Janet's Mercedes was gone. There was a terse little note on the hall table that read, *Gone to Houston shopping, back tomorrow.*

Even as she was reading it, Curt came in the back door, bareheaded and sweaty.

"She's gone?" he asked.

She nodded. "Left a note. She's gone to Houston and won't be back until tomorrow."

"Great. It'll give me time to put locks on the bedroom doors," he said.

She sighed. "Jordan's been talking to you, hasn't he?" she asked.

"Yes, and he's been kissing you, apparently," he murmured, grinning. "Old Harry had to yell himself hoarse to get Jordan's attention when they brought those feed supplements out."

She flushed. She couldn't think of a single defense. But she hadn't heard Harry yelling, except one time. No wonder people were talking.

"Interested in you, is he?" Curt asked softly.

"He wanted me to ask him out on a date and get him lost on a dirt road," she said.

"And you said…?"

She moved restively. "I said that I didn't seduce men in parked cars on deserted roads, of course," she assured him.

He looked solemn. "Sis, we've never really talked about Jordan…."

"And we really don't need to, now," she interrupted. "I'm a big girl and I know all about Jordan. He's only teasing. I'm older and he's doing it in a different way, that's all."

Curt wasn't smiling. "He isn't."

She cleared her throat. "Well, it doesn't matter. He's not a marrying man and I'm not a frivolous woman. Besides, his tastes run to beauty queens and state senators' daughters."

He hesitated.

She smiled before he could say anything else. "Let it drop. We've got enough on our minds now without adding more to them. Let's rush to the hardware store and buy locks before she gets back."

He shrugged and let it go. There would be another time to discuss Jordan Powell.

When Libby got home from work Tuesday evening she was still reeling from the shocking news that a fed-up Violet had quit her job and gone to work for Dick Wright. Blake Kemp had *not* taken the news well. Her mood lifted when she found Jordan's big burgundy double-cabbed pickup truck sitting in her front yard. He was sitting on the side of the truck bed, whittling a piece of wood with a pocket knife, his broad-brimmed hat pushed way back on his head. He looked up at her approach and jumped down to meet her.

"You're late," he complained.

She got out of her car, grabbing her purse on the way. ''I had to stay late and type up some notes for Mr. Kemp.''

He scowled. ''That's Violet's job.''

''Violet's leaving,'' she said on a sigh. ''She's going to work for Duke Wright.''

''But she's crazy for Kemp, isn't she?'' Jordan wondered.

She scowled at him. ''You aren't supposed to know that,'' she pointed out.

''Everybody knows that.'' He looked around the yard. ''Janet hasn't shown up. Curt said she'd gone to Houston.''

''That's what the note said,'' she agreed, walking beside him to the front porch. ''Curt put the locks on last night.''

''I know. I asked him.''

She unlocked the door and pushed it open. ''Want some coffee?''

''I'd love some. Eggs? Bacon? Cinnamon toast?'' he added.

''Oh, I see,'' she mused with a grin. ''Amie's gone and you're starving, huh?''

He shrugged nonchalantly. ''She didn't have to leave. I only yelled a little.''

''You shouldn't scare her. She's old.''

''Dirt's old. Amie's a spring chicken.'' He chuckled. ''Anyway, she was shopping for antique furniture on the Internet and she found a side table she couldn't live without in San Antonio. She drove up to look at it. She said she'd see me in a couple of days.''

''And you're starving.''

''You make the nicest scrambled eggs, Libby,'' he coaxed. ''Nice crisp bacon. Delicious cinnamon toast. Strong coffee.''

''It isn't the time of day for breakfast.''

''No law that you can't have breakfast for supper,'' he pointed out.

She sighed. ''I was planning a beef casserole.''

''It won't go with scrambled eggs.''

She put her hands on her hips and gave him a considering look. "You really are a pain, Jordan."

He moved a step closer and caught her by the waist with two big lean hands. "If you want me to marry you, you have to prove that you're a good cook."

"Marry...?"

Before she could get another word out, his mouth crushed down over her parted lips. He kissed her slowly, tenderly, his big hands steely at her waist, as if he were keeping them there by sheer will when he wanted to pull her body much closer to his own.

Her hands rested on his clean shirt while she tried to decide if he was kidding. He had to be. Certainly he didn't want to marry anybody. He'd said so often enough.

He lifted his head scant inches. "Stop doing that."

She blinked. "Doing what?"

"Thinking. You can't kiss a man and do analytical formulae in your head at the same time."

"You said you'd never marry anybody...."

His eyes were oddly solemn. "Maybe I changed my mind."

Before she could answer him, he bent his head and kissed her again. This time it wasn't a soft, teasing sample of a kiss. It was bold, brash, invasive and possessive. He enveloped her in his hard arms and crushed her down the length of his powerful body. She felt a husky groan go into her mouth as he grew more insistent.

Against her hips, she felt the sudden hardness of his body. As if he realized that and didn't like having her feel it, he moved away a breath. Slowly, he lifted his hard mouth from her swollen lips and looked down at her quietly, curiously.

"This is getting to be a habit," she said breathlessly. Her body was throbbing, like her heart. She wondered if he could hear it.

His dark eyes fell to the soft, quick pulsing of her heart, visible where her loose blouse bounced in time with it.

Beneath it, two hard little peaks were blatant. He saw them and his eyes began to glitter.

"Don't look at me like that," she whispered gruffly.

His eyes shot up to catch hers. "You want me," he said curtly. "I can see it. Feel it."

Her breath was audible. "You conceited…!"

His hands caught her hips and pushed them against his own. "It's mutual."

"I noticed!" she burst out, jerking away from him, red-faced.

"Don't be such a child," he chided, but gently. "You're old enough to know what desire feels like."

Her face grew redder. "I will not be seduced by you in my own kitchen over scrambled eggs!"

His eyebrows arched. "You're making them, then?" he asked brightly.

"Oh!" She pushed away from him. "You just won't take no for an answer!"

He smiled speculatively. "You can put butter on that," he agreed. His eyes went up and down her slender figure while she walked through to the kitchen, leaving her purse on the hall table as she went. "Not going to change before you start cooking?" he drawled, following her in. "I don't mind helping."

She shot him a dark glare.

He held up both hands. "Just offering to be helpful, that's all."

She laughed helplessly. "I can dress myself, thanks."

"I was offering to help you *un*dress," he pointed out.

She had to fight down another blush. She was a modern, independent woman. It was just that the thought of Jordan's dark eyes on her naked body had an odd, pleasurable effect on her. Especially after that bone-shaking kiss.

"You shouldn't go around kissing women like that unless you mean business," she pointed out as she got out a big iron skillet to cook the bacon in.

"What makes you think I didn't mean it?" he probed, straddling a kitchen chair to watch her work.

"You? Mr. I'll-Never-Marry?"

"I didn't say that. I said I didn't want to get married."

"Well, what's the difference?" she asked, exasperated.

His dark eyes slid down to her breasts with a boldness that made her uncomfortable. "There's always the one woman you can't walk away from."

"There's no such woman in your life."

"Think so?" He frowned. "What are you doing with that?" he asked as she put the skillet on the burner.

"You're the one who wanted bacon!" she exclaimed.

"Bacon, yes, not liquid fat!" He got up from the chair, pulled a couple of paper towels from the roll and pulled a plate from the cabinet. "Don't you know how to cook bacon?"

He proceeded to show her, layering several strips of bacon on a paper-towel coated plate and putting another paper towel on top of it.

She was watching with growing amusement. "And it's going to cook like that," she agreed. "Uh-huh."

"It goes in the microwave," he said with exaggerated patience. "You cook it for..."

"What's wrong?"

He was looking around, frowning, with the plate in one big hand. He opened cupboards and checked in the china cabinet. "All right, I'll bite. Where is it?"

"Where is what?"

"Your microwave oven!"

She sighed. "Jordan, we don't have a microwave oven."

"You're kidding." He scowled at her. "Everybody's got a microwave oven!"

"We haven't got one."

He studied her kitchen and slowly he put the plate back on the counter with a frown. The stove was at least ten years old. It was one of the old-fashioned ones that still had knobs instead of buttons. She didn't even have a dishwasher. Everything in the kitchen was old, like the cast-iron skillet she used for most every meal.

"I didn't realize how hard things were for you and Curt," he said after a minute. "I thought your father had all kinds of money."

"He did, until he married Janet," she replied. "She wanted to eat out all the time. The stove was worn out and so was the dishwasher. He was going to replace them, but she had him buy her a diamond ring she wanted, instead."

He scowled angrily. "I'm sorry. I'm really sorry."

His apology was unexpected and very touching. "It's all right," she said gently. "I'm used to doing things the hard way. Really I am."

He moved close, framing her oval face in his big warm hands. "You never complain."

She smiled. "Why should I? I'm healthy and strong and able to do anything that needs doing around here."

"You make me ashamed, Libby," he said softly. He bent and kissed her with aching tenderness.

"Why?" she whispered at his firm mouth.

"I'm not really sure. Do that again."

He nibbled her upper lip, coaxing her body to lean heavily against his. "This is even better than dessert," he murmured as he deepened the pressure of his mouth. "Come here!"

He lifted her against him and kissed her hungrily, until her mouth felt faintly bruised from the slow, insistent pressure. It was like flying. She loved kissing Jordan. She hoped he was never going to stop!

But all at once, he did, with a jerky breath. "This won't do," he murmured a little huskily. "Curt will be home any minute. I don't want him to find us on the kitchen table."

Her mouth flew open. "Jordan!"

He shrugged and looked sheepish. "It was heading that way. Here." He handed her the plate of bacon. "I guess you'd better fry it. I don't think it's going to cook by itself."

She smiled up at him. ''I'll drain it on paper towels and get rid of some of the grease after it's cooked.''

''Why are you throwing those away?'' he asked when she put the bacon on to fry and threw away the paper towels it had laid on.

''Bacteria,'' she told him. ''You never put meat back on a plate where it's been lying, raw.''

''They teach you that in school these days, I guess?''

She nodded. ''And lots of other stuff.''

''Like how to use a prophylactic...?'' he probed wickedly.

She flushed. ''They did not! And I'll wash your mouth out with soap if you say that again!'' she threatened.

''Never mind. I'll teach you how to use it, when the time comes,'' he added outrageously.

''I am not using a prophylactic!''

''You want kids right away, then?'' he persisted.

''I am not having sex with you on my kitchen table!''

There was a sudden stunned silence. Jordan was staring over her shoulder and his expression was priceless. Grimacing, she turned to find her older brother standing there with his mouth open.

''Oh, shut your mouth, Curt,'' she grumbled. ''It was a hypothetical discussion!''

''Except for the part about the prophylactic,'' Jordan said with a howling mad grin. ''Did you know that they don't teach people how to use them in school?''

Curt lost it. He almost doubled over laughing.

Libby threw a dish towel at him. ''Both of you, out of my kitchen! I'll call you when it's ready. Go on, out!''

They left the room obediently, still laughing.

Libby shook her head and started turning the bacon.

''Hasn't Janet even phoned to say if she was coming back today?'' Jordan asked the two siblings when they were seated at the kitchen table having supper.

''There wasn't anything on the answering machine,''

Libby said. "I checked it while the bacon was cooking. Maybe she thinks we're on to something and she's running for it."

"No, I don't think so," Curt replied at once. "She's not about to leave this property to us. Not considering what it would be worth to a developer."

"I agree," Jordan said. "I've given Kemp the phone number of a private detective I know in San Antonio," he added. "He's going to look into the case for me."

"We'll pay you back," Curt promised, and Libby nodded.

"Let's cross our bridges one at a time," Jordan replied. "First order of business is to see if we can find any proof that she's committed a crime in the past."

"Mabel said she was suspected in a death at a nursing home in Branntville," she volunteered.

"So Kemp told me," Jordan said. "This is good bacon," he added.

"Thanks," she said with a smile.

"Violet's father was another one of her victims," Libby added.

Jordan nodded while Curt scowled curiously at both of them. "But they can't prove that. Not unless there's enough evidence to order an exhumation. And, considering the physical condition of Violet's mother," he added, "I'm afraid she'd never be able to agree to it. The shock would probably kill her mother."

Libby sighed. "Poor Violet. She's had such a hard life. And now to have to change jobs..."

"She works for Kemp, doesn't she?" Curt asked.

"She did. She quit today," Libby replied. "She's going to work for Duke Wright."

"Oh, Sherry King's going to *love* that," Curt chuckled.

"She doesn't own Duke," Libby said. "He doesn't even like her."

"She's very possessive about men she wants."

"More power to her if she can put a net over him and lock him in her closet."

Jordan chuckled. "He's not keen on the thought of a second wife."

"He's still trying to get custody of his son, isn't he?" Curt asked. "Poor guy."

"He won't be the first man who lost a woman to a career," Jordan reminded him. "Although it's usually the other way around." He glanced at Libby. "Just for the record, I think you're more important than a new bull, no matter what his ancestry is."

"Gee, thanks," she replied, tongue-in-cheek.

"It never hurts to clear up these little details before they become issues," he said wryly. "On the other hand, it would be nice if you'd tell me if you have plans to go to law school and move to a big city to practice law?"

"Not me, thanks," she replied. "I'm very happy where I am."

"You don't know any other life except this one," he persisted. "What if you regret not spreading your wings further on down the road?"

"We can't see into the future, Jordan," she replied thoughtfully. "But I don't like cities, although I'm sure they're exciting for some people. I don't like parties or business and I wouldn't trade jobs with Kemp for anything on earth. I'm happy looking up case precedents and researching options. I wouldn't like having to stand up in a courtroom and argue a case."

"You don't know that," he mused, and a shadow crossed his face. "What if you got a taste of it one day and couldn't live without it but it was too late?"

"Too late?"

"What if you had kids and a husband?" he prompted.

"You're thinking about Duke Wright," she said slowly.

He drew in a hard breath, aware that Curt was watching him curiously. "Yes," he told her. "Duke's wife was a secretary. She took night courses to get her law degree and then got pregnant just before she started practice. While Duke was giving bottles and changing diapers, she was climbing the ladder at a prestigious San Antonio law firm, living there during the week and coming home on weekends. Then they offered her a job in New York City."

Libby couldn't quite figure out the look on his face. He was taking it all quite seriously and she'd thought he was teasing.

"So you see," he continued, "she didn't know she wanted a career until it was too late. Now she's making a six-figure annual income and their little boy's in her way. She doesn't want to give him up, but she doesn't have time to take care of him properly. And Duke's caught in the middle."

"I hadn't realized it was that bad," she confessed. "Poor Duke."

"He had a choice," he told her. "He married her thinking she wanted what he did, a nice home and a comfortable living, and kids." He drew a breath. "But she was very young," he added, his eyes studying her covertly. "Maybe she didn't really know what she wanted. Then."

"I suppose some women don't," she replied. "It's a new world. Maybe it took her a long time to realize the opportunities and then it was too late to go back."

He lowered his eyes to his boots. "That's very possible."

"But it's Duke's problem," she added, smiling. "Want some pie? I've got a cherry one that I made yesterday in the refrigerator."

He shook his head. "Thanks. But I won't stay." He got to his feet. "I'll tell Kemp to let you know what the private detective finds out. Meanwhile," he added, glancing at Curt, "not a word to Janet. Okay?"

They both nodded.

"Thanks, Jordan," Curt added.

"What are neighbors for?" he replied, and he chuckled. But his eyes didn't quite meet Libby's.

* * *

''Jordan was acting very oddly tonight, wasn't he?'' Libby asked her brother after they'd washed the dishes and put them away.

''He's a man with a lot on his mind,'' he replied. ''Calhoun Ballenger's making a very powerful bid for that senate seat that old man Merrill's had for so many years. They say old man Merrill's worried and so's his daughter, Julie. You remember, she's been pursuing Jordan lately.''

''But he and Calhoun have been friendly for years,'' she said.

''So they have. There's more. Old man Merrill got pulled over for drunk driving by a couple of our local cops. Now Merrill's pulling strings at city hall to try and make the officers withdraw the charges. Merrill doesn't have a lot of capital. Jordan does.''

''Surely you don't think Jordan would go against Cash Grier, even for Julie?'' she wondered, concerned.

He started to speak and then thought better of it. ''I'm not sure I really know,'' he said.

She rubbed at a clean plate thoughtfully. ''Do you suppose he's serious about her? She and her father are very big socially and they have a house here that they stay in from time to time. She has a college degree. In fact, they say she may try her hand at politics. He was talking about marriage and children to us—like he was serious about it.'' She frowned. ''Does that kind of woman settle down? Or was that what he meant, when he said some women don't know what they want until they find it?''

''I don't know that he's got marriage on his mind,'' Curt replied slowly. ''But he's spent a good deal of time with Julie and the senator just lately.''

That hurt. She bit her lower lip, hard, and forced her mind away from the heat and power of Jordan's kisses. ''We've got a problem of our own. What are we going to do about Janet?''

''Kemp's working on that, isn't he? And Jordan's private detective will be working with him. They'll turn up something. She isn't going to put us out on the street, Libby,'' he said gently. ''I promise you she isn't.''

She smiled up at him. ''You're sort of nice, for a brother.''

He grinned. ''Glad you noticed!''

She didn't sleep all night, though, wondering about Jordan's odd remarks and the way he'd looked at her when he asked if she had ambitions toward law practice. She really didn't, but he seemed to think she was too young to know her own mind.

Well, it wasn't really anything to worry about, she assured herself. Jordan had no idea of marrying *her,* regardless of her ambition or lack thereof. But Curt had said he was seeing a lot of Julie Merrill. For some unfathomable reason, the thought made her sad.

Chapter Four

It was late afternoon before Janet came back, looking out of sorts. She threw herself onto the sofa in the living room and lit a cigarette.

"You'll stink up the place," Libby muttered, hunting for an ashtray. She put it on the table.

"Well, then, you'll have to invest in some more air freshener, won't you, darling?" the older woman asked coldly.

Libby stared at her angrily. "Where have you been for three days?"

Janet avoided looking at her. "I had some business to settle."

"It had better not have been any sales concerning this property," Libby told her firmly.

"And who's going to stop me?" the other woman demanded hotly.

"Mr. Kemp."

Janet crushed out the cigarette and got to her feet. "Let him try. You try, too! I own everything here and I'm not letting you take it away from me! No matter what I have to do,'' she added darkly. ''I earned what I'm getting, putting up with your father handling me like a live doll. The repulsive old fool made my skin crawl!''

''My father loved you,'' Libby bit off, furious that the awful woman could make such a remark about her father, the kindest man she'd ever known.

''He loved showing me off, you mean,'' Janet muttered. ''If he'd really loved me, he'd have given me the things I asked him for. But he was so cheap! Well, I'm not being cheated out of what's mine,'' she added, with a cold glare at Libby. ''Not by you or your brother. I have a lawyer, too, now.''

Libby felt sick. But she managed a calm smile. ''We have locks on our bedroom doors, by the way,'' she said out of the blue. ''And Mr. Kemp is having a private detective check you out.''

Janet looked shocked. ''W-what?''

''Violet who works in my office thinks you might have known her father— Mr. Hardy from San Antonio?'' she added deliberately. ''He had a heart attack, just like Daddy…?''

Janet actually went pale. She jumped to her feet as if she'd been stung.

''Where are you going?'' Libby asked seconds later, when the older woman rushed from the room.

Janet went into her bedroom and slammed the door. The sound of objects bouncing off walls followed in a furious staccato.

Libby bit her lip. She'd been warned not to do anything to make Janet panic and make a run for it, but the woman had pricked her temper. She wished she hadn't opened her mouth.

With dark thoughts, she finished baking a ham and made potato salad to go with it, along with homemade rolls. It gave her something to do besides worry.

But when Curt came home to eat, he was met by Janet with a suitcase, going out the door.

"Where are you off to?" he asked her coolly.

She threw a furious glance at the kitchen. "Anywhere I don't have to put up with your sister!" she snarled. "I'll get a motel room in town. You'll be hearing from my attorney in a day or so."

Curt's eyebrows lifted. "Funny. I was just about to tell you the same thing. I had a phone call from Kemp while I was at work. His private investigator has turned up some *very* interesting information about your former employment at a nursing home in Branntville…?"

Janet brushed by him in a mad rush toward her Mercedes. She threw her case in and jumped in behind it, spraying dirt as she spun out of the driveway.

"Well, that's clinched it," Curt mused as he joined his troubled sister in the kitchen. "She won't be back, or I'll miss my bet."

"I don't think it was a good idea to run her off," she commented as she set the table. "I'd already opened my big mouth and mentioned the locks on our bedroom doors and Violet's father to her."

"It's okay," Curt said gently. "I'm doing what Kemp told me to. I put her on the run."

"Mr. Kemp said to do that?"

He nodded, tossing his hat onto a side table and pulling out a chair. "Any coffee going? We've been mucking out line cabins all day. I'm beat!"

"Mucking out line cabins, not stables?"

"The river ran out of its banks right into that cabin on the north border," he said heavily. "We've been shoveling mud all afternoon. Crazy, isn't it? We had drought for four years, now it's floods. God must really be mad at somebody!"

"Don't look at me, I haven't done a single thing out of line."

He smiled. "When have you ever?" He studied her as she put food on the table. "Jordan says he's taking you out to a movie next week…watch it!"

Her hands almost let go of the potato salad bowl. She caught it and put it down carefully, gaping at her brother. ''Jordan's taking *me* to a movie?''

''It's what usually happens when men start kissing women,'' he said philosophically, leaning back in his chair with a wicked grin. ''They get addicted.''

''How did you know he was kissing me last night?''

He grinned wickedly. ''I didn't.''

She cleared her throat and turned away, reddening as she remembered the passionate kiss she and Jordan had shared before the supper he'd coaxed her to cook for him. She hadn't slept well all night thinking about it. Or about what Curt had said, that Jordan was spending a lot of time with Julie Merrill. But he couldn't be interested in the woman, if he wanted to take Libby out!

''You never got addicted to any women,'' she pointed out.

He shrugged. ''My day will come. It just hasn't yet.''

''What were you telling Janet about a private investigator and the nursing home?''

''Oh, yes.'' He waited until she sat down and they said grace before he continued, while piling ham on his plate. ''I'm not sure how much Kemp told you already but it seems that Janet has changed her legal identity since she worked in the nursing home. Also her hair color. She was under suspicion for the death of that elderly patient who liked to play the horses. She was making off with his bank account when it seems she was paid a visit by a gentleman representing a rather shadowy figure who was owed a great deal of money by the deceased. She left everything and ran for her life.'' He smiled complacently. ''You see, there were more debts than money left in the elderly gentleman's entire estate!''

Libby was listening intently.

''There's more.'' He took a bite of ham. ''This is nice!'' he exclaimed when he tasted it.

''Isn't it?'' She smiled. ''I got it from Duke Wright. He's

sidelining into a pork products shop and he's marketing on the Internet. He's doing organic bacon and ham."

"Smart guy."

She nodded. "There's more, you said?"

"Yes. They've just managed to convince Violet's mother that her husband might have been murdered. She's agreed to an exhumation."

"But they said the shock might be fatal!"

"Mrs. Hardy loved her husband. She never believed it was a heart attack. He'd had an echocardiogram that was misread, leading to a heart catheterization. They found nothing that would indicate grounds for a heart attack."

"Poor Violet," Libby said sadly. "It's going to be hard on her, too." She glanced up at her brother. "I still can't believe she quit and is going to work for Duke Wright."

"I know," he said. "She was crazy about Kemp!"

She nodded sadly. "Serves him right. He's been unpleasant to her lately. Violet's tired of eating her heart out for him. And who knows. It might prompt Mr. Kemp to do some soul searching."

"More than likely he'll just hire somebody else and forget all about her. If he wanted to be married, he could be," he added.

"He doesn't date anybody, does he?" she asked curiously.

He shook his head. "But he's not gay."

"I never thought he was. I just wondered why he keeps so much to himself."

"Maybe he's like a lot of other bachelors in Jacobsville, he's got a secret past that he doesn't want to share!"

"We're running out of bachelors," she retorted. "The Hart boys were the last to go and nobody ever thought they'd end up with families."

"Biscuits were their downfall," he pointed out.

"Jordan doesn't like biscuits," she mused. "I did ask, you know."

He chuckled. "Jordan doesn't have a weakness and he's

never lacked dates when he wanted them.'' He eyed her over his coffee cup. ''But he may be at the end of his own rope.''

''Don't look at me,'' she said, having spent too much time lately thinking about Jordan's intentions toward her. ''I may be the flavor of the week, but Jordan isn't going to want to marry down, if you see what I mean.''

His eyes narrowed. ''We may not be high society, but our people go back a long way in Jacobs County.''

''That doesn't put us in monied circles, either,'' she reminded him. Her eyes were dreamy and faraway. ''He's got a big, fancy house and he likes to keep company with high society. Maybe that's why he's been taking Senator Merrill's daughter around. It gets him into places he was never invited to before. We'd never fit. Especially me,'' she added in a more wistful tone than she realized.

''That wouldn't matter.''

She smiled sadly. ''It would and you know it. He'll need a wife who can entertain and throw parties, arrange sales, things like that. Most of all, he'll want a woman who's beautiful and intelligent, someone he'll be proud to show off. He might take me to a movie. But believe me, he won't take me to a minister.''

''You're sure of that?''

She looked up at him. ''You said it yourself— Jordan has been spending a lot of time with the state senator's daughter. He's running for re-election and the latest polls say that Calhoun Ballenger is almost tied with him. He needs all the support he can get, financial and otherwise. I think Jordan's going to help him, because of Julie.''

''Then why is he kissing you?''

''To make her jealous?'' she pondered. ''Maybe to convince himself that he's still attractive to women. But it's not serious. Not with him.'' She looked up. ''And I don't have affairs, whether it's politically correct or not.''

He sighed. ''I suppose we all have our pipe dreams.''

''What's yours, while we're on the subject?''

He smiled. ''I'd like to start a ranch supply company. The last one left belonged to Ted Regan's father-in-law. When he died, the store went bust, and then his daughter Corrie married Ted Regan and didn't need to make her own living. The hardware store can order most supplies, but not cattle feed or horse feed. Stuff like that.''

She hadn't realized her brother had such ambitions. ''If we weren't in such a financial mess, I'd be more than willing to co-sign a loan with the house as collateral.''

He stared at her intently. ''You'd do that for me?''

''Of course. You're my brother. I love you.''

He reached out and caught her hand. ''I love you, too, Sis.''

''Pipe dreams are nice. Don't you give yours up. Eventually we'll settle this inheritance question and we might have a little capital to work with.'' She studied him with pride. ''I think you'd make a great success of it. You've kept us solvent, up until Janet's unexpected arrival.''

''She'll be out for blood. I should probably call Kemp and update him on what's happened.''

''That might not be a bad idea. Maybe we should get a dog,'' she added slowly.

''Bad idea. We can hardly afford to feed old Bailey, your horse. We'd have to buy food for a dog, too, and it would break us.''

She saw his eyes twinkle and she burst out laughing, too.

Janet's attorney never showed up and two days later, Janet vanished, leaving a trail of charges to the Collinses for everything from clothes to the motel bill.

''You won't have to pay that,'' Kemp told Libby when he'd related the latest news to her. ''I've already alerted the merchants that she had no authority to charge anything to you or Curt, or the estate.''

''Thanks,'' she said with relief. ''What do we do now?''

''I've got the state police out looking for her,'' he replied, his hands deep in his slacks' pockets. ''On suspicion of murder. You won't like what's coming next.''

''What?''

''I want to have your father exhumed.''

She ground her teeth together. ''I was afraid of that.''

''We'll be discreet. But we need to have the crime lab check for trace evidence of poisoning. You see, we know what killed the old man at the nursing home where she worked. I believe she did kill him. Poisoners tend to stick to the same routine.''

''Poor Daddy,'' she said, feeling sick. Now she wondered if they might have saved him, if they'd only realized sooner that Janet was dangerous.

''Don't play mind games with yourself, Libby,'' Kemp said quietly. ''It does no good.''

''What a terrible way to go.''

''The poison she used was quick,'' he replied. ''Some can cause symptoms for months and the victim dies a painfully slow death. That wasn't the case here. It's the only good news I have for you, I'm afraid. But after they autopsy Mr. Hardy, there may be more forensic evidence to make a case against her. We've found a source for the poison.''

''But the doctor said that Daddy died of a heart attack,'' she began.

''He might have,'' Kemp had to admit. ''But he could as easily have died of poison or an air embolism.''

''Jordan mentioned that,'' she recalled.

He smiled secretively. ''Jordan doesn't miss a trick.''

''But Janet's gone. What if they discover that Daddy's death was foul play and then they can't find her?'' Libby pointed out. ''She's gotten away with it at least two times, by being cagey.''

''Every criminal eventually makes a mistake,'' he said absently. ''She'll make one. Mark my words.''

She only nodded. She glanced at Violet's empty desk and winced.

"I have an ad in the paper for a new secretary," he said coldly. "Meanwhile, Mabel's going to do double duty," he added, nodding toward Mabel, who was on the phone taking notes.

"It's going to be lonely without her," she said without thinking.

Kemp actually ground his teeth, turned on his heel and went back into his office. As an afterthought, he slammed the door.

Libby lost it. She laughed helplessly. Mabel, off the phone now and aware of Kemp's shocking attitude, laughed, too.

"It won't last long," Mabel whispered. "Violet was the only secretary he's ever had who could make and break appointments without hurting people's feelings. She was the fastest typist, too. He's not going to find somebody to replace her overnight."

Libby agreed silently. But it promised to be an interesting working environment for the foreseeable future.

Libby didn't even notice there was a message on the answering machine until after supper, when she'd had a lonely sandwich after Curt had phoned and said he was eating pizza with the other cowboys over at the Regan place for their weekly card game.

Curious, Libby punched the answer key and listened to the message. In a silken tone, the caller identified himself as an attorney named Smith and said that Mrs. Collins had hired him to do the probate on her late husband's will. He added that the children of Riddle Collins would have two weeks to vacate the premises.

Libby went through the roof. Her hands trembled as she tried to call Kemp and failing to reach him, she punched in Jordan's number.

It took a long time for him to answer the phone and when he finally did, there was conversation and music in the background.

"Yes?" he asked curtly.

Libby faltered. "Am I interrupting? I can call you another time..."

"Libby?" His voice softened. "Wait a minute." She heard muffled conversation, an angry reply, and the sound of a door closing. "Okay," he said. "What's wrong?"

"I can't get Mr. Kemp," she began urgently, "and Janet's attorney just called and said we had two weeks to get out of the house before they did the probate!"

"Libby," he said softly, "just sit down and use your mind. Think. When has anybody ever been asked to vacate a house just so that probate papers could be filed?"

She took a deep breath and then another. Her hands were still cold and trembling but she was beginning to remember bits and pieces of court documents. She was a paralegal. For God's sake, she knew about probate!

She sighed heavily. "Thanks. I just lost it. I was so shocked and so scared!"

"Is Curt there?"

"No, he went to his weekly card game with the cowboys over at Ted Regan's ranch," she said.

"I'm sorry I can't come over and talk to you. I'm having a fund-raising party for Senator Merrill tonight."

Merrill. His daughter Julie was the socialite. She was beautiful and rich and...socially acceptable. Certainly, she'd be at the party, too.

"Libby?" he prompted, when she didn't answer him.

"That's...that's okay, Jordan, I don't need company, honest," she said at once. "I just lost my mind for a minute. I'm sorry I bothered you. Really!"

"You don't have to apologize," he said, as if her statement unsettled him.

"I'll hang up now. Thanks, Jordan!"

He was still talking when she put the receiver down, very quickly, and put the answering machine back on. If he called back, she wasn't answering him. Janet's vicious tactics had unsettled her. She knew Janet had gotten someone to make that phone call deliberately, to upset Riddle's children.

It was her way of getting even, no doubt, for what Libby and Curt had said to her. She wondered if there was any way they could trace a call off an answering machine? A flash of inspiration hit her. Before Jordan would have time to call and foul the connection, she jerked up the phone and pressed the *69 keys. It gave her the number of the party who'd just phoned and she wrote it down at once, delighted to see that it was not a local number. She'd give it to Kemp the next morning and let his private investigator look into it.

Feeling more confident, she went back to the kitchen and finished washing up the few dishes. She couldn't forget Jordan's deep voice on the phone and the sound of a woman's voice arguing angrily when he went into another room to talk to Libby. It must be that senator's daughter. Obviously she felt possessive of Jordan and was wary of any potential rival. But Libby was no rival, she told herself. Jordan had just kissed her. That was all.

If only she could forget how it had felt. Then she remembered something else: Jordan's odd statements about Duke Wright's wife, and how young she was, and how she didn't quite know she wanted a career until she was already married and pregnant. He'd given Libby an odd, searching look when he said that.

The senator's daughter, Julie Merrill, was twenty-six, she recalled, with a degree in political science. Obviously she already knew what she wanted. She wanted Jordan. She was at his house tonight, probably hostessing the party there. Libby looked down at her worn jeans and faded blouse and then around her at the shabby but useful furniture in the old house. She laughed mirthlessly. What in the world would Jordan want with her, anyway? She'd been daydreaming. She'd better wake up, before she had her heart torn out.

* * *

She didn't phone Jordan again and he didn't call her back. She did give the telephone number of the so-called attorney to Mr. Kemp, who passed it along to his investigator.

Several days later, he paused by Libby's desk while she was writing up a precedent for a libel case, and he looked smug.

"That was quick thinking on your part," he remarked with a smile. "We traced the number to San Antonio. The man isn't an attorney, though. He's a waiter in a high-class restaurant who thinks Janet is his meal ticket to the easy life. We, uh, disabused him of the idea and told him one of her possible futures. We understand that he quit his job and left town on the next bus to make sure he wasn't involved in anything she did."

She laughed softly. "Thank goodness! Then Curt and I don't have to move!"

Kemp glared at her. "As if I'd stand by and let any so-called attorney toss you out of your home!"

"Thanks, boss," she said with genuine gratitude.

He shrugged. "Paralegals are thin on the ground," he said with twinkling blue-gray eyes.

"Callie Kirby and I are the only ones that I know of in town right now," she agreed.

"And Callie's got a child," he said, nodding. "I don't think Micah's going to want her to come back to work until their kids are in school."

"I expect not. She's got Micah's father to help take care of, too," she added, "after his latest stroke."

"People die," he said, and his eyes seemed distant and troubled.

"Mabel called in sick," she said reluctantly. "She's got some sort of stomach virus."

"They go around every spring," he agreed with a sigh. "Can you handle everything, or do you want to get a temp? If you do, call the agency. Ask if they've got somebody who can type."

She gave him her most innocent look. ''Of course I can do the work of three women, sir, and even make coffee...''

He laughed. ''Call the agency.''

''Yes, sir.''

He glowered. ''It's Violet's fault,'' he muttered, turning. ''I'll bet she's cursed us. We'll have sick help from now on.''

''I'm sure she'd never do that, Mr. Kemp,'' she assured him. ''She's a nice person.''

''Imagine taking offense at a *look* and throwing in the towel. Hell, I look at people all the time and they don't quit!''

She cleared her throat and nodded toward the door, which was just opening.

A lovely young woman with a briefcase and long blond hair came in. ''I'm Julie Merrill,'' she said with a haughty smile. ''Senator Merrill's daughter? You advertised for a secretary, I believe.''

Libby could not believe her eyes. Jordan's latest love and she turned up here looking for work! Of all the horrible bad luck...

Kemp stared at the young woman without speaking.

''Oh, not me!'' Julie laughed, clearing her throat. ''Heavens, I don't need a job! No, it's my friend Lydia. She's just out of secretarial school and she can't find anything suitable.''

''Can she type?''

''Yes! Sixty words a minute. And she can take shorthand, if you don't dictate too fast.''

''Can she speak?''

Julie blinked. ''I beg your pardon?''

Kemp gave her a scrutiny that would have stopped traffic. His eyes became a wintry blue, which Libby knew from experience meant that his temper was just beginning to kindle.

''I don't give jobs through third persons, Miss Merrill,

and I don't give a damn who your father is,'' he said with a cool smile.

She colored hotly and gaped at him. ''I...I...just thought...I mean, I could ask...!''

''Tell your friend she can come in and fill out an application, but not to expect much,'' he added shortly. ''I have no respect for a woman who has to be helped into a job through favoritism. And in case it's escaped your attention,'' he added, moving a step closer to her, ''nobody works for me unless they're qualified.''

Julie shot a cold glare at Libby, who was watching intently. ''I guess you think she's qualified,'' she said angrily.

''I have a diploma as a trained paralegal,'' Libby replied coolly. ''It's on the wall behind you, at my desk.''

Kemp only smiled. It wasn't a nice smile.

Julie set her teeth together so hard that they almost clicked. ''I don't think Lydia would like this job, anyway!''

Kemp's right eyebrow arched. ''Was there anything else, Miss Merrill?''

She turned, jerking open the door. ''My father will not be happy when I tell him how you've spoken to me.''

''By all means, tell him, with my blessing,'' Kemp said. ''One of his faults is a shameful lack of discipline with his children. I understand you've recently expressed interest in running for public office in Jacobs County, Miss Merrill. Let me give you a piece of advice. Don't.''

Her mouth fell open. ''How dare you...!''

''It's your father's money, of course. If he wants to throw it away, that's his concern.''

''I could win an election!''

Kemp smiled. ''Perhaps you could. But not in Jacobs County,'' he said pleasantly. His eyes narrowed and became cold and his voice grew deceptively soft. ''Closet skeletons become visible baggage in an election. And no one here has forgotten your high-school party. Especially not the Culbertsons.''

Julie's face went pale. Her fingers on the briefcase

tightened until the knuckles showed. She actually looked frightened.

"That was...a terrible accident."

"Shannon Culbertson is still dead."

Julie's lower lip trembled. She turned and went out the door so quickly that she forgot to close it.

Kemp did it for her, his face cold and hard, full of repressed fury.

Libby wondered what was going on, but she didn't dare ask.

Later, of course, when Curt got home from work, she couldn't resist asking the question.

He scowled. "What the hell did Julie want in Kemp's office? Lydia doesn't need a job, she already has a job—a good one—at the courthouse over in Bexar County!"

"She said Lydia wanted to work for Mr. Kemp, but she was giving me the evil eye for all she was worth."

"She wants Jordan. You're in the way."

"Sure I am," she laughed coldly. "What about that girl, Shannon Culbertson?"

Curt hesitated. "That was eight years ago."

"What happened?"

"Somebody put something in her drink—which she wasn't supposed to have had in the first place. It was a forerunner of the date-rape drug. She had a hidden heart condition. It killed her."

"Who did it?"

"Nobody knows, but Julie tried to cover it up, to save her father's senate seat. Kemp dug out the truth and gave it to the newspapers." He shook his head. "A vindictive man, Kemp."

"Why?" she asked.

"They say Kemp was in love with the girl. He never got over it."

"But Julie's father won the election," she pointed out.

"Only because the leading lights of the town supported him and contributed to his reelection campaign. Most of those old-timers are dead or in nursing homes and the gossip around town is that Senator Merrill is already over his ears in debt from his campaign. Besides which, he's up against formidable opposition for the first time in recent years."

Chapter Five

So that was Kemp's secret, Libby thought. A lost love. "Yes, I know," she said. "Calhoun Ballenger has really shaken up the district politically. A lot of people think he's going to win the nomination right out from under Merrill."

"I'm almost sure he will," Curt replied. "The powers that be in the county have changed over the past few years. The Harts have come up in the world. So have the Tremaynes, the Ballengers, Ted Regan, and a few other families. The power structure now isn't in the hands of the old elite. If you don't believe that, notice what's going on at city hall. Chief Grier is making a record number of drug busts and I don't need to remind you that Senator Merrill was arrested for drunk driving."

"That never was in the paper, you know," she said with a wry smile.

"The publisher is one of his cronies—he refused to run the story. But Merrill's up to his ears in legal trouble. So he's trying to get the mayor and two councilmen who owe him favors to fire the two police officers who made the arrest and discredit them. The primary election is the first week of May, you know.''

''Poor police,'' she murmured.

''Mark my words, they'll never lose their jobs. Grier has contacts everywhere and despite his personal problems, he's not going to let his officers go down without a fight. I'd bet everything I have on him.''

She grinned. ''I like him.''

Curt chuckled. ''I like him, too.''

''Mr. Kemp said they traced the lawyer's call to San Antonio,'' she added, and told him what was said. ''Why would she want us out of the house?''

''Maybe she thinks there's something in it that she hasn't gotten yet,'' he mused. ''Dad's coin collection, for instance.''

''I haven't seen that in months,'' she said.

''Neither have I. She probably sold it already,'' he said with cold disgust. ''But Janet's going to hang herself before she quits.'' He gave his sister a sad look. ''I'm sorry about the exhumation. But we really need to know the truth about how Dad died.''

''I know,'' she replied. The pain was still fresh and she had to fight tears. She managed a smile for him. ''Daddy wouldn't mind.''

''No. I don't think he would.''

''I wish we'd paid more attention to what was going on.''

''He thought he loved her, Libby,'' he said. ''Maybe he did. He wouldn't have listened to us, no matter what we said, if it was something bad about her. You know how he was.''

''Loving her blindly may have cost him his life.''

''Try to remember that he died happy. He didn't know what Janet was. He didn't know that she was cheating him.''

''It doesn't help much.''

He nodded. ''Nothing will bring him back. But maybe

we can save somebody else's father. That would make it all worthwhile.''

''Yes,'' she agreed. ''It would.''

That evening while they were watching television, a truck drove up. A minute later, there was a hard knock on the door.

''I've got it,'' Curt said, leaving Libby with her embroidery.

There were muffled voices and then heavy footsteps coming into the room.

Jordan stared at Libby curiously. ''Julie came to your office today,'' he said.

''She was looking for a job for her friend Lydia,'' Libby said in a matter-of-fact tone.

''That's not what she said,'' Jordan replied tersely. ''She told me that you treated her so rudely that Kemp made her leave the office.''

Libby lifted both eyebrows. ''Wow. Imagine that.''

''I'm not joking with you, Libby,'' Jordan said, and his tone chilled. ''That was a petty thing to do.''

''It would have been,'' she agreed, growing angry herself, ''if I'd done it. She came into the office in a temper, glared at me, made some rude remarks to Mr. Kemp and got herself thrown out.''

''That's not what she told me,'' he repeated.

Libby got to her feet, motioning to Curt, who was about to protest on her behalf. ''I don't need help, Curt. Stay out of it, that's a nice brother.'' She moved closer to Jordan. ''Miss Merrill insinuated that Mr. Kemp had better offer Lydia a job because of her father's position in the community. And he reminded her about her high-school graduation party where a girl died.''

''He what?'' he exploded.

''Mr. Kemp doesn't take threats lying down,'' she said, uneasy because of Jordan's overt hostility. ''Miss Merrill was very haughty and very rude. And neither of us can understand why she'd try to get Lydia a job at Kemp's office, because she's already got one in San Antonio!''

Jordan didn't say anything. He just stood there, silent.

''She was with you when I phoned your house, I guess, and she got the idea that I was chasing you,'' she said, gratified by the sudden blinking of his eyelids. ''You can tell her, for me,'' she added with saccharine sweetness, ''that I would not have you on a hot dog bun with uptown relish. If she thinks I'm the competition, all she has to do is look where I live.'' Her face tautened. ''Go ahead, Jordan, look around you. I'm not even in your league, whatever your high-class girlfriend thinks. You're a kind neighbor whom I asked for advice and that's all you ever were. Period,'' she lied, trying to save face.

He still wasn't moving or speaking. But his eyes were taking on a nasty glitter. Beside his lean hips, one of his hands was clenched until the knuckles went white. ''Ever?'' he prodded, his tone insinuating things.

She knew what he meant. She swallowed hard, trying not to remember the heat and power of the kisses they'd shared. Obviously, they'd meant nothing to him!

''Ever,'' she repeated. ''I certainly wasn't trying to tie you down, Jordan. I'm not at all sure that I want to spend the rest of my life in Jacobsville working for a lawyer, anyway,'' she added deliberately, but without looking at him. ''I've thought about that a lot, about what you said. Maybe I do have ambitions.''

He didn't speak for several seconds. His eyes became narrow and cold.

''If you'd like to show your Julie that I'm no competition, you can bring her down here and show her how we live,'' she offered with a smile. ''That would really open her eyes, wouldn't it?''

''Libby,'' Curt warned. ''Don't talk like that.''

''How should I talk?'' she demanded, her throat tightening. ''Our father is dead and it looks like our stepmother killed him right under our noses! She's trying to take away everything we have, getting her friends to call and threaten and harass us, and now here's Jordan's goody-two-shoes girlfriend making me out to be a man-stealer, or somebody. How the hell should I talk?!"

Jordan let out a long breath. "I thought you knew what you wanted," he said after a minute.

"I'm young. Like you said," she said cynically. "Sorry I ever asked you for help, Jordan, and made your girlfriend mad. You can bet I'll never make that mistake twice."

She turned and went into the kitchen and slammed the door behind her. She was learning really bad habits from Mr. Kemp, she decided, as she wiped tears away with a paper towel.

She heard the door open behind her and close again, firmly. It was Curt, she supposed, coming to check on her.

"I guess I handled that badly," she said, choking on tears. "Has he gone?"

Big, warm hands caught her shoulders and turned her around. Jordan's eyes glittered down into hers. "No, he hasn't gone," he bit off.

He looked ferocious like that. She should have been intimidated, but she wasn't. He was handsome, even bristling with temper.

"I've said all I have to say," she began.

"Well, I haven't," he shot back, goaded. "I've never looked down on you for what you've got and you know it."

"Julie Merrill does," she muttered.

His hands tightened and relaxed. He looked vaguely embarrassed. His dark eyes slid past her to the worn calendar on the wall. "You know how I grew up," he said heavily. "We had nothing. I was never invited to parties. My parents were glorified servants in the eyes of the town's social set."

She drew in a short breath. "And now Julie's opening the doors and inviting you in and you like it."

He seemed shocked by the statement. His eyes dropped to meet hers. "Maybe."

"Can't you see why?" she asked quietly. "You're rich now. You made something out of nothing. You have confidence, and power, and you know how to behave in company. But there's more to it than that, where the Merrills are concerned."

"That's not your business," he said shortly.

She smiled sadly. "They need financial backing. Their old friends aren't as wealthy as they used to be. Calhoun Ballenger has the support of the newer wealthy people in Jacobsville and they don't deal in 'good old boy' politics."

"In other words, Julie only wants me for money to run her father's re-election campaign."

"You know better than that," she replied, searching his hard face hungrily. "You're handsome and sexy. Women adore you."

One eyebrow lifted. "Even you?"

She wanted to deny it, but she couldn't. "Even me," she confessed. "But I'm no more in your class, really, than you're in Julie's. They're old money. It doesn't really matter to them how rich you get, you'll never be one of them."

His eyes narrowed angrily. "I am one of them," he retorted. "I'm hobnobbing with New York society, with Kentucky thoroughbred breeders, with presidential staff members—even with Hollywood producers and actors!"

"You could do that on your own," she said. "You don't need the Merrills to make you socially acceptable. And in case you've forgotten, Christabel and Judd Dunn have been hobnobbing with Hollywood people for a year. They're not rich. Not really."

He was losing the argument and he didn't like it. He glared down at her with more riotous feelings than he'd entertained in years. "Julie wants to marry me," he said, producing the flat statement like a weapon.

She managed not to react to the retort, barely. Her heart was sinking like lead in her chest as she pictured Julie in a designer wedding gown flashing diamonds like pennies on her way to the altar.

"*She* doesn't want a career," he added, smiling coldly.

Neither did Libby, really. She liked having a job, but she also liked living in Jacobsville and working around the ranch. She'd have liked being Jordan's wife more than anything else she could think of. But that wasn't going to happen. He didn't want her.

She tried to pull away from Jordan's strong hands, but he wasn't budging.

"Let me go," she muttered. "I'm sure Julie wouldn't like this!"

"Wouldn't like what?" he drawled. "Being in my arms, or having you in them?"

"Are you having fun?" she challenged.

"Not yet," he murmured, dropping his gaze to her full lips. "But I expect to be pretty soon..."

"You can't...!"

But he could. And he was. She felt the warm, soft, coaxing pressure of his hard mouth before she could finish the protest. Her eyes closed. She was aware of his size and strength, of the warmth of his powerful body against hers. She could feel his heartbeat, feel the rough sigh of his breath as he deepened the kiss.

He hadn't really meant to do this. He'd meant it as a punishment, for the things she'd said to him. But when he had her so close that he could feel her heart beating like a wild thing against him, nothing else seemed to matter except pleasing her, as she was pleasing him.

He drew her up closer, so that he could feel the soft, warm imprint of her body on the length of his. He traced her soft mouth with his lips, with the tip of his tongue. He felt her stiffen and then lift up to him. He gathered her completely against him and forgot Julie, forgot the argument, forgot everything.

She felt the sudden ardor of his embrace grow unmanageable in a space of seconds. His mouth was insistent on hers, demanding. His hands had gone to her hips. They were pressing her against the sudden rigidity of his powerful body. Even as she registered his urgent hunger for her, she felt one of his big, lean hands seeking between them for the soft, rounded curve of her breast…

She pulled away from him abruptly, her mouth swollen, her eyes wild. "N-no," she choked.

He tried to pull her back into his arms. "Why not?" he murmured, his eyes on her mouth.

"Curt," she whispered.

"Curt." He spoke the name as if he didn't recognize it. He blinked. He took a deep breath and suddenly realized where they were and what he'd been doing.

He drew in a harsh, deep breath.

"You have to go home," she said huskily.

He stood up straight and stared down his nose at her. "If you will keep throwing yourself into my arms, what do you expect?" he asked outrageously.

She gaped at him.

"It's no use trying to look innocent," he added as he moved back another step. "And don't start taking off your blouse, it won't work."

"I am not…!" she choked, crossing her arms quickly.

He made a rough sound in his throat. "A likely story. Don't follow me home, either, because I lock my doors at night."

She wanted to react to that teasing banter that she'd enjoyed so much before, but she couldn't forget that he'd taken Julie's side against her.

She stared at him coldly. "I won't follow you home. Not while you're spending all your free time defending Julie Merrill, when I'm the one who was insulted."

He froze over. "The way Julie tells it, you started on her first."

"And you believe her, of course. She's beautiful and rich and sophisticated."

"Something no man in his right mind could accuse you

of,'' he shot back. With a cold glare, he turned and went out the door.

He didn't pause to speak to Curt, who was just coming in the front door. He shot him a look bare of courtesy and stormed outside. He was boiling over with emotion, the strongest of which was frustrated desire.

Libby didn't explain anything to her brother, but she knew he wasn't blind or stupid. He didn't ask questions, either. He just hugged her and smiled.

She went to bed feeling totally at sea. How could an argument lead to something so tempestuous that she'd almost passed out at Jordan's feet? And if he really wanted Julie, then how could he kiss Libby with such frustrated desire? And why had he started another fight before he left?

She was still trying to figure out why she hadn't slapped his arrogant face when she fell asleep.

The tension between Jordan and his neighbors was suddenly visible even to onlookers. He never set foot on their place. When he had a barbecue for his ranch hands in April, to celebrate the impressive calf sale he'd held, Curt wasn't invited. When Libby had a small birthday party to mark her twenty-fourth birthday, Jordan wasn't on the guest list. Jacobsville being the small town it was, people noticed.

''Have you and Jordan had some sort of falling out?'' Mr. Kemp asked while his new secretary, a sweet little brunette fresh out of high school named Jessie, was out to lunch.

Libby looked up at him with wide-eyed innocence. ''Falling out?''

''Julie Merrill has been telling people that she and Jordan have marriage plans,'' he said. ''I don't believe it. Her father's in financial hot water and Jordan's rich. Old man Merrill is going to need a lot of support in today's political climate. He made some bad calls on the budget and education and the voters are out to get him."

"So I've heard. They say Calhoun Ballenger's just pulled ahead in the polls."

"He'll win," Kemp replied. "It's no contest. Regardless of Jordan's backing."

"Mr. Kemp, would they really use what happened at Julie's party as a weapon against her father?" she asked carefully.

"Of course they would!" he said shortly. "Even in Jacobs County, dirty laundry has a value. There are other skeletons in that closet, too. Plenty of them. Merrill has already lost the election. His way of doing business, under the table, is obsolete. He's trying to make Cash Grier fire those arresting officers and swear they lied. It won't happen. He and his daughter just don't know it and she refuses to face defeat."

"She's at Jordan's house every day now," she said on a sigh that was more wistful than she knew. "She's very beautiful."

"She's a tarantula," Kemp said coldly. "She's got her finger in a pie I can't tell you about, but it's about to hit the tabloids. When it does, her father can kiss his career goodbye."

"Sir?"

He lifted both eyebrows. "Can you keep a secret?"

"If I can't, why am I working for you?" she asked pertly.

"Those two officers Grier's backing, who caught the senator driving drunk—" he said. "They've also been investigating a house out on the Victoria road where drugs are bought and sold. That's the real reason they're facing dismissal. Merrill's nephew is our mayor."

"And he's in it up to his neck, I guess?" she fished.

He nodded. "The nephew and Miss Merrill herself. That's where her new Porsche came from."

Libby whistled. ''But if Jordan's connected with her...'' she said worriedly.

''That's right,'' he replied. ''He'll be right in hot water with her, even though he's not doing anything illegal. Mud not only sticks, it rubs off.''

She chewed her lower lip. ''You couldn't warn him, I guess?''

He shook his head. ''We aren't speaking.''

She stared at him. ''But you're friends.''

''Not anymore. You see, he thinks I took your side unjustly against Miss Merrill.''

She frowned. ''I'm sorry.''

He chuckled. ''It will all blow over in a few weeks. You'll see.''

She wasn't so confident. She didn't think it would and she hated the thought of seeing Jordan connected with such an unsavory business.

She walked down to Barbara's Café for lunch and ran right into Julie Merrill and Jordan Powell, who were waiting in line together.

''Oh, look, it's the little secretary,'' Julie drawled when she saw Libby in line behind them. ''Still telling lies about me, Miss Collins?'' she asked with a laugh.

Jordan was looking at Libby with an expression that was hard to classify.

Libby ignored her, turning instead to speak to one of the girls from the county clerk's office, who was in line behind her.

''Don't you turn your back on me, you little creep!'' Julie raged, attracting attention as she walked right up to Libby. Her eyes were glazed, furious. ''You told Jordan that I tried to throw my weight around in Kemp's office and it was a lie! You were just trying to make yourself look good, weren't you?!''

Libby felt sick at her stomach. She was no good at dealing with angry people, despite the fact that she had to watch

Kemp's secretaries do it every day. She wasn't really afraid of the other girl, but she was keenly aware of their differences on the social ladder. Julie was rich and well-known and sophisticated. Libby was little more than a rancher's daughter turned legal apprentice.

"Jordan can't stand you, in case you wondered, so it's no use calling him up all the time for help, and standing at his door trying to make him notice you!" Julie continued haughtily. "He wouldn't demean himself by going out with a dirty little nobody like you!"

Libby pulled herself up and stared at the older girl, keenly aware of curious eyes watching and people listening in the crowded lunch traffic. "Jordan is our neighbor, Miss Merrill," she said in a strained tone. Her legs were shaking, but she didn't let it show. "Nothing more. I don't want Jordan."

"Good. I'm glad you realize that Jordan's nothing more than a neighbor, because you're a nuisance! No man in his right mind would look at you twice!"

"Oh, I don't know about that," Harley Fowler said suddenly, moving up the line to look down at Julie Merrill with cold eyes. "I'd say her manners are a damned sight better than yours and your mouth wouldn't get you into any decent man's house in Jacobsville!"

Julie's mouth fell open.

"I wouldn't have her on toast!" one of the Tremaynes' cowboys ventured from his table.

"Hey, Julie, how about a dime bag?" some anonymous voice called. "I need a fix!"

Julie went pale. "Who said that?!" she demanded shakily.

"Julie, let's go," Jordan said curtly, taking her by the arm.

"I'm hungry!" she protested, fighting his hold.

Libby didn't look up as he passed her with Julie firmly at his side. He didn't look at her, either, and his face was white with rage.

As she went out the door, there was a skirl of belligerent

applause from the patrons of the café. Julie made a rude gesture toward them, which was followed by equally rude laughter.

"Isn't she a pain?" The girl from the clerk's office laughed. "Honestly, Libby, you were such a lady! I'd have laid a chair across her thick skull!"

"Me, too," said another girl. "Nobody can stand her. She thinks she's such a debutante."

Libby listened to the talk with a raging heartbeat. She was sick to her stomach from the unexpected confrontation and glad that Jordan had gotten the girl out of the room before things got ugly. But it ruined her lunch. It ruined her whole day.

It didn't occur to Libby that Jordan would be upset about the things that Julie had said in the café, especially since he hadn't said a word to Libby at the time. But he actually came by Kemp's office the next day, hat in hand, to apologize for Julie's behavior.

He looked disappointed when Kemp was sitting perched on the edge of Libby's desk, as if he'd hoped to find her alone. But he recovered quickly.

He gave Kemp a quick glare, his gaze returning at once to Libby. "I wanted to apologize for Julie," he said curtly. "She's sorry she caused a scene yesterday. She's been upset about her father facing drunk-driving charges."

"I don't receive absentee apologies," Libby said coldly. "And you'll never convince me that she *would* apologize."

Kemp's eyebrows collided. "What's that?"

"Julie made some harsh remarks about me in Barbara's Café yesterday," Libby told him, "in front of half the town."

"Why didn't you come and get me?" Kemp asked. "I'd have settled her hash for her," he added, with a dangerous look at Jordan.

"Harley Fowler defended me," Libby said with a quiet

smile. ''So did several other gentlemen in the crowd,'' she added deliberately.

''She's not as bad as you think she is,'' Jordan said grimly.

''The hell she's not,'' Kemp replied softly. He got up. ''I know things about her that you're going to wish you did and very soon. Libby, don't be long. We've got a case first thing tomorrow. I'll need those notes,'' he added, nodding toward the computer screen. He went to his office and closed the door.

''What was Kemp talking about?'' Jordan asked Libby curiously.

''I could tell you, but you wouldn't believe me,'' she said sadly, remembering how warm their relationship had been before Julie Merrill clouded the horizon.

He drew in a long breath and moved a little closer, pushing his hat back over his dark hair. He looked down at her with barely contained hunger. Mabel was busy in the back with the photocopier and the girl who was filling in for Violet had gone to a dental appointment. Mr. Kemp was shut up in his office. Libby kept hoping the phone would ring, or someone would come in the front door and save her from Jordan. It was all she could do not to throw herself into his arms, even after the fights they'd had. She couldn't stop being attracted to him.

''Look,'' he said quietly, ''I'm not trying to make an enemy of you. I like Julie. Her father is a good man and he's had some hard knocks lately. They really need my help, Libby. They haven't got anybody else.''

She could just imagine Julie crying prettily, lavishing praise on Jordan for being so useful, dressing up in her best—which was considerably better than Libby's best—and making a play for him. She might be snippy and aggressive toward other women, but Julie Merrill was a practiced seducer. She knew how to wind men around her finger. She was young and beautiful and cultured and rich.

She knew tricks that most men—even Jordan—wouldn't be able to resist.

''Why are you so attracted to her?'' Libby wondered aloud.

Jordan gave her an enigmatic look. ''She's mature,'' he said without thinking. ''She knows exactly what she wants and she goes after it wholeheartedly. Besides that, she's a woman who could have anybody.''

''And she wants you,'' she said for him.

He shrugged. ''Yes. She does.''

She studied his lean, hard face, surprising a curious rigidity there before he concealed it. ''I suppose you're flattered,'' she murmured.

''She draws every man's eye when she walks into a room,'' he said slowly. ''She can play the piano like a professional. She speaks three languages. She's been around the world several times. She's dated some of the most famous actors in Hollywood. She's even been presented to the queen in England.'' He sighed. ''Most men would have a hard time turning up their noses at a woman like that.''

''In other words, she's like a trophy.''

He studied her arrogantly. ''You could say that. But there's something more, too. She needs me. She said everyone in town had turned their backs on her father. Calhoun Ballenger is drawing financial support from some of the richest families in town, the same people who promised Senator Merrill their support and then withdrew it. Julie was in tears when she told me how he'd been sold out by his best friends. Until I came along, he actually considered dropping out of the race.''

And pigs fly, Libby thought privately, but she didn't say it. The Merrills were dangling their celebrity in front of Jordan, a man who'd been shut out of high society even though he was now filthy rich. They were offering him entry into a closed community. All that and beautiful Julie as well.

''Did you hear what she said to me in Barbara's Café?'' she wondered aloud.

''What do you mean?'' he asked curiously.

''You stood there and let her attack me, without saying a word.''

He scowled. ''I was talking to Brad Henry while we stood in line, about a bull he wanted to sell. I didn't realize what was going on until Julie raised her voice. By then, Harley Fowler and several other men were making catcalls at her. I thought the best thing to do would be to get her outside before things escalated.''

''Did you hear her accuse me of chasing you? Did you hear her warn me off you?''

He cocked his head. ''I heard that part,'' he admitted. ''She's very possessive and more jealous of me than I realized. But I didn't like having her insult you, if that's what you mean,'' he said quietly. ''I told her so later. She said she'd apologize, but I thought it might come easier from me. She's insecure, Libby. You wouldn't think so, but she really takes things to heart.''

A revelation a minute, Libby was thinking. Jordan actually believed what he was saying. Julie had really done a job on him.

''She said that you wouldn't waste your time on a nobody like me,'' she persisted.

''Women say things they don't mean all the time.'' He shrugged it off. ''You take things to heart, too, Libby,'' he added gently. ''You're still very young.''

''You keep saying that,'' she replied, exasperated. ''How old do I have to be for you to think of me as an adult?''

He moved closer, one lean hand going to her slender throat, slowly caressing it. ''I've thought of you like that for a long time,'' he said deeply. ''But you're an addiction I can't afford. You said it yourself—you're ambitious. You won't be satisfied in a small town. Like the old-timers used to say, you want to go and see the elephant.''

She was caught in his dark eyes, spellbound. She'd said

that, yes, because of the way he'd behaved about Julie's insults. She'd wanted to sting him. But she didn't mean it. She wasn't ambitious. All she wanted was Jordan. Her eyes were lost in his.

"The elephant?" she parroted, her gaze on his hard mouth.

"You want to see the world," he translated. But he was moving closer as he said it and his head was bending, even against his will. This was stupid. He couldn't afford to let himself be drawn into this sweet trap. Libby wanted a career. She was young and ambitious. He'd go in headfirst and she'd take off and leave him, just as Duke Wright's young wife had left him in search of fame and fortune. He'd deliberately drawn back from Libby and let himself be vamped by Julie Merrill, to show this little firecracker that he hadn't been serious about those kisses they'd exchanged. He wasn't going to risk his heart on a gamble this big. Libby was in love with love. She was attracted to him. But that wasn't love. She was too young to know the difference. He wasn't. He'd grabbed at Julie the way a drowning man reaches for a life jacket. Libby didn't know that. He couldn't admit it.

While he was thinking, he was parting her lips with his. He forgot where they were, who they were. He forgot the arguments and all the reasons he shouldn't do this.

"Libby," he growled against her soft lips.

She barely heard him. Her blood was singing in her veins like a throbbing chorus. Her arms went around his neck in a stranglehold. She pushed up against him, forcing into his mouth in urgency.

His arms swallowed her up whole. The kiss was slow, deep, hungry. It was invasive. Her whole body began to throb with delight. It began to swell. Their earlier kisses had been almost chaste. These were erotic. They were… narcotic.

A soft little cry of pleasure went from her mouth into

his and managed to penetrate the fog of desire she was drowning him in.

He jerked back from her as if he'd been stung. He fought to keep his inner turmoil from showing, his weakness from being visible to her. His big hands caught her waist and pushed her firmly away.

"I know," she said breathlessly. "You think I've had snakebite on my lip and you were only trying to draw out the poison."

He burst out laughing in spite of himself.

She swallowed hard and backed away another step. "Just think how Julie Merrill would react if she saw you kissing me."

That wiped the smile off his face. "That wasn't a kiss," he said.

"No kidding?" She touched her swollen mouth ironically. "I'll bet Julie could even give you lessons."

"Don't talk about her like that," he warned.

"You think she's honest and forthright, because you are," she said, a little breathless. "You're forgetting that her father is a career politician. They both know how to bend the truth without breaking it, how to influence public opinion."

"Politics is a science," he retorted.

"It can be a horrible corruption, as well," she reminded him. "Calhoun Ballenger has taken a lot of heat from them, even a sexual harassment charge that had no basis in fact. Fortunately, people around here know better, and it backfired. It only made Senator Merrill look bad."

His eyes began to glitter. "That wasn't fiction. The woman swore it happened."

"She was one of Julie's cousins," she said with disgust.

He looked as if he hadn't known that. He scowled, but he didn't answer her.

"Julie thinks my brother and I are so far beneath her that we aren't even worth mentioning," she continued, folding her arms over her chest. "She chooses her friends by their social status and bank accounts. Curt and I are losers in her book and she doesn't think we're fit to associate with you. She'll find a way to push you right out of our lives."

"I don't have social status, but I'm welcome in their home," he said flatly.

"There's an election coming up, they don't have enough money to win it, but you do. They'll take your money and make you feel like an equal until you're not needed anymore. Then you'll be out on your ear. You don't come from old money, Jordan, even if you're rich now..."

"You don't know a damned thing about what I come from," he snapped.

The furious statement caught her off guard. She knew Jordan had made his own fortune, but he never spoke about his childhood. His mother worked as a housekeeper. Everybody knew it. He sounded as if he couldn't bear to admit his people were only laborers.

"I didn't mean to be insulting," she began slowly.

"Hell! You're doing your best to turn me against Julie. She said you would," he added. "She said something else, too—that you're involved with Harley Fowler."

She refused to react to that. "Harley's sweet. He defended me when Julie was insulting me."

That was a sore spot, because Jordan hadn't really heard what Julie was saying until it was too late. He didn't like Harley, anyway.

"Harley's a nobody."

"Just like me," she retorted. "I'd much rather have Harley than you, Jordan," she added. "He may be just a working stiff, but he's got more class than you'll ever have, even if you hang out with the Merrills for the next fifty years!"

That did it. He gave her a furious glare, spit out a word that would have insulted Satan himself and marched right out the door.

"And stay out!" she called after it slammed.

Kemp stuck his head out of his office door and stared at

her. "Are you that same shy, introverted girl who came to work here last year?"

She grinned at him through her heartbreak. "You're rubbing off on me, Mr. Kemp," she remarked.

He laughed curtly and went back into his office.

Later, Libby was miserable. They'd exhumed her father's body and taken it up to the state crime lab in Austin for tests.

Curt was furious when she told him that Jordan had been to her office to apologize for the Merrill girl.

"As if she'd ever apologize to the likes of us," he said angrily. "And Jordan just stood by and let her insult you in the café without saying a word!"

She gaped at him. "How did you know that?"

"Harley Fowler came by where I was working this morning to tell me about it. He figured, rightly, that you'd try to keep it to yourself." He sank down into a chair. "I gave Jordan notice this afternoon. In two weeks, I'm out of there."

She grimaced. "But, Curt, where will you go?"

"Right over to Duke Wright's place," he replied with a smile. "I already lined up a job and I'll get a raise, to boot."

"That's great," she said, and meant it.

"We'll be fine. Don't worry about it." He sighed. "It's so much lately, isn't it, Sis? But we'll survive. We will!"

"I know that, Curt. I'm not worried."

But she was. She hated being enemies with Jordan, who was basically a kind and generous man. She was furious with the Merrills for coming between them for such a selfish reason. They only wanted Jordan's money for the old man's reelection campaign. They didn't care about Jordan. But perhaps he was flattered to be included in such high society, to be asked to hang out with their friends and acquaintances.

But Libby knew something about the people the Merrills associated with that, perhaps, Jordan didn't. Many of them were addicts, either to liquor or drugs. They did nothing for the community; only for themselves. They wanted to know the right people, be seen in the right places, have money that showed when people looked. But to Libby, who loved her little house and little ranch, it seemed terribly artificial.

She didn't have much but she was happy with her life. She enjoyed planting things and watching them grow. She liked teaching Vacation Bible School in the summer and working in the church nursery with little children. She liked cooking food to carry to bereaved families when relatives died. She liked helping out with church bazaars, donating time to the local soup kitchen. She didn't put on airs, but people seemed to like her just the way she was.

Certainly Harley Fowler did. He'd come over to see her the day after Julie's attack in the café, to make sure she was all right. He'd asked her out to eat the following Saturday night.

"Only to Shea's," he chuckled. "I just paid off a new transmission for my truck and I'm broke."

She'd grinned at him. "That's okay. I'm broke, too!"

He shook his head, his eyes sparkling as he looked down at her with appreciation. "Libby, you're my kind of people."

"Thanks, Harley."

"Say, can you dance?"

She blinked. "Well, I can do a two-step."

"That's good enough." He chuckled. "I've been taking these dance courses on the side."

"I know. I heard about the famous waltz with Janie Brewster at the Cattleman's Ball last year."

He smiled sheepishly. "Well, now I'm working on the

jitterbug and I hear that Shea's live band can play that sort of thing.''

''You can teach me to jitterbug, Harley,'' she agreed at once. ''I'd love to go dancing with you.''

He looked odd. ''Really?''

She nodded and smiled. ''Really.''

''Then I'll see you Saturday about six. We can eat there, too.''

''Suits me. I'll leave supper for Curt in the refrigerator. That was really nice of you to go to bat for him with your boss, Harley,'' she added seriously. ''Thanks.''

He shrugged. ''Mr. Parks wasn't too pleased with the way Powell's sucking up to the Merrills, either,'' he said. ''He knows things about them.''

''So do I,'' she replied. ''But Jordan doesn't take well-meant advice.''

''His problem,'' Harley said sharply.

She nodded. ''Yes, Harley. It's his problem. I'll see you Saturday!'' she added, laughing.

When she told Curt about the upcoming date, he seemed pleased. ''It's about time you went out and had some fun for a change.''

''I like Harley a lot,'' she told her brother.

He searched her eyes knowingly. ''But he's not Jordan.''

She turned away. ''Jordan made his choice. I'm making mine.'' She smiled philosophically. ''I dare say we'll both be happy!''

Chapter Six

Libby and Harley raised eyebrows at Shea's Roadhouse and Bar with their impromptu rendition of the jitterbug. It was a full house, too, on a Saturday night. At least two of the Tremayne brothers were there with their wives, and Calhoun Ballenger and his wife, Abby, were sitting at a table nearby with Leo Hart and his wife, Janie.

"I'm absolutely sure that Calhoun's going to win the state senate seat," Harley said in Libby's ear when they were seated again, drinking iced tea and eating hamburgers. "It looks like he's going to get some support from the Harts."

"Is Mr. Parks in his corner, too?" she asked.

He nodded. "All the way. The political landscape has been changing steadily for the past few years, but old man Merrill just keeps going with his old agenda. He hasn't got a clue what the voters want anymore. And, more important, he doesn't control them through his powerful friends."

"You'd think his daughter would be forward-thinking," she pointed out.

He didn't say anything. But his face was eloquent.

''Somebody said she was thinking of running for public office in Jacobsville,'' she began.

''No name identification,'' Harley said at once. ''You have to have it to win an office. Without it, all the money in the world won't get you elected.''

''You seem to know something about politics,'' she commented.

He averted his eyes. ''Do I?'' he mused.

Harley never talked about his family, or his past. He'd shown up at Cy Parks' place one day and proved himself to be an exceptional cowboy, but nobody knew much about him. He'd gone on a gigantic drug bust with Jacobsville's ex-mercenaries and he had a reputation for being a tough customer. But he was as mysterious in his way as the town's police chief, Cash Grier.

''Wouldn't you just know they'd show up and spoil everything?'' Harley said suddenly, glaring toward the door.

Sure enough, there was Jordan Powell in an expensive Western-cut sports coat and Stetson and boots, escorting pretty Julie Merrill in a blue silk dress that looked simple and probably cost the earth.

''Doesn't she look expensive?'' Harley mused.

''She probably is,'' Libby said, trying not to look and sound as hurt as she really was. It killed her to see Jordan there with that terrible woman.

''She's going to find out, pretty soon, that she's the equivalent of three-day-old fish with this crowd,'' Harley predicted coolly, watching her stick her nose up at the Ballengers as she passed them.

''I just hope she doesn't drag Jordan down with her,'' Libby said softly. ''He started out like us, Harley,'' she added. ''He was just a working cowboy with ambition.''

Jordan seated Julie and shot a cool glance in Harley and Libby's direction, without even acknowledging them. He sat down, placing his Stetson on a vacant chair and motioned a waiter.

''Did you want something stronger to drink?'' Harley asked her.

She grinned at him. ''I don't have a head for liquor, Harley. I'd rather stick to iced tea, if you don't mind.''

''So would I,'' he confided, motioning for a waiter.

The waiter, with a fine sense of irony, walked right past Jordan to take Harley's order. Julie Merrill was sputtering like a stepped-on garden hose.

''Two more iced teas, Charlie,'' Harley told the waiter. ''And thanks for giving us preference.''

''Oh, I know who the best people are, Harley,'' the boy said with a wicked grin. And he walked right past Jordan and Julie again, without even looking at them. A minute later, Jordan got up and stalked over to the counter to order their drinks.

''He'll smolder for the rest of the night over that,'' Harley mused. ''So will she, unless I miss my guess. Isn't it amazing,'' he added thoughtfully, ''that a man with as much sense as Jordan Powell can't see right through that debutante?''

''How is it that you can?'' Libby asked him curiously.

He shrugged. ''I know politicians all too well,'' he said, and for a moment, his expression was distant. ''Old man Merrill has been hitting the bottle pretty hard lately,'' he said. ''It isn't going to sit well with his constituents that he got pulled over and charged with drunk driving by Jacobsville's finest.''

''Do you think they'll convict him?'' she wondered aloud.

''You can bet money on it,'' Harley replied. ''The world has shifted ten degrees. Local politicians don't meet in parked cars and make policy anymore. The sunshine laws mean that the media get wind of anything crooked and they report it. Senator Merrill has been living in the past. He's going to get a hell of a wake-up call at the primary election, when Calhoun Ballenger knocks him off the Democratic ballot as a contender.''

"Mr. Ballenger looks like a gentleman," Libby commented, noticing the closeness of Calhoun and his brunette wife Abby. "He and his wife have been married a long time, haven't they?"

"Years," Harley said. "He and Justin are honest and hardworking men. They came up from nothing, too, although Justin's wife Shelby was a Jacobs before she married him," he reminded her. "A direct descendant of Big John Jacobs. But don't you think either of the Ballenger brothers would have been taken in by Julie Merrill, even when they were still single."

She paused to thank the waiter, who brought their two glasses of tall, cold iced tea. Jordan was still waiting for his order at the counter, while Julie glared at Libby and Harley.

"She's not quite normal, is she?" Libby said quietly. "I mean, that outburst in Barbara's Café was so...violent."

"People on drugs usually are violent," Harley replied. "And irrational." He looked right into Libby's eyes. "She's involved in some pretty nasty stuff, Libby. I can't tell you what I know, but Jordan is damaging himself just by being seen in public with her. The campaigns will get hot and heavy later this month and some dirty linen is about to be exposed to God and the general public."

Libby was concerned. "Jordan's a good man," she said quietly, her eyes going like homing pigeons to his lean, handsome face.

He caught her looking at him and glared. Julie, seeing his attention diverted, looked, too.

Once he returned to the table Julie leaned over and whispered something to Jordan that made him give Libby a killing glare before he started ignoring her completely.

"Watch your back," Harley told Libby as he sipped his iced tea. "She considers you a danger to her plans with Jordan. She'll sell you down the river if she can."

She sighed miserably. "First my stepmother, now Julie,"

she murmured. "I feel like I've got a target painted on my forehead."

"We all have bad times," Harley told her gently, and slid a big hand over one of hers where it lay on the table. "We get through them."

"You, too?" she wondered aloud.

"Yeah. Me, too," he replied, and he smiled at her.

Neither of them saw the furious look on Jordan Powell's face, or the calculating look on Julie's.

The following week, when Libby went to Barbara's Café for lunch, she walked right into Jordan Powell on the sidewalk. He was alone, as she was, and his expression made her feel cold all over.

"What's this about you going up to San Antonio for the night with Harley last Wednesday?" he asked bluntly.

Libby couldn't even formulate a reply for the shock. She'd driven Curt over to Duke Wright's place early Wednesday afternoon and from there she'd driven up to San Antonio to obtain some legal documents from the county clerk's office for Mr. Kemp. She hadn't even seen Harley there.

"I thought you were pure as the driven snow," Jordan continued icily. His dark eyes narrowed on her shocked face. "You put on a good act, don't you, Libby? I don't need to be a mind-reader to know why, either. I'm rich and you and your brother are about to lose your ranch."

"Janet hasn't started probate yet," she faltered.

"That's not what I hear."

"I don't care what you hear," she told him flatly. "Neither Curt nor I care very much what you think, either, Jordan. But you're going to run into serious problems if you hang out with Julie Merrill until her father loses the election."

He glared down at her. "He isn't going to lose," he assured her.

She hated seeing him be so stubborn, especially when

she had at least some idea of what Julie was going to drag him down into. She moved a step closer, her green eyes soft and beseeching. "Jordan, you're an intelligent man," she began slowly. "Surely you can see what Julie wants you for..."

A worldly look narrowed his eyes as they searched over her figure without any reaction at all. "Julie wants me, all right," he replied, coolly. "That's what's driving you to make these wild comments, isn't it? You're jealous because I'm spending so much time with her."

She didn't dare let on what she was feeling. She forced a careless smile. "Am I? You think I don't know when a man is teasing me?"

"You know more than I ever gave you credit for and that's the truth," he said flatly. "You and Harley Fowler." He made it sound like an insult.

"Harley is a fine man," she said, defending him.

"Obviously you think so, or you wouldn't be shacking up with him," he accused. "Does your brother know?"

"I'm a big girl now," she said, furious at the insinuation.

"Both of you had better remember that I make a bad enemy," he told her. "Whatever happens with your ranch, I don't want to have a subdivision full of people on my border."

He didn't know that Libby and Curt had already discussed how they were going to manage without their father's life insurance policy to pay the mortgage payments that were still owed. Riddle had taken out a mortgage on the ranch to buy Janet's Mercedes. Janet had waltzed off with the money and the private detective Jordan had recommended to Mr. Kemp had drawn a blank when he tried to dig into Janet's past. The will hadn't been probated, either, so there was no way Riddle Curtis's children could claim any of their inheritance with which to pay bills or make that huge mortgage payment. They'd had to let their only helper—their part-time cowboy—go, for lack of funds to pay him. They only had one horse left and they'd had to sell off most of their cattle. The only money coming in right now was what Curt and Libby earned in their respective jobs, and it wasn't much.

Of course, Libby wasn't going to share that information with a hostile Jordan Powell. Things were so bad that she and Curt might have to move off the ranch anyway because they couldn't make that mortgage payment at the end of the month. It was over eight hundred dollars. Their collective take-home pay wouldn't amount to that much and there were still other bills owing. Janet had run up huge bills while Riddle was still alive.

Jordan felt sick at what he was saying to Libby. He was jealous of Harley Fowler, furiously jealous. He couldn't bear the thought of Libby in bed with the other man. She wasn't even denying what Julie had assured him had happened between them. Libby, in Harley's arms, kissing him with such hunger that his toes tingled. Libby, loving Harley…

Jordan ached to have her for himself. He dreamed of her every night. But Libby was with Harley now. He'd lost his chance. He couldn't bear it!

''Is Harley going to loan you enough money to keep the ranch going until Janet's found?'' he wondered aloud. He smiled coldly. ''He hasn't got two dimes to rub together, from what I hear.''

Libby remembered the mortgage payments she couldn't make. Once, she might have bent her pride enough to ask Jordan to loan it to her. Not anymore. Not after what he'd said to her.

She lifted her chin. ''That's not your business, Jordan,'' she said proudly.

''Don't expect me to lend it to you,'' he said for spite.

''Jordan, I wouldn't ask you for a loan if the house burned down,'' she assured him, unflinching. ''Now, if you'll excuse me, I'm using up my lunch hour.''

She started to go around him, but he caught her arm and marched her down the little alley between her office and the town square. It was an alcove, away from traffic, with no prying eyes.

While she was wondering what was on his mind, he backed her up against the cold brick and brought his mouth down on her lips.

She pushed at his chest, but he only gave her his weight, pressing her harder into the wall. His own body was almost as hard, especially when his hips shifted suddenly, and lowered squarely against her own. She shivered at the slow caress of his hands on her ribcage while the kiss went on and on. She couldn't breathe. She didn't want to breathe. Her body ached for something more than this warm, heady torment. She moaned huskily under the hard, furious press of his mouth.

He lifted his head a bare inch and looked into her wide green eyes with possession and desire. It never stopped. He couldn't get within arm's length of her without giving in to temptation. Did she realize? No. She had no idea. She thought it was a punishment for her harsh words. It was more. It was anguish.

"You still want me," he ground out. "Do you think I don't know?"

"What?" she murmured, her eyes on his mouth. She could barely think at all. She felt his body so close that when he breathed, her chest deflated. Her breasts ached at the warm pressure of his broad chest. It was heaven to be so close to him. And she didn't dare let it show.

"Are you trying to prove something?" she murmured, forcing her hands to push instead of pull at his shoulders.

"Only that Harley isn't in my league," he said in a husky, arrogant tone, as he bent again and forced her mouth open under the slow, exquisite skill of his kisses. "In fact," he bit off against her lips, "neither are you, cupcake."

She wanted to come back with some snappy reply. She really did. But the sensations he was arousing were hypnotic, drugging. She felt him move one long, powerful jean-clad leg in between both of hers. It was broad daylight, in the middle of town. He was making love to her against a wall. And she didn't care.

She moved against him, her lips welcoming, her hands spreading, caressing, against his ribcage, his chest. There was no tomorrow. There was only Jordan, wanting her.

Her body throbbed in time with her frantic heartbeat. She was hot all over, swelling, aching. She wanted relief. Anything…!

Voices coming close pushed them apart when she would have said that nothing could. Jordan stepped back, his face a rigid mask. She looked up at him, her crushed mouth red from the ardent pressure, her eyes soft and misty and dazed.

Her pocketbook was on the ground. He reached down and handed it back to her, watching as she put the strap over her shoulder and stared up at him, still bemused.

She wanted to tell him that Harley was a better lover, to make some flip remark that would sting him. But she couldn't.

He was in pretty much the same shape. He hated the very thought of Harley. But even through the jealousy, he realized that Libby's responses weren't those of any experienced woman. When Julie kissed him, it was with her whole body. She was more than willing to do anything he liked. But he couldn't take Julie to bed because he didn't want her that way. It was a source of irritation and amazement to him. And to Julie, who made sarcastic remarks about his prowess.

It wasn't a lack of ability. It was just a lack of desire. But he raged with it when he looked at Libby. He'd never wanted a woman to the point of madness until now and she was the one woman he couldn't have.

"Women and their damned ambitions," he said under his breath. "Damn Harley. And damn you, Libby!"

"Damn you, too, Jordan," she said breathlessly. "And don't expect me to drag you into any more alleys and make love to you, if that's going to be your attitude!"

She turned and walked away before he had time to realize what she'd said. He had to bite back a laugh. This was no laughing matter. He had to get a grip on himself before Libby realized what was wrong with him.

After their disturbing encounter, she wondered if she and Curt wouldn't do better to just move off their property and live somewhere else. In fact, she told herself, that might not be a bad idea.

Mr. Kemp didn't agree.

"You have to maintain a presence on the property," he told Libby firmly. "If you move out, Janet might use that against you in court."

"You don't understand," she groaned. "Jordan is driving me crazy. And every time I look out the window, Julie's speeding down the road to Jordan's house."

"Jordan's being conned," he ventured.

"I know that, but he won't listen," Libby said, sitting down heavily behind her desk. "Julie's got him convinced that I'm running wild with Harley Fowler."

"That woman is big trouble," he said. "I'd give a lot to see her forced to admit what she did to the Culbertson girl at that party."

"You think it was her?" she asked, shocked.

He shrugged. "Nobody else had a motive," he said, his eyes narrow and cold. "Shannon Culbertson was running against her for class president and Julie wanted to win. I don't think she planned to kill her. She was going to set her up with one of the boys she was dating and ruin Shannon's reputation. But it backfired. At least, that's my theory. If this gets out it's going to disgrace her father even further."

"Isn't he already disgraced enough because of the drunk-driving charges?" she asked.

"He and his cronies at city hall are trying desperately to get those charges dropped, before they get into some newspaper whose publisher doesn't owe him a favor," Kemp replied, perching on the edge of her desk. "There's a disciplinary hearing at city hall next month for the officers involved. Grier says the council is going to try to have the police officers fired.''

She smiled. ''I can just see Chief Grier letting that happen.''

Kemp chuckled. ''I think the city council is going to be in for a big surprise. Our former police chief, Chet Blake, never would buck the council, or stand up for any officer who did something politically incorrect with the city fathers. Grier isn't like his cousin.''

''What if they fire him, too?'' she asked.

He stood up. ''If they even try, there will be a recall of the city council and the mayor,'' Kemp said simply. ''I can almost guarantee it. A lot of people locally are fed up with city management. Solid waste is backing up, there's no provision for water conservation, the fire department hasn't got one piece of modern equipment, and we're losing revenue hand over fist because nobody wants to mention raising taxes.''

''I didn't realize that.''

''Grier did.'' He smiled to himself. ''He's going to shake up this town. It won't be a bad thing, either.''

''Do you think he'll stay?''

Kemp nodded. ''He's put down deep roots already, although I don't think he realizes how deep they go just yet.''

Like everyone else in Jacobsville, Libby knew what was going on in Cash Grier's private life. After all, it had been in most of the tabloids. Exactly what the situation was between him and his houseguest, Tippy Moore, was anybody's guess. The couple were equally tight-lipped in public.

''Could I ask you to do something for me, sir?'' she asked suddenly.

''Of course.''

''Could you find out if they've learned anything about… Daddy at the state crime lab and how much longer it's going to be before they have a report?'' she asked.

He frowned. ''Good Lord, I didn't realize how long it had been since the exhumation,'' he said. ''Certainly. I'll get right on it, in fact.''

''Thanks,'' she said.

He shrugged. ''No problem.'' He got to his feet and hesitated. ''Have you talked to Violet lately?'' he asked reluctantly.

''She's lost weight and she's having her hair frosted,'' she began.

His lips made a thin line. ''I don't want to know about her appearance. I only wondered how she likes her new job.''

''A lot,'' she replied. She pursed her lips. ''In fact, she and my brother are going out on a date Saturday night.''

''Your brother knows her?'' he asked.

She nodded. ''He's working for Duke Wright, too...''

''Since when?'' he exclaimed. ''He was Jordan's right-hand man!''

She averted her eyes. ''Not anymore. Jordan said some pretty bad things about me and Curt quit.''

Kemp cursed. ''I don't understand how a man who was so concerned for both of you has suddenly become an enemy. However,'' he added, ''I imagine Julie Merrill has something to do with his change of heart.''

''He's crazy about her, from what we hear.''

''He's crazy, all right,'' he said, turning back toward his office. ''He'll go right down the tubes with her and her father if he isn't careful.''

''I tried to tell him. He accused me of being jealous.''

He glanced back at her. ''And you aren't?'' he probed softly.

Her face closed up. ''What good would it do, Mr. Kemp? Either people like you or they don't.''

Kemp had thought, privately, that it was more than liking on Jordan's part. But apparently, he'd been wrong right down the line.

''Bring your pad, if you don't mind, Libby,'' he said. ''I

want you to look up a case for me at the courthouse law library.''

''Yes, sir,'' she said, picking up her pad. It was always better to stay busy. That way she didn't have so much time to think.

She was walking into the courthouse when she met Calhoun Ballenger coming out of it. He stopped and grinned at her.

''Just the woman I was looking for,'' he said. ''On the assumption that I win this primary election for the Democratic candidate, how would you like to join my campaign staff in your spare time?''

She caught her breath. ''Mr. Ballenger, I'm very flattered!''

''Duke Wright tells me that you have some formidable language skills,'' he continued. ''Not that my secretaries don't, but they've got their hands full right now trying to get people to go to the polls and vote for me in May. I need someone to write publicity for me. Are you interested?''

''You bet!'' she said at once.

''Great! Come by the ranch Saturday about one. I've invited a few other people as well.''

''Not…the Merrills or Jordan Powell?'' she asked worriedly.

He glowered at her. ''I do not invite the political competition to staff meetings,'' he said with mock hauteur. He grinned. ''Besides, Jordan and I aren't speaking.''

''That's a relief,'' she said honestly.

''You're on the wrong side of him, too, I gather?''

She nodded. ''Me and half the town.''

''More than half, if I read the situation right,'' he said with a sigh. ''A handful of very prominent Democrats have changed sides and they're now promoting me.'' He smiled. ''More for our side.''

She smiled back. ''Exactly! Well, then, I'll see you Saturday.''

''I've already invited your boss and Duke Wright, but Duke won't come,'' he added heavily. ''I invited Grier, and Duke's still browned off about the altercation he had with our police chief.''

''He shouldn't have swung on him,'' she pointed out.

''I'm sure he knows that now,'' he agreed, his eyes twinkling. ''See you.''

She gave him a wave and walked into the courthouse lobby. Jordan Powell was standing there with a receipt for his automobile tag and glaring daggers at Libby.

''You're on a friendly basis with Calhoun Ballenger, I gather?'' he asked.

''I'm going to work on his campaign staff,'' she replied with a haughty smile.

''He's going to lose,'' he told her firmly. ''He doesn't have name identification.''

She smiled at him. ''He hasn't been arrested for drunk driving, to my knowledge,'' she pointed out.

His eyes flashed fire. ''That's a frame,'' he returned. ''Grier's officers planted evidence against him.''

She glared back. ''Chief Grier is honest and openhanded,'' she told him. ''And his officers would never be asked to do any such thing!''

''They'll be out of work after that hearing,'' he predicted.

''You swallow everything Julie tells you, don't you, Jordan?'' she asked quietly. ''Maybe you should take a look at the makeup of our city council. Those were people who once owned big businesses in Jacobsville and had tons of money. But their companies are all going downhill and they're short of ready cash. They aren't the people who have the power today. And if you think Chief Grier is going to stand by and let them railroad his employees, you're way off base.''

Jordan didn't reply at once. He stared at Libby until her face colored.

"I never thought you'd go against me, after all I've done for you and Curt," he said.

She was thinking the same thing. It made her ashamed to recall how he'd tried to help them both when Janet was first under suspicion of murder and fraud. But he'd behaved differently since he'd gotten mixed up with Senator Merrill's daughter. He'd changed, drastically.

"You have done a lot for us," she had to agree. "We'll always be grateful for it. But you took sides against us first, Jordan. You stood by with your mouth closed in Barbara's Café and let Julie humiliate me."

Jordan's eyes flashed. It almost looked like guilt. "You had enough support."

"Yes, from Harley Fowler. At least someone spoke up for me."

He looked ice cold. "You were rude to Julie first, in your own office."

"Why don't you ask Mr. Kemp who started it?" she replied.

"Kemp hates her," he said bluntly. "He'd back your story. I'm working for Senator Merrill and I'm going to get him reelected. You just side with the troublemakers and do what you please. But don't expect me to come around with my hat in my hand."

"I never did, Jordan," she said calmly. "I'm just a nobody around Jacobsville and I'm very aware of it. I'm not sophisticated or polished or rich, and I have no manners. On the other hand, I have no aspirations to high society, in case you wondered."

"Good thing. You'd never fit in," he bit off.

She smiled sadly. "And you think you will?" she challenged softly. "You may have better table manners than I do—and more money—but your father was poor. None of your new high-class friends is ever going to forget that. Even if you do."

He said something nasty. She colored a little, but she didn't back down.

"Don't worry, I know my place, Mr. Powell," she replied, just to irritate him. "I'm a minor problem that you've put out beside the road. I won't forget."

She was making him feel small. He didn't like it.

"Thank you for being there when we needed you most," she added quietly. "We aren't going to sell our land to developers."

"If you ever get title to it," he said coldly.

She shrugged. "That's out of our hands."

"Kemp will do what he can for you," he said, feeling guilty, because he knew that she and Curt had no money for attorneys. He'd heard that Janet was still missing and that Kemp's private detective had drawn a blank when he looked into her past. Libby and Curt must be worried sick about money.

"Yes, Mr. Kemp will do what he can for us." She studied his face, so hard and uncompromising, and wondered what had happened to make them so distant after the heated promises of those kisses they'd exchanged only weeks before.

"Curt likes working for Wright, I suppose?" he asked reluctantly.

She nodded. "He's very happy there."

"Julie had a cousin who trains horses. He's won trophies in steeplechase competition. He's working in Curt's place now, with my two new thoroughbreds."

"I suppose Julie wants to keep it all in the family," she replied.

He glared down at her. "Keep all what in the family?"

"Your money, Jordan," she said sweetly.

"You wouldn't have turned it down, if I'd given you the chance," he accused sarcastically. "You were laying it on thick."

"Who was kissing whom in the alley?" she returned huskily.

He didn't like remembering that. He jerked his wide-brimmed hat down over his eyes. ''A moment of weakness. Shouldn't have happened. I'm not free anymore.''

Insinuating that he and Julie were much more than friends, Libby thought correctly. She looked past Jordan to Julie, who was just coming out of the courthouse looking elegant and cold as ice. She saw Libby standing with Jordan and her lips collided furiously.

''Jordan! Let's go!'' she called to him angrily.

''I was only passing the time of day with him, Julie,'' Libby told the older woman with a vacant smile.

''You keep your sticky hands to yourself, you little liar,'' Julie told her as she passed on the steps. ''Jordan is mine!''

''No doubt you mean his money is yours, right?'' Libby ventured.

Julie drew back her hand and slapped Libby across the cheek as hard as she could. ''Damn you!'' she raged.

Libby was shocked at the unexpected physical reply, but she didn't retaliate. She just stood there, straight and dignified, with as much pride as she could muster. Around the two women, several citizens stopped and looked on with keen disapproval.

One of them was Officer Dana Hall, one of the two police officers who had arrested Senator Merrill for drunk driving.

She walked right up to Libby. ''That was assault, Miss Collins,'' she told Libby. ''If you want to press charges, I can arrest Miss Merrill on the spot.''

''Arrest!'' Julie exploded. ''You can't arrest me!''

''I most certainly can,'' Officer Hall replied. ''Miss Collins, do you want to press charges?''

Libby stared at Julie Merrill with cold pleasure, wondering how it would look on the front page of Jacobsville's newspaper.

''Wouldn't that put another kink in your father's reelection campaign?'' Libby ventured softly.

Julie looked past Libby and suddenly burst into tears.

She threw herself into Jordan Powell's arms. "Oh, Jordan, she's going to have me arrested!"

"No, she's not," Jordan said curtly. He glanced at Libby. "She wouldn't dare."

Libby cocked her head. "I wouldn't?" She glared at him. "Look at my cheek, Jordan."

It was red. There was a very obvious handprint on it.

"She insulted me," Julie wailed. "I had every right to hit her back!"

"She never struck you, Miss Merrill," Officer Hall replied coldly. "Striking another person is against the law, regardless of the provocation."

"I never meant to do it!" Julie wailed. She was sobbing, but there wasn't a speck of moisture under her eyes. "Please, Jordan, don't let them put me in jail!"

Libby and Officer Hall exchanged disgusted looks.

"Men are so damned gullible," Libby remarked with a glare at Jordan, who looked outraged. "All right, Julie, have it your way. But you'd better learn to produce tears as well as broken sobs if you want to convince another *woman* that you're crying."

"Jordan, could we go now?" Julie sobbed. "I'm just sick…!"

"Not half as sick as you'll be when your father loses the election, Julie," Libby drawled sweetly, and walked up the steps with Officer Hall at her side. She didn't even look at Jordan as she went into the courthouse.

Chapter Seven

Calhoun Ballenger's meeting with his volunteer staff was a cheerful riot of surprises. Libby found herself working with women she'd known only by name a few months earlier. Now she was suddenly in the cream of society, but with women who didn't snub her or look down their noses at her social position.

Libby was delighted to find herself working with Violet, who'd come straight from her job at Duke Wright's ranch for the meeting.

"This is great!" Violet exclaimed, hugging Libby. "I've missed working with you!"

"I've missed you, too, Violet," Libby assured her. She shook her head as she looked at the other woman. "You look great!"

Violet grinned. She'd dropped at least two dress sizes. She was well-rounded, but no longer obese even to the most critical eye. She'd had her brown hair frosted and it was waving around her face and shoulders. She was wearing a low-cut dress that emphasized the size of her pretty breasts, and her small waist and voluptuous hips, along with high heels that arched her small feet nicely.

"I've worked hard at the gym," Violet confessed. She was still laughing when her eyes collided with Blake Kemp's across the room. The expression left her face. She averted her eyes quickly. "Excuse me, won't you, Libby? I came with Curt. You, uh, don't mind, do you?" she added worriedly.

"Don't be silly," Libby said with a genuine smile. "Curt's nice. So are you. I think you'd make a lovely couple..."

"Still happy with Duke Wright, Miss Hardy?" came a cold, biting comment from Libby's back.

Blake Kemp moved into view, his pale eyes expressive on Violet's pretty figure and the changes in the way she dressed.

"I'm...very happy with him, Mr. Kemp," Violet said, clasping her hands together tightly. "If you'll excuse me..."

"You've lost weight," Kemp said gruffly.

Violet's eyes widened. "And you actually noticed?"

The muscles in his face tautened. "You look...nice."

Violet's jaw dropped. She was literally at a loss for words. Her eyes lifted to Kemp's and they stood staring at each other for longer than was polite, neither speaking or moving.

Kemp shifted restlessly on his long legs. "How's your mother?"

Violet swallowed hard. "She's not doing very well, I'm afraid. You know...about the exhumation?"

Kemp nodded. "They're still in the process of evaluating Curt and Libby's father's remains, as well, at the crime lab. So far, they have nothing to report."

Violet looked beside him at Libby and winced. "I didn't know, Libby. I'm so sorry."

"So am I, for you," Libby replied. "We didn't want to do it, but we had to know for sure."

"Will they really be able to tell anything, after all this time?" Violet asked Kemp, and she actually moved a step closer to him.

He seemed to catch his breath. He was looking at her oddly. "I assume so." His voice was deeper, too. Involuntarily, his lean fingers reached out and touched Violet's long hair. "I like the frosting," he said reluctantly. "It makes your eyes look...bluer."

"Does it?" Violet asked, but her eyes were staring into his as if she'd found treasure there.

With an amused smile, Libby excused herself and joined her brother, who was talking to the police chief.

Cash Grier noticed her approach and smiled. He looked older somehow and there were new lines around his dark eyes.

"Hi, Chief," she greeted him. "How's it going?"

"Don't ask," Curt chuckled. "He's in the middle of a controversy."

"So are we," Libby replied. "We're on the wrong side of the election and Jordan Powell is furious at us."

"We're on the right side," Cash said carelessly. "The city fathers are in for a rude awakening." He leaned down. "I have friends in high places." He paused. "I also have friends in *low* places." He grinned.

Libby and Curt burst out laughing, because they recognized the lines from a country song they'd all loved.

Calhoun Ballenger joined them, clapping Cash on the back affectionately. "Thanks for coming," he said. "Even if it is putting another nail in your coffin with the mayor."

"They mayor can kiss my..." Cash glanced at Libby and grinned. "Never mind."

They all laughed.

"She's lived with me all her life," Curt remarked. "She's practically unshockable."

"How's Tippy?" Calhoun asked.

Cash smiled. "Doing better, thanks. She'd have come, too, but she's still having a bad time."

"No wonder," Calhoun replied, recalling the ordeal Tippy had been through in the hands of kidnappers. It had been in all the tabloids. "Good thing they caught the culprits who kidnapped her."

"Isn't it?" Cash said, not giving away that he'd caught them, with the help of an old colleague. "Nice turnout, Calhoun," he added, looking around them. "I thought you invited Judd."

"I did," Calhoun said at once, "but the twins have a cold."

"Damn!" Cash grimaced. "I told Judd that he and Crissy needed to stop running that air conditioner all night!"

"It wasn't that," Calhoun confided. "They went to the Coltrains' birthday party for their son—his second birthday—and that's where they got the colds."

Cash sighed. "Poor babies."

"He's their godfather," Calhoun told Libby and Curt. "But he thinks Jessamina belongs to him."

"She does," Cash replied haughtily.

Nobody mentioned what the tabloids had said—that Tippy had been pregnant with Cash's child a few weeks earlier and lost it just before her ordeal with the kidnapping.

Libby diplomatically changed the subject. "Mr. Kemp said that you can put up campaign posters in our office windows," she told Calhoun, "and Barbara's willing to let you put up as many as you like in her café," she added with a grin. "She said she's never going to forgive Julie Merrill for making a scene there."

Calhoun chuckled. "I've had that sort of offer all week," he replied. "Nobody wants Senator Merrill back in office, but the city fathers have thrown their support behind him and he thinks he's unbeatable. What we really need is a change in city government as well. We're on our second mayor in eight months and this one is afraid of his own shadow."

"He's also Senator Merrill's nephew," Curt added.

"Which is why he's trying to make my officers back down on those DWI charges," Cash Grier interposed.

"I'd like see it. Carlos Garcia wouldn't back down from anybody," Calhoun mused. "Or Officer Dana Hall, either."

"Ms. Hall came to my assistance at the courthouse this week," Libby volunteered. "Julie Merrill slapped me. Officer Hall was more than willing to arrest her, if I'd agreed to press charges."

"Good for Dana," Cash returned. "You be careful, Ms. Collins," he added firmly. "That woman has poor impulse control. I wouldn't put it past her to try and run somebody down."

"Neither would I," Curt added worriedly. "She's already told Jordan some furious lies about us and he believes her."

"She can be very convincing," Libby said, not wanting to verbally attack Jordan even now.

"It may get worse now, with all of you backing me," Calhoun told the small group. "I won't have any hard feelings if you want to withdraw your support."

"Do I look like the sort of man who backs away from trouble?" Cash asked lazily, with a grin.

"Speaking of Duke Wright," Libby murmured dryly, "he's throwing his support to Mr. Ballenger, too. But he had, uh, reservations about coming to the meeting."

Cash chuckled. "I don't hold grudges."

"Yes, but he does," Calhoun said on a chuckle. "He'll get over it. He's got some personal problems right now."

"Don't we all?" Cash replied wistfully, and his dark eyes were troubled.

Libby and Curt didn't add their two cents' worth, but they exchanged quiet looks.

The campaign was winding down for the primary, but all the polls gave Calhoun a huge lead over Merrill. Printed materials were ordered, along with buttons, pencils, bumper stickers and keychains. There was enough promotional matter to blanket the town and in the days that followed, Calhoun's supporters did exactly that in Jacobs County and the surrounding area in the state senatorial district that Merrill represented.

Julie Merrill was acting as her father's campaign manager and she was coordinating efforts for promotion with a group of teenagers she'd hired. Some of them were delinquents and there was a rash of vandalisms pertaining to the destruction of Calhoun's campaign posters.

Cash Grier, predictably, went after the culprits and rounded them up. He got one to talk and the newspapers revealed that Miss Merrill had paid the young man to destroy Calhoun's campaign literature. Julie denied it. But the vandalism stopped.

Meanwhile, acting mayor Ben Brady was mounting a fervent defense for Senator Merrill on the drunk-driving charges and trying to make things hot for the two officers. He ordered them suspended and tried to get the city council to back him up.

Cash got wind of it and phoned Simon Hart, the state's attorney general. Simon phoned the city attorney and they had a long talk. Soon afterward, the officers were notified that they could stay on the job until the hearing the following month.

Meanwhile, the state crime lab revealed the results of its report to Blake Kemp. He walked up to Libby's desk while she was on the phone and waited impatiently for her to hang up.

"They can't find any evidence of foul play, Libby," he said at once.

"And if there was any, they would?" she asked quickly.

He nodded. "I'm almost certain of it. The crime lab verified our medical examiner's diagnosis of myocardial infarction. So Janet's off the hook for that one, at least."

Libby sat back with a long sigh and closed her eyes.

"Thank God. I couldn't have lived with it if she'd poisoned Daddy and we never knew."

He nodded. "On the other hand, they hit paydirt with Violet's father," he added.

She sat up straight. "Poison?"

"Yes," he said heavily. "I'm not going to phone her. I'm going over to Duke Wright's place to tell her in person. Then I'll take her home to talk to her mother. She'll need someone with her."

Yes, she would, and Libby was secretly relieved that Kemp was going to be the person. Violet would need a shoulder to cry on.

"I'll phone Curt and tell him," she said.

"Libby, give me half an hour first," he asked quietly. "I don't want him to tell Violet."

She wondered why, but she wasn't going to pry. "Okay."

He managed a brief smile. "Thanks."

"What about Janet?" she wondered miserably. "They still haven't found her."

"They will. Now all we need is a witness who can place her with Mr. Hardy the night of his death, and we can have her arrested and charged with murder," he replied.

"Chance would be a fine thing, Mr. Kemp," she said heavily.

"Don't give up hope," he instructed. "She's not going to get away with your inheritance. I promise."

She managed a smile. "Thanks."

But she wasn't really convinced. She went home that afternoon feeling lost and alone. She'd told Curt the good news after Violet had gone home with Kemp. Curt had been as relieved as she had, but there was still the problem of probate. Everything was in Janet's name, as their father had instructed. Janet had the insurance money. Nobody could do anything with the estate until the will was probated and

Janet had to sign the papers for that. It was a financial nightmare.

There was a message on the answering machine when Libby got home. She pushed the Play button and her heart sank right to her ankles.

"This is the loan officer at Jacobsville Savings and Loan," came the pleasant voice. "We just wanted to remind you that your loan payment was due three days ago. Please call us if there's a problem." The caller gave her name and position and her telephone number. The line went dead.

Libby sat down beside the phone and just stared at it. Curt had told her already that they weren't going to be able to make the payment. Jordan had assured her that he wasn't going to loan her the money to pay it. There was nobody else they would feel comfortable asking. She put her face in her hands and let the tears fall. The financial establishment would repossess the ranch. It wouldn't matter where Janet was or what state the probate action was in. They were going to lose their home.

She went out to the barn and ran the curry comb over Bailey, her father's horse. He was the last horse they had.

The barn leaked. It was starting to rain and Libby felt raindrops falling on her shoulder through a rip in the tin roof from a small tornado that had torn through a month earlier. The straw on the floor of the barn needed changing, but the hay crop had drowned in the flooding. They'd have to buy some. Libby looked down at her worn jeans, at the small hand resting on them. The tiger eye ring her father had given her looked ominous in the darkened barn. She sighed and turned back to the horse.

"Bailey, I don't know what we're going to do," she told the old horse, who neighed as if he were answering her.

The sound of a vehicle pulling up in the yard diverted her. She looked down the long aisle of the barn to see Jordan's pickup truck sitting at the entrance. Her heart skipped as he got out and came striding through the dirty straw, his cotton shirt speckled with raindrops that had escaped the wide brim of his white straw hat.

"What do you want?" she asked, trying to ignore him to finish her grooming job on the horse.

"My two new thoroughbreds are missing."

She turned, the curry comb suspended in her small hand. "And you think we took them?" she asked incredulously. "You honestly think we'd steal from you, even if we were starving?"

He averted his face, as if the question had wounded him.

"Please leave," she said through her teeth.

He rammed his hands into his pockets and moved a step closer, looking past her to Bailey. "That horse is useless for ranch work. He's all of twenty."

"He's my horse," she replied. "I'm not getting rid of him, whatever happens."

She felt his lean, powerful body at her back. "Libby," he began. "About that bank loan..."

"Curt and I are managing just fine, thanks," she said without turning.

His big, strong hands came down heavily on her shoulders, making her jump. "The bank president is a good friend of the Merrills."

She pulled away from him and looked up, her unspoken fears in her green eyes. "They can't do anything to us without Janet," she told him. "She has legal power of attorney."

"Damn it, I know that!" he muttered. "But it's not going to stop the bank from foreclosing, don't you see? You can't make the loan payment!"

"What business is that of yours?" she asked bitterly.

He drew in a slow breath. "I can talk to the president of the Jacobsville Merchant Bank for you," he said. "He might be willing to work out something for the land. You and Curt can't work it, anyway, and you don't have the capital to invest in it. The best you could do is sell off your remaining cattle and give it up.''

She couldn't even manage words. She had no options at all and he had to know it. She could almost hate him.

''We can't sell anything,'' she said harshly. ''I told you, Janet has power of attorney. And she was named in Daddy's will as the sole holder of the property. We can't even sell a stick of furniture. We're going to have to watch the bank foreclose, Jordan, because Janet has our hands tied. We're going to lose everything Daddy worked for, all his life...''

Her lower lip trembled. She couldn't even finish the sentence.

Jordan stepped forward and wrapped her up tight in his arms, holding her while she cried. ''Damn, what a mess!''

She beat a small fist against his massive chest. ''Why?'' she moaned. ''Why?''

His arms tightened. ''I don't know, baby,'' he whispered at her ear, his voice deep and soothing. ''I wish I did.''

She nuzzled closer, drowning in the pleasure of being close to him. It had been so long since he'd held her.

His chest rose and fell heavily. ''Kemp's detective hasn't tracked her down yet?''

''Not yet. But she didn't...kill Daddy. The autopsy showed that he died of a heart attack.''

''That's something, I guess,'' he murmured.

''But Violet's daddy was poisoned,'' she added quietly, her eyes open as they stared past Jordan's broad chest toward his truck parked at the front of the barn. ''So they'll still get her for murder, if they can ever find her.''

''Poor Violet,'' he said.

''Yes.''

His hand smoothed her hair. It tangled in the wavy soft strands. ''You smell of roses, Libby,'' he murmured deeply, and the pressure of his arms changed in some subtle way.

She could feel the sudden tautness of his lean body against her, the increasing warmth of his embrace. But he'd taken Julie's side against her and she wasn't comfortable being in his arms anymore.

She tried to pull away, but he wouldn't let her.

"Don't fight me," he said gruffly. "You know you don't want to."

"I don't?"

He lifted his head and looked down into her misty and wet green eyes. His voice was deep with feeling. "You haven't stopped wanting me."

"I want hot chocolate, too, Jordan, but it still gives me migraine, so I don't drink it," she said emphatically.

His dark eyebrows lifted. "That's cute. You think you convinced me?"

"Sure," she lied.

He laughed mirthlessly, letting his dark eyes fall to her lips. "Let's see."

He bent, drawing his lips slowly, tenderly, across her mouth in a teasing impression of a kiss. He was lazy and gentle and after a few seconds of imitating a plank of wood, her traitorous body betrayed her.

She relaxed into the heat of his body with a shaky little sigh and found herself enveloped in his arms. He kissed her again, hungrily this time, without the tenderness of that first brief exchange.

She moaned and tried to protest the sudden crush of his lean hand at the base of her spine, rubbing her body against him. But he didn't give her enough breath or strength to protest and the next thing she knew, she was on her back in a stall of fresh hay and his body was completely covering hers.

"No, Jordan," she protested weakly.

"Yes," he groaned. His long leg slid lazily against hers, and between them, while his big, warm hands smoothed blatantly over her ribcage, his thumbs sliding boldly right over her breasts. "Don't think," he whispered against her parted lips. "Just give in. I won't hurt you."

"I know that," she whispered. "But..."

He nibbled on her lower lip. His thumbs edged out gently and found her nipples. They moved lazily, back and forth, coaxing the tips into hard little nubs. She shivered with unexpected pleasure.

He lifted his head and looked into her eyes while he did it again. If she was used to this sort of love play, it certainly didn't show. She was pliable, yielded, absolutely fascinated with what he was doing to her body. She liked it.

That was all he needed to know. His leg became insistent between hers, coaxing them to move apart, to admit the slow, exquisite imprint of his hips between her long legs. It was like that day in the alley beyond her office, when she hadn't cared if all of Jacobsville walked by while he was pressing her aching body against the brick wall. She was drowning in pleasure.

Surely, she thought blindly, it couldn't be wrong to give in to something so sweet! His hands on her body were producing undreamed of sensations. He was giving her pleasure in hot, sweeping waves. He touched her and she ached for more. He kissed her and she lifted against him to find his mouth and coax it into ardor. One of her legs curled helplessly around his powerful thigh and she moaned when he accepted the silent invitation and moved into near intimacy with her.

He was aroused. He was powerful. She felt the hard thrust of him against her body and she wanted to rip off her clothes and invite his hands, his eyes, his body, into complete surrender with her. She wanted to feel the ecstasy she knew he could give her. He was skilled, masterful. He knew what she needed, what she wanted. He could give her pleasure beyond bearing, she knew it.

His lean hands moved under her blouse, searching for closeness, unfastening buttons, invading lace. She felt his fingers brush tenderly, lovingly, over her bare breasts in an intimacy she'd never shared with anyone.

Her dreams of him had been this explicit, but she'd never thought she would live them in such urgent passion. As he touched her, she arched to help him, moved to encourage him. Her mouth opened wide under his. She felt his tongue suddenly thrust into it with violent need.

She moaned loudly, her fingertips gripping the hard muscle of his upper arms as he thrust her blouse and bra up to her throat and bent at once to put his mouth on her breasts.

The warm, moist contact was shattering. She stiffened with the shock of pleasure it produced. He tasted her in a hot, feverish silence, broken only by his urgent breathing and the rough sigh of her own voice in his ear.

''Yes,'' he groaned, opening his mouth. ''Yes, Libby. Here. Right here. You and me. I can give you more pleasure than damned Harley ever dreamed of giving you!''

Harley. Harley. She felt her body growing cold. ''Harley?'' she whispered.

He lifted his head and looked down at her breasts with grinding urgency. ''He's had you.''

''He has not!'' she exclaimed, shocked.

He scowled, in limbo, caught between his insane need to possess her and his jealousy of the other man.

She took advantage of his indecision by jerking out of his arms and pulling her blouse down as she dragged herself out of the stall. She groped for fastenings while she flushed with embarrassment at what she'd just let him do to her.

She looked devastated. Her hair was full of straw, like her clothes. Her green eyes were wild, her face flushed, her mouth swollen.

He got to his feet, still in the grip of passion, and started toward her. His hat was off. His hair was wild, from her searching fingers, and his shirt was half-open over hair-matted muscle.

''Come back here,'' he said huskily, moving forward.

''No!'' she said firmly, shivering. ''I'm not standing in for Julie Merrill!''

The words stopped him in his tracks. He hesitated, his brows meeting over turbulent dark eyes.

"Remember Julie? Your girlfriend?" she persisted shakily. Throwing his lover in his face was a way to cover her hurt for the insinuation he'd made about her and Harley. "What in the world would she think if she could see you now?"

He straightened, but with an effort. His body was raging. He wanted Libby. He'd never wanted anyone, anything, as much as he wanted her.

"Julie has nothing to do with this," he ground out. "I want you!"

"For how long, Jordan?" she asked bitingly. "Ten minutes? Thirty?"

He blinked. His mind wasn't working.

"I am nobody's one-night stand," she flashed at him. "Not even yours!"

He took a deep breath, then another one. He stared at her blankly while he tried to stop thinking about how sweet it was to feel her body under his hands.

"I want you to leave, now," she repeated, folding her arms over her loose bra. She could feel the swollen contours of her breasts and remembered with pure shame how it felt to have him touching and kissing them.

"That isn't what you wanted five minutes ago," he reminded her flatly.

She closed her eyes. "I'm grass-green and stupid," she said curtly. "It wouldn't be the first time an experienced man seduced an innocent girl."

"Don't make stupid jokes," he said icily. "You're no innocent."

"You believe what you like about me, Jordan, it doesn't matter anymore," she interrupted him. "I've got work to do. Why don't you go home?"

He glared at her, frustrated desire riding him hard. He cursed himself for ruining everything by bringing up Harley Fowler. "You're a hard woman, Libby," he said. "Harder than I ever realized."

"Goodbye, Jordan," she said, and she turned away to pick up the curry comb she'd dropped.

He gave her a furious glare and stormed out of the barn to his truck. Bailey jumped as Jordan slammed the door and left skid marks getting out of the driveway. She relaxed then, grateful that she'd managed to save herself from that masterful seduction. She'd had a close call. She had to make sure that Jordan never got so close to her again. She couldn't trust him. Not now.

Chapter Eight

Janet was still in hiding before the primary election and probate hadn't begun. But plenty had changed in Jacobsville. Libby and Curt had been forced to move out of the farmhouse where they'd grown up, because the bank had foreclosed.

They hadn't said a word to Jordan about it. Curt moved into the bunkhouse at the Wright ranch where he worked. Libby moved into a boardinghouse where two other Jacobsville career women lived.

Bailey would have had to be boarded and Libby didn't have the money. But she worked out a deal with a dude ranch nearby. Bailey would be used for trail rides for people who were nervous of horses and Libby would help on the weekends. It wasn't the ideal solution, but it was the only one she had. It was a wrench to give up Bailey, even though it wasn't going to be forever.

Jordan and Julie Merrill were apparently engaged. Or so Julie was saying, and she was wearing a huge diamond on her ring finger. Her father was using every dirty trick in the book to gain his party's candidacy.

Julie Merrill was vehemently outspoken about some unnamed dirty tactics being used against her father in the primary election campaign, and she went on television to make accusations against Calhoun Ballenger.

The next morning, Blake Kemp had her served as the defendant in a defamation lawsuit.

"They're not going to win this case," Julie raged at Jordan. "I want you to get me the best attorney in Austin! We're going to put Calhoun Ballenger right in the gutter where he belongs, along with all these jump-up nouveau riche that think they own our county!"

Jordan, who was one of those jump-ups, gave her a curious look. "Excuse me?" he asked coolly.

"Well, I'm not standing by while Ballenger talks my father's constituents into deserting him!"

"You're the one who's been making allegations, Julie," Jordan said quietly. "To anyone who was willing to listen."

She waved that away. "You have to do that to win elections."

"I'm not going to be party to anything dishonest," Jordan said through his teeth.

Julie backed down. She curled against him and sighed. "Okay. I'll tone it down, for your sake. But you aren't going to let Calhoun Ballenger sue me, are you?"

Jordan didn't know what he was going to do. He felt uneasy at Julie's temperament and her tactics. He'd taken her side against Kemp when she told him that one of the boys at her graduation party had put something in the Culbertson girl's drink and she couldn't turn him in. She'd cried about Libby Collins making horrible statements against her. But Libby had never done such a thing before.

He'd liked being Julie's escort, being accepted by the social crowd she ran around with. But it was getting old and he was beginning to believe that Julie was only playing up to him for money to put into her father's campaign.

Libby had tried to warn him and he'd jumped down her throat. He felt guilty about that, too. He felt guilty about a lot of things lately.

"Listen," he said. "I think you need to step back and take a good look at what you're doing. Calhoun Ballenger isn't some minor citizen. He and his brother own a feedlot that's nationally known. Besides that, he has the support of most of the people in Jacobsville with money."

"My father has the support of the social set," she began.

"Yes, but Julie, they're the old elite. The demographics have changed in Jacobs County in the past ten years. Look around you. The Harts are a political family from the roots up. Their brother is the state attorney general and he's already casting a serious eye on what's going on in the Jacobsville city council, about those police officers the mayor's trying to suspend."

"They can't do anything about that," she argued.

"Julie, the Harts are related to Chief Grier," he said shortly.

She hesitated. For the first time, she looked uncertain.

"Not only that, they're related to the governor and the vice president. And while it isn't well-known locally, Grier's people are very wealthy."

She sat down. She ran a hand through her blond hair. "Why didn't you say this before?"

"I tried to," he pointed out. "You refused to listen."

"But Daddy can't possibly lose the election," she said with a child's understanding of things. "He's been state senator from this district for years and years."

"And now the voters are looking for some new blood," he told her. "Not only in local government, but in state and national government. You and your father don't really move with the times, Julie."

"Surely, you don't think Calhoun can beat Daddy?" she asked huskily.

"I think he's going to," he replied honestly, ramming his hands into his pockets. "He's way ahead of your father in the polls. You know that. You and your father have made some bad enemies trying to have those police officers fired. You've gotten on the wrong side of not only Cash Grier, but the Harts as well. There will be repercussions. I've already heard talk of a complete recall of the mayor and the city council."

"But the mayor is Daddy's nephew. How could they...?"

"Don't you know anything about small towns?" he ground out. "Julie, you've spent too much time in Austin with your father and not enough around here where the elections are decided."

"This is just a hick town," she said, surprised. "Why should I care what goes on here?"

Jordan's face hardened. "Because Jacobs County is the biggest county in your father's district. He can't get re-elected without it. You've damaged his campaign by the way you've behaved to Libby Collins."

"That nobody?" she scoffed.

"Her father is a direct descendant of old John Jacobs," he pointed out. "They may not have money and they may not be socially acceptable to you and your father, but the Collinses are highly respected here. The reason Calhoun's got such support is because you've tried to hurt Libby."

"But that's absurd!"

"She's a good person," he said, averting his eyes as he recalled his unworthy treatment of her—and of Curt—on Julie's behalf. "She's had some hard knocks recently."

"So have I," Julie said hotly. "Most notably, having a lawsuit filed against me for defamation of character by that lawyer Kemp!" She turned to him. "Are you going to get me a lawyer, or do I have to find my own?"

Jordan was cutting his losses while there was still time. He felt like ten kinds of fool for the way he'd behaved in the past few weeks. "I think you'd better do that yourself," he replied. "I'm not going against Calhoun Ballenger."

She scoffed. "You'll never get that Collins woman to

like you again, no matter what you do,'' she said haughtily. ''Or didn't you know that she and her brother have forfeited the ranch to the bank?''

He was speechless. ''They've what?''

''Nobody would loan them the money they needed to save it,'' she said with a cold smile. ''So the bank president foreclosed. Daddy had a long talk with him.''

He looked furious. His big fists clenched at his hips. ''That was low, Julie.''

''When you want to win, sometimes you have to fight dirty,'' she said simply. ''You belong to me. I'm not letting some nobody of a little dirt rancher take you away from me. We need you.''

''I don't belong to you,'' he returned, scooping up his hat. ''In fact, I've never felt dirtier than I do right now.''

She gaped at him. ''I beg your pardon! You can't talk to me like that!''

''I just did.'' He started toward the door.

''You're no loss, Jordan,'' she yelled after him. ''We needed your money, but I never wanted you! You're one of those jump-ups with no decent background. I'm sorry I ever invited you here the first time. I'm ashamed that I told my friends I liked you!''

''That makes two of us,'' he murmured icily, and he went out the door without a backward glance.

Kemp was going over some notes with Libby when Jordan Powell walked into the office without bothering to knock.

''I'd like to talk to Libby for a minute,'' he said solemnly, hat in hand.

Libby stared at him blankly. ''I can't think what you have to say,'' she replied. ''I'm very busy.''

''She is,'' Kemp replied. ''I'm due in court in thirty minutes.''

''Then I'll come back in thirty minutes,'' Jordan replied.

''Feel free, but I won't be here. I have nothing to say to

you, Jordan,'' she told him bluntly. ''You turned your back on me when I needed you the most. I don't need you now. I never will again.''

''Listen,'' he began impatiently.

''No.'' She turned back to Kemp. ''What were you saying, boss?''

Kemp hesitated. He could see the pain in Jordan's face and he had some idea that Jordan had just found out the truth about Julie Merrill. He checked his watch. ''Listen, I can read your writing. Just give me the pad and I'll get to the courthouse. It's okay,'' he added when she looked as if he were deserting her to the enemy. ''Really.''

She bit her lower lip hard. ''Okay.''

''Thanks,'' Jordan said stiffly, as Kemp got up from the desk.

''You owe me one,'' he replied, as he passed the taciturn rancher on the way out the door.

Minutes later, Mabel went into Kemp's office to put some notes on his desk, leaving Jordan and Libby alone.

''I've made some bad mistakes,'' he began stiffly. He hated apologies. Usually, he found ways not to make them. But he'd hurt Libby too badly not to try.

She was staring at her keyboard, trying not to listen.

''You have to understand what it's been like for me,'' he said hesitantly. He sat down in a chair next to her desk, with his wide-brimmed hat in his hands. ''My people were like yours, poor. My mother had money, but her people disinherited her when she married my dad. I never had two nickels to rub together. I was that Powell kid, whose father worked for wages, whose mother was reduced to working as a housekeeper.'' He stared at the floor with his pride aching. ''I wanted to be somebody, Libby. That's all I ever wanted. Just to have respect from the people who mattered in this town.'' He shrugged. ''I thought going around with Julie would give me that.''

''I don't suppose you noticed that her father belongs to

a group of respectable people who no longer have any power around here,'' she said stiffly.

He sighed. ''No, I didn't. I had my head turned. She was beautiful and rich and cultured, and she came at me like a hurricane. I was in over my head before I knew it.''

Libby, who wasn't beautiful or rich or cultured, felt her heart breaking. She knew all this, but it hurt to hear him admit it. Because it meant that those hungry, sweet kisses she'd shared with him meant nothing at all. He wanted Julie.

''I've broken it off with her,'' he said bluntly.

Libby didn't say anything.

''Did you hear me?'' he asked impatiently.

She looked up at him with disillusioned eyes. ''You believed her. She said I was shacking up with Harley Fowler. She said I attacked her in this office and hurt her feelings. You believed all that, even though you knew me. And when she attacked me in Barbara's Café and on the courthouse steps, you didn't say a thing.''

He winced.

''Words don't mean anything, Powell,'' she said bitterly. ''You can sit there and apologize and try to smooth over what you did for the rest of your life, but I won't listen. When I needed you, you turned your back on me.''

He drew in a long breath. ''I guess I did.''

''I can understand that you were flattered by her attention,'' she said. ''But Curt and I have lost everything we had. Our father is dead and we don't even have a home anymore.''

He moved his hat in his hands. ''You could move in with me.''

She laughed bitterly. ''Thanks.''

''No, listen,'' he said earnestly, leaning forward.

She held up a hand. ''Don't. I've had all the hard knocks I can handle. I don't want anything from you, Jordan. Not anything at all.''

He wanted to bite something. He felt furious at his own

stupidity, at his blind allegiance to Julie Merrill and her father, at his naivete in letting them use him. He felt even worse about the way he'd turned on Libby. But he was afraid of what he'd felt for her, afraid of her youth, her changeability. Now he only felt like a fool.

"Thanks for the offer and the apology," she added heavily. "Now, if you'll excuse me, I have to get back to work."

She turned on the computer, brought up her work screen and shut Jordan out of her sight and mind.

He got up slowly and moved toward the door. He hesitated at it, glancing back at her. "What about the autopsy?" he asked suddenly.

She swallowed hard. "Daddy died of a heart attack, just like the doctors said," she replied.

He sighed. "And Violet's father?"

"Was poisoned," she replied.

"Riddle had a lucky escape," he commented. "So did you and Curt."

She didn't look at him. "I just hope they can find her, before she kills some other poor old man."

He nodded. After a minute, he gave her one last soulful glance and went out the door.

Life went on as usual. Calhoun's campaign staff cranked up the heat. Libby spent her free time helping to make up flyers and make telephone calls, offering to drive voters to the polls during the primary election if they didn't have a way to get to the polls.

"You know, I really think Calhoun's going to win," Curt told Libby while they were having a quick lunch together on Saturday, after she got off from work.

She smiled. "So do I. He's got all kinds of support."

He picked at his potato chips. "Heard from Jordan?"

She stiffened. "He came by the office to apologize a few days ago."

He drew in a long breath. ''Rumor is that Julie Merrill's courting Duke Wright now.''

''Good luck to her. He's still in love with his wife. And he's not quite as gullible as Jordan.''

''Jordan wasn't so gullible,'' he defended his former boss. ''When a woman that pretty turns up the heat, most normal men will follow her anywhere.''

She lifted both eyebrows. ''Even you?''

He grinned. ''I'm not normal. I'm a cowboy.''

She chuckled and sipped her iced tea. ''They're still looking for Janet. I've had an idea,'' she said.

''Shoot.''

''What if we advertise our property for sale in all the regional newspapers?''

''Whoa,'' he said. ''We can't sell it. We don't have power of attorney and the will's not even in probate yet.''

''She's a suspected murderess,'' she reminded him. ''Felons can't inherit, did you know? If she's tried and convicted, we might be able to get her to return everything she got from Daddy's estate.''

He frowned, thinking hard. ''Do you remember Dad telling us about a new will he'd made?''

She blinked. ''No.''

''Maybe you weren't there. It was when he was in the hospital, just before he died. He could hardly talk for the pain and he was gasping for breath. But he said there was a will. He said he put it in his safest place.'' He frowned heavily. ''I never thought about that until just now, but what if he meant a *new* will, Libby?''

''It wouldn't have been legal if it wasn't witnessed,'' she said sadly. ''He might have written something down and she found it and threw it out. I doubt it would stand up in court.''

''No. He went to San Antonio without Janet, about two days before he had the heart attack,'' he persisted.

''Who did he know in San Antonio?'' she wondered aloud.

''Why don't you ask Mr. Kemp to see if his private detective could snoop around?'' he queried softly.

She pursed her lips. ''It would be a long shot. And we couldn't afford to pay him....''

''Dad had a coin collection that was worth half a million dollars, Libby,'' Curt said. ''It's never turned up. I can't find any record that he ever sold it, either.''

Her lips fell open. In the agony of the past few months, that had never occurred to her. ''I assumed Janet cashed it in....''

''She had the insurance money,'' he reminded her, ''and the property—or so she assumed. But when we were sorting out Dad's personal belongings, that case he kept the coins in was missing. What if—'' he added eagerly ''—he took it to San Antonio and left it with someone, along with an altered will?''

She was trying to think. It wasn't easy. If they had those coins, if nothing else, they could make the loan payment.

''I can ask Mr. Kemp if he'll look into it,'' she said. ''He can take the money out of my salary.''

''I can contribute some of mine,'' Curt added.

She felt lighter than she had in weeks. ''I'll go ask him right now!''

''Finish your sandwich first,'' he coaxed. ''You've lost weight, baby sister.''

She grimaced. ''I've been depressed since we had to leave home.''

''Yeah. Me, too.''

She smiled at him. ''But things are looking up!''

She found Kemp just about to leave for the day. She stopped him at the door and told him what she and Curt had been discussing.

He closed the door behind them, picked up the phone, and dialed a number. Libby listened while he outlined the case to someone, most likely the private detective he'd hired to look for Janet.

"That's right," he told the man. "One more thing, there's a substantial coin collection missing as well. I'll ask." He put his hand over the receiver and asked Libby for a description of it, which he gave to the man. He added a few more comments and hung up, smiling.

"Considering the age of those coins and their value, it wouldn't be hard to trace them if they'd been sold. Good work, Libby!"

"Thank my brother," she replied, smiling. "He remembered it."

"You would have, too, I expect, in time," he said in a kindly tone. "Want me to have a talk with the bank president?" he added. "I think he might be more amenable to letting you and Curt back on the property with this new angle in mind. It might be to his advantage," he added in a satisfied tone.

"You mean, if we turn out to have that much money of our own, free and clear, it would make him very uncomfortable if we put it in the Jacobsville Municipal Bank and not his?"

"Exactly."

Her eyes blazed. "Which is exactly where we *will* put it, if we get it," she added.

He chuckled. "No need to tell him that just yet."

Her eyebrows lifted. "Mr. Kemp, you have a devious mind."

He smiled. "What else is new?"

Libby was furious at herself for not thinking of her father's impressive coin collection until now. She'd watched those coins come in the mail for years without really noticing them. But now they were important. They meant the difference between losing their home and getting it back again.

She sat on pins and needles over the weekend, until Kemp heard from the private detective the following Monday afternoon.

He buzzed Libby and told her to come into the office.

He was smiling when she got there. ''We found them,'' he said, chuckling when she made a whoop loud enough to bring Mabel down the hall.

''It's okay,'' Libby told her coworker, ''I've just had some good news for a change!''

Mabel grinned and went back to work.

Libby sat down in the chair in front of Kemp's big desk, smiling and leaning forward.

''Your father left the coins with a dealer who locked them in his safe. He was told not to let Janet have them under any circumstances,'' he added gently. ''Besides that, there was a will. He's got that, too. It's not a self-made will, either. It was done by a lawyer in the dealer's office and witnessed by two people who work for him.''

Libby's eyes filled with tears. ''Daddy knew! He knew she was trying to cut us out of the will!''

''He must have,'' he conceded. ''Apparently she'd made some comments about what she was going to do when he died. And she'd been harassing him about his health, making remarks about his heart being weak, as well.'' His jaw clenched. ''Whatever the cause, he changed the will in your favor—yours and Curt's. This will is going to stand up in a court of law and it changes the entire financial situation. You and Curt can go home and I'll get the will into probate immediately.''

''But the insurance...''

He nodded. ''She was the beneficiary for *one* of his insurance policies.'' He smiled at her surprise. ''There's another one, a half-a-million dollar policy, that he left with the same dealer who has the will. You and Curt are co-beneficiaries.''

''He didn't contact us!'' she exclaimed suddenly.

''Yes, and that's the interesting part,'' he said. ''He tried to contact you and Janet told him that you and Curt were out of the country on an extended vacation. She planned to go and talk to him the very day you made the remarks about

Violet's father and having locks put on your bedroom doors. She ran for her life before she had time to try to get to the rest of your inheritance.'' He chuckled. ''Maybe she had some idea of what the seller was guarding and decided that the insurance policy would hold her for a while without risking arrest.''

''Oh, thank God,'' she whispered, shivering with delight. ''Thank God! We can go home!''

''Apparently,'' he agreed, smiling. ''I'm going to drive up to San Antonio today and get those documents and the coin collection.''

She was suddenly concerned. ''But what if Janet hears about it? She had that friend in San Antonio who called and tried to get us off the property...'' She stopped abruptly. ''That's why they were trying to get us out of the house! They knew about the coin collection!'' She sat back heavily. ''But they could be dangerous....''

''Cash Grier is going with me.''

She pursed her lips amusedly. ''Okay.''

He chuckled. ''Nobody is going to try to attack me with Grier in the car. Even if he isn't armed.''

''Good point,'' she agreed.

''So call your brother and tell him the news,'' he said. ''And stop worrying. You're going to land on your feet, Libby.''

''How's Violet?'' she asked without thinking.

He stood up, his hands deep in his pockets. ''She and her mother are distraught, as you might imagine. They never realized that Mr. Hardy had been the victim of foul play. I've tried to keep it out of the papers, but when Janet's caught, it's going to be difficult.''

''Is there anything I can do?''

He smiled. ''Take them a pizza and let Violet talk to you about it,'' he suggested. ''She misses working here.''

''I miss her, too.''

He shifted, averting his gaze. ''I offered to let her come back to work here.''

''You did?'' she asked, enthused.

''She's going to think about it,'' he added. ''You might, uh, tell her how short-handed we are here, and that the temporary woman we got had to quit. Maybe she'll feel sorry for us and come back.''

She smiled. ''I'll do my best.''

He looked odd. ''Thanks,'' he said stiffly.

Chapter Nine

The very next day, Kemp came into the office grinning like a lottery winner. He was carrying a cardboard box, in which was a mahogany box full of rare gold coins, an insurance policy, a few personal items that had belonged to Riddle Collins and a fully executed new will.

Libby had to sit down when Kemp presented her with the hard evidence of her father's love for herself and Curt.

"The will is legal," he told her. "I'm going to take it right to the courthouse and file it. It will supercede the will that Janet probably still has in her possession. You should take the coins to the bank and put them in a safe-deposit box until you're ready to dispose of them. The dealer said he'll buy them from you at market value any time you're ready to sell them."

"But I'll have to use them as collateral for a loan to make the loan payment..."

"Actually, no, you won't," Kemp said with a smile, drawing two green-covered passbooks out of the box and handing them to her.

"What are these?" she asked blankly.

"Your father had two other bank accounts, both in San Antonio." He smiled warmly. "There's more than enough there to pay off the mortgage completely so that the ranch is free and clear. You'll still have a small fortune left over. You and your brother are going to be rich, Libby. Congratulations."

She cried a little, both for her father's loving care of them even after death and for having come so close to losing everything.

She pulled a tissue out of the pocket of her slacks and wiped her red eyes. "I'll take these to the Jacobsville Municipal Bank right now," she said firmly, "and have the money transferred here from San Antonio. Then I'll have them issue a cashier's check to pay off the other bank," she added with glee.

"Good girl. You can phone the insurance company about the death benefit, too. How does it feel, not to have to worry about money?"

She chuckled. "Very good." She eyed him curiously. "Does this mean you're firing me?"

"Well, Libby, you won't really need to work for a living anymore," he began slowly.

"But I love my job!" she exclaimed, and had the pleasure of watching his high cheekbones go ruddy. "Can't I stay?"

He drew in a long breath. "I'd be delighted if you would," he confessed. "I can't seem to keep a paralegal these days."

She smiled, remembering that Callie Kirby had been one, until she'd married Micah Steele. There had been two others after her, but neither had stayed long.

"Then it's settled. I have to go and call Curt!"

"Go to the bank first, Libby," he instructed with a grin.

"And I'll get to the courthouse. Mabel, we're going to be out of the office for thirty minutes!"

"Okay, boss!"

They went down the hall together and they stopped dead.

Violet was back at her desk, across from a grinning Mabel, looking radiant. "You said I could come back," she told Kemp at once, looking pretty and uncertain at the same time.

He drew in a sharp breath and his eyes lingered on her. "I certainly did," he agreed. "Are you staying?"

She nodded.

"How about making a fresh pot of coffee?" he asked.

"Regular?" she asked.

He averted his gaze to the door. "Half and half," he murmured. "Caffeine isn't good for me."

He went out the door, leaving Violet's jaw dropped.

"I told you he missed you," Libby whispered as she followed Kemp out the door and onto the sidewalk.

Libby and Curt were able to go home the next morning. But their arrival was bittersweet. The house had been ransacked in their absence.

"We'd better call the sheriff's office," Curt said angrily, when they'd ascertained that the disorder was thorough. "We'll need to have a report filed on this for insurance purposes."

"Do we even have insurance?"

He nodded. "Dad had a homeowner's policy. I've been keeping up the payments, remember?"

She righted a chair that had been turned over next to the desk her father had used in his study. The filling cabinet had been emptied onto the floor, along with a lot of other documents pertaining to the ranch's business.

"They were looking for that coin collection," Curt

guessed as he picked up the phone. "I'll bet anything Janet knew about it. She must be running short of cash already!"

"Thank God Mr. Kemp was able to track it down," she said.

"Sheriff's department?" Curt said into the telephone receiver. "I need you to send someone out to the Collins ranch. That's right, it's just past Jordan Powell's place. We've had a burglary. Yes. Okay. Thanks!" He hung up. "I talked to Hayes. He's going to come himself, along with his investigator."

"I thought he was overseas with his army unit in Iraq," she commented.

"He's back." He glanced at her amusedly. "You used to have a case on him, just before you went nuts over Jordan Powell."

She hated hearing Jordan's name mentioned. "Hayes is nice."

"So he is." He toyed with the telephone cord. "Libby, Jordan's having some bad times lately. His association with the Merrills has made him enemies."

"That was his choice," she reminded her brother.

"He was good to us, when Dad died."

She knew that. It didn't help. Her memories of Jordan's betrayal were too fresh. "Think I should do anything before they get here?"

"Make coffee," he suggested dryly. "Hayes's investigator is Mack Hughes, and he lives on caffeine."

"I'll do that."

Sheriff Hayes Carson pulled up at the front steps in his car, a brightly polished black vehicle with all sorts of antennae sticking out of it. The investigator, Mack Hughes, pulled up beside it in his black SUV with a deck of lights on the roof.

"Thanks for coming so quickly," Curt said, shaking hands with both men. "You remember my sister, Libby."

"Hello, Elizabeth," Hayes said with a grin, having always used her real first name instead of the nickname most people called her by. He was dashing, with blond hair and dark eyes, tall and muscular and big. He was in his mid-thirties; one tough customer, too. He and Cash Grier often went head-to-head in disputes, although they were good colleagues when there was an emergency.

"Hi, Hayes," she replied with a smile. "Hello, Mack."

Mack, tall and dark, nodded politely. "Let's see what you've got."

They ushered the law enforcement officers inside and stood back while they went about searching for clues.

"Any idea who the perpetrators were?" Hayes murmured while Mack looked around.

"Someone connected to our stepmother, most likely," Libby commented. "Dad had a very expensive coin collection and some secret bank accounts that even we didn't know about. If that's what they were looking for, they're out of luck. Mr. Kemp tracked them to San Antonio. Everything's in the bank now and a new will we recovered is in the proper hands."

Hayes whistled softly. "Lucky for you."

There was a sudden commotion in the front yard, made by a truck skidding to a stop between the two law enforcement vehicles. A dusty, tired Jordan Powell came up the steps, taking them two at a time, and stopped abruptly in the living room.

"What's happened?" he asked at once, his eyes homing to Libby with dark concern.

"The house was ransacked," Hayes told him. "Have you seen anything suspicious?"

"No. But I'll ask my men," Jordan assured them. He looked at Libby for a long time. "You okay?"

''Curt and I are fine, thanks,'' she said in a polite but reserved tone.

Jordan looked around at the jumble of furniture and paper on the floor, along with lamps and broken pieces of ceramic items that had been on the mantel over the fireplace.

''This wasn't necessary,'' Jordan said grimly. ''Even if they were looking for something, they didn't have to break everything in the house.''

''It was malicious, all right,'' Hayes agreed. He moved just in front of Libby. ''I heard from Grier that you've had two confrontations with Julie Merrill, one of them physically violent. She's also been implicated in acts of vandalism. I want to know if you think she might have had any part in this.''

Libby glanced at Jordan apprehensively.

''It could be a possibility,'' Jordan said, to her dismay. ''She was jealous of Libby and I've just broken with Julie and her father. She didn't take it well.''

''I'll add her to the list of suspects,'' Hayes said quietly. ''But I have to tell you, she isn't going to like being accused.''

''I don't care,'' Curt replied, answering for himself as well as Libby. ''Nobody has a right to do something like this.''

''Boss!'' Mack called from the back porch. ''Could you ask the Collinses to come out here, please?''

Curt stood aside to let Libby go first. On the small back stoop, Mack was squatting down, looking at a big red gas can. ''This yours?'' he asked Curt.

Curt frowned. ''We don't have one that big,'' he replied. ''Ours is locked up in the outbuilding next to the barn.''

Mack and Hayes exchanged curious looks.

''There's an insurance policy on the house,'' Libby remarked worriedly. "It's got Janet, our stepmother, listed as beneficiary."

"That narrows down the suspects," Hayes remarked.

"Surely she wouldn't..." Libby began.

"You've made a lot of trouble for her," Jordan said grimly. "And now she's missed out on two savings accounts and a will that she didn't even know existed."

"How did you know that?" Libby asked belligerently.

"My cousin owns the Municipal Bank," Jordan said nonchalantly.

"He had no business telling you anything!" Libby protested.

"He didn't, exactly," Jordan confessed. "I heard him talking to one of his clerks about opening the new account for you and setting up a safe-deposit box."

"Eavesdropping should be against the law," she muttered.

"I'll make a note of it," Hayes said with a grin.

She grinned back. "Thanks, Hayes."

He told Mack to start marking evidence to be collected. "We'll see if we can lift any latent prints," he told the small group. "If it was Janet, or someone she hired, they'll probably have been wearing gloves. If it was Julie Merrill, we might get lucky."

"I hope we can connect somebody to it," Libby said wearily, looking around. "If for no other reason than to make them pay to help have this mess cleaned up!"

"I'll take care of that," Jordan said at once, and reached for his cell phone.

"We don't need—!" Libby began hotly.

But Jordan wasn't listening. He was talking to Amie at his ranch, instructing her to phone two housekeepers she knew who helped her with heavy tasks and send them over to the Collins place.

"You might as well give up," Hayes remarked dryly.

"Once Jordan gets the bit between his teeth, it would take a shotgun to stop him. You know that."

She sighed angrily. "Yes. I know."

Hayes pushed his wide-brimmed hat back off his forehead and smiled down at Libby. "Are you doing anything Saturday night?" he asked. "They're having a campaign rally for Calhoun's supporters at Shea's."

"I know, I'm one of them," she replied, smiling. "Are you going to be there?"

He shrugged. "I might as well. Somebody'll have a beer too many and pick a fight, I don't doubt. Tiny the bouncer will have his hands full."

"Great!" she said enthusiastically.

Jordan was eavesdropping and not liking what he heard. He wanted to tell Hayes to back off. He wanted to tell Libby what he felt. But he couldn't get the words out.

"If you two are moving back in," Hayes added, "I think we'd better have somebody around overnight. I've got two volunteer deputies in the Sheriff's Posse who would be willing, I expect, if you'll keep them in coffee."

She smiled. "I'd be delighted. Thanks, Hayes. It would make me feel secure. We've got a shotgun, but I don't even know where it is."

"You could both stay with me until Hayes gets a handle on who did this," Jordan volunteered.

"No, thanks," Libby said quietly, trying not to remember that Jordan had already asked her to do that. No matter how she felt about the big idiot, she wasn't going to step into Julie Merrill's place.

"This is our home," Curt added.

Jordan drew in a long, sad breath. "Okay. But if you need help…"

"We'll call Hayes, thanks," Libby said, turning back to the sheriff. "I need to tidy up the kitchen. Is it all right?"

Hayes went with her into the small room and looked

around. There wasn't much damage in there and nothing was broken. "It looks okay. Go ahead, Libby. I'll see you Saturday, then?"

She grinned up at him. "Of course."

He grinned back and then rejoined the men in the living room. "I'm going to talk to my volunteers," he told Curt. "I'll be in touch."

"Thanks a lot, Hayes," Curt replied.

"Just doing my job. See you, Jordan."

"Yeah." Jordan didn't offer to shake hands. He glared after the other man as he went out the front door.

"I can clean my own house," Libby began impatiently.

Jordan met her eyes evenly. "I've made a lot of mistakes. I've done a lot of damage. I know I can't make it up to you in one fell swoop, but let me do what I can to make amends. Will you?"

Libby looked at her brother, who shrugged and walked away, leaving her to deal with Jordan alone.

"Some help you are," Libby muttered at his retreating back.

"I don't like the idea of that gas can," Jordan said, ignoring her statement. "You can't stay awake twenty-four hours a day. If Janet is really desperate enough to set fire to the house trying to get her hands on the insurance money, neither you nor Curt is going to be safe here."

"Hayes is getting us some protection," she replied coolly.

"I know that. But even deputies have to use the bathroom occasionally," he said flatly. "Why won't you come home with me?"

She lifted her chin. "This is my place, mine and Curt's. We're not running anymore."

He sighed. "I admire your courage, Libby. But it's misplaced this time."

She turned away. "I've got a lot to do, Jordan. Thanks anyway."

He caught her small waist from behind and held her just in front of him. His warm breath stirred the hair at the back of her head. "I was afraid."

"Of...what?" she asked, startled.

His big hands contracted. "You're very young, even for a woman your age," he said stiffly. "Young women are constantly changing."

She turned in his hold, curious. She looked up at him without understanding. "What has that got to do with anything?"

He reached out and traced her mouth with his thumb. He looked unusually solemn. "You really don't know, do you?" he asked quietly. "That's part of the problem."

"You aren't making any sense."

"I am. You're just not hearing what I'm saying." He bent and kissed her softly beside her ear, drawing away almost at once. "Never mind. You'll figure it out one day. Meanwhile, I'm going to do a better job of looking after you."

"I can—"

He interrupted at once. "If you say 'look after myself,' so help me, I'll...!"

She glared at him.

He glared back.

"You're up against someone formidable, whoever it is," he continued. "I'm not letting anything happen to you, Libby."

"Fat lot you cared before," she muttered.

He sighed heavily. "Yes, I know. I'll eat crow without catsup if it will help you trust me again."

"Julie's very pretty," she said reluctantly.

"She isn't a patch on you, butterfly," he said quietly.

She hesitated. But she wasn't giving in easily. He'd hurt

her. No way was she going to run headfirst into his arms the first time he opened them.

She watched him suspiciously.

His broad chest rose and fell. ''Okay. We'll do it your way. I'll see you at Shea's.''

''You're the enemy,'' she pointed out. ''You're not on Calhoun's team.''

He shrugged. ''A man can change sides, can't he?'' he mused. ''Meanwhile, if you need me, I'll be at the house. If you call, I'll come running.''

She nodded slowly. ''All right.''

He smiled at her.

Curt came back in. He was as cool to Jordan as his sister. The older man shrugged and left without another word.

''Now he's changed sides again,'' Libby told Curt when Jordan was gone.

''Jordan's feeling his age, Libby,'' Curt told her. ''And some comments were made by his cowboys about that kiss they saw.''

Her eyebrows arched. ''What?''

He sighed. ''I never had the heart to tell you. But one of the older hands said Jordan was trying to rob the cradle. It enraged Jordan. But it made him think, too. He knows how sheltered you've been. I think he was trying to protect you.''

''From what?''

''Maybe from a relationship he didn't think you were ready for,'' he replied. ''Julie was handy, he'd dated her a time or two, and she swarmed all over him just about the time he was drawing back from you. I expect he was flattered by her attention and being invited into that highbrow social set that shut out his mother after she was disinherited because she married his father. The local society women just turned their backs on her. She was never invited anywhere ever again. Jordan felt it keenly, that some of his playmates weren't allowed to invite him to their houses."

"I didn't know it was so hard on him. He's only told me bits and pieces about his upbringing."

"He doesn't advertise it," he added. "She gave up everything to marry his father. She worked as a housekeeper in one of the motels owned by her father's best friend. It was a rough upbringing for Jordan."

"I can imagine." She sighed, unable to prevent her heart from thawing.

Shea's was filled to capacity on Saturday evening. Cash Grier got a lot of attention because he brought Tippy with him. She looked good despite her ordeals, except for the small indications of healing cuts on her lovely face. She was weak and still not totally recovered and it showed. Nevertheless, she was still the most beautiful woman in the room. But she had eyes only for Cash and that showed, too.

When they got on the dance floor together, Libby was embarrassed to find herself staring wistfully at them. Tippy melted into Cash's tall body as if she'd found heaven. He looked that way as well. They clung together to the sound of an old love song. And when she looked up at him, he actually stopped dancing and just stared at her.

"They make a nice couple," Jordan said from behind her.

She glanced up at him. He looked odd. His dark eyes were quiet, intent on her uplifted face.

"Yes, they do," she replied. "They seem to fit together very well."

He nodded. "Dance with me," he said in a deep voice, and drew her into his arms.

She hesitated, but only for a few seconds. She'd built dreams on those kisses they'd shared and she thought it was all over. But the way he was holding her made her knees weak. His big hand covered hers against his chest and pressed it hard into the warm muscle.

''I've been an idiot,'' he said at her ear.

''What do you mean?'' she wondered aloud, drugged by his closeness.

''I shouldn't have backed off,'' he replied quietly. ''I got cold feet at the very worst time.''

''Jordan…''

''…mind if I cut in?'' Hayes Carson asked with a grin.

Jordan stopped, his mind still in limbo. ''We were talking,'' he began.

''Plenty of time for that later. Shall we, Libby?'' he asked, and moved right in front of Jordan. He danced Libby away before she had a chance to stop him.

''Now that's what I call a jealous man,'' Hayes murmured dryly, glancing over her shoulder at Jordan. ''No need to ask about the lay of the land.''

''Jordan doesn't feel that way about me,'' Libby protested.

''He doesn't?''

She averted her eyes to the crowded dance floor. ''He isn't a marrying man.''

''Uh-huh.''

She glanced up at Hayes, who was still grinning.

She flushed at the look in his eyes.

Across the room, Jordan Powell saw that flush and had to restrain himself from going over there and tearing Libby out of Hayes's embrace.

''What the devil are you doing here?'' Calhoun Ballenger asked abruptly.

Jordan glanced at him wryly. ''Not much,'' he murmured. ''But I came to ask if you needed another willing ally. I've, uh, changed camps.''

Calhoun's eyebrows went up almost to his blond hairline.

''I do like to be on the winning side,'' Jordan drawled.

Calhoun burst out laughing. ''Well, you're not a bad diplomat, I guess,'' he confessed, holding out his hand. ''Welcome aboard.''

''My pleasure.''

Jordan contrived to drive Libby and Curt home, but he was careful to let Curt go into the ranch house before he cut off the engine and turned to Libby.

''There's been some news,'' he said carefully.

''About Janet?'' she exclaimed.

''About Julie,'' he corrected. He toyed with a strand of her hair in the dim light of the car interior. ''One of Grier's men saw her with a known drug dealer earlier today. She's put her neck in a noose and she doesn't even know it.''

''She uses, doesn't she?'' she asked.

He shrugged. ''Her behavior is erratic. She must.''

''I'm sorry. You liked her...''

He bent and kissed her hungrily, pulling her across his lap to wrap her up in his warm, strong arms. ''I like you,'' he whispered against her mouth. ''More than I ever dreamed I could!''

She wanted to ask questions, but she couldn't kiss him and breathe at the same time. She gave up and ran her arms up around his neck. She relaxed into his close embrace and kissed him back until her mouth grew sore and swollen.

He sighed into her throat as he held her and rocked her in his arms in the warm darkness.

''Libby, I think we should start going out together.''

She blinked. ''You and me?''

He nodded. ''You and me.'' He drew back and looked down at her possessively. ''I could give up liver and onions, if I had to. But I can't give you up.''

''Listen, I don't have affairs...''

He kissed her into silence. ''Neither do I. So I guess maybe we won't sleep together after all.''

"But if we go out together..." she worried.

He grinned. "You have enough self-restraint for both of us, I'm sure," he drawled. "You can keep me honest."

She drew back a little and noted the position of his big lean hands under her blouse. She looked at him intently.

He cleared his throat and drew his hands out from under the blouse. "Every man is entitled to one little slip. Right?" His eyes were twinkling.

She laughed. "Okay."

He touched her mouth with his one last time. "In that case, you'd better rush inside before I forget to be honest."

"Thanks for bringing us home."

"My pleasure. Lock the doors," he added seriously. "And I'm only a phone call away if you need me. You call me," he emphasized. "Not Hayes Carson. Got that?"

"And since when did I become your personal property?" she asked haughtily.

"Since the minute you let me put my hands under your blouse," he shot right back, laughing. "Think about it."

She got out of the vehicle, dizzy and with her head swimming. In one night, everything had changed.

"Don't worry," he added gently, leaning out the window. "I have enough restraint for both of us!"

Before she could answer him, he gunned the engine and took off down the road.

Chapter Ten

For the next few days, Jordan was at Libby's house more than at his own. He smoothed over hard feelings with her brother and became a household fixture. Libby and Curt filed the insurance claim, paid off the mortgage, and started repurchasing cattle for the small ranch.

Janet was found a couple of days later at a motel just outside San Antonio, with a man. He turned out to be the so-called attorney who'd phoned and tried to get Libby and Curt out of their home. She was arrested and charged with murder in the death of Violet's father. There was DNA evidence taken from the dead man's clothing and the motel room that was directly linked to Janet. It placed her at the motel the night Mr. Hardy died. When she realized the trouble she was in, she tried to make a deal for a reduced sentence. She agreed to confess to the murder in return for a life sentence without hope of parole. But she denied having a gas can. She swore that she never had plans to burn down Riddle Collins's house with his children in it. Nobody paid her much attention. She'd told so many lies.

It was a different story for Julie Merrill. She continued

to make trouble, and not only for Calhoun Ballenger. She was determined that Jordan wasn't going to desert her for little Libby Collins. She had a plan. Two days before the hearing to decide the fate of the police officers who'd arrested her father— Saturday, she put it into practice.

She phoned Libby at work and apologized profusely for all the trouble she'd caused.

"I never meant to be such a pain in the neck," she assured Libby. "I want to make it up to you. You get off at one on Saturdays, don't you? Suppose you come over here for lunch?"

"To your house?" Libby replied warily.

"Yes. I've had our cook make something special," she purred. "And I can tell you my side of the story. Will you?"

Dubious, Libby hesitated.

"Surely you aren't afraid of me?" Julie drawled. "I mean, what could I do to you, even if I had something terrible in mind?"

"You don't need to feed me," Libby replied cautiously. "I don't hold grudges."

"You'll come, then," Julie persisted. "Today at one. Will you?"

It was against her better judgment. But it wasn't a bad idea to keep a feud going, especially now that Jordan seemed really interested in her.

"Okay," Libby said finally. "I'll be there at one."

"Thanks!" Julie said huskily. "You don't know how much I appreciate it! Uh, I don't guess you'd like to bring your brother, too?" she added suddenly.

Libby frowned. "Curt's driving a cattle truck for Duke Wright up to San Antonio today."

"Well, then, another time, perhaps! I'll see you at one." Julie hung up, with a bright and happy note in her voice.

Libby frowned. Was she stupid to go to the woman's home? But why would Julie risk harming her now, with the primary election so close? It was the following Tuesday.

She phoned Jordan. ''Guess what just happened?'' she asked.

''You've realized how irresistible I am and you're rushing over to seduce me?'' he teased. ''Shall I turn down the covers on my bed?''

''Stop that,'' she muttered. ''I'm serious.''

''So am I!''

''Jordan,'' she laughed. ''Julie just called to apologize. She invited me to lunch.''

''Did she?'' he asked. ''Are you going?''

''I thought I might.'' She hesitated. ''Don't you think it's a good idea, to mend fences, I mean?''

''I don't know, Libby,'' he replied seriously. ''She's been erratic and out of control lately. I don't think it's a good idea. I'd rather you didn't.''

''Are you afraid she might tell me something about you that I don't know?'' she returned, suspicious.

He sighed. ''No. It's not that. She wasn't happy when I broke off with her. I don't trust her.''

''What can she do to me in broad daylight?'' she laughed. ''Shoot me?''

''Of course not,'' he scoffed.

''Then stop worrying. She only wants to apologize.''

''You be careful,'' he returned. ''And phone me when you get home. Okay?''

''Okay.''

''How about a movie tonight?'' he added. ''There's a new mystery at the theater. You can even have popcorn.''

''That sounds nice,'' she said, feeling warm and secure.

''I'll pick you up about six.''

''I'll be ready. See you then.''

She hung up and pondered over his misgivings. Surely he was overreacting. He was probably afraid Julie might make up a convincing lie about how intimate they'd been. Or perhaps she might be telling the truth. She only knew that she had to find out why Julie wanted to see her in person. She was going.

But something niggled at the back of her mind when she drove toward Julie's palatial home on the Jacobs River. Julie might have wanted to invite Libby over to apologize, but why would she want Curt to come, too? She didn't even know Curt.

Libby's foot lifted off the accelerator. Her home was next door to Jordan's. Julie was furious that Jordan had broken off with her. If the house was gone, Libby and Curt would have to move away again, as they had before...!

Libby turned the truck around in the middle of the road and sped toward her house. She wished she had a cell phone. There was no way to call for help. But she was absolutely certain what was about to happen. And she knew immediately that her stepmother hadn't been responsible for that gas can on the porch.

The question was, who had Julie convinced to set that fire for her? Or would she be crazy enough to try and do it herself?

Libby sped faster down the road. If only there had been state police, a sheriff's deputy, a policeman watching. She was speeding. It was the only time in her life she'd ever wanted to be caught!

But there were no flashing lights, no sirens. She was going to have to try and stop the perpetrator all by herself. She wasn't a big woman. She had no illusions about being able to tackle a grown man. She didn't even have a weapon. Wait. There was a tire tool in the boot! At least, she could threaten with it.

She turned into the road that led to the house. There was no smoke visible anywhere and no sign of any traffic. For the first time, she realized that she could be chasing make-believe villains. Why would she think that Julie Merrill would try to burn her house down? Maybe the strain of the past weeks was making her hysterical after all.

She pulled up in front of the house and got out, grabbing the tire tool out of the back. It wouldn't hurt to look around, now that she was here.

She moved around the side of the house, her heart beating wildly. Her palms were so sweaty that she had to get a better grip on the tire tool. She walked past the chimney, to the corner, and peered around. Her heart stopped.

There was a man there. A young, dark man. He had a can of gasoline. He was muttering to himself as he sloshed it on the back porch and the steps.

Libby closed her eyes and prayed for strength. There was nobody to help her. She had to do this alone.

She walked around the corner with the tire tool raised. "That's enough, you varmint! You're trespassing on private property and you're going to jail. The police are right behind me!"

Startled, the man dropped the gas can and stared wild-eyed at Libby.

Sensing an advantage, she started to run toward him, yelling at the top of her lungs.

To her amazement, he started running down a path behind the house, with Libby right on his heels, still yelling.

Then something happened that was utterly in the realm of fantasy. She heard an engine behind her. An accomplice, she wondered, almost panicking.

Jordan Powell pulled up right beside her in his truck and threw open the passenger door. "Get in!" he called.

She didn't need prompting. She jumped right in beside him, tire tool and all, and slammed the door. "He was dousing the back porch with gas!" she panted. "Don't let him get away!"

"I don't intend to." His face was grim as he stood down

on the accelerator and the truck shot forward on the pasture road, which was no more than tracks through tall grass.

The attempted arsonist was tiring. He was pretty thick in the middle and had short legs. He was almost to a beat-up old car sitting out of sight of the house near the barn when Jordan came alongside him on the driver's side.

"Hold it in the ruts!" he called to Libby.

Just as she grabbed the wheel, he threw open the door and leaped out on the startled, breathless young man, pinning him to the ground.

By the time Libby had the truck stopped, Jordan had the man by his shirt collar and was holding him there.

"Pick up the phone and call Hayes," he called to Libby.

Her hands were shaking, but she managed to dial 911 and give the dispatcher an abbreviated account of what had just happened. She was told that they contacted a deputy who was barely a mile away and he was starting toward the Collins place at that moment.

Libby thanked her nicely and cut off the phone.

"Who put you up to this?" Jordan demanded of the man. "Tell me, or so help me, I'll make sure you don't get out of prison until you're an old man!"

"It was Miss Julie," the young man sobbed. "I never done nothing like this in my life. My daddy works for her and he took some things out of her house. She said she'd turn him over to the police if I didn't do this for her."

"She'd have turned him over anyway, you fool," Jordan said coldly. "She was using you. Do you have any idea what the penalty is for arson?"

He was still sobbing. "I was scared, Mr. Powell."

Jordan relented, but only a little. He looked up as the sound of a siren was heard coming closer.

Libby opened the door of the truck and got out, just as a sheriff's car came flying down the track and stopped just behind the truck.

The deputy was Sammy Tibbs. They both knew him. He'd been in Libby's class in high school.

''What have you got, Jordan?'' Sammy asked.

''A would-be arsonist,'' Jordan told him. ''He'll confess if you ask him.''

''I caught him pouring gas on my back porch and I chased him with my tire tool. I almost had him when Jordan came along,'' Libby said with a shy grin.

''Whew,'' Sammy whistled. ''I hope I don't ever run afoul of you,'' he told her.

''That makes two of us,'' Jordan said, with a gentle smile for her.

''I assume you'll be pressing charges?'' Sammy asked Libby as he handcuffed the young man, who was still out of breath.

''You can bet real money on it,'' Libby agreed. ''And you'll need to pick up Julie Merrill as well, because this man said she told him to do it.''

Sammy's hands froze on the handcuffs. ''Julie Merrill? The state senator's daughter?''

''That's exactly who I mean,'' Libby replied. ''She called and invited me over to lunch. Since she doesn't like me, I got suspicious and came home instead, just in time to catch this weasel in the act.''

''Is this true?'' the deputy asked the man.

''Mirandize him first,'' Jordan suggested. ''Just so there won't be any loopholes.''

''Good idea,'' Sammy agreed, and read the suspect his rights.

''Now, tell him,'' Libby prodded, glaring at the man who'd been within a hair of burning her house down.

The young man sighed as if the weight of the world was sitting on his shoulders. ''Miss Merrill had something on my daddy, who works for her. She said if I'd set a fire on Miss Collins's back steps, she'd forget all about it. She just wanted to scare Miss Collins is all. She didn't tell me to burn the whole place down."

"Arson is arson," Sammy replied. "Don't touch anything," he told Libby. "I'll send our investigator back out there and call the state fire marshal. Arson is hard to prove, but this one's going to be a walk in the park."

"Thanks, Sammy," Libby said.

He grinned. "What for? You caught him!"

He put the scared suspect in the back of his car and sped off with a wave of his hand.

"That was too damned close," Jordan said, looking down at Libby with tormented eyes. "I couldn't believe it when I saw you chasing him through the field with a tire iron! What if he'd been armed?"

"He wasn't," she said. "Besides, he ran the minute I chased him, just like a black snake."

He pulled her into his arms and wrapped her up tight. There was a faint tremor in those strong arms.

"You brave idiot," he murmured into her neck. "Thank God he didn't get the fire started first. I can see you running inside to grab all the sentimental items and save them. You'd have been burned alive."

She grimaced, because he was absolutely right. She'd have tried to save her mementos of her father and mother, at any cost.

"Libby, I think we'd better get engaged," he said suddenly.

She was hallucinating. She said so.

He pulled back from her, his eyes solemn. "You're not hallucinating. If Julie realizes how serious this is between us, she'll back off."

"She's going to be in jail shortly, she'll have to," she pointed out.

"They can afford bail until her hearing, even so," he replied. "She'll be out for blood. But if she hears about the engagement, it might be enough to make her think twice."

"I'm not afraid of her," she said, although she really was.

"Humor me," he coaxed, bending to kiss her gently.

She smiled under the warm, comforting feel of his hard mouth on her lips. "Well..."

He nibbled her upper lip. "I'll get you a ring," he whispered.

"What sort?"

"What do you want?"

"I like emeralds," she whispered, standing on tiptoe to coax his mouth down again.

"An emerald, then."

"Nobody would know?"

He chuckled as he kissed her. "We might have to tell a few hundred people, just to make it believable. And we might actually have to get married, but that's okay, isn't it?"

She blinked. "Get...married?"

"That's what the ring's for, Libby," he said against her warm mouth. "Advance notice."

"But...you've always said you never wanted to get married."

"I always said there's the one woman a man can't walk away from," he added. He lifted his head and looked down at her, all the teasing gone. "I can't walk away from you. The past few weeks have been pure hell."

Her eyes widened with unexpected delight.

He traced her eyebrows with his forefinger. "I missed you," he whispered. "It was like being cut apart."

"You wanted Julie," she accused.

He grimaced. "I wanted you to think about what was happening. You've been sheltered your whole life. Duke Wright's wife was just like you. Then she married and had a child and got career-minded. That poor devil lives in hell because she didn't know what she wanted until it was too late!"

She searched his face quietly. "You think I'd want a career."

"I don't know, Libby," he bit off. He looked anguished. "I'm an all-or-nothing kind of man. I can't just stick my toe in to test the water. I jump in headfirst."

He...loved her. She was stunned. She couldn't believe she hadn't noticed, in all this time. Curt had seen it long before this. He'd tried to tell her. But she hadn't believed that a man like Jordan could be serious about someone like her.

Her lips fell apart with a husky sigh. She was on fire. She'd never dreamed that life could be so sweet. "I don't want a career," she said slowly.

"What if you do, someday?" he persisted.

She reached up and traced his firm, jutting chin with her fingertips. "I'm twenty-four years old, Jordan," she said. "If I don't know my own mind by now, I never will."

He still looked undecided.

She put both hands flat on his shirt. Under it, she could feel the muted thunder of his heartbeat. "Why don't we go to a movie?" she asked.

He seemed to relax. He smiled. "We could grab a hamburger for lunch and talk about it," he prompted.

"Okay."

"Then we'll go by the sheriff's department and you can write out a statement," he added.

She grimaced. "I guess I'll have to."

He nodded. "So will I." His eyes narrowed. "I wish I could see the look on Julie's face when the deputy sheriff pulls up in her driveway."

"I imagine she'll be surprised," Libby replied.

Surprised was an understatement. Julie Merrill gaped at the young man in the deputy sheriff's uniform.

"You're joking," she said haughtily. "I...I had nothing to do with any attempted arson!"

‘‘We have a man in custody who’ll swear to it,’’ he replied. ‘‘You can come peacefully or you can go out the door in handcuffs,’’ he added, still pleasant and respectful. ‘‘Your choice, Miss Merrill.’’

She let out a harsh breath. ‘‘This is outrageous!’’

‘‘What’s going on out here?’’ Her father, the state senator, came into the hall, weaving a little, and blinked when he saw the deputy. ‘‘What’s he doing here?’’ he murmured.

‘‘Your daughter is under arrest, senator,’’ he was told as the deputy suddenly turned Julie around and cuffed her with professional dexterity. ‘‘For conspiracy to commit arson.’’

‘‘Arson?’’ The senator blinked. ‘‘Julie?’’

‘‘She sent a man to burn down the Collins place,’’ he was told. ‘‘We have two eyewitnesses as well.’’

The senator gaped at his daughter. ‘‘I told you to leave that woman alone,’’ he said, shaking his finger at her. ‘‘I told you Jordan would get involved if you didn’t! You’ve cost me the election! Everybody around here will go to the polls Tuesday and vote for Calhoun Ballenger! You’ve ruined me!’’

‘‘Oh, no, sir, she hasn’t,’’ the deputy assured him with a grin. ‘‘Your nephew, the mayor, did that, by persecuting two police officers who were just doing their jobs.’’ The smile faded. ‘‘You’re going to see Monday night just how much hot water you’ve jumped into. That disciplinary hearing is going to be remembered for the next century in Jacobsville.’’

‘‘Where are you taking my daughter?’’ the senator snorted.

‘‘To jail, to be booked. You can call your attorney and arrange for a bail hearing whenever you like,’’ the deputy added, with a speaking glance at the older man’s condition. ‘‘If you’re able.’’

‘‘I’ll call my own attorney,’’ Julie said hotly. ‘‘Then I’ll sue you for false arrest!’’

''You're welcome to try,'' the deputy said. ''Come along, Miss Merrill.''

''Daddy, do try to sober up!'' Julie said scathingly.

''What would be the point?'' the senator replied. ''Life was so good when I didn't know all about you, Julie. When I thought you were a sweet, kind, innocent woman like your mother...'' He closed his eyes. ''You killed that girl!''

''I did not! Think what you're saying!'' Julie yelled at him.

Tears poured down his cheeks. ''She died in my arms...''

''Let's go,'' the deputy said, tugging Julie Merrill out the door. He closed it on the sobbing politician.

Julie Merrill was lodged in the county jail until her bail hearing the following Monday morning. Meanwhile, Jordan and Libby had given their statements and the would-be arsonist was singing like a canary bird.

The disciplinary hearing for Chief Grier's two police officers was Monday night at the city council meeting.

It didn't take long. Within thirty minutes, the Council had finished its usual business, Grier's officers were cleared of any misconduct, and the surprise guests at the hearing had Jacobsville buzzing for weeks afterward.

Chapter Eleven

Jordan drove Libby to his house in a warm silence. He led her into the big, elegant living room and closed the door behind them.

"Want something to drink?" he asked, moving to a pitcher of iced tea that Amie had apparently left for them, along with a plate of homemade cake, covered with foil. "And a piece of pound cake?"

"I'd love that," she agreed.

He poured tea into two glasses and handed them to her, along with doilies to protect the coffee table from spots. He put cake onto two plates, with forks, and brought them along. But as he bent over the coffee table, he obscured Libby's plate. When he sat down beside her, there was a beautiful emerald solitaire, set in gold, lying on her piece of cake.

"Look at that," he exclaimed with twinkling dark eyes. "Why, it's an engagement ring! I wonder who could have put it there?" he drawled.

She picked it up, breathless. "It's beautiful."

''Isn't it?'' he mused. ''Why don't you try it on? If it fits,'' he added slyly, ''you might turn into a fairy princess and get your own true prince as a prize!''

She smiled through her breathless delight. ''Think so?''

''Darlin', I can almost guarantee it,'' he replied tenderly. ''Want to give it a shot?''

He seemed to hold his breath while he waited for her reply. She had to fight tears. It was the most poignant moment of her entire life.

''Why don't you put it on for me?'' she asked finally, watching him lift the ring and slide it onto her ring finger with something like relief.

''How about that?'' he murmured dryly. ''It's a perfect fit. Almost as if it were made just for you,'' he added.

She looked up at him and all the humor went out of his face. He held her small hand in his big one and searched her eyes.

''You love emeralds. I bought this months ago and stuck it in a drawer while I tried to decide whether or not it would be suicide to propose to you. Duke Wright's situation made me uncertain. I was afraid you hadn't seen enough of the world, or life, to be able to settle down here in Jacobsville. I was afraid to take a chance.''

She moved a step closer. ''But you finally did.''

He cupped her face in his big, warm hands. ''Yes. When I realized that I was spending time with Julie just to keep you at bay. If she'd been a better sort of person, it would have been a low thing to do. I was flattered at her interest and the company I got to keep. But I felt like a traitor when she started insulting you in public. I was too wrapped up in my own uncertainties to do what I should have done.''

''Which was what?'' she asked softly.

He bent to her soft mouth. ''I should have realized that if you really love someone, everything works out.'' He kissed her tenderly. "I should have told you how I felt and given you a chance to spread your wings if you wanted to. I could have waited while you decided what sort of future you wanted."

She still couldn't believe that he didn't know how she felt. "I was crazy about you," she whispered huskily. "Everybody knew it except you." She reached up and linked her arms around his neck. "Duke's wife wasn't like me, Jordan," she added, searching his dark eyes. "She lived with a domineering father and a deeply religious mother. They taught her that a woman's role in life was to marry and obey her husband. She'd always done what they told her to do. But after she married Duke, she ran wild, probably giving vent to all those feelings of suffocated restriction she'd endured all her life. Getting pregnant on her wedding night was a big mistake for both of them, because then she really felt trapped." She took a deep breath. "If Duke hadn't rushed her into it, she'd have gone off and found her career and come back to him when she knew what she really wanted. It was a tragedy in the making from the very beginning."

"She didn't love him enough," he murmured.

"He didn't love her enough," she countered. "He got her pregnant, thinking it would hold her."

He sighed. "I want children," he said softly. "But not right away. We need time to get to know each other before we start a family, don't we?"

She smiled. "See? You ask me about things. You don't order me around. Duke was exactly the opposite." She traced his mouth with her fingertips. "That's why I stopped going out with him. He never asked me what I wanted to do, even what I wanted to eat when we went out together. He actually ordered meals for me before I could say what

I liked.'' She glowered. ''He ordered me liver and onions and I never went out with him again.''

He lifted an eyebrow and grinned. ''Darlin', I swear on my horse that I will *never* order you liver and onions.'' He crossed his heart.

He was so handsome when he grinned like that. Her heart expanded like a balloon with pure happiness. ''Actually,'' she whispered, lifting up to him. ''I'd even eat liver and onions for you.''

''The real test of love,'' he agreed, gathering her up hungrily. ''And I'd eat squash for you,'' he offered.

She smiled under the slow, sweet pressure of his mouth. Amie said he'd actually dumped a squash casserole in the middle of the living room carpet to make the point that he never wanted it again.

''This is nice,'' he murmured, lifting her completely off the floor. ''But I can do better.''

''Can you really?'' she whispered, biting softly at his full lower lip. ''Show me!''

He laughed, even though his body was making emphatic statements about how little time there was left for teasing. He was burning.

He put her down on the sofa and crushed her into it with the warm, hard length of his body.

''Jordan,'' she whispered breathlessly when he eased between her long legs.

''Don't panic,'' he said against her lips. ''Amie's a scream away. Lift up.''

She did, and he unfastened the bra and pushed it out of the way under her blouse. He deepened the kiss slowly, seductively, while his lean hands discovered the soft warmth of her bare breasts in a heated silence.

Her head began to spin. He was going to be her husband. She could lie in his arms all night long. They could have children together. After the tragedy of the past few months, it was like a trip to paradise.

She moaned and wrapped her long legs around his hips, urging him even closer. She felt the power and heat of him intimately. Her mouth opened, inviting the quick, hard thrust of his tongue.

"Oh, yes," she groaned into his hard mouth. Her hips lifted into his rhythmically, her breath gasping out at his ear as she clung to him. "Yes. That feels...good!"

A tortured sound worked out of his throat as he pressed her down hard into the soft cushions of the sofa, his hands already reaching for the zipper in the front of her slacks, so far gone that he was mindless.

The sound of footsteps outside the door finally penetrated the fog of passion that lay between them. Jordan lifted his head. Libby looked up at him, dazed and only half aware of the sound.

"Amie," Jordan groaned, taking a steadying breath. "We have to stop."

"Tell her to go away," she whispered, laughing breathlessly.

"You tell her," he teased as he got to his feet. "She gets even in the kitchen. She can make squash look just like a corn casserole."

"Amie's Revenge?"

He nodded. "Amie's Revenge." Jordan paused. "I want to marry you," he said quietly. "I want it with all my heart."

She had to fight down tears to answer him. "I want it, too."

He drew her close, over his lap, and when he kissed her, it was with such breathless tenderness that she felt tears threatening again.

She slid her arms around his neck and kissed him back with fervent ardor. But he put her gently away.

''You don't want to ravish me?'' she exclaimed. ''You said once that you could do me justice in thirty minutes!''

''I lied,'' he said, chuckling. ''I'd need two hours. And Amie's skulking out in the hall, waiting for an opportunity to congratulate us,'' he added in a whisper. ''We can't possibly shock her so soon before the wedding.''

She hesitated. ''So soon...?''

''I want to get married as quickly as possible,'' he informed her. ''All we need is the blood tests, a license, and I've already got us a minister. Unless you want a formal wedding in a big church with hundreds of guests,'' he added worriedly.

''No need, since you've already got us a minister,'' she teased.

He relaxed. ''Thank God! The idea of a morning coat and hundreds of people...''

She was kissing him, so he stopped talking.

Just as things were getting interesting, there was an impatient knock at the door. ''Well?'' Amie called through it.

''She said yes!'' Jordan called back.

The door opened and Amie rushed in, grinning from ear to ear.

''She hates squash,'' he said in a mock whisper.

''I won't ever make it again,'' Amie promised.

He hugged her. After a minute, Libby joined them. She hugged the housekeeper, too.

''Welcome to the family!'' Amie laughed.

And that was the end of any heated interludes for the rest of the evening.

The next few days went by in a blur of activity. When the votes were counted on Tuesday at the primary election,

Senator Merrill lost the Democratic candidacy by a ten-to-one margin. A recall of the city fathers was announced, along with news of a special election to follow. Councilman Culver and the mayor were both implicated in drug trafficking, along with Julie Merrill. Julie had managed to get bail the day before the primary, but she hadn't been seen since. She was also still in trouble for the arson conspiracy. Her father had given an impressive concession speech, in front of the news media, and congratulated Calhoun Ballenger with sincerity. It began to be noticed that he improved when his daughter's sins came to light. Apparently he'd been duty-bound to try and protect her, and it had almost killed his conscience. He'd started drinking heavily, and then realized that he was likely to lose his state senate seat for it. He'd panicked, gone to the mayor, and tried to get the charges dropped.

One irresponsible act had cost Senator Merrill everything. But, he told Calhoun, he still had his house and his health. He'd stand by his daughter, of course, and do what he could for her. Perhaps retirement wouldn't be such a bad thing. His daughter could not be reached for comment. She was now being hunted by every law enforcement officer in Texas and government agents on the drug charges, which were formidable. Other unsavory facts were still coming to light about her doings.

Jordan finally understood why Libby had tried so hard to keep him out of Julie's company and he apologized profusely for refusing to listen to her. Duke Wright's plight had made him somber and afraid, especially when he realized how much he loved Libby. He was afraid to take a chance on her. He had plenty of regrets.

Libby accepted his apology and threw herself into politics as one of Calhoun's speechwriters, a job she loved. But, she told Jordan, she had no desire to do it for a profession. She was quite happy to work for Mr. Kemp and raise a family in Jacobsville.

On the morning of Libby's marriage to Jordan, she was almost floating with delight. ''I can't believe the things that have happened in two weeks,'' Libby told her brother at the church door as they waited for the music to go down the aisle together. ''It's just amazing!''

''For a small town, it certainly is,'' he agreed. He grinned. ''Happy?''

''Too happy,'' she confessed, blushing. ''I never dreamed I'd be marrying Jordan.''

''I did. He's been crazy about you for years, but Duke Wright's bad luck really got to him. Fortunately, he did see the light in time.''

She took a deep breath as the first strains of the wedding march were heard. ''I'm glad it's just us and not a crowd,'' she murmured.

He didn't speak. His eyes twinkled as he opened the door.

Inside, all the prominent citizens of Jacobsville were sitting in their pews, waiting for the bride to be given away by her brother. Cash Grier was there with Tippy. So were Calhoun Ballenger and Abby, Justin Ballenger and Shelby Jacobs Ballenger. And the Hart brothers, all five of them including the attorney general, with their wives. The Tremaynes. Mr. Kemp, with Violet! The Drs. Coltrain and Dr. Morris and Dr. Steele and their wives. Eb Scott and his wife. Cy Parks and his wife. It was a veritable who's who of the city.

''Surprise,'' Curt whispered in her ear, and tugged her along down the aisle. She was adorned in a simple white satin gown with colorful embroidery on the bodice and puffy sleeves, a delicate veil covering her face and shoulders. She carried a bouquet of lily of the valley and pink roses.

Jordan Powell, in a soft gray morning coat and all the trappings, was waiting for her at the altar with the minister. He looked handsome and welcoming and he was smiling from ear to ear.

Libby thought back over the past few agonizing weeks and realized all the hardships and heartache she'd endured made her truly appreciate all the sweet blessings that had come into her life. She smiled through her tears and stopped at Jordan's side, her small hand searching blindly for his as she waited to speak her vows. She'd never felt more loved or happier than she was at that moment. She only wished her parents had lived to see her married.

Just after the wedding, there was a reception at the church fellowship hall, catered by Barbara's Café. The wedding cake was beautiful, with a colorful motif that exactly matched the embroidery on Libby's wedding gown.

She and Jordan were photographed together cutting the cake and then interacting with all their unexpected guests. The only sticky moment was when handsome Hayes Carson bent to kiss Libby.

"Careful, Hayes," Jordan said from right beside him. "I'm watching you!"

"Great idea," Hayes replied imperturbably and grinned. "You could use a few lessons."

And he kissed Libby enthusiastically while Jordan fumed.

When they were finally alone, hours later in Galveston, Jordan was still fuming about that kiss.

"You know Hayes was teasing," she said, coaxing him into her arms. "But I'm not. I've waited twenty-four years for this,'' she added with a wry smile. ''I have great expectations.''

He drew her close with a worldly look. ''And I expect to satisfy them fully!''

''I'm not going to be very good at this, at first,'' she said breathlessly, when he began to undress her. ''Is it all right?''

He smiled tenderly. ''You're going to be great at it,'' he countered. ''The only real requirement is love. We're rich in that.''

She relaxed a little, watching his dark eyes glow as he uncovered the soft, petal-pink smoothness of her bare skin. She was a little nervous. Nobody had seen her undressed since she was a little girl.

Jordan realized that and it made him even more gentle. He'd never been with an innocent, but he knew enough about women that it wasn't going to be a problem. She loved him. He wanted nothing more than to please her.

When she was standing in just her briefs, he bent and smoothed his warm mouth over the curve of her breasts. She smelled of roses. There was a faint moisture under his lips, which he rightly attributed to fear.

He lifted his head and looked down into her wide, uncertain eyes. ''Women have been doing this since the dawn of time,'' he whispered. ''If it wasn't fun, nobody would want to do it. Right?''

She laughed nervously. ''Right.''

He smiled tenderly. ''So just relax and let me drive. It's going to be a journey you'll never forget.''

Her hands went to his tie. ''Okay. But I get to make suggestions,'' she told him impishly, and worked to unfasten the tie and then his white shirt. She opened it over a bronzed chest thick with dark, soft hair. He felt furry. But under the hair was hard, warm muscle. She liked the way he felt.

He kissed her softly while he coaxed her hands to his belt. She hesitated.

''Don't agonize over it,'' he teased, moving her hands aside to unfasten it himself. ''We'll go slow.''

''I'm not really a coward,'' she whispered unsteadily. ''It's just uncharted territory. I've never even looked at pictures...''

He could imagine what sort of pictures she was talking about. He only smiled. ''Next time, you'll be a veteran and it won't intimidate you.''

''Are you sure?'' she asked.

He bent to her mouth again. ''I'm sure.''

His warm lips moved down her throat to her breasts, but this time they weren't gently teasing. They were invasive and insistent as they opened on the hard little nubs his caresses had already produced. When his hands moved her hips lazily against the hard thrust of his powerful body, she began to feel drugged.

She'd thought it would be embarrassing and uncomfortable to make love in the light. But Jordan was slow and thorough, easing her into an intimacy beyond anything she'd ever dreamed. He cradled her against him on the big bed, arousing her to such a fever pitch that when he removed the last bit of her clothing, it was a relief to feel the coolness of the room against her hot skin. And by the time he removed his own clothes, she was too hungry to be embarrassed. In fact, she was as aggressive as he was, starving for him in the tempestuous minutes that followed.

She remembered the first kiss they'd shared, beside her pickup truck at his fence. She'd known then that she'd do anything he wanted her to do. But this was far from the vague dreams of fulfillment she'd had when she was alone.

She hadn't known that passion was like a fever that nothing could quench, that desire brought intense desperation. She hadn't known that lovemaking was blind, deaf, mute slavery to a man's touch.

"I would die for you," Jordan whispered huskily at her ear as he moved slowly into total possession with her trembling body.

"Will it…hurt?" she managed in a stranger's voice as she hesitated just momentarily at the enormity of what was happening to her.

He laughed sensuously as he began to move lazily against her. "Are you kidding?" he murmured. And with a sharp, deft movement, he produced a sensation that lifted her clear of the bed and against him with an unearthly little cry of pleasure.

From there, it was a descent into total madness. She shivered with every powerful thrust of his body. She clung to him with her arms, her legs, her soul. She moaned helplessly as sensation built on sensation, until she was almost screaming from the urgent need for satisfaction.

She heard her own voice pleading with him, but she couldn't understand her own words. She drove for fulfillment, her body demanding, feverishly moving with his as they climbed the spiral of passion together.

She felt suddenly as if she'd been dropped from a great height into a hot, throbbing wave of pleasure that began and never seemed to end. She clung to him, terrified that he might stop, that he might draw back, that he might pull away.

"Shh," he whispered tenderly. "I won't stop. It's all right. It's all right, honey. I love you…so much!"

"I love you, too!" she gasped.

Then he began to shudder, even as she felt herself move from one plane of ecstasy to another, and another, and another, each one deeper and more satisfying than the one before. At one point she thought she might actually die from the force of it. Her eyes closed and she let the waves wash over her in succession, glorying in the unbelievably sweet aftermath.

Above her, Jordan was just reaching his own culmination. He groaned harshly at her ear and shuddered one last time before he collapsed in her arms, dead weight on her damp, shivering body.

"And you were afraid," he chided in a tender whisper, kissing her eyes, her cheeks, her throat.

She laughed. "So that's how it feels," she said drowsily. "And now I'm sleepy."

He laughed with her. "So am I."

"Will you be here when I wake up?" she teased.

He kissed her swollen mouth gently. "For the rest of my life, honey. Until the very end."

Her arms curved around him and she curled into his powerful body, feeling closer to him than she'd ever felt to another human being. It was poignant. She was a whole woman. She was loved.

"Until the very end, my darling," she repeated, her voice trailing away in the silence of the room.

She slept in his arms. It was the best night of her life. But it was only the beginning for both of them.

* * * * *

Kiss Me, Cowboy!

MAUREEN CHILD

MAUREEN CHILD

is a California native who loves to travel. Every chance they get, she and her husband are taking off on another research trip. The author of more than sixty books, Maureen loves a happy ending and still swears that she has the best job in the world. She lives in Southern California with her husband, two children and a golden retriever with delusions of grandeur.

Visit her website at www.maureenchild.com.

One

Being a virgin wasn't all it was cracked up to be.

But then, Nora Bailey was about to change all that, wasn't she? The question was, just who could she find to help her get rid of her chastity belt? Pickin's were slim, as they say.

Staring out the gleaming front window of her bakery, Nora watched the citizens of Tesoro, California, enjoying a beautiful spring morning. With a calculating eye, she studied only the men walking along the crowded, narrow main street.

First, she spotted Dewy Fontaine, ninety if he was a day, heading into the pharmacy across the street. He stopped to say hello to Dixon Hill, father of six, working on his third wife. Nora shuddered.

Trevor Church raced by on his skateboard. Cute, but eighteen, for pity's sake. The kid popped a wheelie as he slipped around the corner and disappeared.

Harrison DeLong, sixty and just a little too spry, stopped to shake hands and kiss babies. Running for mayor…*again,* and who trusts politicians?

Mike Fallon. Nora sighed. Nope. Her gaze lingered on him for a moment or two as he strolled down the street toward the ice-cream parlor. Tall, he wore faded denims and a short-sleeved, dark red shirt. His boots were scuffed, his dark hair was ruffled in the breeze, and Nora knew, without even being able to see them, that his green eyes would be shuttered. Wary. Heck, the only female Mike trusted was his five-year-old daughter, Emily. Just then, the little girl raced up to her father and grabbed his hand with both of hers. Mike glanced down and gave his pretty daughter one of his rare yet breathtaking smiles.

A darn shame that Mike wasn't in the running.

"Wouldn't you know it?" she muttered. "I'm finally ready to 'do the deed' and there's no one left to do it *with.*"

Way back in high school, she'd made the decision to remain a virgin until she was married. At the time, it had seemed like the smart thing to do. But she hadn't counted on being the only twenty-eight-year-old virgin in the country, for crying out loud.

She'd expected to graduate from college, find Mr. Right, get married and have babies. Pretty old-fashioned dreams, she supposed, in the grand scheme of things. But then, she'd been born and raised in Tesoro, a tiny coastal town in central California, where people still had bake sales to raise money for the school. Where neighbors looked out for one another and doors were mostly left unlocked.

Where single men were now harder to find than a calorie-free chocolate chip cookie.

So here she stood, eleven years after high school, as pure as the day she was born. The whole celibacy thing had really lost most of its shine. Nora had clung to her vow through the years, despite the fact that both of her younger sisters were married, with a baby each. She'd told herself repeatedly that the right man would come along. But honestly, she'd begun to doubt it lately. After all, she'd never been the kind of woman men lusted after.

Her sisters were small and pretty. Nora was tall, too forthright for her own good and stubborn to boot. She was terrible at flirting, too honest to play games and too busy building her business to kill time at bars or dance clubs.

But the kicker, the impetus to call this whole virginity thing off, had strolled into Nora's bakery only the day before. Becky Sloane was getting married. The kid Nora used to baby-sit had come in to order her wedding cake. A four-tiered, white chocolate number with pink and yellow roses. Becky—or rather her mother—was sparing no expense. At nineteen, Becky was on engagement number two, and Nora was willing to bet she hadn't said no to number one yet, either.

And that's when Nora first wondered just who she'd been saving her virginity for. At the rate she was going, she would be able to be buried "intact" and her headstone could read Returned, Unopened. Depressing. Which was why she was now so determined to leave the ranks of the pure and unsullied behind.

After all, just how much was a woman expected to take?

Naturally, she'd talked her decision over with her best friend, Molly, over lunch yesterday, mentioning her encounter with Becky Sloane.

"Becky Sloane?" Molly repeated, "I remember when the kid couldn't tie her shoe."

"I know. So how old does that make us?"

"God, how humiliating for you," Molly muttered, and took another long drink of the frosty concoction in front of her. "Becky's getting married and here you sit, as pure as the driven—whatever the heck that means—snow."

"Gee, thanks," Nora said. "I feel so much better now."

She winced. ''Sorry.'' Green-eyed Molly Jackson's red hair was short and cut into a pixielike do with sharp edges and twisted curls that somehow looked great on her. Loyal to the bone, Molly was funny, impatient and creative enough to have launched her own greeting card company that she ran from her home. She also happened to be the mother of the world's cutest six month old girl and was married to the town sheriff, a man who absolutely adored her.

''When's the wedding?'' Molly asked.

''Next week,'' Nora told her. ''Saturday.''

Two red eyebrows arched. ''That's fast.''

''Yes,'' Nora said, and twirled her straw through the slushy drink in front of her. ''And honestly, Becky didn't look so good. A little green around the gills.''

''Hmm. So maybe there's a reason for the big hurry, huh?''

''I don't know,'' Nora said. ''But if Becky is pregnant, then that puts her way ahead of me, doesn't it?''

Molly smiled and shook her head. ''This is a contest, then?''

''No.'' Nora sighed and leaned back in her seat. ''It's just that I used to baby-sit her and now she's starting out on her life while I...''

''Bake a mean cinnamon roll?''

''Exactly.''

''Well, you know how much I love to say 'I told you so,''' Molly said. ''But I won't this time. All I will say is it's past time that you did something about this, Nora. You know darn well that most men avoid virgins like the plague. They figure virgins are too romantic. Too willing to build picket fences around a man."

"True."

So to find Mr. Right—if he existed—she needed to be rid of the whole virgin thing. Surely an experienced woman would have better luck.

From the back of the bar, an old jukebox blasted out sixties tunes. Along one wall, a row of booths with scarred red vinyl seats marched in a line. Each table held a candle covered by red plastic netting that was supposed to have added atmosphere. But, over the years, the patrons had peeled away so much of the netting that now the candles simply looked like they had acne.

She and Molly sat at a table on the far side of the room, hidden by the shadows and practically covered by the silk vines of trailing ivy plants hanging from pots overhead. A few regulars were sitting on stools at the bar while couples occupied the booths and snuggled in close together.

Nora sighed, tore her gaze away from the most amorous couple in the bunch and looked seriously at her friend. "What I have to do then is become an ex-virgin."

"Haven't I been saying that for the last five years?"

"You said no 'I told you so's.'"

"My bad." Molly held up a hand as if taking an oath and swore solemnly, "I will never again point out to you that you took so long coming to the conclusion that single, unattached males in Tesoro are almost extinct. Still, you're better off shopping at home. Who knows what kind of man you'd find in the city?"

Nora had to smile. If there was one thing in her life she could count on, it was Molly being absolutely honest with her. Even when she didn't want to hear it.

"Well, I feel better."

"You will," Molly promised as she finished off her margarita. "As soon as you get past this one little roadblock."

"Little?"

"Okay not so little. But we'll find you a man. You wait and see. I mean, it's not as if you're an old maid or something. Not yet, anyway."

Nora shivered. There was a horrible thought. She got an instant mental image of herself, forty years from now, living alone except for the dozen cats crawling all over her doily-covered furniture. Nope. That's not the life she wanted. She wanted a family. She wanted love. And it was high time she went out and started looking for it.

"I can do this, right?"

"Absolutely."

But before Nora could relax a little, Molly asked, "What's the time limit on this?"

"Time limit?"

Molly nodded. "I know you, Nora. If given half a chance, you'll talk yourself out of it. If we don't set a timer on this, you won't get moving. You'll end up sitting back and waiting for Mr. Right again."

"Do you really think there *is* a Mr. Right?" Nora asked quietly. She'd always believed there was someone for everyone. The older she got, though, the less likely that theory looked.

"Yeah," Molly said after a couple of minutes' thought. "I do." The soft smile on her face forced a tiny pang of—not jealousy, because Nora would never begrudge her best friend the happiness she'd found with Jeff—but maybe a little envy.

"How is your Mr. Right, anyway?"

Molly grinned. "Terrific. He's watching the baby down at the office." She checked her watch then and gulped. "And I'd better get down there and rescue him so he can get back to business. But before I go…time limit?"

"How do I know how long it'll take?"

"Uh-huh. How about three months?"

Nora thought about it. Could she really do this? Set herself out to trap some guy into helping her rid herself of what she'd come to think of as an albatross hanging from her neck? And if she didn't do it? Then what? Start shopping for cats? Oh, no. "Okay. Three months."

"Atta girl." Molly grinned. "Before you know it, you'll be living happily ever after, Nor. You wait and see."

A timer went off, ending Nora's thoughts about yesterday's conversation with Molly and bringing her back to the moment at hand. Hurrying through the swinging door into the kitchen, she snatched up a hot pad, yanked open the oven door and pulled out a tray of steaming cinnamon sticky buns.

She smiled as she set them on the cooling tray, then in a smooth, practiced motion, slid the next baking pan into the oven. As the scent of toasted pecans and warm cinnamon filled the room, Nora leaned back against the marble mixing counter and looked around the room.

Small but efficient, her little kitchen was outfitted with the very best equipment she could afford. She'd made a name for herself in Tesoro over the last few years. Her bakery was becoming so popular that she was even drawing customers in from Carmel and Monterey. Her business was thriving, she had a great little house just a block from the bakery and parents and two sisters she loved. All that was missing was a family of her own.

And that was a gnawing, constant ache in the bottom of her heart.

She'd always thought there would be time. During college, she'd been too focused on graduating to do much dating. And after graduation, she'd attended chef's school and pastry classes. Then she'd concentrated on opening her business. And once the bakery was open, it had taken every moment of her time to get it up and running and make it successful.

Now that it was, she had time to notice what she was missing. The years had swept by so quickly, she hadn't realized that most of the women she'd grown up with were married and had children already. And as her biological clock—God, she hated that phrase—raced on, her time was running out. She didn't want to be forty and just starting her family. Yes, it worked for a lot of women, she knew that. It just wasn't what she'd wanted or expected her life to be.

As much as she loved being Aunt Nora to her sisters' two little girls, it just wasn't enough. And if she was going to change the situation, she had to do something about it now.

There was one bright spot in all this. Everyone for twenty miles around would be invited to Becky Sloane's wedding. Surely she'd be able to find at least one single, available male there.

''For heaven's sake Nora, when was the last time you had a manicure?''

Nora snatched her hand free of her sister's and examined her less than perfect nails. "I've been busy. You know, working?"

"Nobody's that busy," Jenny snapped. She grabbed her sister's hand again and, scowling, began to file.

"What is up with your hair?" Frannie stared at her older sister in the mirror, her pale eyes reflecting an appalled fascination. "Have you been hacking at it with scissors again?"

Nora flinched and lifted her free hand to defensively smooth down the rough edges of her so-called "hairdo." "I resent the word, *hacking*."

"As a beautician, I resent what you did to your hair."

Her sisters. Nora sighed and looked at them. Petite and blond, the two of them looked like cheerleader bookends. Jenny and Frannie, at twenty-four and twenty-three respectively, had each married their high school sweethearts and were blissfully happy. Nora didn't begrudge either of them. But, as their older sister, she wouldn't mind having a little bliss herself. As close as twins, her sisters had always been a twosome. Pretty, popular and confident, they'd had the males of Tesoro eating out of their hands since kindergarten.

Now, Nora had never had any problem with self-confidence, either, but she'd always been more comfortable playing a sport rather than standing on the sidelines shaking pom-poms. And while her sisters used charm to sway opinion, Nora was more likely to argue a point until her opponent was simply too worn down to care anymore.

So why was she here in the tiny shop connected to Frannie's house, putting herself through this?

Okay, Nora told herself, maybe this hadn't been such a good idea, after all. She'd thought that the fastest, easiest way to whip herself into shape was to go to her sisters for help. But was the torture worth the end result?

''I can't believe you're finally letting me do your hair.''

''Just don't get crazy,'' Nora warned.

Frannie snorted a laugh. ''Don't panic. I promise not to introduce you to real *style.*''

''Funny.''

''Thanks.''

''I think we'll do acrylic nails on you,'' Jenny said, clearly disgusted. ''Your own are hopeless and too far gone to be saved.''

Nora shot her a look. ''Why not just cut my hands off?''

''I should. They're so chapped, it's a disgrace.''

Okay, help was one thing. Sitting here being humiliated was another. Pushing herself up, Nora said, ''That's it. I'm out of here.''

Frannie held her down and caught her gaze in the mirror. ''We promise to stop picking on you, but I'm not letting you out of my shop with your hair like that.

People will think I did it and my reputation will be shot.''

''That's not picking?''

''Last dig, I swear.''

''Me, too.'' Jenny's gaze met Nora's in the mirror. ''Stay, okay? We'll make you so gorgeous you'll outshine the bride.''

Nora eased back down, and as she did, the tension in the room dropped away and Frannie chuckled.

''That won't be hard. From what I hear, morning sickness may have Becky hurling all the way down the aisle.''

''Her mother insists it's the flu,'' Jenny said.

''Yeah, a nine-month virus.''

That comment sent Jenny off on more local gossip, and as her sisters' voices drifted around her, Nora closed her eyes and hoped to high heaven she'd recognize herself once her sisters were through working their ''magic.''

Two

Mike Fallon pulled at the dark blue necktie that was damn near strangling him and told himself that attending the wedding was good for business. In a town the size of Tesoro, it didn't pay to alienate any of your potential customers. Besides, he couldn't hide away on his ranch. He had Emily to think about. Whether he liked it or not, she would grow up. And he didn't want her to be known as the ''hermit's daughter.''

Though, God knew, if he had his choice, he'd just as soon stay out on the ranch as come into town and make small talk. But then, that was one of the reasons his ex-wife, Vicky, had divorced him, wasn't it?

Don't go there, he silently warned himself. Don't start thinking about Vicky and the mistake that had been their marriage. Hell, wasn't he miserable enough? He took a sip of beer, leaned one shoulder against a flower-bedecked wall and, to distract himself, looked out over the crowd wandering around the country club's reception room.

Almost instantly, his gaze locked on Nora Bailey. Now, *there* was a distraction.

His gaze swept over her, from the top of her perfectly done hair, down to the curves hidden beneath her sexy little black dress and right to the tips of her three inch heels. When he'd first caught a glimpse of her in the church, he'd had to do a double take. This was a Nora he'd never seen before.

He was used to seeing her standing behind her bakery counter, giving out free cookies to the kids and running her hands through hair that looked as though she'd taken her electric mixer to it.

Tonight, she was different. Mike's hand tightened on the beer bottle, and when he took another drink, he had to force the icy liquid past the hard knot lodged in his throat. Damn, she looked good. Her honey-blond hair was shorter and danced around her face in a mass of loose curls. Her dark blue eyes looked somehow smokier, and her legs were displayed to awesome perfection. Who would have guessed that beneath her usual uniform of apron, jeans and T-shirt, she was hiding such an amazing figure?

He watched her as she moved through the crowd, laughing, talking...*drinking.* Her steps a little unsteady, she tended to wobble, then catch herself as she moved toward him with the deliberately careful walk of a drunk trying to look sober. Frowning, Mike told himself it was none of his business if Nora wanted to have a few.

"Room tilting?" he asked as she came closer.

Nora stopped dead, lifted her chin and squinted to get a good look at him. She blinked and tried to clear her vision. But it was no use. Mike Fallon definitely had not one, but *two* gorgeous faces. And the harder she tried, the blurrier he got. At last, she gave it up.

Maybe she shouldn't have had that last margarita, she thought as a flush of heat swept through her.

"Hi, Mike." She blew out a breath. "And no, it's not tilting. Swaying a little, maybe." Narrowing her eyes, she looked him up and down. "I'm surprised to see you here."

"The whole town's here."

"Yeah," she said, shifting her gaze to let it slide across the crowd. Just as her sisters had predicted, the bride was a lovely shade of green. Becky's new groom danced attendance on her while her mother told everyone who would stand still enough to listen about the virulent flu her poor daughter had caught.

Except for the tasty margaritas, the night, as far as Nora was concerned, had been a bust. She hadn't found anyone willing to take her virginity out for a spin, so to speak. Still, the reception wasn't over yet.

Her gaze slid back to Mike. Even blurry, he was too handsome for his own good. His rugged jaw and deep green eyes really were fantasy material. And though she preferred him in his jeans and boots, a suit jacket looked pretty good on him, too. Good enough that she was willing to give it a shot.

Leaning in toward him, she smiled and batted her eyelashes.

"You have something in your eyes?"

"No," she said, and reared back to glare at him. "I was flirting."

"Badly."

"Gee, thanks."

"Nora, what's going on?"

She sighed and reached up to push her hand through her hair until she remembered that Frannie had sprayed it into a football helmet. Letting her hand drop to her side again, she muttered, "Nothing. Absolutely *nothing* is going on."

And, the way things were looking, she was pretty sure she was headed for that house full of cats.

"If you don't mind my saying so," Mike said softly, his voice just carrying over the rock and roll blasting from the speakers at the front of the reception hall, ''you're acting a little...weird.''

''Weird?'' She put one hand on his chest and shoved. He didn't move. ''*I'm* acting weird?'' Nora laughed shortly. ''You come to a big party and stand in a corner by yourself and *I'm* the one acting weird?'' She shook her head and immediately regretted the action. ''Whoa,'' she whispered. Then, when the room righted itself again, she continued. ''You know,'' she said, taking a deep breath, ''you can go to a party, but if you're not *at* the party, then you might as well not have gone to the party. You know what I mean?''

''Not a clue.''

She huffed out a breath. Pointless to try to get through to him, she thought. And while she stood here talking to the statue that was Mike Fallon, she was missing opportunities. ''Never mind. We are *so* not comoon-commuti—'' she paused to corral her tongue around the word—''*communicating.*''

His lips twitched into what might have been a smile, but it flashed across his face and disappeared again so quickly, she couldn't be sure. It *was* a great face, she thought. Heck, even blurry, he looked good. ''It's a shame,'' she muttered.

''What is?''

Nora shook her head and waved one hand at him. ''Nothing. Nothing. See you, Mike.''

She walked away then and his gaze dropped to the

curve of her behind. Hell, what man's wouldn't? It was a great behind. But Mike frowned to himself as he wondered what she'd meant by *it's a shame*.

Over the next couple of hours, he watched Nora laughing and talking with her friends, and a part of him envied how comfortable she was with people. Socializing had never come easily to Mike and he figured it was too late now to change that. Even if he'd wanted to.

He took a sip of his second beer of the night and realized it had gone warm. Setting it down on the table in front of him, he forgot about it and focused instead on the tall blonde in black. Strange, but he couldn't seem to stop watching Nora. Or thinking about her. He could have left the reception an hour ago. Ordinarily, he would have. But for some reason, tonight, he just wasn't ready to leave yet.

Bill Hammond, Tesoro's self-described ladies' man, moved in on Nora. When she threw her head back to look at him, Mike's gaze fixed on the elegant line of her throat.

Bill's gaze was focused a little lower.

''Nora,'' someone close by said in a deep voice, ''you look amazing.''

''Thank you.'' Actually, even she'd had to admit that her sisters' handiwork had turned out pretty well. Though she did have to fight the urge to pull down on her hem and up on her neckline. Before this, she'd never owned anything that exposed so much skin—except a swimsuit. Turning around to thank whoever it was talking to her, she smiled up at Bill Hammond and hoped he didn't notice her disappointment.

As the local ladies' man, Bill considered any single female between the ages of eighteen and eighty fair game. Getting a compliment from him was as special as seeing a snowflake in a blizzard. Still, she felt she was in no position to be choosy.

His dark brown hair was styled just right, his dark brown eyes skimmed over her in appreciation, then slipped past her, as if making sure there was no one more interesting around. A small part of her sizzled in annoyance, but she smothered it. Nora had come to the wedding with one thought in mind: find a suitable guy to help her out of celibacy.

And since Bill seemed to be the only one offering…

"Would you like to dance?" he asked.

Before her rational mind could react and tell him to go away, Nora spoke up. "You bet."

She stumbled slightly but told herself it was because her new shoes hurt her feet. Who on earth had ever decided women should wear high heels?

Nora swayed slightly, but, since she was dancing, she hoped no one would notice. Oh, she really shouldn't have had that last margarita. But she'd needed a little false courage to deal with this whole man hunt. Now that she'd actually caught a man's interest, she wasn't at all sure she was pleased about it.

Bill's hands seemed to be everywhere. Instead of being excited, Nora just wanted him to stop it. But she swallowed back the no she wanted to give him. After all, this had been the plan all along, right? Now wasn't the time to get nervous. Instead she told herself to get in the spirit of things.

He guided her into a turn around the dance floor, and the crowd surrounding them seemed to blur into a wash of color and motion. Yet, somehow, she managed to spot one pair of deep green eyes watching her from across the room.

Mike.

Her heart did a strange little bump and roll as she locked gazes with him. A moment later, that feeling was gone as Bill whispered, "Let's step outside for some fresh air."

Fresh air. That's probably all she needed. Good idea.

"Okay," she said, and walked beside him, the heavy weight of his arm draped across her shoulders as he steered her through the crowd and out the French doors.

Night air rushed toward them, cool and sweet, with the scent of the flower gardens just beyond the brick patio. Nora slipped free of Bill's arm and immediately felt lighter and more free as she crossed the patio and came to a stop at the river-stone balustrade.

She tipped her head back to look up at the sky, sprinkled with diamond-like stars. A soft sea breeze drifted past her, tugging at her hair, caressing her skin and even, she thought wryly, clearing away some of the haze in her brain.

Enough so that when Bill approached her from behind, she wished she were anywhere but there.

''Did I tell you that you look great tonight?'' he asked.

''Probably.''

''Well,'' he said, sliding one hand down the length of her bare arm, ''just in case I didn't, I'll say it now. Man, Nora, I had no idea you could look like this.''

Well, there was a backhanded compliment if she'd ever heard one. What did she look like usually, she wondered, a gargoyle?

''Thanks.''

''You're just as sweet as one of your pastries.''

She winced. Did lines like that really work?

''Now I want to see if you taste as good as you look.''

And with that smooth come-on, he turned her around and stared down into her eyes with a hunger she'd never seen directed at her before. A deep, dark hole opened up in the pit of Nora's stomach, and for one shining moment, she thought for sure she'd be thoroughly and violently ill. Then Bill grabbed her close with all the sensitivity of a starving man reaching for the only steak left in the world.

Her hands flat against his chest, she tried to hold him off, but with his arms pinning her to him, it was useless. Her mind raced with a speed that surprised her, considering just how wobbly she'd been a moment before. How could she have allowed herself to get into this position? Heck, forty cats were suddenly looking pretty good.

Before she could do anything to stop him, his mouth was coming down on hers and all Nora could think was that she'd never noticed just how thick and wet Bill's lips were. She felt...nothing. No excitement. No anticipation. Not even fear or anxiety. Just a mild sort of revulsion that she was pretty sure she'd have to get over if she ever wanted to lose her "virgin" status.

"Let her go."

A deep voice. Close by.

Nora's eyes wheeled as she searched the dimly lit patio for the intruder. A second later, Bill was plucked off of her and effortlessly tossed to one side.

He staggered slightly, regained his footing and scowled at the man standing protectively close to Nora.

"Back off, Bill," Mike said.

"Who invited you into this?"

"I didn't have to be invited." Clearly disgusted,

Mike added, ‘‘Can’t you see she’s had too much to drink?’’

‘‘Mike...’’ Nora said, grabbing at his arm.

He shrugged her off, never taking his eyes off of Bill, who didn’t look at all happy about having his romantic moves interrupted.

‘‘This is between me and Nora.’’

‘‘Ordinarily,’’ Mike said, ‘‘I’d agree. Not tonight.’’

‘‘Who’re you?’’ Bill demanded. ‘‘Her father?’’

She felt as though she were trapped in an old movie. Hero and villain were squaring off, with the heroine standing on the sidelines, wringing her hands. Well, she’d never been much of a hand wringer.

‘‘Okay,’’ Nora piped up again. ‘‘Why don’t you guys—’’

‘‘Shut up a minute, all right?’’ Mike said, not even glancing at her.

‘‘Shut up?’’ She glared at him and only got angrier when she noticed he was paying no attention to her at all. ‘‘You’re telling me to shut up?’’

He finally shot her a quick look. ‘‘Just sit down, will you?’’

‘‘Look, I don’t need you to—’’

‘‘It’s okay, Nora. This’ll only take a minute.’’

But her protests came a little late as Bill suddenly charged. Mike stepped to the left, drew his right arm back and landed a solid punch to the other man’s jaw. Bill did a strange, almost ballet-like spin and crumpled into the nearby shrubbery without a sound. Stunned, Nora stared down at her would-be lover, now sprawled in the well-tended bushes. She noted that music was still playing inside. The crowd was still celebrating. No one but she and the two men involved had any idea of what was going on out here in the shadows.

That was some consolation, she guessed. At least half the town hadn't witnessed this little scene.

Everything was ruined now. Her plan shot, she turned and looked up at the man who had inadvertently kept her a virgin one more night. She'd have had to have been blind not to see the flash of satisfaction in Mike's eyes. How very…male of him. Planting one hand in the center of his chest, she gave him a shove and was pleased to see him back up a little.

"What do you think you're doing?"

Clearly bewildered, Mike just gaped at her for a moment or two before saying, "I think I'm saving you from a jerk."

"Did I ask to be saved?"

"No, but—"

"Did I look scared? Panicked?"

"No," he admitted, pushing the edges of his jacket back to shove both hands in his pants pockets. "You looked a little disgusted."

"And that requires rescue?"

When he didn't say anything, Nora threw both

hands in the air and started pacing. Her heels clicked menacingly on the bricks, keeping time with her fury.

Mike watched her warily but had to admit that she looked good with the fire of rage in her cheeks. What she was so mad about, he hadn't a clue. Hell, he'd thought he was doing her a favor. Usually, Nora was sensible. Reasonable. Tonight, though, she hadn't been acting at all like herself. When he saw Bill steer her out into the night, he knew the man was about to make a play. And since Mike also knew that Nora'd had one too many celebratory drinks, he'd figured she might need a hand peeling Bill's hands off her body.

Of course, he hadn't counted on the quick rush of...something that had filled him the minute he spotted Bill Hammond draped across Nora's frame. And he didn't want to explore that feeling at the moment, either. Right now, he was more concerned with staying out of her reach.

"Three hundred dollars," she was saying. "Counting the manicure and the haircut—I mean, they're my sisters, but it's their job, right? They have a right to be paid. Plus the new dress—and I hate shopping."

A woman? Who hated shopping?

"What are you talking about?" His gaze followed her as she marched back and forth past Bill's prone body.

"This." She waved her hands up and down her body, indicating the whole package. "The dress, the hair, the makeup, these stupid, too expensive shoes that are killing me. Not to mention this purse. It's only big enough to hold my keys and my driver's license! How can they charge seventy-five bucks for that?''

''How the hell should I know, but—''

She cut him off again. ''That's not the point, though, is it?''

No, the point was that he'd come out here to be a rescuer and she was making him feel like Typhoid Mike. He should have gone with his first instinct. To mind his own business. What was it his father used to say? Oh, yes. ''No good deed goes unpunished.'' He could almost hear the old man laughing at him.

He folded his arms across his chest, bit down on the anger rumbling through him and said, ''Why don't you tell me what the point is, exactly?''

''Fine.''

She stopped right in front of him, tilted her head back to look into his eyes and wobbled unsteadily. She hardly blinked when he moved quickly to grab hold of her upper arms to steady her.

''The point is,'' she said, ''I had a plan. A perfectly good plan and you've ruined it.'' She half turned, looked over her shoulder to where Bill was just stirring and pushing himself out of the hedges.

Mike followed her gaze. ''Bill was your plan?''

''Certainly a big part of it,'' she countered, then frowning, turned back to Mike. A drooping blond curl fell across her forehead and she blew out a breath, sending it out of her eyes.

Her cheeks flushed, her eyes dancing with impatience, frustration and anger, she made a hell of a picture. It was damn near enough to make Mike's mouth water. Which worried him enough to let her go and take a long step backward.

"Okay fine. Bill's waking up. I'll just get out of here and you can go back to your...plan."

Bill muttered under his breath, rubbed his jaw and slowly climbed out of the bushes. Once he was on his feet again, he gave Mike a hot glare, avoided looking at Nora altogether and headed back toward the reception. His steps were steady, but the greenery stuck in his hair spoiled his attempt at dignity.

When they were alone on the patio again, Nora threw her hands high and let them slap down against her sides again. "See? Ruined. Now I'll have to find someone else."

But apparently, Mike thought, not tonight, since she walked past him and started down the brick walkway that ringed the clubhouse. Faux antique lampposts lined the walk, dropping small puddles of light into the shadows. Nora walked unevenly, wobbling from one side of the bricks to the other. Mike glanced over his shoulder at the crowded room behind him, then back to Nora. No contest.

He caught up to her in a few long strides. She was moving slowly, carefully, and limping painfully.

"These things are killing me," she complained just before she kicked first her right shoe, then the left, into the ivy lining the walkway. She sighed in satisfaction and started walking again, leaving the hated shoes behind. Mike chuckled to himself, scooped up her shoes in one hand and followed, wondering what in the hell had happened to turn the ever-sensible Nora into a beautiful, exasperating stranger.

He was about to find out.

Three

Mike kept a wary eye on Nora as she moved farther away from the wedding reception, still in full swing just twenty feet from them. Her steps wobbly on the brick walkway, she seemed to sway through the puddles of light dropped by the tall lamps lining the path. The night air was thick with the scent of flowers, and the dance music from inside came muted and soft, like a delicate backdrop. Nora kept muttering under her breath, and though he couldn't make out what she was saying, the tone of her voice told him it was probably just as well. Shaking his head, he followed her, tucking her shoes into the pockets of his jacket. She probably wouldn't thank him, but he figured the best thing he could do now was to get her into his car and take her home.

Then she stopped suddenly, turned, and before he could react, she slammed into his chest. Staggering slightly, she lifted her chin, looked into his eyes and blinked, as if trying to bring him into focus. He knew the feeling. It was as if he were seeing her for the first time. Her blue eyes were dreamy and her skin looked like fine porcelain in the dim, soft light. A slight sea breeze kicked in from the ocean only a mile or two away, and ruffled her hair with a lover's caress. For one brief moment, Mike thought about pulling her close, slanting his mouth over hers and—

"This is your fault," she said.

He laughed, the romantic image he'd been building, shattered. "You drinking too much is my fault?"

"Not that." She waved a hand at him, scowling. "You're not paying attention."

True. He hadn't been paying attention to her words. He'd been too distracted by her curves. "Okay, now I'm listening."

She inhaled deeply, then let her breath out in a rush, ruffling the blond curl hanging over her forehead. He'd never seen her so...*loose*. Usually, Nora was friendly but businesslike as she stood behind her counter at the bakery. Tonight was a revelation in a lot of ways.

Frustration bubbled inside Nora. Not that she'd been

all that excited about being kissed by Bill Hammond. Actually, just remembering the feel of his mouth on hers was enough to give her a cold chill. But he had, after all, been the only man offering. She swiped one hand across her forehead, pushing that one drooping curl back into place, and as she did, her brain seemed to clear briefly.

"What was I thinking?" she muttered.

"Sort of what I was wondering," Mike said.

She looked up at him, grateful to see that he was just a shade less blurry than before. But blurry or focused, he was more than worth a look or two. And it wasn't just his good looks or forest-green eyes. There was just something about Mike. Something…solid, dependable. As sturdy as a brick wall and just about as funny. Mike generally wasn't much of a smiler. "Okay, fine, Bill was a mistake."

"Granted. The question is, why were you about to make it?"

Nora huffed out a breath. "It's not like I had a lot of choices, you know."

Mike shook his head. "I still don't have a clue what you're talking about."

"What I'm talking about is, you ruined the plan."

"*What* plan?"

"It's your fault," she said again. "You messed it up, so you owe me."

"I peeled a jerk off you."

"Exactly," she snapped, and narrowed her gaze on him as he swayed back and forth. "And stand still."

"I'm not moving."

"Oh, boy. That can't be good." She frowned at him. "Are you laughing at me?"

He held both hands up in mock surrender and shook his head, while managing to hide his smile. "Not a chance."

"You have to promise to help me."

"Help you what?"

"I'll tell you after you promise to help."

"I don't do blind promises."

"But you owe me."

"Stop saying that."

"Then promise."

Mike glanced around. Everyone else was still inside, but he didn't know how long that was going to last. Nora was still unsteady on her feet and her blue eyes were just a little hazy from too many margaritas. Plus, it seemed as though she was willing to stand here and argue forever. He figured the only way out of this was to promise to whatever it was she wanted. Then he could pour her into his car and take her home. Hell, she'd probably forget all about this mess when she sobered up, anyway.

"Okay, fine. I promise." Taking her arm, he steered her toward the parking lot again.

She pulled free.

Stubborn, he thought, and waited for whatever was coming next.

"Oh." She blinked, then smiled. "Well, good then. That's better." She reached out and patted his chest with the flat of her hand. "You are a prince among tides...no...a prince among...princes!"

"That's me. Prince Mike." He took her hand in his and tried not to think about the flash of heat that stabbed through him with that simple touch. It had been way too long since he'd felt the kind of electrical charge that was even now sizzling along his bloodstream. Hell, until that moment, he'd have been willing to bet his "lust-o-meter" was broken. But apparently not. Oh, yeah. Best to get her home fast. Best for both of them. She was too tipsy for him to be thinking what he was thinking. "Now, I'll take you home before you get into more trouble."

"I wasn't *in* trouble," she argued.

"Not what it looked like to me."

"Hey, you think it was easy for me, flirting with everybody in the room?" Nora pulled her hand free of his and poked him in the chest with the tip of her forefinger. "You think it's easy to pretend to be interested in how Adam Marshal tunes an engine? Or to look fascinated when Dave Edwards described his white-water rafting trip for the fifth time?" She sighed heavily. "And that's not even counting the times I had to hear the mayor practice his Founders Day speech."

"Sounds pretty bad."

"You have no idea."

"So why do it?"

She shifted her gaze to look out over the darkened clubhouse grounds. "Because I'm twenty-eight-years-old and the kid I used to baby-sit just got married."

"And that means..."

Disgusted, she turned her gaze back to his. "It means, that unless I make some changes, I'm looking at old-maidhood."

"Are you nuts?" Mike took a good, hard look at her. Every one of her curves was outlined to perfection. Her blue eyes flashed in the dim light tossed by the lamps overhead and her honey-blond hair shone like gold.

"Nuts? Probably," she said on a heavy sigh. "But this is *so* much worse. I am the last of a dying breed. A dinosaur. A...what else is extinct?"

"What the hell are you talking about?"

"I'm a virgin."

"A *virgin?*" Well, she had his attention now. He took an instinctive step backward, as if trying to keep a safe distance between them.

"Say it a little louder. I don't think the folks in the back row quite caught it." Then she laughed, but there was no humor in the sound as she studied his expression. "Ah, and there's the 'look.' Honesly—honestly...poker? Not your game. All of you guys react to a virgin like a vampire to sunlight.'' She turned her back on him and started off down the walkway toward the parking lot again, muttering with every step. ''That is so like a man. Say the word *virgin* and he leaps out of the way as if a bullet's aimed at his heart.''

''I didn't leap.''

''Hah!''

Mike followed after her and when he caught up, he grabbed her upper arm and spun her around to look at him. Then he reached up, shoved one hand through his hair and tried to concentrate. But hey, it wasn't easy. He hadn't guessed there *were* any virgins over the age of twenty.

''You caught me off guard, Nora.''

''Yeah,'' she said glumly, lifting her gaze to his. ''It's a real icebreaker.'' Sucking in a gulp of jasmine-scented air, she continued. ''Anyway, the point is, I was trying to find someone to help me with my…situation.''

''Bill?'' he asked, astonishment coloring his tone. ''Bill's the guy you picked?''

Instead of answering that question, she asked one of her own. ''I look pretty good, right?''

His gaze swept her up and down before settling back on her face again. ''Oh, yeah.''

''I'm reasonably intelligent.''

''I thought so, until a few minutes ago.''

She gave him a tight, un-amused smile. ''So getting rid of my...*problem* should be fairly easy, right?''

He wasn't so sure about that. Speaking for himself, he wasn't about to get too close to a virgin. For her, sex would take on more meaning than it should. It would evolve into white-picket fences and family dinners and babies and—he slammed a mental door on his thoughts. No way was he going to get wrapped up in this. Nora was a nice-enough woman and, God knew, she filled out a little black dress better than anyone he'd ever seen before, but he just wasn't the man for her.

For anyone.

''Nora...''

''You said you'd help.''

Panic reared its ugly head. ''I promised to help,'' he qualified. ''Not to—'' He stopped talking and stared at her for a long minute.

But she wasn't listening. Stepping up close to him, she fisted both of her hands on his lapels and went up on her toes until she was looking directly into his eyes. ''I don't wanna be an old maid. I don't wanna bunch of cats. I want babies. I want family. I—''

Even in the dim light, he saw her face pale and her eyes go wide and round. ''Are you okay?''

''Oh,'' she said softly, letting him go and lifting one hand to cover her mouth. ''I am *so* far from okay.''

Nora's stomach rolled uneasily and she swallowed

hard, fighting for control. Deep breaths, she told herself, and tried to put that thought into action. But it didn't seem to be helping. Her head was swimming, and her stomach pitched and dived as if it were a tiny boat in the middle of a stormy sea. "Oh, boy," she muttered, concentrating on the misery sliding through her body.

"Maybe I should just take you home."

"Yeah. Good idea."

With his warm hand cupping her elbow, she focused on the heat of his skin to fight against the chills sweeping through her. Tipping her face back into the breeze, she pulled in several deep breaths and told herself silently that nausea was just mind over matter. Mind over matter. Mind over—

"Oh, God." She pulled away from him, leaned into the shrubbery and was thoroughly, violently ill. Her brain raced, pointing out all the ways she'd managed to humiliate herself on this one glorious night.

She'd flirted shamelessly—and badly. She'd allowed Bill Hammond, of all people, to kiss her. And, to put a cap on the evening, she was throwing up a lung in front of Mike Fallon. Oh, yeah. This had gone well. She might as well go buy her first starter cat.

Her big night of seduction had turned into a cautionary tale.

But as the spasms of sickness slowly passed, Nora became aware of a cool, dry hand on her forehead and the sound of Mike's soft, soothing whispers. As embarrassing as this moment was, she was glad he was there. The only thing worse than being sick in front of someone was being sick all alone.

Straightening up, she inhaled deeply and noticed that the haze in her brain was completely gone. It had been replaced by a pounding bass drum, but at least she could think and see again.

Mike handed her a handkerchief. As she took it, she smiled. ''Thanks. I didn't think anyone carried these anymore.''

He shrugged. ''Just an old-fashioned guy, I guess.''

And, apparently, a nice-enough guy to completely avoid mentioning her most recent humiliation.

''So,'' he said. ''You still want that ride home?''

''Yeah. Thanks.''

On the short ride to Nora's place, Mike studied her. With most of the alcohol out of her system, he was guessing she was beginning to regret telling him all about the whole ''virgin thing.'' And frankly, he'd be just as happy to forget about it himself. As it was, he'd been doing too much thinking about Nora now that he'd seen her out of her jeans and into something he couldn't help imagining getting her out of.

Hell.

His fists tightened around the steering wheel and he told himself to just keep his mind on the road. To not think about the swell of her breasts above the low cut neckline of that dress. And, while he was at it, he really should keep the image of her legs out of his brain. And just to be on the safe side, he figured he'd start forgetting about the curve of her rear and the soft shine of her hair and—

Hell.

He steered the car down her street and barely glanced at the tidy lawns and picture-perfect houses as he drove down to the middle of the block. Pulling into her driveway, he threw the car into Park, cut the engine and turned in his seat to look at her.

Damn. Even in the shadows, she was way too pretty for his peace of mind.

"Thanks," she said, turning her head to look at him.

"Want me to arrange to get your car back tonight?"

"No," she said, opening the car door and stepping out. "I can walk into the bakery tomorrow and then pick up my car later."

Mike got out of the car and walked up the driveway, just a step or two behind her. She'd left the front porch light on and a soft, golden glow streamed from the Tiffany style glass shade and dazzled the small space with slices of color. He noticed some kind of flower trailing from a series of hanging pots and a short glider swing that was dotted with comfy-looking cushions.

Sort of made him curious as to what the inside of her house looked like. But it wasn't likely he'd be finding out. She might not want to think about what she'd said when the margaritas were doing her thinking for her, but he remembered it all.

She wanted love. Family. Babies.

And that was enough to convince him to keep his distance.

Nora opened her front door and more light spilled into the darkness, like a warm, golden path laid out to welcome him. This could be serious trouble.

"I'm going to make me some strong coffee," Nora said, looking over her shoulder at him. "Want a cup?"

Say no, his brain screamed. One last stab at rational thinking echoed over and over through his brain, and for some unknown reason, Mike vetoed it. "Sure."

He followed her inside and she shut the door behind him. Mike fought down the feeling of being a prisoner hearing a cell door slamming closed.

Nora walked past him and headed down a short hallway. Mike stayed right behind her, and when she hit a switch, he blinked at the bright light ricocheting off the kitchen's sunshine-yellow walls. A white pedestal table surrounded by four captain's chairs sat in front of a bay window. Plants lined the windowsills, and the gleaming countertops boasted an assortment of top-of-the-line appliances.

She moved around the room in her stocking feet as Mike watched her. Every movement was smooth, no motion was wasted. This was a woman who spent a lot of time in her kitchen. She seemed far more at home here than she had at that party.

Something they had in common.

When she had the coffee brewing, she turned around to face him. ''I'm just going to go freshen up. Have a seat, I'll be back in a minute.''

As she left the room, Mike glanced at the table and chairs and beyond the shining window panes into the darkness outside. A cozy setup, he thought, and told himself again he should be going. After all, Emily was at home with a baby-sitter and he had an early day waiting for him tomorrow. But, for some reason, he wasn't ready to leave yet. He told himself he was only sticking around to make sure she was all right.

But even he was having trouble believing that.

''Sorry I made you miss the reception,'' Nora called from the other room.

''No problem,'' he answered. ''I'm not really much of a party guy.''

''Well, duh.''

He smiled to himself and took a seat at the table.

A few minutes later, Nora breezed back into the kitchen. She'd changed into a pair of denim shorts and a short-sleeved, deep blue T-shirt that clung to her body with the same tempting allure that black dress had displayed. Her legs looked long and lean and slightly tanned. Her bare feet were decorated with a silver toe ring on her left foot and pale pink polish on her toenails.

And Mike knew he was getting in deeper here every damn minute.

The coffeepot hissed and steamed, sounding like an old woman shushing a crowd. Nora pulled two thick yellow mugs out of a cabinet and poured them each a cup of coffee.

"You take it black, right?"

He arched a brow. "Impressive."

Nora smiled, sat down opposite him and pushed one hand through hair that now looked soft and untamed. "Hey, a good businesswoman remembers how her customers like their coffee." She took a sip, closed her eyes and said, "Let's see, you prefer the cinnamon buns and Emily loves my chocolate chip cookies and you come in every Wednesday afternoon when you pick her up from school."

He didn't know whether to be further impressed or a little irritated that he'd become such a creature of habit that a storekeeper could set her watch by him. When had that happened?

"So," Nora was saying, and Mike listened up. Already that night he'd learned that it was important to stay on his toes when she was talking. "You've seen me at my worst tonight, that's for sure."

"Nora," he said, fingering the handle of his coffee

cup, ''why don't we just forget about everything that happened and—''

''No way.''

''What?''

''You heard me,'' Nora said, leaning back in her chair to give him a slow smile that damn near set fire to his insides. ''You promised to help and I'm holding you to it.''

Four

He squirmed uneasily in his chair. Now that he knew just what she was looking for, he was a little warier than usual. There wasn't a chance in hell he was going to get involved with a virgin looking to explore sex. Down that road lay—well, all kinds of things he wasn't interested in.

"Exactly what kind of 'help' are we talking about here?" Mike asked, determinedly keeping his gaze locked with hers. Despite the fact that her blue eyes looked soft and tempting, it was still safer than letting his gaze drift over that body she'd managed to hide until tonight.

Nora laughed, the sound rising up, filling the quiet room and settling over him like a promise.

"Jeez, relax, Mike." She lifted her cup and took a long sip of the fragrant coffee. "You look like a man who's just been stood up against a wall, given a blindfold and asked for his last words."

"No, I don't." He was better at hiding his emotions than *that,* wasn't he?

"Right." Nora shook her head, and he refused to notice how many different colors of blond her hair really was. Besides, she was talking. Again.

"It's not like I want *you* to do the deed personally."

In fact, she sounded pretty damn appalled at the notion. "Well," he said, pretty sure he'd just been insulted. "That's good."

Nora got up, walked to the cookie jar and filled a plate with a dozen or so of her fresh baked cookies. Carrying them back to the table, she set them down in front of him, took one for herself and sat down again.

Mike glanced at the plate. Chocolate chip, peanut butter, cinnamon sugar. If he *was* looking for a wife...which he wasn't...he'd still avoid Nora. Being married to a woman who could bake like this could put five hundred pounds on a guy.

"I mean, everyone in town knows that you're not interested in women."

He froze, startled. "Excuse me?"

She laughed again. ''Sorry. That came out wrong. I just meant that you're not interested in commitment. I mean, ever since Vicky left, you've practically had Stay Away tattooed on your forehead.''

Everything inside him went cold and still. It took every ounce of his self-control not to crumble the cookie he held into a pile of crumbs. He wasn't going to get drawn into a discussion about his ex-wife. Not with anyone. And apparently, Nora could see that fact in his expression as well.

''Oops.'' She covered a flash of embarrassment by taking another gulp of coffee. Then cradling the cup in her hands, she lifted her gaze to his and, wincing, said, ''Sorry about that.''

''No problem.''

''Yeah, so I see. Look, I didn't mean to mention the *V* word.''

Mike willed his hands to relax. Willed his muscles to unclench. Willed his apparently clear-as-glass expression to shift into one of complete ambivalence. ''I told you. No problem. Vicky's in the past.''

Mike was the first to admit that since Vicky packed up, picked up and left two years ago, he hadn't exactly been a social animal. He preferred life on the ranch. There, all he had to deal with were the animals, the price of oranges and frost. And of course, Emily. His brain fuzzed out a little as he thought of his daughter.

Five years old and the one good thing he and Vicky had managed to do together.

He could understand how a woman could get fed up with marriage, with ranch life…hell, with *him.* What he'd never be able to comprehend is how a woman could walk away from her own daughter without a backward glance. But then Vicky had never wanted to be a mother, had she? And when she left, she'd told him flat out that he could have sole custody.

Which worked out fine as far as Mike was concerned. One day, he'd have to find a way to explain to Emily just why her mother had chosen to abandon her. But until then, the two of them were a team and he'd protect that child with everything he had. And if that meant steering clear of women until his daughter was eighteen, then that was a small price to pay. He didn't want a string of women going in and out of Emily's life. He wanted her to have stability. Security. But most of all, he didn't want her heart broken because she'd become attached to daddy's girlfriend only to have that woman disappear from their world.

Nope. And if that made him a hermit, then he'd just have to live with it.

Still, just because he wasn't looking for a relationship, that didn't make him *dead.*

"Uh-huh. If she's in the past, why does just the mention of her name freeze you over?" She looked at him for a long, slow minute. He could almost feel the seconds ticking past as he stared into those blue eyes of hers. A part of his mind wondered why he'd never noticed before just how many shades of blue were centered in her gaze.

Focus, he told himself again.

"I just don't like to be reminded, that's all."

She turned her coffee cup idly. "Emily's a fairly big reminder, don't you think?"

"That's different. Emily is...*Emily.*"

Nora nodded slowly. "She's a sweetheart."

He relaxed a little. "Yeah, she is."

One second ticked past, then two, then three, while they stared at each other across the kitchen table. With the darkness crouched just beyond the window, and the silence hovering in the room, they sat together in the warm, cozy kitchen and it felt...*intimate,* somehow.

"Anyway," Nora said, a bit louder than necessary as she forced the word *intimate* out of her brain, "back on target. The point is, you're not looking for a wife, so you're safe."

One corner of his mouth tipped up. "Just what every man wants to hear."

"At least you can relax knowing you're out of the running."

"But every other man in town is fair game?"

"Hey, a girl's gotta plan ahead," Nora said, ignoring the decidedly insulted tone of his voice. "This is not only about losing my virginity—it's about finding Mr. Right.''

''In Tesoro?''

She frowned to herself. ''True, the options are a little limited, but I'm sure I can make this work. I know the men here. I don't know anyone in the city. And I'm not the kind of woman who can stroll into a bar and pick up a stranger. That would just be too...icky.'' She sighed and picked up her coffee cup again. ''Besides, my mother's been reading the singles ads and assures me that there are *lots* of nice men in Monterey.''

''Singles ads? You?''

He sounded so genuinely surprised by that notion, Nora felt a bit better. ''Thanks for that,'' she said, flashing him a quick smile. ''But my mother's more eager to find me a man than I am. The woman's just dying for more grandchildren.''

''You have sisters,'' he pointed out.

''Yeah, but Frannie and Jenny have done their part already. I'm the last holdout.'' Disgusted, she leaned back in her chair, folded her arms beneath her breasts and propped her bare feet up on the chair closest to her. ''I swear, this whole 'virtue thing' has gotten way out of hand. It's become a liability instead of an asset.''

''You could just keep the whole 'virgin thing' a secret.''

''Thought about that,'' she admitted, shaking her head again. ''But it's no good. I think guys have radar about this sort of thing. They home right in on a virgin and then steer a wide path around her.'' She shot him a knowing look.

''Point taken.''

''So, since you owe me one, for breaking up my little plan…''

''Some plan—''

''And—'' she raised her voice to talk over him ''—since you personally are out of the running, I think it's only fair that you help me find 'the guy.'''

''Now I'm a matchmaker?''

''More of a trapper.''

''I think this is against the rules for a member of the male gender.''

She smiled again and he felt the warmth of it slap into him.

''I won't tell if you don't.''

''Trust me,'' he vowed. ''I'm not telling.''

''Good. Then, between the two of us, we should be able to find the right guy.''

How this had happened, Mike had no idea. All he'd done was try to do the right thing. Help her out of a bad situation. And now he was stuck in a situation that made her little scene with Bill Hammond look like a picnic.

''Then it's a deal?'' She held out one hand across the table.

He thought about making one last stab at getting out of this. But then he looked into those eyes of hers again and he knew it was a lost cause. Mike took her hand in his, ignored that soul-searing flash of warmth and muttered ''Deal'' before quickly releasing her again.

But the warmth stayed with him and Mike had the distinct feeling that he was going to regret this deal for a long, long time.

''So, what happened with Bill?''

It was late afternoon the day after the reception and business was pretty slow. Nora had had only one or two customers since noon, so she took a seat behind the counter, balanced the phone receiver on her shoulder and answered Molly's question. ''Nothing. Absolutely nothing.''

There was a long, thoughtful silence before her best friend said, ''But you left with him. And you never came back.''

''Yeah, well,'' Nora said, checking off a list of grocery supplies as she talked, ''there was a slight hitch in the plan.''

''What kind of hitch?''

''Mike showed up out of nowhere and sent Bill into the bushes.''

''Mike Fallon?''

''The one and only.''

''Oooh. Now this is getting interesting.''

''Not really.'' Although sitting with Mike at her kitchen table last night had been...nice. In the last few years, they'd hardly talked at all, except for the few words they exchanged over her counter. And maybe it was the margaritas talking, but he'd seemed so... different last night. More approachable. More... lustable. Jeez. Was that even a word?

''Oh, come on, let an old married woman enjoy her fantasies, will ya? Gorgeous Mike Fallon, riding to the rescue—he did ride to the rescue, right?''

''Oh, yeah. I'm guessing Bill's not real fond of him today.''

''Well good. I mean, Bill Hammond isn't exactly the stuff dreams are made of.''

''I know, but—''

''No buts. You deserve better, Nor.''

True. Not that Bill was a troll or anything, but for heaven's sake. Did she really want to give up her long-held virginity to a man who wouldn't even notice? Funny how your ideas could change in one evening. Just yesterday, she'd been ready to do almost anything to leave chastity behind. Today, she wanted a little...more.

Behind her, the bell attached to the front door jangled out a welcome and announced a customer's arrival.

"Someone's here," she told Molly. "Gotta go."

"Okay, but I demand up-to-the-minute reports."

"Promise," Nora said, and hung up the phone smiling. Standing up, she turned around to greet...an empty store. Frowning, she moved around the counter, and as soon as she did, she spotted her customer.

"Well, hi," she said. "I didn't see you."

Emily Fallon smiled at her and Nora's heart melted. "That's 'cuz I'm still really little."

"I guess you are," Nora said, nodding. "So what can I do for you today, Miss Fallon?"

The little girl giggled and held out her closed right fist. When she opened it, she revealed a crumpled-up one dollar bill. "Daddy says I can have two cookies."

"He did, did he?" Nora said thoughtfully, and let her gaze slide past the child to the wide front windows and the street beyond. Mike stood just outside, and for a second, Nora noticed her heartbeat quicken. Which was weird. After all, she'd known Mike for years, and until last night, she'd never thought of him as more than Emily's dad and a pretty nice guy.

Suddenly, though, those long legs of his looked delectable in his worn jeans. His scuffed boots, crossed at the ankle, looked...sexy. The worn, long-sleeved blue shirt he wore only made his already-broad chest look wider, more muscular. And his green eyes as he watched her through the window seemed deeper, more mysterious, than she remembered.

Her stomach pitched suddenly and Nora pulled in a long, steadying breath in a futile attempt to get a grip on her wildly raging hormones.

This is ridiculous, she told herself. Mike wasn't interested in her. Or anyone. He wasn't going to be the man to help her through her ''problem.'' So there was absolutely no point in indulging in what could probably be staggeringly wonderful fantasies.

''Miss Nora...''

She shook her head, but didn't manage to dislodge any of said fantasies. Determined, though, she looked back at his daughter. Good. Focus there. On a sweet face, with freckles dotting a tiny nose. On a pair of lopsided pigtails and a wide grin that displayed one dimpled cheek. On green eyes that were so like her father's...

Cut it out, Nora.

''Two cookies. Chocolate chip, right?'' she asked unnecessarily as she walked behind the counter and filled the order. Like every other child Nora had ever known, Emily had particular likes and dislikes, with chocolate chip cookies being high on the approved list.

''Yes'm.''

She smiled to herself at the polite and grownup-sounding child, then walked back to Emily and handed her a small white bag. ''Here you go, honey.''

"Thank you."

"Shall we see if your daddy wants a cookie, too?"

Emily laughed. "Oh, he doesn't. I heard him tell Rick he wasn't gonna eat sugar anymore."

"Is that right?" Nora looked from the girl to the man still standing safely outside the bakery. Telling his foreman that he was swearing off sugar, was he? And apparently he figured if he didn't actually step inside the bakery, he'd be safely out of reach. Did he really think she'd let him off the hook that easily?

"Let's go talk to your daddy and see if we can't change his mind." Nora took Emily's small hand in hers and kept hold of it while she pushed through the door and stepped onto the sidewalk.

Mike straightened up instantly, coming out of the lazy lean against a light pole like a man ready to bolt. Late-afternoon sunshine spilled down on the street from a cloudless blue sky, and all around them, the town was bustling.

"Hi, Nora."

"Mike."

"Miss Nora says you should have a cookie." Emily looked from one adult to the other, her pigtails swinging as she turned her head from side to side.

"Swearing off sugar, huh?"

Mike scowled. "Just cutting back."

"Sugar in general, or just my bakery?"

"Nora," he said, "I just figured that after you slept

it off—'' He broke off, glanced at his daughter and reworded that. ''After a good night's sleep, you'd see that this whole idea is crazy and want to forget about it.''

''You figured wrong.''

''Apparently.''

''So,'' Nora said, gently running one hand across the top of Emily's head, ''I was thinking I'd come out to the ranch tonight and we could make some plans.''

He squinted into the sunlight, scraped one hand across his jaw and said, ''You're not going to let go of this at all, are you?''

''Not a chance,'' she said.

He sighed heavily and said, ''Fine. Tonight.''

''Are you gonna come over and bring cookies, Miss Nora?''

Nora looked down at the little girl and smiled. ''How about I come over early and you and I can make cookies together?''

''Oh, you don't have to—'' he started to say.

''Goody,'' Emily crowed, her small voice undermining her father's protest.

''Terrific,'' Nora said, lifting her gaze to meet Mike's. ''Then I'll see you in an hour or two, okay?''

He just stared at her for a long minute before caving. ''I'm outmanned and outgunned. Guess we'll see you at the ranch in a while.''

''Can't wait,'' she assured him.

As Mike took his daughter's hand and headed toward their car, he felt Nora's gaze on him as surely as he would have her touch. With Emily's chatter rattling around him, he tried to tell himself that having Nora in his house would be no big deal.

But his heartbeat quickened at the thought and his body felt suddenly tight and uncomfortable. He figured his hormones were fighting it out with his brain.

He just didn't know which was going to win.

Five

"An' can we make some with little candies on 'em?"

"You bet we can," Nora said, and wiped a splotch of flour off the tip of Emily's nose.

"This is fun, Nora," the little girl said, and slapped her small hands down onto the dough. "Daddy doesn't let me cook 'cuz I'm too small."

Oops. Nora inwardly cringed a bit. Maybe she should have checked this out with Mike first. On the other hand, he wasn't here and she was. So, as long as they weren't cooking over an open fire on the linoleum, she didn't really see a problem. Although, she thought, glancing down at the worn, faux-brick flooring…maybe an open fire wouldn't be such a bad idea.

"Well, we'll just have to tell him what a good job you did, won't we?"

Emily gave her a grin filled with absolute delight, and Nora figured that reward would be worth any hassle she had to face later with Mike.

And speaking of Mike, where the heck was he, anyway? Nora had already been at the ranch for two hours and there was still no sign of him. Donna Dixon, the ranch foreman's wife, had been here watching Emily when Nora arrived. At eight months pregnant, the woman had been only too happy to turn Emily's care over to Nora so she could go home and lie down.

Left to their own devices, Nora and Emily had played two games, colored pictures and then had tea with her favorite dolls. When tea time was over, the child took Nora on a tour of the house, and Nora was surprised to note that except for Emily's room, which was every little girl's fantasy bedroom, the ranch house was very plainly decorated.

For Emily, there were soft blue walls, a canopy bed, lace and ruffles, bookcases stuffed with the classics along with dozens of nighttime storybooks. Not to mention enough dolls and stuffed animals to populate Santa's workshop. But the rest of the house was simply furnished, with no little touches that added warmth. The great room held a couple of comfortable-looking sofas and one worn chair facing a huge open hearth. The minute she saw it, Nora's brain started whirling with ideas to cozy up the big space. She'd like to be turned loose on the house with a few gallons of paint and a little imagination.

But it was the kitchen that really called to her. It was a terrific room, with all kinds of potential. But the beige walls and plain pine cabinets practically screamed for attention. In her mind's eye, she saw what it could look like and her mouth nearly watered with her itch to do something about it. Still, it wasn't her business, was it? Mike hadn't invited her in to redecorate his house. Heck, he hadn't *invited* her at all. She'd practically forced herself on him.

"Are the cookies done yet?"

"Hmm?" Nora dragged her mind back to the present and looked at Emily. "Oh. Cookies. Let's check, okay?"

The little girl hopped down from her stool and hurried to the oven door.

"Don't touch it now, it's hot."

Emily practically danced in place, but she slapped her tiny hands together and held on tight, as if to keep from reaching for the cookies.

Grinning, Nora picked up a hot pad, opened the oven door and was instantly greeted by a wave of heat and the glorious scent of hot chocolate chips. "Done," she pronounced, and pulled the tray out. In a few seconds, she had the cookies scooped up and onto a cooling tray, the next batch loaded and the oven door shut again.

Emily breathed deep and then looked at Nora. ''Can we have one?''

Any reasonable adult would no doubt say, *Of course not. You have to wait until after dinner so you won't spoil your appetite.* Nora's own mother was a big believer in the ''no snack'' theory. But Nora wasn't about to look into those shining green eyes and say no.

''Sure we can,'' she said instead. ''Nothing better than gooey, warm cookies.''

Emily sucked in a gulp of air and held it while Nora picked up the tray and held it out to the little girl. ''They're hot, so be careful.''

''I will.'' She plucked a nice fat one from the rack and waited until Nora picked one for herself, then set the rack back on the counter before biting into it. Grinning, she mumbled, ''S'good.''

''It sure is,'' Nora said, smiling at the smear of chocolate on the child's mouth and the glint of pride in her eyes. Poor little thing. No mom to share these little adventures with. And a father, who though loving, was obviously a late worker. True, Emily did have Donna during the day, but since the foreman's wife was really centered on her own coming child, she didn't have the attention to give Emily. Nora felt a small twinge in her heart as she smiled and said softly, ''You're a good baker.''

''I am, huh?'' The girl wiped her free hand on the apron that was tied around her chest and hung almost to her feet. ''I can tell Daddy I'm a good cook, can't I?''

''I'm sure he'll be very impressed,'' Nora assured her, and made a mental note to make sure Mike was suitably proud of Emily's accomplishment.

''Can we make some more?''

Nora laughed and stood up, brushing one hand across the girl's forehead, lifting straw-colored bangs that felt like silk. ''Let's finish these first, okay?''

'''Kay,'' Emily agreed, and climbed the stool again to take her place beside the oak cooking island. Carefully, just as Nora had shown her, the little girl scooped out spoonful after spoonful of cookie dough and gently dropped them onto another cookie sheet.

Nora kept one eye on the child and one eye on the kitchen window. Outside, twilight deepened. Across the ranch yard, she could see lamplight glinting in Rick and Donna's windows. She was used to looking out her own windows and seeing streetlamps and cars passing along the road. Here, on the edges of town, darkness was more complete. More...*dark.* Walking across the kitchen, she opened the back door and let the cool evening breeze drift past her.

Except for the sound of Emily singing to herself

under her breath, the silence was awesome. Nora would have thought this much quiet would be unnerving. Instead she found it…soothing. There was a sense of peacefulness about the whole place, the silent house and the wide openness surrounding it that seemed almost magical.

She glanced at her watch.

And wondered again where Mike was and just how long he was going to stall before coming home.

Mike stayed out on the ranch until it was too damn dark to get anything else done. Rick, his foreman, had called it a day more than an hour ago, heading back to the small house on the ranch that he shared with his pregnant wife. But then Rick was eager to get home. He didn't have a woman on a mission waiting for him.

The first few stars winked into existence and glittered against a deep purple sky. He pulled off his hat, raked his fingers through his hair and told himself that he had to go home sometime. It wasn't just Nora sitting in his house waiting. Emily would be wondering where he was pretty soon.

He climbed into the truck, slammed the door and fired up the engine. He'd stalled as long as he could. If he stayed out here much later, he'd need a sleeping bag. Besides, why should he let Nora keep him away from his own house? Throwing the truck into gear, he flicked on the headlights and headed toward home. The ruts in the road rattled the truck and shook the rocks in Mike's head.

"Idiot," he muttered, and braced his left arm on the window ledge. "It's just Nora Bailey. You've seen her at least a couple of times a week for years. Now all of a sudden you can't be in the same room with her?"

He slapped his hand against the steering wheel and made a sharp right into the drive leading to the house. Gravel crunched beneath the tires and ground out a familiar welcome. As he shut off the engine and climbed out of the truck, he told himself again that there was no reason to be wary of Nora. She'd made it plain enough that he wasn't in the running for the task she needed done. And that was just fine with him. So fine. He snatched his hat off, crumpled the brim in one tight fist and stopped dead outside the kitchen window.

Inside, two blond heads were bent together. Nora and Emily, side by side at the cooking island, were laughing together and making cookies. At that moment, Mike's daughter lifted her head, looked into Nora's eyes and damn near *beamed.* Her little face was lit from within. Delight sparkled in her eyes and the dimple in her cheek had never looked deeper. There was only one word to describe the expression on his little girl's face. *Adoration.* Clearly, she'd found her hero in Nora.

But before he could wonder if that was a good thing or a bad thing, Emily spotted him and whooped out a welcome. She clambered off the kitchen stool and he headed for the door. His long legs couldn't carry him as fast as an excited little girl could move. In seconds, she had the door open and was jumping at him, arms wide.

Mike scooped her up, swung her around in a tight circle, then propped his forearm beneath her bottom to support her as she clung to him like a burr. Her small arms wrapped around his neck and hugged tight. And just as it did every night, Mike's heart melted. He held his whole world in his arms, and he never forgot to thank whatever gods had sent this child. She was everything to him.

''Daddy, I *cooked!*'' She pulled her head back to look at him and gave him a smile that always turned him into a soft lump of clay that Emily could push and shove around any way she wanted to.

''You did, huh?''

She nodded so fiercely that her pigtails swung wildly around her head. ''I made cookies.'' Emily turned her head to look at the woman just stepping around the oak island. ''Nora helped, but I did it and everything.''

Before he could speak, Nora's voice cut across his child's high-pitched words.

''Emily told me that she's not allowed to cook, but

I thought that just this once wouldn't be so bad and that you'd understand and—''

Mike held up one hand to cut the stream of conversation off. It sounded as though she was warning him not to be mad. As though she thought he might come down on Emily for a decision an adult made. Did she really think he was that big a jerk? Besides, even if he'd wanted to, he wouldn't have been able to maintain anger while looking into Emily's happy face. She was just so proud of her accomplishment.

''Do you want one, Daddy?''

He tore his gaze from Nora to look into the eyes so much like his own. ''Absolutely.'' Mike lifted her off his hip, set her on her feet and gave her backside a pat. ''Go pick me a good one, okay?''

''I'll get you the best one of all,'' she promised, and practically skipped over to the cooling rack.

While Emily was busy, Nora sidled up to him. ''Thanks for not spoiling her good time by being mad.''

''I'm not an ogre, y'know.''

''Never said you were,'' she countered. ''But Emily told me you don't want her cooking and—''

He hung his hat on the rack just inside the door, then shoved both hands into his jeans pockets before saying, ''That's because Donna's not much of a cook. Almost burned down the kitchen once when she forgot and left a pan on the stove.''

"Yikes."

"Exactly."

"Okay then, so you won't mind if Emily and I do a little baking from time to time?"

From time to time? So then this wasn't a one-time-only visit? He looked at her through narrowed eyes. "You figuring on being here a lot, are you?"

"Well, at least until we solve my problem," she said, half turning to keep an eye on Emily, who was examining each and every cookie. "How long do you figure that'll take?"

How long to find a man worthy of Nora Bailey?

He was just beginning to suspect that it might be an impossible task.

Then Emily was back, carrying two cookies. She handed one each to the adults. "Taste it, Daddy."

Nora lifted hers and took a small, dainty bite of the chocolate chip cookie. He watched her mouth and felt tortured as she licked warm chocolate off her bottom lip with a long, slow sweep of her tongue.

"Aren't you hungry, Daddy?" Emily demanded.

"I sure am," he said tightly. But not for cookies. Nora gave him a knowing look and a quick smile, then turned and walked across the kitchen. His gaze dropped to the sway of her behind, and he wondered if jeans that tight shouldn't be illegal.

To distract himself, he shoved the cookie in his mouth and chewed with a vengeance. Emily was delighted. But Mike was still hungry—and there weren't enough chocolate chips in the country to ease the ache building inside him.

For the next couple of weeks, Nora spent nearly as much time at the ranch as she did at the bakery. She was still up before dawn to do the baking, but nearly every day she left the bakery in the early afternoon to make the drive out to the Fallon ranch. And, each time she did, she caught herself closing just a bit earlier than the last time. Heck, if this kept up, she'd soon be serving the breakfast crowd, then shutting down for the day.

But she couldn't seem to help herself. Sure, it had all started with the idea of Mike helping her find a man. But it was developing into so much more than that. She really looked forward to spending time with Emily. The little girl touched corners of Nora's heart she hadn't even known were lonely. The child was so hungry for a mother's love and attention that she soaked up whatever affection Nora gave her and then handed it back ten times over.

Mike, though, was a different story. Nora leaned her forearms on the tall, whitewashed rail fence surrounding a paddock. In the center of the wide ring, Mike stood, holding a long leather leash in one hand. On the other end of the leash, a beautiful horse cantered around the edges of the circle, tossing its head as if trying to shake him.

But Mike kept up a steady stream of soothing words as he worked the animal. Most of it was nonsense, but the rhythm of his speech and the deep rumble of his voice combined to nearly hypnotize the horse…and Nora. Her gaze locked on him, she followed him as he turned in a slow circle. His faded blue work shirt was worn and sweat-stained. His jeans were covered in dirt and grime. His boots were filthy, and the hat he wore was tilted low over his eyes, shading them to the point where she couldn't even see them. But, then, she didn't have to. She knew only too well the power of that direct stare.

Hadn't she been dreaming about those eyes of his for nearly a week? Her mouth went dry and her stomach swirled with nerves and anticipation, and with something tight and dark and hot that made every cell in her body sit up and weep for mercy.

It was torture, pure and simple. But it was also a torture she willingly put herself through every afternoon. It had become a routine. Something she looked forward to. Spending this time with Mike, watching him work the animals with a sure and steady hand was—okay, exciting.

She shifted her gaze to take in the ranch yard and the wide-open spaces beyond. It was just so beautiful out here. She couldn't imagine being able to wake up every morning and have this be the first thing you saw. Being away from town felt energizing. The lack of people and noise gave her the chance to think. And the slower pace gave way to time for daydreams.

And that thought brought her right back to Mike. Her favorite daydream.

''Okay, that's enough for today,'' Mike called out, and Nora blinked, dismissing those late-night fantasies as the product of a *way*-overworked imagination. She willed her nerves into submission and watched as Mike tossed the leather leash to Rick, then turn and headed toward her.

''Pretty horse,'' she said when she was sure her voice would work.

''Stubborn, too,'' Mike pointed out, and, grinning, tugged leather gloves off his hands. ''It's going to take me forever to convince that mare to wear a saddle and bridle.''

He sounded disgusted, but Nora wasn't fooled. She'd noted the gleam of admiration in his eyes as he watched the horse being led back to the stable. Chuckling, she said, ''You love it.''

Mike glanced at her, almost surprised. ''Yeah. Guess I do.'' Pulling his hat off, he ran one hand through his hair, then leaned an elbow on the top rung of the fence. ''Boarding and training horses are the fun part of living on the ranch.''

''And what's the part you don't love?''

His gaze locked with hers. ''Not a damn thing. I like being out here. I like everything about living on the ranch. I don't plan on moving to a town. *Ever.*''

Nora had the distinct impression that there was a message in that last statement. But since she hadn't a clue what that might be, she took what he'd said at face value. ''I don't blame you.''

''Huh?''

She glanced at him, then turned her face into the wind and stared out beyond the paddock and the ranch yard. Off in the distance, the orchards spread out in neat, orderly rows like soldiers lined up for inspection. Overhead, the sky was a deep, vivid blue, with a handful of marshmallow clouds scuttling across its surface.

''I said I don't blame you,'' she repeated. ''It's beautiful here. And so quiet.''

''Yeah.''

''I mean,'' she went on, ''I know Tesoro's a small town, but still, sometimes the noise and all the people get to me.''

''Uh-huh.''

Reacting to the tone of his voice, she turned her head to look at him. ''You don't believe me.''

''Let's just say, I've heard that one before.''

''Is that right?'' she asked. ''From who?''

''Vicky.'' He bit off the word and his mouth looked as if he'd tasted something bitter.

Nora's stomach jittered and she told herself she

should let it go. Heck, the look in his eyes told her he clearly didn't want to talk about it. But there was something else there, too. Some echo of disappointment. Some lasting shred of hurt that tugged at her and wouldn't allow her to keep quiet.

"What didn't she like?"

He inhaled slowly, deeply, and shifted his gaze from hers to stare out over the ranch. "Asking me what she did like would take less time."

"Okay," she said. "Consider it asked."

Slowly, he turned his head until he was looking at her again. "Nothing. Not the quiet, not the solitude, not Emily—and at the end, not me, either."

"She was an idiot."

He shrugged, but Nora wasn't fooled. Old pain was still too close to the surface here. "So was I," he said. "I thought desire was a good start for a marriage." He turned his gaze directly on her and Nora read regret shining clearly in those dark green depths. "I let my hormones guide me once. I won't do it again."

"Nobody's asking you to," she reminded him. Though that wasn't really accurate. Since her own hormones were singing, she wouldn't mind a bit if his did a quick dance or two.

"You seem to like it out here," he said, and the abrupt change of subject startled her for an instant.

But she went with it and saw relief crowd his features. "I do. It's gorgeous. And the ranch house is so big. The whole place feels big, though. Wide open—you know, 'where the buffalo roam' kind of feel.''

He laughed shortly and Nora relished the deep rumble of sound. ''No buffalo. Just horses, a few orchards—''

''It's enough,'' she interrupted him, and let her gaze wander briefly again before looking back at him. ''It's a great place to raise kids.''

Oops. There went that thundercloud chasing across his face again.

''That was the plan,'' he admitted. ''But things don't always work out like you think they will.''

His voice had dropped so low that she barely heard the last few words he uttered. It must have cost him to talk about his ex-wife. A part of Nora wanted to go find Vicky and give her a good, swift kick. But since she couldn't very well do that, she settled for changing the subject one more time. The instant she did, she saw relief flood his eyes.

''Well, you'll just have to do a better job of finding me a man than you did in finding yourself a wife.''

''Shouldn't be tough,'' he muttered.

''Good.'' Resting her chin on her forearms, she looked at him through wide, innocent eyes. ''I've been thinking. What about Tony Diaz?''

He pulled his head back and looked at her as though her hair was on fire. ''Are you nuts? He's twenty years older than you.''

Nora hid an inward smile and congratulated herself on obviously striking a nerve. ''Experienced.''

''Old.''

''Then he'd probably consider me a sweet young thing,'' she pointed out, thoroughly enjoying herself now. ''That's a definite plus.''

''You're twenty-eight. Not exactly ready for medicare.''

''Hey, age is in the eye of the beholder.''

''Tony sells shoes at a department store.''

Okay, this wasn't really fair. Nora was getting way too big a kick out of teasing him. She was no more interested in Tony Diaz than she was in dancing naked down Main Street. ''A steady job,'' she said. ''People with feet will always need shoes.''

''And the fact that he has a daughter the same age as you?''

''We can raid each other's closets.''

Mike stared at her for a long minute, until he finally noticed the gleam in her eyes and then he bit back the laugh crawling up his throat. ''You're pulling my chain.''

Blond eyebrows lifted and one corner of her mouth twitched. ''Not yet. Would you like me to?''

Six

He was pretty sure his heart stopped for a second. Images filled his brain, racing through his mind at top speed. He had a feeling she knew it, too. She chewed at her bottom lip and, with every tug, he felt a like tug somewhere deep inside him.

Mike shifted uncomfortably, scowled a bit and refused to take the bait. Instead, he asked, a bit harsher than he'd planned to, "Why are you here?"

The slight smile on her face faded slowly. "Do you mean existentially speaking or literally, *here?*"

"Literally, thanks," he ground out.

"Our bargain," she reminded him.

The damn bargain. Talk about making deals with the devil. He hadn't had a minute's peace since agreeing to this whole thing. "You know, that's not really working out so well."

"Only because every man I suggest, you shoot down."

True. Damn it. *He'd* noticed that, but he'd been sort of hoping she hadn't. It's not that he didn't want to help her find some guy—or maybe it was. He couldn't be sure anymore. All he knew was that whenever she suggested one of the men in town, he had a ready reason why she should stay the hell away from the guy.

Too old.

Too young.

Too fat.

Too poor.

Drank too much.

Hell, it was ridiculous. Most of the men they'd talked about had been Mike's friends for years. He'd never had a problem with any of them. Until it came time to set Nora up with one of them.

For some reason or other, he just didn't like the idea of her being with…*hell, admit it. Anyone.* Which made for a big problem. Because he wasn't going to be sucked into trouble by his hormones again.

When he'd first met Vicky, his body had gone on high alert and all he could think about was having her.

Then, once he *had* her, everything had gone straight down the tubes. There was no way he was going to let his body do the thinking for him again.

So why the heck didn't he find Nora a nice guy and get her out of his hair? His mind? His dreams?

Pushing away from the fence, he took a step or two farther, as if that extra foot of space between them would make all the difference. Then he looked at her again. "You're right."

"I am?"

"Absolutely."

"You have no idea just how much a woman loves hearing a man say that," she said, "but in the interest of clarity, I'm right about *what,* exactly?"

"About me shooting down your suggestions."

She nodded sagely. "Ah. So you're in favor of Tony, then?"

He snapped her a quick look. "No. He *is* too old for you. God, Nora, you're looking for a man. Not a father figure."

"Okay," she said, with a little shrug that caused the rounded neckline of her T-shirt to slide off her left shoulder. Mike's gaze locked on that patch of creamy skin and he wondered if it felt as smooth as it looked. He fisted his hands to keep from reaching for her to find out. "So who'd you have in mind?"

He racked his brain, trying to come up with somebody he hadn't already dismissed. And just when he figured he was going to come up dry, a name occurred to him. ''Seth,'' he blurted, grateful for the inspiration. ''Seth Thomas.''

Nora frowned thoughtfully. ''The deputy?''

''Why not?'' Mike countered, forcing himself to push the idea. ''He's new in town. Probably doesn't know too many people yet.''

She looked at him, and for one long moment, he lost himself in those blue eyes of hers. But then he remembered that Nora wasn't for him. He reminded himself that the last two weeks didn't mean squat. She'd been coming out here to have him help her find someone *else*. The fact that he'd gotten used to having her around meant nothing. The fact that she and Emily had become the best of friends—well, that did worry him. Sooner or later, Nora would stop hanging around out here so much—and for the sake of his sanity, it had better be sooner—and then Emily would be hurt, missing her friend.

But just think, he told himself, how much worse she'd be hurt if she thought she had a shot at getting a brand-new mother only to be let down.

Nope. Better this way. Better for everyone. Especially for Seth Thomas, the lucky bastard.

''You know what?'' Nora said after a long minute or two of strained silence. ''You're right. Seth is new in town. Who better for me to try my 'wiles' on?''

She stepped back from the fence, an unreadable expression on her face. But all Mike could see were her eyes. Eyes that suddenly looked huge and innocent and...*disappointed?*

''Nora...'' Mike started, but a second later he was interrupted, and it was just as well, since he didn't know what the hell he'd been about to say.

''Nora!'' Emily's high, thin voice floated out of the house, and a half second later, the girl herself came sprinting into the yard.

Nora broke eye contact with Mike and turned to look at the little girl eagerly racing toward her. ''What is it, sweetie?''

''I finished my picture,'' Emily called out, nearly breathless with excitement. She skidded to a stop beside Nora, grabbed her hand and started tugging the woman toward the house. ''You hafta see. I made it for you. Special.''

''Well, I can't wait to see it, then,'' Nora told her, and scooped the child up to prop her on one hip. Gently, she smoothed the child's flyaway blond hair back from her face. Then, without looking back at him, Nora lifted one hand in a salute. ''See you around, Mike. This is girl stuff.''

''Yeah, Daddy,'' Emily repeated with a smile, watching him from over Nora's shoulder. ''Girl stuff.''

He took a step after them, then stopped himself. His gaze locked on the two of them, and for a second he felt like the outsider here. Nora and his daughter had somehow become a ''team'' in the last couple of weeks. They were drawing a circle of warmth around each other and it was all Mike could do to keep from stepping into the center of it.

And before he could forget all of his hard-won lessons, he turned his back on the house and walked, alone, to the cold, dark barn.

The bakery was busy.

Both of Nora's part-time employees were racing around, filling orders, pouring coffee and making change. Outside, morning sunlight lit up Main Street like a spotlight. On the sidewalks, people were hustling through their shopping chores and stopping to chat with old friends.

But, at Nora's, there was no time for chatting. And she was grateful. As long as she kept busy, she didn't have to think about last night.

Stupid, she told herself, and sliced up another steaming pan of lemon rolls. She made quick, deft cuts, moving on instinct, as her brain rattled noisily in her head.

''Pulling my chain?''

''Not yet. Want me to?''

Oh, God. She'd made an idiot of herself.

Why in heaven's name was she even *trying* to flirt with Mike? She wasn't supposed to be developing ''feelings'' for Mike Fallon. He was just the means to an end. Her little helper. An elf in Santa's workshop, for goodness' sake.

She stopped slicing for a second and in that blink of time saw again Mike's reaction to her teasing. If she'd been blind, she would still have seen the Go Away sign in his eyes. And what had she done? Kept talking, that's what. Tell him he had lousy taste in wives. ''Good going, Nora. That was thoughtful.''

Grumbling, she finished slicing the lemon rolls, set the knife down and reached for a spatula. ''You're an idiot, Nora,'' she muttered, then shifted to one side and used the spatula to scoop up the rolls and set them on a paper-doily-covered platter.

''Terry,'' she called. When a short teenager with freckles poked her head around the door, she said, ''Here're the rolls.''

''Good,'' the girl said, stepping into the room to take the tray. ''The natives are getting restless.''

''Ooh,'' Molly said as she, too, stepped into the kitchen, ''then I'd better grab one of those before the slavering hordes get them all.'' She plucked a lemon roll off the top of the plate and grinned as Terry disappeared back into the main room.

''Hi,'' Nora said, then looked for the stroller Molly usually had with her. ''Where's the baby?''

''With Donna Dixon, out front. She wanted to see the baby and I wanted to see you.'' Licking icing off her fingers, Molly walked across the kitchen, leaned one hip on the counter and stared at her best friend. ''So, Jeff tells me that you've got a date with the new deputy tonight.''

Nora dusted her hands with flour, then plunged both fists into a mound of dough that had been set aside to rise. Kneading always worked out her tensions and today she needed the outlet more than usual. Seth Thomas. The guy Mike had thrown at her like a bone tossed to a guard dog to distract the animal long enough so you could escape. Ah, yes. So romantic.

''News travels fast.''

''Could have been faster,'' Molly pointed out, then took a bite of lemon roll. ''I mean, I would have thought my very best friend would tell me herself when she's got a hot date. But noooo...I have to hear it from my husband.''

''Jeff's got a big mouth.''

''Yeah, I know. One of the reasons I love him. Can't keep a secret, so I find out everything.'' She walked around the kitchen island, grabbed a coffee mug and poured herself a cup. ''Except, of course, why said best friend didn't call me.''

Nora winced. True. She'd been letting a lot of things slide the last couple of weeks. Her business. Her friends. Her family. All to spend time with a man who so clearly wasn't interested in her. *Idiot.* ''Sorry,'' she said lamely. ''I meant to call, but I've been busy and—''

''Yeah,'' Molly interrupted around another bite of lemon roll, ''busy hanging out at Mike Fallon's place.''

''There's that news bulletin again,'' Nora muttered. Honestly, it was impossible to keep things quiet in Tesoro. Everyone knew everyone else's business and felt justified in spreading that knowledge everywhere they went. But then, she'd been spending so much time at Mike's place, it was a wonder her mother hadn't had wedding invitations printed up.

''Just what's been going on out there, anyway?'' Molly asked. Then she gasped as an idea struck and she nearly choked on a piece of pastry. After the resulting coughing fit ended, she asked breathlessly, ''You didn't—you haven't—not with Mike Fallon?''

''No.'' Nora's denial was flat and too disgusted to be taken for a lie. ''I'm still in the ranks of the 'virgins-this-old-should-be-shot category.' ''

''Oh.'' She took a sip of coffee. ''Well, that's disappointing.''

Nora stopped kneading, pulled one fist out of the glutinous mass and punched it. ''*You're* disappointed?''

Molly laughed. ''Hey, I'm an old married woman. I have to live vicariously through *somebody.*''

''Well, you won't find much excitement through me, believe me.''

Molly walked closer, still clutching her coffee cup and roll. ''Nora, what's going on? Is there something you're not telling me?''

Nora stalled. Tipping the huge mound of dough on its side, she twisted and pulled and dug her fingers in, squeezing for all she was worth. She wasn't about to admit, even to Molly, that she was getting hung up on a man she knew darn well was a dead end. Heck, she didn't want to admit that to *herself.*

''There is something.''

Before she could surrender to the inquisition and blurt out the truth, a high-pitched wail rose up from the front room. Cocking her head, Nora grinned. ''That sounds like Tracy.''

''Yep. I'd better go rescue Donna Dixon. Have to take the baby over to Jeff's mom's this morning, anyway.'' She headed for the swinging door, but before she left, she turned and looked back over her shoulder. ''But I still want to know what's going on with you. And I want to hear about tonight's date. So call me, okay?''

As her friend left, Nora nodded. ''I'll be sure to tell you everything. As soon as I figure it out myself.''

Mike wandered through the darkened house trying not to think about what Nora was doing. Or who she was doing it *with.*

With Emily asleep and the house so quiet it was driving him nuts, he had no distractions to keep his mind from drifting straight to the one woman it shouldn't be drifting to. She would be out on her date with the deputy by now, he thought, stopping in front of the wide front windows.

He looked past his reflection in the glass to the darkness beyond and the images his brain insisted on creating. With no trouble at all, he saw her, in that little black dress she'd worn to the wedding. The one that clung to her every curve and made a man's mouth water at the thought of peeling it off her body. He imagined it clearly, seeing the deputy leaning across a dinner table, smiling into Nora's eyes. He saw him stroke her hand with a lingering touch. He watched as Nora smiled at a man who wasn't *him* and felt his insides tighten into a knot he thought might choke him.

Virgin.

She was a lamb being tossed to the wolves.

What if the deputy got as grabby as Bill Hammond had the night of the wedding? What if Nora said no and the guy didn't listen? What if she needed Mike's help and he was all the way out here, on the ranch?

''That settles it,'' he muttered, and marched to the telephone on a table beside a sofa. As he hit speed dial and waited for the call to connect, he noticed the small vase of flowers and traced the tip of one finger along a fragile petal.

Flowers.

That was Nora's doing.

In the last two weeks, he'd noticed little changes in his house. She brought fresh flowers and dotted the place with them in vases and jars and drinking glasses. She'd bought a few throw pillows to soften the lines of the old leather sofas in the great room. She'd hung curtains and rearranged framed pictures on the wall. She'd brought hair ribbons for Emily and had lately taken to making dinner for the three of them. Her touch was everywhere. She permeated the house. There was no escaping her, even when she wasn't here. Her perfume lingered in the air and taunted his dreams. Her memory danced in his brain and he heard the echoes of her laughter playing over and over again in his mind.

His hand tightened on the receiver when someone picked up the other end and said, "Hello?"

"Rick, it's me," Mike ground out tightly. "Can you come over here and sit with Emily for a while? I've gotta make a run to town."

Seth Thomas was a perfectly nice man.

Cute, too.

So why was it, Nora wondered, halfway through

their date, that there were no bells ringing in her mind? No slow sizzle in her blood? No pitch and swirl in the pit of her stomach? She sat across the table from him and listened with half an ear as he told her about the sheriff's academy training program. She nodded in all the right places and gave him an encouraging smile, but the truth of the matter was, she was so not interested. Okay, maybe she wasn't looking to marry Seth. But was a little excitement too much to ask?

What she really wanted to do was go home, put her jammies on and watch an old movie.

Or better yet, go to Mike's house, take her jammies *off* and—she put the mental brakes on that train of thought.

''So,'' Seth was saying, ''when Jeff offered me this job in Tesoro, I grabbed it.'' He leaned back in his chair and folded his arms across his chest. ''Because I think the secret to good law enforcement is...''

She tuned him out again and wondered what Mike was doing right at the moment. Did he miss her? Was he wondering how the date was going?

An hour later, Mike was sitting in his truck outside Nora's house. His gaze locked on the front window, he saw two people through the haze of the curtains. Blurred images, but enough to tell him that Nora had invited her date inside.

Mike's fingers curled around the steering wheel and

squeezed. He should have stayed home. He had no business sitting out here watching her like some damn stalker or something. Nora meant nothing to him. Hell, he'd practically forced her into this date with the new deputy. So he had no one to blame but himself.

But who was talking about blame, here?

Not him.

He was fine.

Just fine.

And firing up the engine, he peeled away from the curb and drove home.

Alone.

Seven

"But he's so cute," Molly said, staring up at Nora as though her best friend was nuts.

"And boring," Nora said with a sigh as she slumped down onto Molly's burgundy-colored sofa. Just thinking about her date last night made her tired. Not that he was a bad guy, but even if it was just about sex then she'd like to go out with a guy who had the ability to heat her blood with a single look. And that wasn't Deputy Thomas. "All night, all he did was tell me about the academy. How he won the fitness medal and that he was top of his sharpshooter class, about how to handcuff a person—"

"Really? Hmm..."

Nora laughed. "Cut it out."

"Just thinking out loud," Molly told her.

"The point is, there was just no..."

"Spark?"

"Exactly," Nora sighed.

"And suddenly you're requiring sparks. I guess I'm not a one night stand kind of woman."

"Well, duh."

Nora shifted uneasily on the couch and let her gaze slide around the room. Cozy, comfortable, Molly's house was cluttered, lived-in. There were fingerprints on the windows, books stacked on tables and a layer of dust on just about everything. Martha Stewart, she wasn't. But as she told anyone who'd listen, she'd have plenty of time to clean house, but her daughter would only be a baby for a little while.

The absolutely perfect Tracy, six months old and growing like...well, okay, a weed, crawled across the toy-strewn floor, gurgling and muttering to herself. Nora's gaze locked on the little sweetheart and her insides ached. The way things were going, she might never have her own children. And the thought of that just made her heartsick.

"Hello?" Molly prompted. "You were saying..."

She glanced at her friend. "I was saying that your daughter gets more gorgeous every day."

Molly practically beamed. ''She does, doesn't she?''

But she wasn't distracted for long. Molly had a streak of pit bull in her. ''So have you got a spark-worthy someone in mind?''

''Sort of.''

''And would this sort of guy be a handsome rancher with a five-year-old daughter?''

Nora's gaze snapped to her friend. ''What're you, psychic?''

''Oh, yeah, just call me Molly the Magnificent.'' Laughing, she propped her feet up on the coffee table. ''Honestly, Nora, you've been spending nearly every waking minute with the man for the last two weeks. Who the heck else would it be?''

''For sanity's sake?'' Nora countered. ''Just about anyone else.''

''Mike's a nice guy.''

''Oh, he's terrific. He just looks at me and sees Typhoid Mary.''

''Okay, this tendency to exaggerate is getting a little out of hand.''

''I'm not,'' Nora said, remembering just how fast Mike had tossed Seth Thomas at her. ''He does everything he can to keep me at arm's length.''

Molly sat forward and grinned. ''If you're at arm's length, honey, he can still reach you.''

"Easy for you to say. Jeff melts into a puddle whenever he looks at you."

"Honey, up the temperature and every man will eventually dissolve."

Nora laughed at the thought, though, even as she did, she remembered flashes of heat dazzling Mike's eyes when he looked at her. She recalled standing close beside him and feeling his tension mount until he would stomp off to go somewhere...anywhere, else. Nora smiled to herself and wondered. If she could make him hot enough...maybe even Mike could melt.

The afternoon sun baked the earth and seemed to simmer on Mike's bare back. Heat rippled through him, fueling the fires within that had been raging since the night before. He never should have gone into town. Never should have driven past Nora's place. Never should have tortured himself by imagining her with the deputy.

Because, all night long, his mind had taunted him, drawing up image after image of Nora being kissed and held and touched by someone who wasn't *him.* His grip tightened on the hammer in his right fist. He slammed it against a nail head with enough strength to push it right through the fence plank and out the other side. His right arm sang with the contact, and for one brief second, it took his mind off what he shouldn't be thinking about, anyway.

Small consolation.

When he heard a car pull into the drive, something in the pit of his stomach skittered at the familiar sound of the engine. Mike turned slowly, warily, as if he turned too quickly, that car might disappear. Then he'd be in real trouble. When your imaginings took on solid shape and sound, it was ''rubber room'' time.

The car door opened and Nora climbed out. Sunlight danced on the edges of her hair, making the carelessly tousled mass shine like gold. She looked right at him, as if her gaze had been magnetically drawn to his. Even from across the distance separating them, Mike felt the solid punch of those blue eyes hit him hard and leave him breathless.

She came around the front of the car, all slow moves and a smile, and his gaze swept over her as if he was a blind man who was suddenly given the power to see. He noticed everything about her. A scoop-neck, pale yellow tank top displayed enough creamy, sun-kissed skin on her chest, shoulders and arms to tantalize him. The hem of the darn thing stopped short above the waistband of her grass-green capris, giving him a peek at her belly button and a slash of tanned flesh that made him want to see more. He sucked in a gulp of air, choked it down and kept looking. She wore sandals that displayed that toe ring of hers, and his mouth went dry as he watched her hips sway with each slow, deliberate step toward him.

She didn't stop until she came to the paddock fence. Then she rested her forearms on the top rail, inching the hem of that tank top up a bit more. Mike closed his eyes, hoped for strength, then opened them again to stare directly into hers.

"Who's next?" she asked.

"What?" Blood rushed and pumped through his body, thundering in his ears, and he had to force himself to hear her when she repeated her question.

"I said, who's next on your list?"

He cleared his throat, stuck the claw of the hammer through one of his belt loops and walked toward her. Damned if he'd let her know what just looking at her was doing to him. "What list?"

"You know, prospective deflowerers," Nora said. She tipped her head to one side and asked, "Is that even a word?"

Who cared? "What are you talking about?" He deliberately kept his gaze locked with hers. Way less dangerous than allowing himself another glimpse of tanned, creamy skin.

She smiled and it sucker punched him.

"C'mon, Mike. Seth Thomas couldn't have been your best shot."

The knot that had been lodged in the center of his chest since the night before slowly dissolved. "Didn't like him?"

"Oh, he's nice," she said, "but when push came to shove—or rather when touch came to pawing..."

"He *pawed* you?"

"That was the idea, wasn't it?" She shifted and ran her fingertips along the edge of the fence rail. "I mean, I can't really lose the whole virginity banner unless some touching is involved."

"Right." His gaze slipped and followed the languorous movement of her fingers until he clenched his jaw and had to look away again.

"But it just didn't feel..." She shrugged, and the clingy material of her blouse tightened across her breasts.

"You know?"

All he knew for sure was, if he didn't get the hell away from her, damn fast, she wouldn't have to worry about finding somebody to "deflower" her. She'd be flat on her back in the paddock, with him right on top of her.

That image flashed into his mind and held there, freeze-framed.

"Mike?" Nora said, waving one hand in front of his face.

"Yeah!" He snapped out of it instantly, shook his head and blew out a rush of air.

"You okay?"

"Fine," he muttered, and snatched his hat off to stab his fingers through his hair. At least, he would be fine as soon as he could find enough cold water to soak his body in. The Arctic Ocean ought to be big enough.

"Well, you don't look okay," Nora said, inwardly smiling. Ah, it was good to know that even if she wasn't much of a flirt, she was girl enough to bring a man to his knees. Figuratively, if not literally. Feigning concern, she suggested, "Maybe you've had too much sun today."

"I'm fine," he insisted.

"It's really hot, though," she said on a soft moan, tilting her head back and stroking her neck with the tips of her fingers. "Feels like my skin's on fire."

He inhaled slowly, deeply. She heard the deliberate intake of air, and it did her a world of good to know that he was totally affected by her.

"I gotta get back to work," he said tightly, and turned away, headed back for the far side of the paddock.

"Oh, okay then," Nora said, shifting her gaze to meet his. "I'll just go on inside and say hi to Emily."

He stopped dead and half turned to look at her over his shoulder. "You're staying?"

"Sure," she said, smiling at him. "We've still got to find me a man, don't we?" Then she spun around and walked toward the house, intentionally swaying her hips in what she hoped was a provocative move. She felt his gaze on her as she walked, and if she'd been made of straw, she'd have burst into flame from the heat of his stare. As it was, her skin hummed, her insides churned, her knees wobbled and places in her body that had yet to be introduced to passion sat up and begged.

So just *who* was torturing *whom* here?

Mike stayed outside working as long as he could, but, eventually, he had to give it up and go inside. Rick was spending more and more time with Donna, as he should be, Mike thought. But that meant more work for him and less time with Emily.

So, he should be grateful that Nora had come back, right? At least his daughter was happy and well-looked-after. What did it really matter, in the grand scheme of things, that he was going slowly insane?

He stepped into the kitchen, hung his hat on the wall peg and looked around the empty room. A casserole dish, covered with foil, sat on the stove top. Dishes had been washed and put away, but there was a single place setting, for him, waiting on the table. Apparently Emily and Nora had already eaten.

And despite the fact that he'd stayed out late on purpose, he was disappointed to realize he'd missed dinner with them. The clock over the sink read seven-fifteen and Mike felt a stab of guilt. Nearly Emily's bedtime and he'd hardly seen her all day. He could take care of that, though. Just grab a quick shower and—

"Mike?"

Nora's voice, coming from the great room.

He got a grip on his hormones and walked through the doorway and down the hall. "Yeah, I just came in and—" He stopped as he entered the room. Emily lay on one of the sofas, cuddled up beneath a blanket. Nora was sitting right beside her.

Worry and fear roared to life inside him as he crossed the room in a few long strides. Dropping to one knee beside his daughter, he looked up into Nora's worried gaze and asked, "What's wrong?"

She shook her head and shrugged. "I don't know. She was fine a few minutes ago and now—"

"Daddy—" Emily's voice came soft and tired "—I don't feel good."

"What hurts, baby?" he asked, his tone gentle, crooning as he stroked her bangs back from her forehead. "Your tummy?"

"No," she whined, and cupped one small hand around her neck. "My froat's sore."

"Mike, I swear," Nora was saying, and he heard the tension in her voice, "up until a few minutes ago, she was fine. We were coloring." She waved one hand at the abandoned coloring books and crayons lying scattered across the coffee table.

"Kids get sick fast," he muttered, and spared a

quick look at the beautiful blonde beside him. ‘‘Don’t worry about it.’’

‘‘Daddy, it hu-u-urts….’’

Despite the concern washing through him, Mike could still appreciate how a kid was able to shove three syllables into a one-syllable word. ‘‘It’s okay, baby. Daddy’ll fix it.’’

Emily closed her eyes and turned onto her side, curling up into a tiny cocoon. Mike bent down, planted a kiss on the top of her head and stood up, motioning Nora to follow him as he moved across the room. She did, reluctantly, continually glancing back at the child lying so uncharacteristically still.

‘‘Nora,’’ he said, and she focused on him. ‘‘Look, I don’t want to ask, but I’m filthy. Will you stay with Emily while I take a quick shower? Then I’ll take over caring for Emily and you can go home.’’

She looked at him as if he had two heads. ‘‘I’m not going anywhere,’’ she said after a long minute of stunned silence.

‘‘You don’t have to stay,’’ he said tightly. ‘‘Emily’s had these before. It’s just a sore throat. I just have to keep her fever down. She’ll be fine.’’

‘‘I’m sure she will,’’ Nora agreed, folding her arms beneath her breasts and shooting him a look that told him she was going to be stubborn about this. ‘‘And I’ll be right here with her to see it for myself.’’

''No-o-ora'' came a soft wail from the couch, ''read to me....''

Nora winced slightly and sympathy shone in her eyes as she called back, ''I'll be right there, sweetie.'' Then, turning back to Mike, she lowered her voice and added, ''Go ahead. Get cleaned up. Have dinner. And get used to me. Because I'm not leaving her.''

Then before he could argue, or tell her that he could take care of his own child, Nora was gone, hurrying back to the sofa. Picking up Emily's favorite book, she began to read, and the sound of her voice—calm, loving, gentle—filled the room. Mike simply stood in the shadows, watching the two of them. He was still standing there when Emily reached out and Nora folded that tiny hand in hers.

A pang of something sweet and just a little terrifying ricocheted around the inside of his heart. It had been just he and Emily for so long, he wasn't used to sharing the care of her. But clearly, his little girl had found something in Nora that she needed. Responded to.

And that worried him. Because eventually, Nora would leave and what would that do to Emily?

Two hours later, Nora was a wreck. All thoughts of hot seduction were long since banished from her mind and every ounce of her concentration was focused on Emily. She looked so small, so helpless, lying in her bed surrounded by her stuffed animals. The little girl's cheeks were flushed and her eyes held the glassy sheen of a fever.

''Read it again,'' she whispered, and the scratchy sound of her voice brought a sympathetic ache to Nora's throat.

''Okay, sweetie,'' she said, and drew the child in close, wrapping her arm around her. Emily nestled her head on Nora's chest, and even through the fabric of her shirt, Nora felt the heat radiating from the small body pressed close to her.

Worry tugged at her heart and tore at the edges of her mind. But she read the storybook one more time, trying to keep Emily's mind off her own misery. And while she read the story about a sick little bunny and his friends, Nora concentrated on the feel of Emily's slight body curled into hers. Though she hated that the child was sick, Nora loved feeling needed, loved that Emily felt comforted by her presence.

''Will I still be sick on Friday?''

Nora stopped reading and shifted her gaze to the wide blue eyes looking up at her. ''I don't know, honey, why?''

'''Cuz Mandy in my class is having her birthday and we get to sleep over at her house and everything.'' Emily's bottom lip curled and one fat tear slipped from her left eye and rolled along her cheek.

''Aw, sweetie, don't cry....''

''Who's crying?'' Mike asked.

Nora turned to look at the doorway, where Mike stood, leaning against the jamb, hands in his jeans pockets, bare feet crossed at the ankle.

How long had he been standing there?

''Me, Daddy,'' Emily said as more tears joined the first one.

He smiled softly and pushed away from the door, walking into the room to take a seat across from Nora, next to Emily. ''Don't worry about the party, baby,'' he said softly, and ran his fingertips along her cheek. ''You'll be okay by then.''

''Really?'' A half smile curved her mouth.

''Really. Now, why don't you try to sleep, okay?''

'''Kay,'' she said, and cuddled in closer to Nora.

Mike watched her and shook his head. ''Maybe you should lie down?''

''Nora's readin' to me.''

''Yeah,'' Nora said, smiling. ''I'm readin' to her.''

One corner of Mike's mouth tilted into a smile that set off firecrackers deep inside Nora. She felt the pop and sizzle of them as they scattered, throughout her bloodstream. Pulling in a long, slow breath, she forced her gaze from his and looked instead at the pages of the book she could barely see through the haze of desire clouding her vision.

How did he do that? How did he look at her and

make her want to rip her clothes off and throw herself at him?

''Mind if I listen, too?'' he asked, his voice a low rumble of sound that rippled along her spine and settled into an ache deep inside her.

''You can cuddle with Nora, too, Daddy,'' Emily offered.

Nora sucked in a gulp of air.

Mike heard her.

And gave her a look that made her head spin.

In a good way.

Eight

Emily was sound asleep and her fever was down. But Nora still refused to leave. Mike watched her from the hall doorway, and in the soft glow of the princess night-light gleaming in the corner of the room, she looked…too damn good.

He leaned forward, bracing his hands on either side of the doorway and squeezed until he wouldn't have been surprised to hear the old wood snap in his grip. To indulge himself, he let his gaze slide over her. That fresh-as-a-daisy outfit she'd been wearing when she arrived was now wrinkled and stained with a few drops of liquid ibuprofen. She'd raked her hands through her hair so often it was a tangled mess, and her eyes looked tired and worried.

Still, desire flashed inside him, even brighter and stronger than it had that afternoon. This was more than a reaction to her good looks, though God knew that was there, too. He was responding to who she *was.* How she'd cared for Emily. How she'd worried and fretted and read one story time after time until he was pretty sure she knew it by heart.

This desire raging and pulsing inside him was fueled by what he'd seen of her in the last few weeks. It was the flowers in his house. The laughter that had brightened every corner of a home that had grown too dark. The warmth that had invaded his soul no matter how much he tried to fight it.

And he knew there would be no relief from the wanting because he couldn't give her what she was looking for. Couldn't take that kind of risk. If he only had to consider his own happiness, then he might surrender to these feelings. But he had Emily to think about, too. And to protect her from another possible rejection, he would do anything. Even if it meant denying himself the one woman he wanted more than his next breath.

As if she sensed him watching her, she shifted her gaze to him. When their gazes locked, Mike knew he was in deep trouble. She stood up, bent down and stroked Emily's forehead, then straightened again and moved across the room.

Mike stepped aside as she got closer. When she passed him, she brushed against his body and his skin caught fire. That was the only explanation for the sudden explosion of heat that damn near swamped him. Shaking his head, he gave his sleeping daughter one last look, then turned and followed Nora out into the great room.

She kept walking until she stood in front of the now-cold hearth. On the mantel above the stone fireplace was a line of framed photos. Most were of Emily, but there were a few others, too.

''Are these your parents?'' she asked without turning around.

''Yeah,'' he said, and stopped a good five feet from her. Couldn't hurt to keep a little distance between them. ''They live up north. Near Reno.''

''Pretty up there,'' she said, and let her fingers trail along the oak mantel, sliding up to the next picture. ''And this?''

''My sister,'' he said, shoving his hands into his jeans pockets. ''She and her family live in Montana.''

''You're spread out far and wide, aren't you?''

''Just worked out that way.'' But his family had never really been close, anyway. Oh, they visited, called and e-mailed. But tight, they weren't.

''That's a shame,'' she mused, her voice quiet,

thoughtful. ''My family drives me nuts occasionally, but I can't imagine not having them close by.''

''I have Emily.''

''And she's enough?''

''She's everything.''

Finally, Nora turned to look at him. There were tears in her eyes, and since he hadn't been expecting it, those tears hit him hard. He took a step toward her, then stopped again, unsure just what to do. Damn it, tears always threw him for a loop.

She used both hands to swipe her cheeks dry, then sniffed and gulped in air like a drowning woman. Shaking her head, she gave him a watery smile and said, ''She is everything to you. I can see that when you're together.''

She took another deep, shuddering breath and continued. ''I envy you that, you know?''

What was he supposed to say to that? he wondered. *Thank you?*

But she didn't give him a chance to think of something to say. Instead, she kept talking, her words rushing from her, tumbling over one another into a long, blurred stream of sound. He listened hard, straining to keep up, to hear everything.

''I watched you with her and you were so good, so gentle, and you knew exactly what to do and you weren't scared. You weren't worried. I saw your eyes,'' she said, wagging a finger at him as if accusing him of something dire. ''You weren't worried. Concerned, maybe, but not scared. I was so scared, I didn't know what to do. She got that fever in just a few minutes. It came up out of nowhere and...'' She shrugged, threw her hands high and then let them slap down to her sides again. ''If you hadn't walked in the door when you did, I would have been running out into the dark to find you. I was terrified. I mean, I've been sick and that's no biggie. I can take aspirin and tuck myself into bed. But watching Emily cry and seeing her face flushed and her eyes go all glassy...'' She cringed even at the memory. ''It was terrible. I felt so helpless. So stupid. How can you deal with that so easily? How do you watch a kid be perfectly healthy one minute and then sick in the next?''

''Nora...'' Eventually, he had to try to stop the flow of words. Her tears were running again, coursing down her cheeks in a flood of misplaced guilt.

''My God,'' she whispered as her voice wound down into a hoarse echo of what it had been, ''I have no business wanting a family. Kids of my own? If I react like this, what good would I be to them? I mean, what if they fell and cut themselves? Would I faint at the sight of blood? Would I just sit on the floor and cry with them?'' She pushed her hands through her hair. ''Yeah, I'm the one you want around in a crisis.''

''That's bull.''

''What?'' Her head snapped up and her gaze shot to his.

Mike looked at her and felt his heart squeeze at the sight of her tear-streaked face and misery-filled eyes. He just couldn't stand it another minute. In three long strides, he was beside her. Grabbing her upper arms in a firm yet gentle grip, he drew her up onto her toes and stared deeply into her eyes.

He felt a tremor race through her body and skip into his. This close, her eyes looked as blue as a lake—and just as fathomless. She chewed at her bottom lip in a ridiculous attempt to stem the tears that were still raining down her face. Her breath came in short, hard gulps.

He squeezed her arms a bit tighter and said again, ''It's bull, Nora. All of it. At least,'' he said with a shake of his head, ''what I caught of that monologue. You talk so damn fast, it's hard to be sure.''

A tremulous smile flitted across her face and was gone again in an instant. ''My mom always said that when I was nervous she couldn't hear a word I was saying.''

''I know what she meant,'' he grumbled. ''But the upshot of this is, you're blaming yourself because you panicked.''

''Exactly,'' she said, and tried to worm out of his grasp. But there was no way someone as small as Nora was going to get away from Mike if he didn't want her to. And damn it, he didn't.

''You didn't panic, Nora. You took care of her. You read to her. The same damn story over and over until I would have pulled my hair out in frustration.'' He gave her a small smile and was rewarded with one just like it.

''That's not true,'' she said, leaning into him. ''Emily already told me you read her that story every night.''

''Wrong,'' he said on a sigh, enjoying too much the feel of her body pressed along his. ''I *recite* it. I learned it by heart months ago.''

She laughed. The sound was hesitant, unsure, but it was there, however briefly.

Mike's gaze swept over her face, her hair, and came back to her eyes. So deep. So blue. So...innocent. Hell, he never would have believed that in the twenty-first century, you could find an *innocent* over the age of fifteen. Yet here she stood.

In his arms.

His thumbs moved back and forth over her bare arms, and the feel of her skin beneath his sent a rush of fire pouring through him. His body tightened and breathing became a real issue.

But he wasn't holding her for his own satisfaction, right? He was supposed to be consoling her. He got back to the subject at hand and tried to tell his body to chill out.

"Kids get sick fast, Nora. But they heal just as quick, most of the time." He shrugged helplessly. "And, nine times out of ten, all you can do is stand there and watch over them. Try to make them more comfortable."

Her gaze dropped.

He dipped his head to reestablish the connection. "*Read* to them."

She smiled again.

"You did good."

Nora sucked in a long deep gulp of air and blew it out again, ruffling the stray curl draped over her forehead. "If you're lying to make me feel better," she said, "I want you to know you're doing a great job."

His mouth quirked. "I'm not lying."

She studied his features for a long minute, as if trying to read the truth in his expression. What she saw must have convinced her finally because she nodded and whispered, "Thanks."

"No problem." His thumbs moved over her skin again, and this time she shivered and he felt her reaction kick around inside him. Deliberately, his grip loosened as he told himself to take a step back. That they were too close, standing here in the dimly lit room. Moonlight streamed through the uncurtained front windows and lay in a silvery pattern on the worn rugs and hardwood floors.

The one lamp burning in the room cast a small circle of golden light that came nowhere near them as they stood locked together near the hearth.

"Mike..." she whispered, and her voice seemed to dance at the back of his neck, sending every damn one of his nerve endings onto red alert.

While he still could, Mike let her go and took a half step backward. Scrubbing one hand across his face, he told himself to ignore her perfume—some delicate flowery scent—as it surrounded him, filling the air with a power that threatened to rock him to his knees. "Look," he said tightly, remembering that there was no future in this, "Emily's asleep. She's going to be fine by morning. Maybe you should be headed home."

"I don't want to leave just yet," she said, and took a step closer.

Now, she might be a virgin, but Mike certainly wasn't, and he'd seen that determined look on a woman's face before. She'd made up her mind about something, and he had a feeling that once Nora had set her course it would take more than logic to change it.

"Nora, this isn't a good idea," he said, feeling it only fair that he try, anyway, despite the low chance of success.

"See," she said, coming even closer, "that's where you're wrong, cowboy. I think it's a great idea."

And then she was in his arms, pressing her body into his, wrapping her arms around his neck and going up on her toes until their mouths were just a kiss apart.

Mike's body went hard and tight. Every muscle, every cell, sizzled and burned. He clenched his jaw and fought against grabbing her. His hands fisted at his sides even as he felt his blood boil.

Her breath dusted his face. Her fingers stroked through his hair and he felt her touch right down to his bones. She shifted a little, rubbing her abdomen against him. She smiled knowingly.

"You know, Mike, I think you think it's a better idea than you think you do."

He blinked, shook his head and ground out, *"What?"*

"Oh," she said, running the tip of one finger around the inside collar of his dark red T-shirt. "I think you understand me."

He shuddered and, in self defense, grabbed her tight, holding her still, with his arms locked around her waist and tightening like a vise.

"Oomph." Her breath was squeezed from her lungs, but it didn't seem to be bothering her any.

"Nora," Mike said, forcing his voice to work around the huge knot of need lodged in his throat, "I'm not the one you want."

She tipped her head to one side and gave him a crooked smile that stabbed right to the heart of him. "How do you know what I want, cowboy?"

"Quit calling me that," he grumbled. "I'm a rancher."

"You're a cowboy," she murmured, and let her fingers trail through his hair again, sending tiny lightning bolts blasting throughout his body.

"I'm not gonna do this."

"Oh, I think you will."

Damn it, he thought. She was way more right than he was.

"C'mon cowboy," she murmured, moving her mouth even closer to his. "Be a hero, kiss the girl."

His right hand swept up her spine. Threading his fingers through her fine, silky blond hair, he cupped the back of her head and held her still for one long, heart-stopping second. Staring down into her blue eyes, he felt himself fall, and the last rational thought that darted through his brain was *What the hell. What harm can one kiss do?*

"Yes ma'am," he muttered, and took her mouth in a fiery kiss that slammed into both of them with the strength and raw fury of a runaway train.

Nora held on tight and enjoyed this new experience. She'd been on a roller-coaster ride of emotions all night. First teasing Mike, then sitting beside Emily's sickbed, then here again, in the dark, with Mike. Talking to him, watching him, feeling the power of his forest-green eyes were all enough to send any healthy woman over the edge.

But seeing him in action as a tender, loving father had just topped off what she'd felt building inside her for weeks now. Mike Fallon was more man than she'd ever hoped to find. Her body hummed when he was around. She hated leaving him at night and couldn't wait to see him again. Was that love? She didn't know. Didn't want to think about it. At least not now. For now, all she wanted to do was *feel.*

She'd saved herself for years, hoping, praying the one special man might come along. Then, she'd given up hope. Now, here, tonight, she'd found him.

The fact that he wasn't interested in love or forever was something she'd worry about tomorrow. Tonight, she wanted his arms around her. She wanted to taste and feel and experience everything she'd been missing all these years.

His mouth opened over hers, his tongue parting her lips, sweeping into her mouth to dazzle her even further. She'd been kissed before, her brain screamed out, but her body knew better. She might have been kissed, but she'd never been *kissed.*

And Mike was a man with a real gift for kissing.

She groaned softly as he took more of her, tasting, exploring, delving deep into the heart of her. His breath brushed her cheek, his tongue entwined with hers, dazzling her, stealing her breath and sending her pulse beat into a rapid dance that pounded in her ears and left her shivering.

Again and again, he explored her, while his hands moved up and down her back, along her curves, finding their way along her body, driving the heat swamping her into an inferno. Nora held on to him, clinging to his broad shoulders as if her life depended on him.

Dazzling fireworks exploded behind her closed eyes, and the falling sparks seemed to shatter and spill throughout her body. Her brain shut down, but that didn't matter. No thought was necessary. She forgot to breathe and didn't care. Everything else in the world fell away as she stood wrapped in the center of his warm, solid strength. She wanted that kiss to go on and on. She wanted his hands on her body, and the fire inside quickened until she felt flushed from head to toe. Still, she wanted more.

A moment later, he broke the kiss, dragging his mouth from hers. She struggled for air and rested her head on his chest, trying to get her balance back, comforting herself with the ragged beat of his heart. Standing on her own two feet again, she swayed into him, afraid that if he moved away too quickly, she'd fall flat on her face.

Noodly knees would do that to a person.

He drew in a long, deep breath and let it shudder

through him as he rested his chin on top of her head. "Nora, do us both a favor and go home. Now."

"I don't think I can walk," she confessed.

"I'll carry you to your car."

She leaned her head back to stare up at him. When she saw the dark swirl of desire gleaming in his eyes, her knees went weak again. "Mike, you don't want me to leave. I can see it in your eyes."

"What I want and what I'm going to do are two different things."

Disappointment welled inside her. "They don't have to be."

"Yeah," he said, "they do." And he let her go, taking a step back that was as much mental as it was physical. She felt him withdraw, pull away from the closeness they'd just shared. Nora wanted to kick him.

"You can just shut it off. Just like that." Shaking her head, she glared at him and tried not to think about the fact that her mouth was still humming, her blood still racing.

"If you think this is easy, you're nuts."

"Then why do it?" she demanded, anger and frustration coloring her voice.

"Because one of us has to think clearly."

"Ahhh..." she said on a long, slow inhalation. She dropped both hands to her hips, tapped her left foot against the rug beneath her and snapped, "So what you're saying is, you'll do the thinking for the poor, weak little female who doesn't know her own mind?''

His jaw tightened, the muscle twitching spasmodically. ''I didn't say that.''

''Sure you did, Mike.'' In a slow, measured walk, she moved in a circle around him, forcing him to turn his head just to keep his eye on her. ''You're so tall and strong and smart and everything. And you've had sex...at least *once,* for sure.''

''Hey...''

''So of course you should take charge here, right?''

''I didn't say I was—''

''So, yeah, Mike. Fine. I'll leave, because I'm not really feeling romantic anymore, anyway, in case you didn't guess that by the way I'm talking and how fast the words are coming out—''

His features tight, he muttered, ''I got it, but—''

''But you know something?'' Nora said, moving close enough to poke her index finger into his chest with the force of a nail being pounded into a piece of oak. ''You're going to regret this, Mike.'' She moved in closer still, keeping her gaze locked with his, then, her voice low and husky with choked-off need, she whispered, ''When you're lying there alone in your bed tonight, Mike, I want you to remember that you sent me home.'' She ran her fingers down the front of his shirt, then fisted her hands in the material, pulling his head down to hers. ‘‘You’ll miss me, cowboy. You know you will.’’

Then she kissed him, hard, slanting her mouth over his and pouring everything she was feeling into that one, last kiss. She felt him give, surrender to the moment, and when his hands came up to her back, she let him go and moved out of his reach. It was small consolation that he looked like he’d been hit on the head.

‘‘This is over for tonight, cowboy,’’ she said, mustering what little dignity she could. Lifting her chin, she met his gaze coolly. ‘‘But *just* for tonight.’’

Then, with her insides churning and her brain spinning, she left him standing there in the dim light and didn’t look back.

Nine

"You've got to set the hook and reel him in." Nora's mother glanced at her briefly, then turned her gaze back to the crochet project on her lap.

"Exactly," Frannie piped up, and wiped her baby's drooly chin.

"Honestly, Nora," Jenny complained, hefting her daughter up to her shoulder to be burped. "How have you managed to live this long without knowing the game?"

Nora's gaze drifted from one member of her family to the next. Her mom, Rose, sat in a wing chair with sunlight pouring over her shoulder and onto the spill of garnet yarn cascading off her lap to pool at her feet. Frannie and Jenny were each busy with their kids, but apparently still had plenty of time to give Nora the advice they were so sure she desperately needed.

The house where she grew up hadn't changed much over the years. Oh, it had newer furniture and the carpet had been replaced once or twice. The absence of her father was still felt five years after his passing. But, basically, it was the same old comfortable Victorian. Where she came every two weeks to be harassed over lunch whether she needed it or not.

For the last half hour, the hot topic of discussion was her relationship—or lack thereof—with Mike Fallon. Apparently, the whole darn town was talking about her and Mike. Not so surprising, really. There wasn't a lot going on in Tesoro, so having a new piece of gossip was almost enough reason to throw a carnival. With Nora spending as much time with Mike as she had in the last few weeks, it was no wonder people were speculating.

''Who says you have to play games?'' she suddenly asked of no one in particular.

All three of them snorted muffled laughs.

Gritting her teeth, Nora defended her position. ''Game playing is for kids. Men and women should be honest with each other.''

''Ah, so speaks the still unattached sister,'' Frannie muttered.

''Wisdom from the virgin goddess.'' Jenny rolled her eyes and congratulated her little daughter on a burp well done.

Nora gritted her teeth, but before she could shoot back some pithy retort, another voice interrupted.

''You girls stop it,'' their mother said, and Nora shifted her gaze to the woman with softly graying blond hair. ''Nora, honey, what works for some doesn't necessarily work for others.'' Pulling a stitch tight, she laid her silver hook down and rested her hands in her lap. Smiling, she continued. ''You've always been as honest as the day is long, Nora. No sense in trying to change now.''

''Thank you, Mom,'' she said, giving her sisters a meaningful look.

''But,'' Rose said quickly, drawing her daughter's gaze back to hers. ''Honesty surely isn't always the easiest policy when dealing with a man.''

''Amen,'' Frannie muttered.

Their mother ignored her and focused on Nora. ''Pay no attention, honey. What I'm trying to say is, it won't be easy, but if you want Mike, then you have to figure out how to convince him of that in your own way.'' She leaned forward, bracing her elbows on her knees, and smiled at her eldest daughter. ''I know you, Nora. Where you love, you love strong and deep. If this is really love, then go for it, honey. Find your own way and do what you think best.''

Tears stung the backs of Nora's eyes as she looked into her mother's warm, soft blue gaze. It was good, she thought, to have a place where you were known so well. Where, no matter what, you belonged and people understood.

"Really, Nora, all you have to do is make up your mind and then convince him that his mind is made up, too." Jenny grinned at her from across the room.

Now, that sounded so much easier than it was probably going to be, Nora thought.

"Oh!" Frannie squealed. "Look. Look." She pointed at her little son. The eleven-month-old had pulled himself to his feet. While the women in the room held their collected breaths, tiny hands fisted in the fabric of the sofa cushion. And with his proud family looking on, little Jake took his first toddling steps.

When he dropped onto his well-padded bottom, his delighted mother scooped him up, cheering for his victory. Nora sat on the floor, watching her sisters and her mother congratulating the little boy. Tears filled her eyes, and she felt a raw, open tide of love rush through her, so thick, so powerful, it nearly choked her.

Family.

That's what mattered.

That's what she wanted most.

And she knew just what she had to do to get it.

* * *

Things were getting back to normal.

At least, that's what Mike kept telling himself. He hadn't seen Nora in nearly two days. Not since she'd set his body on fire and then walked out of his house to let him burn to a crisp alone.

"Just as well," he said, throwing Emily's sleeping bag and balloon-decorated overnight case into the back of the truck. Nora had obviously finally accepted that whatever there was between them just wasn't going to go any further.

"Hey, boss!"

Mike's head jerked up and he squinted into the afternoon sunlight to watch Rick approach. "What's up?"

Rick shook his head and snapped his thumb toward his own house at the other end of the ranch yard. "You coming right back from town?"

"Yeah. Be gone about a half hour."

"Excellent. On your way back, will you stop and pick up some tacos for Donna?"

Mike smiled to himself. "Thought she was craving ice cream?"

"Last week," Rick said on a sigh. "This week, it's tacos."

"Sure, I'll get 'em."

"Thanks," Rick said, already heading for the barn. "I owe you."

''No problem,'' Mike said, remembering all too well what it was like to deal with a pregnant wife. Of course, Vicky had pretty much resented the whole situation. She'd complained for nine long months. She'd hated the changes in her body. Hated the baby. Most especially, though, she'd hated *Mike* for creating the child in the first place.

And as long and miserable as that pregnancy had been, none of it had mattered the minute the nurse handed his new daughter to him. Mike could still see Emily—tiny, red, screaming her head off. It was still a moment he thought of as miraculous. Hell, he'd had just about had *sucker* stamped on his forehead from the moment he took his first look at his little girl.

He'd always wanted three or four kids. He smiled at the thought of the ranch ringing with the sound of squeals and laughter. But, an instant later, that smile disappeared as he reminded himself that Emily would be his one and only child. And that was a shame, he admitted, if only to himself. Mike hadn't counted on living the rest of his life alone. He'd wanted a wife. A big family.

But he'd messed it all up so badly, so completely, that he figured he'd had his shot and blown it. Now it wasn't his turn to go out and try to find happiness. He wouldn't let Emily care about someone else, only to be abandoned again. His daughter had to be his priority. Now it was Emily's turn. And he'd do everything he could to make sure his little girl was happy.

Nora had a plan.

She'd even called in the big guns. Making Jenny and Frannie go shopping with her, she'd picked out lingerie that was so sexy she was half surprised it hadn't burned a hole right through the bag she'd carried it home in. With her hair and nails done, she felt pampered and pretty and, let's face it…ready to do battle.

She only wished her nerves were as rock steady as her eyeliner. Her stomach swirled with what felt like hundreds of butterflies, and her mouth was so dry it hurt to swallow.

Inhaling sharply, deeply, she muttered encouragement to herself. "Come on, Nora. You can do this." She laid the flat of her hand at the base of her throat and picked up the staccato beat of her own pulse. Okay, the plan wouldn't get a chance to work if she passed out before she even got started.

She stared through her windshield at the ranch house sitting dark and silent at the end of the drive. A single light in the kitchen told her exactly where Mike was in the big old house—and her heartbeat quickened even further. He was alone. Tonight was Emily's big sleepover party.

Nora swallowed again and tried to steady her

breathing. She steered the car down the drive, following the twin slashes from her headlights. The now familiar sound of gravel crunching beneath her tires seemed…welcoming, somehow. Parking the car, she grabbed her purse and climbed out, closing the door behind her.

She shot a quick look at Rick and Donna's little house and was reassured to see several lights on, plus the flickering of a TV set. There would be no interruptions from that quarter. Now all she needed was to find the nerve to carry out the plan.

The kitchen door opened and a slice of yellow light stabbed through the darkness, silhouetting Mike standing in the doorway. He looked huge. Tall, broad shouldered and exactly what she wanted.

"Nora?" he said, and his voice, though low pitched, carried easily in the quiet she'd learned to appreciate out here, so far from Tesoro.

"Surprise."

He stepped out onto the porch and the light fell on him. With his features half in shadow, he looked mysterious, untouchable. A part of Nora wanted to just say "forget the whole thing" and go home, but she'd come too far to back out now. Besides, that tiny, cowardly voice in the back of her mind was easy to ignore, buried as it was beneath the roaring of her own blood.

"I didn't expect to see you out here again," he said, and folded both arms across his chest.

She came around the front of the car and stepped carefully on the gravel as she felt her high heels wobble unsteadily. The cool night air slipped up beneath the hem of the knee-length linen coat she wore belted around her waist and sent a shiver up the length of her spine. But she was pretty sure it wasn't only the air making her feel the tingle of goose bumps on her skin.

''We should talk,'' she said softly, stepping up onto the porch to stand alongside him. The three-inch heels made her nearly tall enough to look him square in the eye. Nora noticed that despite his lack of welcome, there was a flash of...something in his eyes that gave her the courage to take the next step.

Pulling in a deep breath, she moved past him into the well-worn kitchen. A white take-out bag sat in the middle of the table. The scent of Mexican spices filled the air, and Nora smiled to herself as she looked around the big room. It was homey and familiar and about to become the site of Nora's first attempt at seduction.

''If you're here to talk about the other night...'' he started.

''No,'' she said, cutting him off as she dropped her purse onto the table and turned to face him. ''I'm here to talk about tonight.''

Mike kept his distance. For all the good it did him. Just seeing her here again was enough to stir up every ounce of the desire he'd spent the last two days trying to ignore. Her short blond hair was softly curled and fell around her face in a wild, tangled halo. Her blue eyes looked dark, smoky and dangerous as hell. She was wearing those strappy high heels that had looked so good on her the night of the wedding. And even her pale blue linen coat looked sexy belted tight around her narrow waist.

A coat, though? Spring evenings were cool, but not cold enough to warrant bundling up.

Not the point, he told himself. The main thing here was to get Nora out of the house before—

Her hands dropped to the knotted belt at her waist and he watched as she tugged at it. Apparently she planned on staying awhile.

''What are you doing?''

''Setting the stage for our little talk.''

''The stage?'' he asked, and before he could figure out what she meant exactly, Nora shrugged out of the coat to let it fall to the floor.

Mike's heart stopped.

Under that simple linen coat she was wearing the most amazing combination of silk and lace he'd ever seen. Red-wine-colored silk caressed her body, skimming along her skin, hugging her curves before ending in a short skirt that just covered the tops of her thighs. Slender straps smoothed across her shoulders and across her breasts; the silk gave way to a fragile lace that managed to both hide and display her breasts. Her legs looked long and lean and tanned and his hands itched to touch her, to explore every inch of her.

Reaching out blindly, he slammed the back door closed and wished he had curtains to close, too. ''Oh, man.''

''You like it?'' she asked, and Mike thought that had to be the dumbest question he'd ever heard.

He sucked in air through gritted teeth and finally lifted his gaze to hers. ''Like it? Yeah, I guess you could say that.''

''Good.'' Her mouth, that fabulous mouth, curved in a soft smile that let Mike know she was completely aware of the effect she was having on him.

She did a slow, lazy turn in a tight circle, giving him enough time to appreciate her from every angle. And damned if she didn't look fantastic from every angle. His body went tight and hard. His blood pumped viciously and his heartbeat raced until he was sure it would jump right out of his chest.

''I was hoping you'd like it. Sort of makes up for standing here freezing.''

''Nora—''

She met his gaze and tilted her head to one side to look at him. ''You're not going to try to tell me to leave, are you, Mike?''

''Would it work?'' he ground out tightly.

''Not a chance.'' She moved a little closer to him, and damned if he could convince himself to back up.

Her scent reached him first. That delicate blend of flowers that he would know in the dark and be able to find her by following it.

Oh, man.

"But you could warm me up a little."

"Warm?" A strained, harsh laugh shot from his throat. "Honey, if you're not careful, you're gonna end up in the middle of a forest fire."

Her eyes flashed and her lips parted in a half smile that fed the flames licking at his insides. Mike knew he was a dead man. There was just no way he could let her go. No way he could face the rest of this night without touching her. No way he could last another ten seconds without having her.

"That's why I'm here, Mike," she said, and came close enough to skim her hands up his chest.

His body flashed with an inner heat. Her hands went up, wrapped around his neck and her fingers threaded through his hair. A low grumble of need and want erupted inside him and Mike fought to keep it under control. To keep from losing himself.

"I want you," she said. "I want you to make love to me, Mike."

"Nora, this is crazy."

She nodded, never taking her gaze off his. "I know. It has been right from the start."

"I'm not the man you need."

"You're exactly the man I want, though."

He sucked in another gulp of air and released it in a rush of frustration. Grabbing her around the waist, he slid his fingers along her silk-clad body and felt her tremble at his touch.

She went up on her toes and planted a quick kiss at the corner of his mouth, and he felt himself weaken even further. He'd been fighting this for weeks. Desire had become a constant companion, and frustration a way of life. Well, damn it, a man could take just so much.

"Nora, are you sure?"

She actually laughed, and he watched her eyes dazzle with pleasure. "Are you kidding? I dressed up like this, drove out to your house, stripped in your kitchen and you're asking if I'm *sure?* Jeez, Mike, I'm practically attacking you."

His mouth quirked into a half smile. She had a point.

Nora kissed him then, long and hard and deep, and when it was finally over, she pulled her head back to look at him. "Well, cowboy?"

Shaking his head, Mike told himself that by tomorrow, he'd probably be able to think of hundreds of reasons why he shouldn't be doing this. But tonight he couldn't even think of one.

Still holding her at the waist, he shifted his grip, scooped her up into his arms, and when she laughed in delight, he told himself not to think beyond tonight.

To take this time with Nora as a gift and not question it.

''Hang on, little lady,'' he said in his best cowboy drawl, ''it's gonna be a long night.''

''Promises, promises.'' Nora laughed and wrapped her arms around his neck as he stalked across the kitchen and through the house to his bedroom.

Ten

Those butterflies in Nora's stomach took flight all at once and swirled in circles.

Mouth dry, nerves strained to the aching point, she clung to Mike as he moved quickly through the dark house. Outside his bedroom, he stopped, reached for the knob and threw the door open with so much force it smacked against the wall behind it. He stepped into the room and his arms tightened around her.

Moonlight slanted into the room through the uncurtained window and spread across the wide bed, extending a pale invitation. The handmade quilt covering the mattress looked soft, welcoming. He carried her to the bed and stopped alongside it. Looking down at her, he again asked, ''You're sure about this?''

Nora slid the flat of her hand down his chest and tweaked open one of his shirt buttons. ''I told you. I'm sure. Not a doubt in my mind. Uh-huh, this is what I want. Right now. You. Here. With me. On that bed. I mean it—''

He grinned and Nora's heart did a wild, staggering dance.

''I get it,'' he said, and, still holding her, bent down and reached with one hand to throw the quilt to the foot of the bed. ''You're sure.''

''Oh, yeah.''

''Good,'' he muttered, and knelt on the bed so he could stretch her out across the mattress. '''Cause I'm not sure I could take it if you changed your mind now.''

''No problem there,'' she told him. Her butterflies had butterflies. Every inch of her skin felt alive. Sizzling. One look from him and she felt the fire inside her erupt into a volcano of pulsing need and hunger that she'd never expected to be so strong. And soon, very soon, she'd be leaving virginity behind. She'd take the step she'd been waiting so long for. And best of all, it would be Mike showing her the secret handshake.

His hand swept beneath the hem of her impossibly

expensive nightie and caressed her bare skin and...

"My purse!"

"What?" His fingers stilled on her abdomen.

"I need my purse. I left it in the kitchen—"

"Going somewhere?" he asked lazily, dragging his fingertips across her belly.

She sucked in air, blew it out and shivered as she said, "No. It's just—I didn't want to buy them in Tesoro, because you know this town, and everyone would be talking and they'd all figure out what I was doing...I mean what we were doing, so I stopped at a store in Monterey this afternoon and picked up—"

"You're babbling," he pointed out, and she heard the smile in his voice.

"I'm lucky I can talk," she said, and sucked at air again as his fingertips danced along the edges of her panties.

"Then don't," he said, dipping his head to take her mouth with a series of brief, tantalizing, nibbling kisses. "Don't talk. Just feel. Just—"

"Oh, I like that," she whispered, and wondered if he heard her over the roar of her heartbeat.

"Good," he said, "so do I."

Another nibble. Another taste. Another too quick kiss that left her hungry, frantic, for more.

His mouth dipped to the line of her jaw and down her throat. She felt his lips, his teeth, his tongue, drawing a line of fire across her skin. Her brain blurred.

She'd needed to tell him something. Started to tell him about the store...*oh, my*...and that she had some...*wow*... Air. She needed air. Silently, Nora reminded herself to breathe, but there was just so much more going on in her brain right now, she was afraid that order was going to come in low on her list of priorities.

"So soft," he murmured, and his breath dusted warmth against her skin.

"Mike..." *Think,* she told herself. "In my purse..."

He rose up, looked down at her and smiled. "What could possibly be so important about your purse?"

Her eyes were rolling. That was the only explanation for the fact that his face looked blurry. She inhaled sharply, deeply, and focused. When she found her voice again, she managed to say, "Condoms. There're condoms in my purse."

That slow smile of his deepened as he shook his head. "You're amazing, you know that?"

A flutter of something delicious wafted through her. "Because I can shop?"

"Yeah," he murmured, letting his gaze slide over her and following that trail with his fingertips. He barely touched her, caressing her so gently it was as if a feather was dancing across her skin. Tendrils of expectation unwound throughout her body. Her blood went to a slow simmer and a deep, throbbing ache settled low in her body, making Nora want to twitch and writhe beneath him.

Her eager responses fed Mike's hunger until he could barely see her through the haze of want and need that nearly blinded him. His heart crashed against his rib cage and breathing was damn near impossible. He felt tight and hard and ready to roll. But he had to control his own desires. Had to slow things down. Had to make sure he took his time.

It'd been years since he'd been with a virgin. And hell, he'd been a virgin himself then. But he'd learned plenty over the years and he was determined to see to it that Nora's first time was a hell of a lot more memorable than his had been.

The condoms could wait, though he was grateful she'd thought of them. Especially since he didn't have his own stash. He hadn't exactly been a social animal the last couple of years.

But none of that mattered now. The only thing on his mind was Nora. How best to show her everything. How to take her high enough that she wouldn't mind the fall.

Skimming his hands beneath the hem of that incredible nightie, Mike relished the feel of her soft, smooth skin beneath his palms. Her curves were generous, and he followed every line until he knew her body by touch and she was squirming beneath him.

"I want to touch you, too," she said, and Mike had to smile.

He wanted her hands on him as much as she did, so he stood up and quickly stripped, tearing his clothes and boots off and tossing them into a corner of the room. He watched her watching him and saw her eyes widen.

When he lay down beside her again, she reached up and ran her hands across his chest, skimming her fingers through the short, dark hair and dragging her nails against his skin until he was pretty sure she'd branded him. He gritted his teeth, pulled in air like a drowning man and fought for control. It was a hard-won battle.

Finally, when he couldn't take another second of her gentle torture, he took her hands in one of his and pinned them behind her head on the mattress. She arched her back and her breasts pushed against their lace prison. Her nipples peaked and Mike's mouth watered.

Using his free hand, he pushed the hem of her nightie high until her breasts lay bare in the moonlight. Nora twisted slightly, moving into him, and her breath came in short, hard gasps. She trembled, and he felt the shudder of her movement move through him as well, touching the dark and lonely heart of him.

He dipped his head.

She held her breath.

He took first one nipple, then the next into his

mouth and Nora groaned aloud, arching into him, pushing herself at him as if afraid he would stop. But there was no chance of that.

"Perfect," he murmured, and ran the tip of his tongue across the dark pink, rigid tip of her breast.

"Mike...oh my...Mike..."

He smiled against her flesh. So Nora, to keep talking. He tasted her again, pulling her nipple deep into his mouth, suckling her, teasing her with the edges of his teeth, driving her into a frenzy of need that had her bucking beneath him in a futile attempt to ease the ache within.

"So good," she said brokenly. "It feels so...good. So...right."

His own body tightened as she moved into him again and again, seeking something she'd never known before. He felt her frustration and shared it. He wanted to be inside her, pushing himself home, deep into her warmth. He wanted to claim her for his own.

"Mike...I need—I need—"

"I know, honey," he whispered, lifting his mouth just long enough to shift and taste her other breast. She rocked and moved beneath him again. She tried to pull her hands free of his grip, but Mike held her tighter. He didn't want her touching him now. If she did, he'd lose all semblance of control.

While he tasted her breasts, he slid his free hand down the length of her body. Hooking his fingers beneath the edge of her panties, he pushed them down, over her hips, and as she lifted herself off the bed, he scooped them down and off her legs. Then slowly, teasingly, he ran his hand up the length of her leg, up her calf, past her knee and up along the inside of her thigh. His fingertips blazed a trail of heat and need and she responded eagerly, frantically.

Twisting her head from side to side on the bed, she swallowed hard, licked her lips and gave up trying to escape Mike's strong grip on her wrists.

"Please," she whispered, her voice carrying an ache that echoed inside him. "Please, I need..."

"This," he said, rising up to look into her eyes. His fingertips found her center, damp and hot and ready. Her body jerked at his first intimate touch and a shuddering groan slipped past her throat.

"Oh, Mike..."

"Just feel it, honey," he urged, bending his head to kiss her mouth, her cheeks. "Let it come, then let go and enjoy the ride."

"But...I...can't...breathe...."

A slow grin teased the corner of his mouth. "For this, you don't need air."

Her eyes flashed from blue to smoky-gray as she twisted beneath him. Planting her feet on the mattress, she lifted her hips, welcoming him deeper, faster.

Nora forgot about trying to breathe. All she wanted to think about was what was happening to other parts of her body. She'd never known this wild, frenzied sense of anticipation. Nothing in her life had prepared her for the sheer, raw power of sex. Her brain blurred. Thoughts whisked in and out of her mind so quickly she couldn't have caught one if she'd been trying.

His fingers, magical fingers, touched her, dipping into her body with a maniacal rhythm that pulsed and pounded deep within her. His thumb brushed against a single, unbelievably sensitive spot and Nora nearly screamed. Or would have, if she'd had enough air.

Mike was everything.

His touch.

His kiss.

His body, pressed to hers.

He pushed her higher and higher, and when she thought she'd reached her limit, he pushed her over the edge and her body erupted into a startling burst of sensation that rippled and poured through her in a stream of pleasure so deep, so wide, her only choice was to sink into it and drown.

"I'll be right back," he whispered huskily close to her ear.

Nora couldn't move. Couldn't see. Oh. Open your eyes, Nora. She did and stared blindly up at the ceiling. It was spinning. No, *she* was spinning.

"Mike?" She was pretty sure she said it out loud. But her hearing seemed to be gone, too.

''I'm here,'' he said a second later, and she felt him join her on the bed.

''Where'd you go?''

''To get your purse.''

Her eyes widened and she turned her head to look at him. One dark eyebrow arched and his mouth was curved into that half grin she'd come to love. Instantly, her body went on full alert again. She wouldn't have believed it possible, but she was ready for more.

''I want you inside me, Mike,'' she said, and watched his features tighten. ''I want to feel you within me.''

He pushed one hand through her hair, scooping it back from her face, and his thumb traced a slow pattern on her temple. ''You're killin' me, Nora.''

She smiled. ''Oh, not yet.''

He grinned again. ''Not through with me, then?''

''Not a chance, cowboy,'' she promised, and rolled onto her side so she could wrap her arms around his neck and pull his head to hers for a kiss. She slanted her mouth over his and slid her tongue past his parted lips. She took his breath and was grateful for it. She smoothed her hands over his bare back, loving the feel of his hard, muscled flesh. She pressed her body close, smashing her breasts against his chest, and then moved, rubbing her sensitized nipples until spirals of newly awakened need erupted inside her.

Mike took all she had and then offered it back to

her. His hands moved over her body, defining every curve, exploring every valley. He couldn't touch her enough. Couldn't feel enough of her silky, flower scented skin. And when neither of them could wait another moment, he pulled away from her long enough to snatch up one of the condoms she'd brought with her and put it on.

Then he laid her back against the mattress and knelt between her upraised thighs, spread open for him. He looked down at her and touched her gently, gingerly, and felt her tremble from head to foot.

He moved then, covering her body with his, pushing himself into her damp heat, claiming her as she wanted to be claimed.

Nora dug her fingers into his shoulders and held on as she stared up into his forest-green eyes. She felt him take her. Inch by glorious inch. Slowly, deliberately, he moved deeper, closer. She rocked her hips, trying to accommodate him, trying to ease his passage, trying to ease the ache building all over again inside her.

Then he paused for a moment and in one smooth, long stroke entered her fully, completely. A quick flash of pain rose up and was gone again. Nora winced, then shifted her hips and relished the amazing sensation of actually being joined with Mike. Having him a part of her. Locked together.

''You okay?''

''I'm way better than okay,'' she managed to say around the knot lodged in her throat.

Lifting herself up from the bed, she kissed him. And when he followed her back down, she gave him everything she had to give. His hips set a rhythm that was fast and sure and solid. She moved with him, aching to feel that explosion of power within her again. This time, as it built and roared to a crest inside her, she knew what was coming and didn't fight it. Didn't fear it. Didn't hold back.

She opened herself to the feelings. To him. This was what she'd been waiting for. This magic. This wonder. Electricity hummed through her veins. Anticipation swelled inside her. She held her breath when the first tremor shook her soul, then screamed as it tore through her with a wildness she hadn't known existed.

''Mike!'' She yelled his name, and her voice seemed to echo in the moonlit room.

''Come with me,'' he murmured, levering himself up on one elbow so he could catch her gaze with his. ''Come with me, Nora. Fly.''

''Take me with you,'' she said on a sigh that dissolved into a moan.

He took her higher still, and when he felt her body's surrender, he gave himself up to the release that had been building for weeks. He shouted her name into the moonlight, and together they fell into the heart of the storm.

Eleven

"Wow." Nora's voice sounded froggy even to her. But she was pretty impressed with herself that she'd managed to get that word out, anyway. Of course, it didn't come close to describing what she was feeling.

"Same to you," Mike whispered, and rolled to one side of her before lying there gasping for air like a dying man.

Nora stared up at the ceiling and waited until the overhead beams stopped swimming before she spoke again. "I realize," she said, "that I have no frame of reference. But I think that was pretty good."

He laughed shortly. "Yeah, I'd say so."

"Oh, man, I never thought I'd hear myself ask this. I sound like some dumb old movie, but I just can't help myself, because I really want to know and how will I know if I don't ask, so it's not really dumb if you think about it and—"

Mike held up one hand. "Nora, what?"

"Was it good for you?"

He shot her a look that told her plainly he thought she was nuts to have to ask. And that one incredulous stare did more for her than anything he could say. Still, it was nice to hear the words.

"It was...great." He kept staring at her as if seeing her for the first time. "Amazing."

He reached out and skimmed one hand down the length of her body and Nora's skin tingled expectantly. Her breath caught and a now-familiar aching want began to grow deep within her. "Oh, boy," she whispered, and moved beneath his touch, silently encouraging him.

Mike smiled knowingly. "What is it?"

Nora gulped in air, then blew it out again. "I just had no idea I could go from vestal virgin to wanton woman in the space of an hour."

"Wonton woman?"

She laughed. "Not wonton. *Wanton.* And I know that's a word."

"Is it ever?" he groaned as he pulled her close and then maneuvered her until she was lying on top of him. Stretched out, skin to skin, heartbeat to heartbeat. His hands skimmed down her back and over the curve of her bottom.

Nora closed her eyes as his fingers kneaded her tender flesh. Beneath her, she felt his body stirring to life again. Instantly, she flushed with a rush of heat so powerful, she was pretty sure the ends of her hair were singed. "Whoa."

"'Whoa' as in stop?" he teased.

She took his face between her palms, and looking him square in the eye, she said softly, "Don't you dare." Then she bent her head and kissed him. Mouths melded, tongues explored and twisted together, joined in a dance designed to stir bodies into life. Nora moved atop him, straddling him, and as their kiss deepened, she slid her hands down, across his chest, loving the feel of his hard, strong body.

Loving.

She loved the way he touched her. She loved the sound of his voice. His booming laugh. She loved his tenderness with Emily. The strength he'd shown in rebuilding his life. She loved his sense of humor and his sense of responsibility.

She loved him.

That thought hit her with a startling blast of clarity just as his hands swept down her body to once again explore her intimately. Breaking their kiss, she went up on her knees and watched him watching her. She saw his green eyes darken with desire, passion, and her breath caught at the rush of female power that swept through her.

She wiggled her hips and saw him gasp, closing his eyes as if praying for strength. But his hope went unanswered as she moved again, deliberately lifting her hips high enough to take his body into hers again. Slowly, proudly, she lowered herself onto his length, taking him deep within her. He filled her, reaching into the dark, empty parts of her heart and soul that she'd once feared would always be left wanting.

Her breasts ached for his touch. Her heart ached to hear words he wasn't willing to say.

Nora moved in a slow, rocking motion that set off sparklers of pleasure inside her. She felt the glorious bursts of sensation exploding inside, and even while her brain focused on the pleasure, she tried to memorize it all, to put it down in stone somewhere in her brain. Because she never wanted to forget this moment. The moment when she'd realized her love for Mike and celebrated that love by taking him deeper inside her than she'd ever believed possible.

Mike's hands swept up and down her body. Tweaking her nipples until she arched into his touch, demanding more. In the bright moonlight, her hair shone like silver, her skin gleamed like porcelain, and when she moved on him again, she looked like some otherworldly goddess. His blood boiled, his body ached and his brain shut down. All he could think about was touching her, feeling her, tasting her. He wanted her flat on her back and under him. He wanted to part her legs and taste her secrets. He wanted it all. And he wanted it with Nora.

He'd thought that tonight, he would be the teacher. But instead, she'd taught him just how much he still had to learn. He'd never felt this way before. Never experienced this...connection with any other woman. And now was not the time to try to make sense of it.

Dropping one hand to the spot where their bodies joined, he rubbed her most sensitive spot with a delicate touch that nearly sent her through the ceiling. Her body tightened around him, squeezing him hard and sure in a warm, velvety grip.

And when he couldn't take it another minute, he flipped her onto her back and stared down into her wide, surprised eyes.

"Mike—"

"Nora," he said with a tense smile, "do us both a favor and be quiet."

"Right," she said, and lifted her legs to lock them around his hips. She pulled him against her, moving with his rocking hips, holding on to him, digging her short nails into his back. He felt it all, relished it all. And when the first tremor started inside her, he gave himself up to the same wonder and, with one long thrust, pushed them both over the edge into oblivion.

* * *

An hour or two later...who could be sure?—Nora stumbled from the bedroom into the kitchen. She needed water. And maybe food. She'd never felt so energized and so tired and so...sore in her life. Sex was probably the best exercise in the world. She wondered why no one ever mentioned *that* in all of those videos and books.

She shivered and pulled the edges of Mike's tattered terry-cloth robe tighter around her waist. She'd found the worn black thing hanging on a hook in the master bathroom, and since Mike was still snoozing, she'd helped herself. Nora stubbed her toe as she crossed the hall and did a little half dance as she waited for her toe to stop aching.

"Serves you right for not leaving another light on," she muttered as she rounded a corner into the still brightly lit kitchen. She headed right for the refrigerator and pulled the door open. It was pretty well stocked, considering a man did all the shopping. *And what a man,* she thought as she reached for a fried chicken leg and a bottle of water.

Shutting the refrigerator, she carried her prize to the kitchen table and sat down. She reached for a napkin, then uncapped the bottle of water and took a long, satisfying drink. Her body was still humming and her brain was still trying to decide what to do about the whole "I love Mike" situation when the back door flew open.

Hand at her throat, Nora jumped to her feet just as Rick shouted, "Mike!"

"Oh, my..." Nora's voice trailed off into an embarrassed silence. Not only was she naked under Mike's robe, but the robe was ratty and threadbare and—oh, for heaven's sake. Did it really matter how tacky the robe was?

An instant later, he noticed her. Snatching his hat off, Rick looked her up and down and then quickly ducked his head and shifted his gaze to anywhere but at her. "Sorry, Nora. I uh...didn't know you were here and I..."

Why was *he* embarrassed? At least *he* was dressed!

"What the hell's all the shouting about?" Mike grumbled as he rushed into the kitchen. Bare-chested, he'd taken the time to pull on a pair of jeans, but they were unbuttoned and he was barefoot. His dark hair was ruffled from Nora's crazed fingers and he looked...well, she thought, he looked like he'd just been doing a happy dance on *her*.

Could this get any better?

Rick looked at Mike and scraped one hand over his face. "I'm sorry about interrupting you and—look, I just wanted to tell you that Donna's in labor and we're headed to the hospital. Probably won't be here in the morning."

Mike's gaze shifted from Rick to Nora and back again. Slapping the other man on the back, he said,

"That's great, Rick. Give Donna a good-luck kiss from me."

"I will." Rick deliberately kept his gaze from Nora as he turned and headed back to the door. Before he stepped outside, he said, "'Night, Nora."

Once the back door was closed and they were alone again, Nora glanced at him. "Well, that was fun."

A smile twitched at the corner of his mouth. "You know, even if he hadn't seen you tonight, he would have spotted your car first thing in the morning. He'd have known you spent the night."

"Yeah," she admitted. "But he wouldn't have a mental photo of me in your robe." She ran her fingers down what used to be a lapel. "And speaking of robes, cowboy…you really ought to splurge and buy a new one."

"Why?" he asked, and moved toward her slowly. "From where I'm standing, it looks pretty good."

"Really?"

"Oh, yeah," he assured her. When he stopped directly in front of her, his hands dropped to the knotted belt at her waist. Tugging it open, he pushed the edges of the robe wide and cupped her breasts in his palms.

"Oh, my," Nora sighed, and leaned into him, loving the feel of his fingers on her nipples. The light, teasing touch. The gentle pull and tug on her flesh that brought a wild response to completely unrelated parts of her body.

"You were hungry, huh?" he asked, glancing at the now-forgotten chicken leg on the table.

"Mmm-hmm..."

"Me, too," he murmured, and before she could wonder what he was up to, he'd picked her up and plopped her down on the edge of the table.

"Mike..." Nora's heart rate quickened until she thought it just might leap from her throat—and then where would she be? As he dropped to his knees in front of her, she fought for breath. *What was he...?* She fought for strength. Fought to keep from reaching for him. "Mike, what're you—"

"I told you," he said, and gently parted her thighs, "I just want a little snack."

She gasped as he bent and took her with his mouth. Incredible sensations pooled at her center and then sent long, winding ribbons of need spooling throughout her body. Air staggered in and out of her lungs. She couldn't look away. She watched him as he gave her the most intimate of kisses. She saw him taste her, savor her, and felt herself dissolve in a fresh explosion of desire.

Nora clutched at the edge of the old oak pedestal table. She rocked into him and nearly fell over when she felt his tongue slide across her flesh and dip into the heart of her. Too much, she thought. Too much and not nearly enough. *Never stop,* she silently pleaded. She moaned frantically as he lifted her legs and rested them on his shoulders. His arms came around her bottom and held her firmly in place while his mouth took her places she'd never dreamed existed.

And this time, when she shattered, she wasn't thinking clearly enough to keep her mouth shut. This time when she shouted his name, it changed everything.

"Mike..." she called out, "I love you."

A few minutes later, the words were still hanging in the air like a neon sign. They couldn't be ignored. Mike helped her down from the table, then turned and walked across the room, trying to think of something to say that wouldn't hurt her. But there wasn't a thing he could do to ease this.

"Nora," he said as he trained his gaze on one of the windows and the darkened yard beyond. "I told you before—I'm not the man you need."

He heard her approach, her bare feet making almost no sound on the linoleum. She stood behind him, and he saw her reflection in the window glass. Her eyes looked overly bright and he prayed desperately that it wasn't the gleam of tears he was seeing.

Damn it. He'd blown it good this time. He never should have given into the desire swamping him. He should have sent her home when she showed up in his kitchen looking like every man's fantasy. But to do that he would have had to be a saint. And God knew he was no saint.

She put her hand on his arm, and the warmth of her fingers seemed to spear deeply inside him. It had been so long since he'd felt...anything...that having her touch him so completely was a danger that rocked him even as it enticed him.

"Relax, Mike," she said, smiling, and leaned her forehead against his bare shoulder. "I didn't propose."

"I don't want to hurt you, Nora," he said tightly, and knew he was about to do just that. "But you're making too much of this. It was sex. Great sex, but sex. Desire. Not love."

She didn't say anything, so he kept talking. For the first time in three weeks, she was being quiet. And that pretty much unnerved him. Turning around to face her, he forced himself to look down into her eyes. No tears. Good. "You're a virgin and—"

"*Was* a virgin," she interrupted.

"Exactly. You're emotional. I mean, I'm your first, so you're making more of this than there is."

Nora straightened the robe and tightened the belt around her waist. It couldn't have been easy for a woman to look regal in his worn-out bathrobe. But she managed.

"Don't start treating me like I'm an idiot, Mike, or I'm really going to get mad."

That he didn't need. "Fine. The point is, I like you, Nora. Hell, I'm real fond of you."

"Gee, be still my heart. Oh. Wait a minute. It is."

He ignored the sarcasm and tried again. "You're a hell of a woman, Nora. I admire you a lot. I like spending time with you." He cupped her shoulders and held her in a firm grip that kept him somehow from pulling her close and wrapping his arms around her. "But love's just not in the picture."

Nora looked up at him, saw the regret in his eyes and felt something inside her shatter. Disappointment welled up, sure and strong. For some stupid reason, she'd thought that once she'd said the words, he'd be able to admit that there was more here than desire. But, clearly, he was determined to ignore the very real hum of electricity arcing between them.

Well, fine. But she wouldn't have him feeling sorry for her. She didn't want his sympathy. She wanted his love. And if she couldn't get that, then she wouldn't let him know that it hurt. Sure, she usually believed in honesty. But sometimes even the most honest person had to lie.

Pulling in a deep breath, she blew it out again, met his gaze and told the biggest whopper of her life. "It's okay, Mike. It's not like I want anything from you." She reached up and laid one hand on his cheek. Her heart ached, but her voice was clear. "I love you, but I'll get over it."

He blinked, flinched and shifted position uneasily. Strangely enough, that made her feel better. So she went with it.

''Really. I mean, you were a big help. Now that I'm not a virgin anymore, I'm sure I'll be able to find someone else.''

Did his eyes narrow, or was that wishful thinking?

She rose up on her toes and gave him a brief, hard kiss that practically burned her mouth. ''I'm sure that once I get into the 'swinging single' life, I'll get over you.'' Oh, boy, lying was becoming easier. That couldn't be a good sign.

Nora was amazed that he was buying this. Did he really believe that she could respond to him the way she had and then go to someone else? She'd never forget his touch. Never forget the magic she'd found in his arms. And she couldn't even imagine letting anyone else touch her.

But he didn't need to know that, did he?

''Swinging single?'' he asked tightly, and a muscle in his jaw twitched.

''You know what I mean,'' she said, and ran one hand through her hair as she kept talking. ''I mean, we both knew this was temporary, and I guess I'll have to find my own man after this, because it's probably not a good idea for you and me to keep spending time together and—''

''You're babbling,'' he growled, and pulled her close.

Pressed flat against him, she gloried in the hard, solid strength of him and hoped desperately it wouldn't be for the last time.

His gaze moved over her features. ''If things were different—''

''Things are different,'' she pointed out. ''I'm not Vicky.''

''I know that,'' he snapped. ''But I thought that would work out, too, and it didn't. I can't risk Emily's happiness.''

Damn his ex-wife, Nora thought. The woman was gone, but her legacy lingered. She'd burned Mike so thoroughly he was willing to lock his heart away forever rather than take a chance.

''I'm not asking you to.''

''You're asking for something.''

Yes, she was. She was asking for his heart, but he wasn't ready or willing to give it. So she settled for one more piece of magic. ''Another kiss?'' she said. ''One for the road?''

''Nora—''

''Shut up, cowboy, and kiss me.''

His mouth came down on hers and she gave herself over to the joy of the moment. And when he carried her back down the hall to the bedroom, she tried not to think about the fact that it was probably for the last time.

All night, they came together in a wild tangle of desire and need, and in the morning, when Mike woke up, Nora was gone.

He was alone.

Nora buried herself in pastries.

Well, baking them, anyway.

For the first time in her life, she wasn't hungry. The next few days stumbled along, one after the other, and she told herself that it would get easier. All she had to do was forget Mike.

No problem.

Shouldn't be any more difficult than, say, forgetting how to breathe.

The shop kept her busy during the day, but at night, alone in her house, she felt surrounded by memories. Her body burned for Mike's touch and she caught herself straining to hear the sound of his truck coming down the street. She thought about calling him, but she drew the line at being that pathetic.

She wouldn't become a whiny, needy female. She'd survived twenty-eight years without a man and she could do it again. ''Although,'' she muttered as she pulled yet another pan of cinnamon rolls from the oven, ''it's easy enough to live without something you never had. But once you've had it, you kind of miss it.''

''Talking to yourself again?''

She shot a glance at the swinging door and gave Molly a half smile as she stepped into the kitchen.

''Hi.''

''Wow. Now, there's a greeting designed to make a person feel all warm and toasty.''

''You want warm toast?'' Nora asked, and pointed to another tray. ''There you go.''

Molly shook her head, grabbed a chair and dragged it over to the counter where Nora was busy slicing a log of cookie dough. ''Criminy it's hot in here.'' She tugged at the scoop neck of her tank top.

''Oven,'' Nora said shortly. Her own tank top and shorts helped beat the heat inside the bakery, but in some ways, she found the heat comforting.

''You've been in hiding,'' her friend accused.

''Not hiding,'' Nora told her. ''Just working.''

''You didn't let me know how it went with Mike the other night.''

Nora lifted her gaze to her friend's.

''Ah,'' Molly said sympathetically. ''Not so good.''

''Actually, it was—'' Nora paused, holding the knife's edge on the dough ''—amazing.''

''Congrats. The deed is done.''

''Well and completely done,'' Nora said. ''Several times.''

"Wow." Envy colored Molly's voice.

"Everything was great." She sighed. "Until I told him I loved him."

"Ouch."

"That about sums it up."

Being a true and loyal friend, Molly said the perfect thing. "He's an idiot."

"Agreed," Nora said, and finished her slicing. Then, picking up the slices, she spread them on a cookie sheet with practiced ease. "But he's *my* idiot."

"Uh-huh," Molly said, and reached for one of the still-hot cinnamon rolls. "So, what are you doing about it?"

"I'm letting him miss me."

"Is it working?"

"I miss *him,*" she said. "Does that count?"

Molly pulled off a small piece of the pastry, popped it in her mouth and said thoughtfully, "My guess is, if you're missing him, then he's missing you."

Small consolation, she thought as she turned and slid the cookie tray into the oven. He wasn't missing her enough to come to town. She hadn't seen him or Emily in the last three days.

Nora straightened up, turned around and looked at her friend. "Love's not for sissies, is it?"

Molly shook her head. "Nope. But it's worth it, if you hang in there."

"I don't know, Moll." Nora took a seat opposite

the other woman. Bracing her elbows on the marble counter, she let the coolness slip into her skin and hoped it would chill the fires still burning inside her. "I finally found love—with the one man who doesn't want me."

A hard thing to admit. Her sisters were furious at Mike, her mother was reading the singles ads again and her customers were whispering whenever she walked into the front room. Everyone in Tesoro was talking about her and Mike.

And she didn't care. All she knew was that her business wasn't as much fun if she couldn't tell Mike about her day. Her afternoons dragged on forever because she couldn't go to the ranch to help Mike exercise his horses. Her evenings were empty because she wasn't reading bedtime stories to Emily, tucking her in or getting good-night kisses.

But the nights were the worst. Alone in the dark, she relived that one night with Mike. She recalled every kiss, every touch. What it felt like to stretch out her hand to find him right there. She remembered his heartbeat in the night, his arms closing around her and his body sliding into hers.

Molly suddenly blurred and Nora blinked away the tears welling in her eyes.

"He makes me so mad, Moll," Nora said sadly. "We could have had everything, if he'd just been willing to risk his heart."

Twelve

The longest three days of Mike's life crawled past at a snail's pace.

His mood was black as sin, and anyone with half a brain would have steered clear. But Rick, still flying high from the birth of his son, was apparently oblivious to the warning signs.

''I'm tellin' you, Mike, that boy of mine can eat his weight in formula.''

''Swell.'' Mike concentrated on the fence post, putting his shoulder against it and leaning. The damn thing had to come out before he could replace it—and it looked as though he would be doing all the work around here himself today. He glanced at Rick. The other man was leaning against the truck fender, ankles crossed, arms folded over his chest and a stupid smile on his face.

Funny. Mike had never really noticed just how irritating someone else's happiness could be.

''Donna did a great job,'' Rick was saying, his voice wistful as he strolled down memory lane. ''You should have seen her. No tears. No screams. Some woman down the hall was shouting loud enough to bring down the hospital.''

Mike winced. He remembered Emily's birth clearly, too. Vicky had been that woman screaming. She'd called him every name in the book and then some. She'd screamed at the nurses and the doctors and then hadn't even been interested in her child when she was finally born.

Maybe it would have been better for Vicky if their ''accidental'' pregnancy hadn't happened. But he'd never regret Emily. And, in a way, Emily's birth had cleared the air with Vicky, too. The woman had shown her true colors and then done him the favor of disappearing from his life.

And he and his daughter had been just fine on their own. Until Nora. Mike's mind instantly conjured her laughing image and he gritted his teeth in response. Damn it. He'd been happy. Well, content, at least. And then she'd come along and made him look forward to seeing her. Hearing her.

She'd brought flowers into his house and light into his heart. And damn it...he hadn't *asked* her to.

"Donna was just amazing," Rick was repeating, still awed by the whole miracle of his son's birth.

Caught by the wonder in the other man's voice, Mike found himself imagining what it might have been like if Nora had been Emily's mother. He couldn't picture Nora screaming and cursing at him. He couldn't even pretend to imagine Nora turning away from her child.

He stopped in his efforts to dislodge the fence post and let his mind wander further. He saw images of Nora, pregnant with his child. Nora holding Emily's hand and laughing. The three of them sitting at the kitchen table at dinner. And then his brain picked up speed and apparently decided that if torturing him was the object of this little fantasy, then it ought to do it right.

As clear as day, he saw four or five kids, running wild on the ranch. He saw Nora and him sitting on the porch in the evening, with her on his lap as they laughed at the kids playing with a litter of puppies. In his mind, the old house was lit up like a Christmas tree and the sounds of laughter surrounded it like a protective halo.

Then just as quickly as it came, the vision ended

and he was back in the field, straining against a fence post, listening to Rick ramble. His temper suddenly flared, sharp and hot, and he glared at the other man.

''You gonna help me with this or just stand there holding up that truck all day?''

''Sorry.'' Rick jumped away from the truck, took up a position on the other side of the fence post and started shoving. But while he worked, Rick decided to take his life in his hands. ''Haven't seen Nora in a while,'' he said. ''Everything all right?''

Mike shot him a look that should have fried him. ''Everything's just dandy. Can we work now?''

''Yes, sir, boss.'' Rick ducked his head, but not before Mike saw the flash of annoyance in his friend's eyes.

Great. Now not only was he without Nora, but if this kept up he wouldn't have any friends left, either. Oh, yeah, this was working out fine.

''These cookies are yucky,'' Emily complained, and dropped her half-eaten chocolate chip cookie back into the bag sitting on the front seat of the truck.

''They're your favorite,'' Mike argued.

''Nora's are better.''

Yeah, they were, he silently agreed. He'd taken Emily to a bakery in Monterey, but it just wasn't the same. It had been five days now since he'd seen Nora and Mike was busy convincing himself that it was for the best. To help himself, he'd been avoiding her like the plague. But it just wasn't any good. He could keep from seeing her, but her presence continued to be felt. She'd infiltrated every corner of his world.

Her love for his daughter.

The paintings she'd done with Emily.

Hell, her scent was still lingering in his bedroom.

"Nora says she's gonna help me make a costume for the spring play."

"What?" Mike shifted his brain back into gear and focused on his daughter.

Emily sighed dramatically and gave him one of those patient looks that he swore females were born knowing how to deliver.

"Nora says she's gonna help me—"

"Yeah, I heard that part," he said, wanting to catch his favorite little girl before she launched into a long, detailed explanation. "When did you see Nora?"

"Yesterday," she said, and licked chocolate off her fingertips.

"Yesterday?"

"Uh-huh."

Scowling, Mike asked, "Where did you see her?"

"At school. She comes and has lunch with me."

Nora went to Emily's school? "How long's she been doing this?"

"A *really* long time," Emily said, as if she and

Nora had been doing lunch for centuries. ''I like Nora. She's nice, Daddy.''

Mike just stared at his daughter for a minute. How long had Nora been meeting Emily at school for lunch? Why had no one told *him?* And why was Nora *still* going to the school? Their little bargain was finished. She was no longer a virgin, so the very reason they'd been spending time together was finished. Nora hadn't been to the ranch in five long days. He'd been avoiding her and he was pretty sure she'd been doing the same. But, apparently, she hadn't cut her ties to Emily.

Something warm and bright and a lot like hope rose up inside him. At the same time, he had to face the realization that he'd been a class A jerk. He'd cut Nora off at the knees. Turned his back on what had happened between them because he'd convinced himself it was the only way to protect Emily. But Nora, it seemed, had her own way of taking care of the child. And that involved maintaining ties that Mike had been so intent on cutting.

''Daddy,'' the little girl beside him asked in a voice filled with confusion, ''how come Nora doesn't come out to the ranch anymore?''

Hmm. How to answer that one? The truth? Obviously not. After all, he couldn't very well admit to his only child that she had an idiot for a father. So what could he say?

"Well, Nora's really busy and—"

"Did you ask her to stay with us?" Emily interrupted, and gave him a look that demanded an answer.

"No, honey," he said. "I didn't."

"How come?" she asked, and wiped her mouth, dragging a line of chocolate from her lips halfway up her cheek.

Good question. How come, indeed?

"People won't stay if you don't ask 'em to," she pointed out with all the sweet wisdom of a child.

"I guess you're right," he said. If he had taken Nora's declaration of love and returned it, would she have stayed? Would she have taken a chance on him and a ready-made family?

Hell, he knew the answer to that question without even thinking about it. Of course she would. Nora wasn't Vicky. Nora was funny and smart and kind and she already loved Emily as if she were her own child. And she'd shown *him* more love in the last several weeks than he'd known in years.

A knot formed in the pit of his stomach, and he had to grit his teeth to keep from spitting at himself in disgust. He'd blown it. Big time. He'd been so busy protecting himself and using Emily as an excuse for hiding from the world that he'd missed his chance at *real* love. The happily-ever-after kind.

And he had only himself to blame for it.

Damn it, he'd lost at love before and been burned badly enough to convince him to avoid it. But it had found him again, anyway—he'd just been too damn scared to risk it. And this time, the pain of losing what he might have had was so much worse. Because what he felt for Nora was so much bigger and deeper than anything he'd ever known before.

Grumbling under his breath, he fired up the engine. "Fasten your seat belt, Em," he said.

"Are we gonna go see Nora?" she asked hopefully, and snapped the strap into the buckle.

"Nope," he said, and watched her face fall. Reaching over, he tipped her chin up with the tips of his fingers and smiled at her. "*You're* going home. *I'm* going to see Nora." Some things you just had to do on your own. Though he thought he might stand a better chance of winning Nora over if Emily was with him, Mike discarded the notion. He wanted her to take *him.* Not just his child. He knew she loved Emily.

Now he had to know if she still *loved* him enough to give him a second chance.

"Are you gonna ask her to stay with us, Daddy?"

Ask.

Beg.

Argue.

Whatever it took, he told himself, and steered the truck into traffic.

* * *

Nora looked around at her customers, then shifted her gaze to the wide front window that opened onto Main street. Spring sunshine sprinkled the ground like a promise of coming summer.

The crowds were thick, business was brisk, and all Nora wanted to do was close up shop and head out to the ranch. She leaned her elbows on the counter and brought up the image of her watching Mike working on his horses. If she tried, she could almost feel the sun on her face and hear the wind brushing through the trees. Imaginary Mike turned and gave her a blinding smile that sent bolts of heat shooting through her bloodstream.

"Well, hi Nora," a deep voice murmured from close by.

She jerked out of her lovely daydream to face Bill Hammond. His interested brown gaze swept over her quickly and thoroughly, and Nora felt the sudden urge to cross her arms over her breasts.

"Hi, Bill. What can I get for you?" She nearly winced at the simple question she asked daily.

"Well, now," Bill said as he leaned over the top of the glass display case and gave her a look she was willing to bet he considered one of his best *"Hello Baby"* come-ons.

"I can think of quite a few things that you could get for me."

Nora plastered a polite smile on her face but inwardly hurried him along. Her heart just wasn't in the flirting mood anymore.

Mike stood outside the bakery and rehearsed for the tenth time in the last fifteen minutes exactly what he wanted to say to Nora. That was assuming she'd be in the mood to listen to him at all.

Finally, he decided to just go with his gut. He reached for the doorknob. That's when he spotted Bill leaning in toward Nora and leering at her. A string of warning bells went off in Mike's mind. If he didn't fight for what he wanted *now,* then he'd spend the rest of his life regretting it. Mike watched Bill trying to make one of his patented moves, and in response, frustration and anger bubbled together inside him.

This was his future. If he couldn't convince Nora that he did love her, then he was going to be sentenced to seeing her with some other guy. A guy who would have the right to hold her, love her. A guy who would hear her secrets and share her dreams.

A guy who wasn't him.

Jerking the door open, Mike stepped inside. Ignoring the roomful of customers sitting at the small tables, he stalked directly to the counter.

Nora's gaze snapped to his, but she managed to hide whatever she was feeling. And that worried him. Still, just looking into those blue eyes of hers was enough to convince him to stand his ground and fight for the chance to win her back.

But first things first.

Mike dropped one hand on Bill's shoulder. When the other man shot him a wary glance, Mike said shortly, "Get lost, Bill."

"What?" The man pulled away and took a step back. "You can't make me leave. This is Nora's place and I'm a customer."

All around them, people were beginning to stare. Mike felt their interested gazes but couldn't seem to care.

"The only one around here who could make me leave is Nora," Bill said.

Both men looked at her.

Nora stared at Mike. "Get lost, Bill."

Clearly disgusted, the man slapped both hands on the display case, did a quick U-turn and stormed out. In the stunned silence that followed his exit, Mike kept his gaze locked on Nora as he walked around the counter, came right up to her and took her face between his palms. He kissed her hard and long and deep, and put everything he felt, everything he'd just discovered, into the effort.

When the applause from the customers started, he broke the kiss, and ignoring the crowd, he said, "I need to talk to you."

She swayed a little, but, then, Mike's kisses always

made her a little wobbly. Add that to the complete shock of having him stride into the shop and kiss her in front of God and everyone, and was it any wonder she was a little shaky? And now he wanted to talk. Talk about what? That he wanted her? That he missed her? All good things, but she wanted more. Now she had to find out how badly Mike wanted her. She rubbed her fingers across her mouth, took a slow, deep breath and said, ''So talk.''

Mike glanced at the customers. ''In private.''

Private. When the whole town knew what had been going on between them. She glanced at the customers watching them with avid interest and then looked back at Mike. Whatever he had to say to her, he could say here. In front of witnesses. ''Nope.''

''No?''

Someone behind him chuckled.

Nora shook her head and stuck to her guns. ''If you've got something to say to me, just say it.''

Mike scraped one hand across his face, then rubbed his neck. ''Not going to make this easy, are you?''

''Nothing worth having is easy, Mike,'' she said.

''Okay, fine.'' He nodded, waved one hand at the customers and said, ''If you need to hear me say this in front of the whole damn town, then that's just what I'll do.''

''I'm listening,'' she said, keeping her gaze locked on his.

"I was wrong," he blurted, figuring the best way to start was to admit the worst right up front.

"Wrong about what?"

"Hell, you name it," he muttered.

"No, Mike," she said, and tilted her head to one side, watching him carefully, "I think you should."

"You're right." He laughed shortly, shook his head and threw his hands high before letting them slap against his thighs. "Again. You were right about everything else, too."

Nora's eyes sparkled and her smile widened. That small bubble of hope that had risen in her the moment he walked into the shop now seemed to fill her heart. "So far, I like this talk."

"There's more," he promised, and reached for her.

His hands came down on her shoulders, his fingers pressing into her skin, driving wedges of heat deep into every corner of her soul.

"I finally figured it out, Nora," he said, and his voice dropped to the low, husky tone that had haunted her dreams. "I need you."

Nora swallowed hard and bit down on her bottom lip to keep herself from talking. Now was the time to just listen and pray that he said what she needed to hear.

"Nothing that happened before you matters. Everything's better with you. *I'm* better with you." He rubbed his hands up and down her arms, creating a physical link between them that reached into her soul and locked on. ''I *love* you, Nora.''

She inhaled sharply, sweetly, and savored the words she'd hoped to hear.

''I didn't expect to—didn't want to.'' He shook his head and held her tighter, as if she might try to escape him. ''But it's there, Nora. It's real and it's more than I ever thought I could feel.''

Biting her lip was getting harder and harder. But she needed to hear one more thing, so she kept quiet.

''Marry me, Nora. Marry me and build a family with me. Be Emily's mother and help me give her brothers and sisters.''

Nora released a breath she hadn't even realized she'd been holding. Suddenly, her world looked brighter. She could see the future she'd always wanted, stretching out in front of her. She looked up into those forest-green eyes of his and, for the first time, she saw love shining there. And still, she heard herself ask, ''Before I answer you, I have to know, Mike. What changed your mind?''

He shot a quick glance at the people watching them, then shifted Nora to one side so that his back was to their audience and only he could see her face. ''I finally understood something very simple.''

''What?''

''I was...afraid to love you.'' He blew out a rush of breath as if admitting that had taken a lot out of him. But once he started, he kept talking. ''I was scared to believe again. To take a chance again. And then today I realized that if I don't take the risk, then I'll lose you.'' He pulled her close and wrapped his arms around her tightly. When she tipped her face up to his, he said softly, ''And living without you is just not something I want to do.''

''Mike, I—''

He grinned down at her. ''Hey, I know what it's cost you to be quiet for the last few minutes. But keep it up until I can do this right, okay?''

Nora clamped her mouth shut, smiled through her tears and nodded.

''I love you, Nora,'' he said, and she read the truth in his eyes. ''Will you marry me?''

''Can I talk now?''

''That depends on what you want to say.''

''I want to say yes, cowboy.''

That grin of his widened and her stomach did that oh-so-familiar pitch and roll.

''Then talk, Nora.''

''Yes.''

His arms tightened around her as he lifted her off her feet. ''I think that's the shortest speech I've ever heard from you.''

She wrapped her arms around his neck and planted a quick, hard kiss on his mouth. Then, smiling, she said, ''Well, don't get used to it, because I have to tell you, it about killed me to be quiet this long when I have so much to tell you and ask you—like how's Emily and would she like to be a flower girl and—''

Mike laughed. ''You're babbling, Nora.''

''Then kiss me, cowboy. And don't you dare ever stop.''

He claimed that kiss.

And the crowd went wild.

* * * * *

A Cowboy's Pursuit

ANNE McALLISTER

Dear Reader,

If anyone had ever told me I'd write fifty books, I wouldn't have believed them. There was a time I didn't think I'd get through the first one!

It seemed so daunting – trusting two characters I barely knew to find their way to true love and take me along for the ride. What if they got lost? I wondered. What if they expected *me* to help them find their way? What if they decided they couldn't stand each other? Or, worse, what if they fell madly in love on page nineteen? What was I going to do for another one hundred and seventy or so pages?

But the desire to find out what happened between those two people was greater than the fears about the answers to those questions. And so I began…

A year later (it takes longer when you only write during your two-year-old's naptime), I had a book. Amazed and pleased, I sent it off to a publisher and did the smartest thing I've done in my career – I started another book. I stopped thinking about the first one and got busy on the second. I found new characters to fascinate me, a new story to develop, and I started to write.

I've been doing that now for a lot of years. The two-year-old grew up. Lots of characters have told me their stories and I've enjoyed a lot of happily-ever-afters. But the most exciting one is always the one I'm working on now.

I hope you enjoy Jace's pursuit of Celie in my latest story, *A Cowboy's Pursuit*. He's been in love with her almost as long as I've been writing books, and he's finally going to get a chance to win her! Meanwhile, I'll be at work on the next one.

I couldn't possibly write a hundred, could I?

All the best,

Anne McAllister

ANNE McALLISTER

RITA® Award-winning author Anne McAllister has never managed to pigeonhole the sorts of stories she likes to write. You can write to her at PO Box 3904, Bozeman, MT 59772, USA (SAE with return postage appreciated) or e-mail her at anne@annemcallister.com, she promises to answer. Even if you don't write, drop by and visit her at www.annemcallister.com. You're always welcome!

For Lyle May,
cowboy and friend

One

The slam of the back door stirred Artie Gilliam from his catnap in the armchair in his living room. He blinked, glanced at his watch, then frowned as he heard booted feet cross the kitchen and stomp in his direction.

"Bit early for lunch, ain't it?" he said when Jace Tucker appeared, glowering from the doorway. "Or did my watch stop?" His daddy had given it to him right after the First World War and Artie supposed it could have given up the ghost by now, but he hoped it hadn't. He was counting on something outlasting his ninety-year-old bones.

"I didn't come for lunch," Jace growled. He stalked into the room, still scowling, his hands jammed into the pockets of his jeans, his shoulders hunched. He strode clear to the end of the room before he turned and nailed Artie with a glare. "She's back."

"She," Artie echoed with interest. It wasn't a question. He knew damned well which "she" Jace meant.

As far as Jace Tucker was concerned, there was only one female in the whole universe: Celie O'Meara. Not that Jace had ever said as much to him. Or to anyone.

If there was ever anyone more likely to make a hash of his love life—besides himself, Artie reckoned, and that had been a good sixty-odd years ago now—it was Jace. For a smart, good-lookin' feller who oughta be able to sweep a woman off her feet without half tryin', Jace didn't have the skills of a push broom.

Artie sighed inwardly and shook his head.

Misinterpreting the head shake, Jace enlightened him. "Celie," he spat.

"Ayah." Artie tried to look as if he hadn't already figured that out. He smiled gently. "How nice."

Jace's shoulders seemed to tighten more. "Ha," he said. He did another furious lap around the living room. The young fool would wear out the rug at the rate he was going, and that would be something else that wouldn't survive him, Artie thought glumly.

Now he raised his brows. "Thought you was lookin' forward to her comin' back."

Jace, being Jace, of course, hadn't said anything of the sort.

But every day when he'd come back from working at the hardware store or from training horses out at the ranch, he'd asked if Artie had heard from any of Celie's family. The whole O'Meara clan had gone to Hawaii ten days ago for the wedding of Celie's sister, Polly, to Sloan Gallagher.

Artie was sorry he'd missed it, but the ol' ticker had durn near give out on him this past winter, and the doc had said he wasn't up for flying halfway around the world yet. Didn't matter, really, as they'd kept him posted. He'd heard all about the wedding on the beach and the party with Sloan's film crew afterwards, and he'd always shared the news with Jace.

He'd relayed every scrap of information he'd got after phone calls from Celie's mother, Joyce; from Polly and Sloan; from Polly's oldest daughter, Sara; and once from Celie herself.

''Huh,'' Jace had said when Artie told him about Celie's phone call. ''Managed to tear herself away from all those beach bums long enough to see if you were still among the livin', did she?''

Artie had grinned. ''She's a sweetheart, all right,'' he had agreed, knowing that wasn't what Jace had meant at all.

Jace had scowled then.

Jace was scowling now, hands jammed in the pockets of his jeans as he rocked back on the heels of his well-worn cowboy boots.

''Reckoned you'd be glad to see her,'' Artie said, lifting a quizzical brow.

''That was when I thought she'd come to her senses!'' Jace's boots came down flat with a thump.

''What do you mean?'' Artie frowned. ''She didn't cause no problems at Polly and Sloan's weddin', did she?''

Everyone in Elmer knew that Celie had had a crush on cowboy-turned-actor Sloan Gallagher for years. She'd even bid her life's savings to win a Hollywood weekend with him at that cowboy auction they'd held back in February.

What's more, she'd won! But if she'd gone out there starry-eyed over Sloan—and Artie wasn't absolutely sure she had—she'd sure seemed to come back cured. She'd had nothing but good things to say about Sloan, but she'd treated him more like a brother after that.

And a good thing, too, as Sloan had been sweet on her sister, Polly. It could have been sticky, but it hadn't been. Far as he knew Celie had been delighted to be asked to be the maid of honor at Polly and Sloan's wedding.

"She behaved herself at the weddin', didn't she?" he demanded now.

"Guess so." Jace turned and glowered out the window. He rubbed the back of his neck, clenched his fists at his sides, then hunched his shoulders again. To an old rough-stock rider like Artie, he looked exactly like a bull about to blow.

"She ain't gone back to hankerin' after Matt Williams!" he said, aghast.

Matt Williams had jilted Celie ten years ago. At the time she'd been little more than a child—barely twenty and besotted with a foolish footloose boy who didn't know a good thing when he had it. But telling her so hadn't helped. Matt's rejection had liked to killed her. It had sure as shootin' made her scared of trustin' men.

To Artie's way of thinking, if you got bucked off, you had to just get right back on again, meet other guys, go out on dates. But Celie hadn't seen it that way. She'd holed up with her magazines and her videos and had spent the past ten years dreamin' about Sloan Gallagher.

As far as Artie knew, she hadn't had a date since Matt had dumped her—not until February, anyway, when she'd got up the gumption to bid on Sloan. Of course by then Sloan had already set his sights on Polly.

Artie hoped to goodness that, her dreams of Sloan thwarted, she hadn't decided to start thinking about Matt again.

"Make more sense if she had," Jace muttered.

That made Artie's brows lift. "Since when did you become a Matt Williams fan?"

They'd been buddies back then, of course, Jace and Matt—traveling partners, in fact—going down the road from rodeo to rodeo. But Jace hadn't agreed with Matt's way of breaking his engagement. Of course, that could have been because he'd left it up to Jace to call Celie and tell her it was off.

"Matt's a jerk," Jace said now. He yanked off his straw cowboy hat and raked a hand through his hair. "But then we all know that."

Artie had a terrible thought. "She didn't get engaged to no surfer!"

Jace snorted. He scowled. He strangled the brim of his hat. "No."

"Well then, what the devil's the problem? She's back. It's what you been waitin' for." He held up a hand to forestall Jace's protest. "Don't tell me you two are fightin' already?"

It wasn't any secret that Celie and Jace didn't see eye-to-eye. Course that was on account of Celie always having been a sweet, proper-brought-up girl and Jace being something of a hell-raiser. And if that hadn't been enough, Artie knew Celie had always considered Jace the inspiration for Matt's going astray.

"Matt's role model," she'd called him. *Role model* was one of the nicer terms she'd used.

And there was some truth to her accusation. Any young cowpoke with a hankering for women and the wild side could've learned a few things from Jace Tucker. Even now he still liked to have a good time. But he'd settled down a good bit, to Artie's way of thinking.

The Jace he'd got to know over these past few months drank a few beers and shot a few games of pool at the Dew Drop, but he never came home drunk—and he *always* came home. Didn't bring no girls with him, either.

He was true to Celie. Not that she knew it.

Jace wasn't the sort of feller who wore his heart on his sleeve. Most of the time, Artie reckoned, the young fool had it wrapped up in barbed wire and duct tape and buried it under six feet of sarcasm. So it wasn't real surprising that Celie didn't think he had one.

"You two," Artie muttered, shaking his head in dismay as Jace began pacing again, "are enough to try the patience of a saint. You ain't seen her but a few minutes this morning, Jace! You couldn't have, bein's how it's only just past ten o'clock. So what the dickens has she done to tick you off now?"

"She's leavin'!"

"What?"

"You heard me. She's leavin'!" Jace looked halfway between angry and anguished. His blue eyes, generally light and sunny as a summer sky, were now the color of a storm. He flung his battered hat onto the davenport and cracked his knuckles furiously.

"What the devil do you mean, she's leavin'? Where in tarnation would she go?"

"Remember her singles cruise?" Jace fairly spat the words.

Artie's eyes bugged. Of course he remembered the singles cruise. When Celie had come home from her weekend in Hollywood with Sloan, heart whole and over her crush at last, she'd been determined to get on with her life.

Jace, who had darned near driven Artie crazy all the time she was gone, had barely breathed a sigh of relief when he'd discovered that just because Celie was over Sloan, it didn't mean she was going to fall into *his* arms.

No sir. Instead in April she'd gone on a singles cruise.

"What the hell does she need a singles cruise for?" Jace had wanted to know. He'd been doin' laps in the living room then, too.

"What indeed," Artie had murmured, "when she's got a single feller who loves her right here?"

Jace had stopped dead at that. He'd spun around and

leveled a glare at Artie. ''What the hell are you talkin' about?''

Artie, no fool but no chicken, either, had shrugged lightly. ''Seems to me it's obvious,'' he'd said.

A muscle had ticked furiously in Jace's jaw. He'd ground his teeth, but he hadn't denied it. He'd rubbed a hand against the back of his neck and had shaken his head as if to clear it. And then he'd dug the toe of his boot into the rug and muttered, ''Damn fool thing to do.''

''Is this the singles cruise we're talkin' about or you bein' in love with Celie?'' Artie had asked with a smile.

''What do you think?'' Jace had muttered.

He was muttering again now.

''Don't see how she can go on another one,'' Artie said. ''Them things are expensive.''

''She can afford it,'' Jace said through his teeth, ''if they hire her.''

''Hire her?''

''That's what she came in this morning to say. Just waltzed in, pretty as you please, and handed in her notice. 'Just wanted you to know I'll be leavin' in two weeks,''' Jace mimicked Celie's soft tones. '''Got a job on a cruise ship,''' Jace went on in the same furious sing-song voice, '''so I won't be around to annoy you anymore.''' He slammed his fist into his palm to punctuate the end of the quote.

Artie's heart kicked over in his chest. It worried him a little when his heart did that, but not as much as he was worried about Jace. And about what Jace would do now.

Artie might be closing in on ninety-one, but he wasn't dead yet. He remembered what it felt like to look at a woman and want her. He remembered what that hungry, hollow feeling was like, how it made a guy follow a woman with his eyes and fall over his own feet if he wasn't careful. He'd done it a time or two himself.

That was one of the reasons, after his heart attack, that he'd taken Jace on to work for him. To give him a chance.

Even though she had her own business—C&S Spa and Video, where she cut hair and gave therapeutic massages and Sara, her niece, rented videos—she still came in most mornings and worked at the hardware store with him.

Artie knew she could have handled the store when he'd had his heart attack. That was the kind of girl Celie was—thoughtful, generous, kind—the sort who'd do an old man a favor, who'd help out wherever she could. The sort of gal who would make somebody a good wife.

Who would make Jace Tucker a good wife.

When Artie saw that Jace was sweet on her, Artie reckoned the least he could do was to throw them together. So he had.

He'd got Jace to fill in for him when he was in the hospital. He'd acted weaker and more frail than he really was when he came home, all so's those two could spend some time together and get their love life sorted out.

But they hadn't.

Two more stubborn people than Celie O'Meara and Jace Tucker—when it came to falling in love—would be hard to find. Celie persisted in believing that Jace was no different than he had been at twenty-three, and Jace persisted in remaining stubbornly silent instead of admitting how he felt. They'd been working together four months now, almost five. And as far as Artie could see, things had gone from bad to worse.

Well, maybe Celie's new job would be the wake-up call, Artie thought, taking a deep breath and sitting up straight. Maybe Jace would finally say something that would stop her from going.

''So,'' Artie challenged him, ''what're you gonna do about it?''

Jace slapped his hat back on his head and jerked it down

hard. ''Get drunk,'' he said furiously. ''Then go find me some other girl!''

He turned on his heel and banged out the door. All the windows rattled.

Artie sighed and shook his head. Life really was wasted on the young.

For as long as she could remember, Celie O'Meara had been in love with the idea of love and marriage. As a little girl, she'd played ''wife'' and ''mommy'' while Polly and Mary Beth had played cowboys and Indians and doctor and nurse. It was possible, she thought when she was being brutally honest with herself, that she'd still been ''playing'' the role when, at nineteen, she'd got engaged to Matt.

She hadn't thought so at the time, of course. She'd thought she loved Matt Williams. Worse, she'd thought he loved her.

She had been devastated when he'd jilted her. Her world had come crashing down. All her hopes, her dreams, her expectations had been destroyed. She'd felt like a fool.

Even more, she'd felt like a failure. In Celie's mind, Matt's rejection had publicly branded her as a woman unable to satisfy a man.

''You've just got to meet some other guys,'' her sister Mary Beth had said, doing her best to console her.

''Better guys,'' her sister Polly had insisted firmly.

''Exac'ly. It's like fallin' off a horse,'' Artie Gilliam had told her. ''You jest gotta pick yerself up an' get back on.''

''Of course you do. And you will. You'll find the right man someday,'' her mother had said, then she'd given Celie a hug of encouragement.

But Celie wouldn't even look. She wasn't about to ''get back on.'' She'd been humiliated once. She'd trusted a man. She'd given him her heart and he'd trampled it into the dirt. Get back on and let another one do the same thing?

No way. Once was enough for any lifetime, thank you very much.

But even though she'd vowed never to trust another man, her old dreams of love and marriage had died hard. In fact they hadn't died at all. And even though Celie had given up on "real men," she'd kept her fantasies.

Like Sloan Gallagher.

Sloan was everything she'd ever dreamed of in a man. He was handsome. Strong. Brave. Resolute. Clever. Determined. Sexy.

But mostly he had been safe.

She'd seen him in theaters and on television, had read about him in magazines and allowed herself to imagine what loving him would be like. It had been wonderful—because it had been impossible—until Sloan agreed to come to Elmer for the Great Montana Cowboy Auction to save Maddie Fletcher's ranch.

Then Celie's fantasy world had collided with her real one. Her two-dimensional Sloan was in danger of becoming a real person. Her dreams were no longer merely dreams, they were possibilities—if she let them be. For weeks before the auction they had tormented her, taunted her, challenged her. And in wrestling with them, she'd realized what a hollow empty place her real life had become. She might have been able to ignore that realization, to pretend it didn't matter—if it hadn't been for Jace Tucker.

She might have been able to ignore herself—but she couldn't ignore Jace.

No one *ever* ignored Jace!

He was too vital, too intense, too…too everything. She remembered him from childhood, watching him from afar, always aware of him—*wary* of him—because he seemed different. Fascinating. Bigger, tougher, louder, rougher. Alien. Other.

Unlike Polly, who had been her dad's sidekick, and Mary

Beth, who had tagged along after them, Celie had always been a ''girly'' girl. She'd never been entirely comfortable at the brandings, hanging around the fire teasing with the cowboys. She'd never wrestled with the boys on the playground. She'd liked Matt because he hadn't been as rough as some of them. He'd been quieter. Gentler.

A man after her own heart, she'd thought.

But even Matt had rejected her.

And it had been all Jace Tucker's fault! Matt had come home from the Wilsall Rodeo that summer, saying he'd been talking to Jace and he was thinking maybe he'd go down the road with Jace for a spell.

''Sow me a few wild oats,'' he'd said with a grin, ''before you tie me down.''

She should have worried then, but she hadn't. She hadn't believed he really meant it. But she also hadn't been thrilled about him going down the road with Jace Tucker.

''Don't let Jace lead you astray,'' she'd warned him.

And Matt had laughed. ''No fear.''

But it turned out that all her fears had been realized when two months later Matt hadn't come home to get married. Instead, fifteen minutes before the ceremony was to start, Jace Tucker had called to say Matt wasn't coming.

''He says he's not ready,'' Jace had told her.

''What do you mean, not ready?'' Celie could still remember her high, tight voice. But even then she'd been like an ostrich, head in the sand, believing that Jace must mean that Matt simply hadn't figured out how to tie his tie or button his suit coat yet.

''To get hitched,'' Jace had spelled it out. ''He says he can't do it. That he's got places to go, things to do, to see...'' Jace's voice had faded, and there had been a considerable pause during which he obviously expected her to say something.

But Celie had been incapable of speech.

She'd been strangling the receiver in disbelief. There were close to a hundred people just up the street going into the church at that very moment, for goodness' sake!

Her mother had been calling to her to get off the phone and hurry up. Her dad had been standing in the doorway wearing a wholly uncharacteristic suit and tie of his own as he'd grinned at her.

But Celie hadn't grinned back. She'd stood there staring at the phone in disbelief, listening to Jace Tucker sigh and mutter under his breath, then say, ''For crying out loud, Celie, say something!''

''It's a lie,'' Celie had said, because that was all she could think right then. This was Jace, after all! She knew Jace would think getting married was a joke. She hated him right then more than she'd ever hated anyone.

''It's not a lie, Celie,'' he'd said, his voice harsh. ''Matt isn't coming! He doesn't want to get married. Call the wedding off.''

Mortified, she'd banged down the receiver. Then, numbly, she'd done exactly that. And all the while she'd burned with a white-hot fury at Jace's impatience. As if she should have known! As if she should have been expecting it. As if it were obvious that no man in his right mind would want to marry her!

Jace hadn't even said he was sorry.

Why should he be? He'd been with Matt the last time they'd come through Elmer. He'd stood in the kitchen, shifted from one booted foot to the other, impatient to be gone, barely even looking at her. He'd obviously thought she was a loser from the very start. And somehow he'd managed to convince Matt.

He'd influenced Matt. *Inspired* Matt!

And Celie still resented that. But mostly she resented Jace because every time she saw him she was reminded of her failure.

She was not the person she wanted to be. She was a reasonably successful businesswoman. She was the owner of Elmer's only hair salon and video store. She was a volunteer at the library, the doting aunt of six nieces and a nephew, and the person that Sid the cat liked better than anyone else on earth.

But she didn't have a boyfriend. Or a husband. Or a child.

She wasn't a wife. Or a mother.

She was a reject. And every time she saw Jace Tucker, she remembered that.

For most of the past ten years she hadn't had to see him. Footloose rodeo cowboys like Jace didn't hang around hair salons in Elmer, even if their sister and her family still lived on the family ranch five miles north of town. A year could go by and she might only catch a glimpse of him once or twice.

She heard about him now and then, of course. She knew he'd done well over the years in rodeo. He'd never been the world-champion bronc rider like Noah Tanner, who lived west of Elmer. But he'd got to the National Finals several years, and this past year Celie knew he'd gone to Las Vegas in the number-one spot.

''Jace says this is his year,'' his sister, Jodie, who was Celie's age, had said proudly when she'd come into The Spa just before Thanksgiving to get her hair cut. ''Maybe if he wins in Vegas next month at the NFR he'll retire and move back to town.''

Celie's heart had jerked in her chest at the very thought of running into Jace Tucker every time she turned around. But she hadn't said a word. She'd kept right on clipping, pleased that at least her fingers hadn't jerked.

''Maybe he'll be ready to settle down,'' Jodie had speculated. ''Find himself a good woman and have a passel of kids.''

Celie couldn't help snorting at that.

Jodie had looked in the mirror and their eyes had met. She'd smiled mischievously. "Maybe I'll send him around."

"No, thanks," Celie had said as fast as she could get the words out of her mouth.

"You used to think he was sort of cute," Jodie reminded her. That was the trouble with living in the same place your whole life. People remembered all kinds of foolishness—like the fact that in sixth grade at a slumber party Celie had once let slip that she'd thought Jodie's big brother was kind of cute.

"I've developed a bit of taste since then," Celie had said sharply.

Jodie's brows lifted at Celie's tone. "He's not that bad," she'd defended her brother.

You could also count on Jodie *not* remembering that Jace had been the one who'd broken the news to Celie about Matt. Unless he hadn't told her.

Of course he'd told her! Celie couldn't imagine that he wouldn't have. But she didn't say anything. She made herself focus on Jodie's hair again, only replying, "I'm not interested in your brother."

She had, however, said a fleeting prayer that Jace Tucker would *not* become the World Champion Bronc Rider in December. And she remembered feeling a momentary pang of guilt when a couple of weeks later she heard that he'd been injured at the NFR. She hadn't wanted him to win, but she hadn't expected he'd wind up in the hospital.

Not that it had been *her* fault!

If her God were the sort who exacted divine retribution for such selfish behavior, though, putting Jace to work in the hardware store after Artie had his heart attack would have been right up His alley. But if Celie wasn't blaming herself for Jace's getting injured, she could hardly blame

God for Jace being in the store on that January day when Artie had had his attack or for his being with her at the hospital when the old man had been determined to have someone take over the store.

It hadn't been necessary!

Heaven knew she could have handled the hardware store herself. She'd said so. But Artie hadn't listened. He was stubborn and set in his ways, and even though he counted on Celie and her mother and her sister and nieces to do a lot of things, he was obviously old-fashioned enough to think a man ought to be in charge.

He'd thought *Jace* ought to be in charge!

Since then she'd had to deal with Jace Tucker. And it was having to deal with Jace on a daily basis that had made her furious enough to bid on Sloan.

Seeing Jace day after day, being treated to his teasing, his knowing winks and gleeful grins had driven her right up the wall. A day hadn't gone by that he hadn't made some remark about Sloan Gallagher—and her!

Celie had seethed and fumed. She'd felt first hollow and then angry and then desperate. She'd tried to cling to her dreams, but reality—and Jace—had kept getting in the way.

As the Valentine cowboy auction had drawn closer, Jace had even turned up in her dreams as often as Sloan! It was transference, she'd assured herself. He was good-looking, damn him, though she'd never ever admit that out loud. He had thick dark hair and blue eyes very much like Sloan's. But while Sloan's were warm and tender—at least in his films—Jace's laughed and crinkled at the corners whenever he grinned and teased her, which was almost all the time.

Celie wanted to throw things at him. She wanted to kick his shins. Mostly she tried to stay out of his way. But that didn't mean she didn't notice him.

How could she not?

And when he wasn't teasing her about Sloan, he was

busy flirting with all the women who came into the store. There were, it seemed, hundreds of them. Not just the locals girls, whom he flirted with as a matter of course, but all the ones who'd come to Elmer to bid on Sloan.

"You'd think they came to bid on you," she'd said to him once.

"I'm not for sale," he'd said smugly.

"No one would buy you," she'd retorted.

Jace had just laughed. But Celie hadn't thought it was funny. She also knew it wasn't true. If Jace Tucker had been auctioned off, she was quite sure lots of women would bid on him. He'd certainly had plenty of women clamoring to stay with him in the extra rooms at Artie's house while they waited for the auction.

Celie had muttered something disparaging about Jace and his harem in the days right before it.

He'd just laughed. "Jealous? Want to join?"

"Never!" Celie had snapped. "I won't share my man."

"If you ever get another one," Jace said. He'd said, "Sorry," quick enough right after, when he'd seen the look on her face.

But the shock of what he'd said had struck her to the core.

And that was when Celie had actually begun to consider bidding on Sloan. At first the idea was so wild and preposterous that she couldn't believe she'd ever thought it. But the more she did think about it, the more she realized that she had to do something. If she didn't, they'd be nailing her in her coffin and they'd write on her tombstone, "Here Lies Cecilia O'Meara—She Died Before She Lived."

And Celie wanted to live.

Fantasies weren't enough anymore. Dreams didn't suffice.

And so, on the day of the auction, she'd mustered her

courage, marched into the town hall and had bid her bank balance on Sloan Gallagher down to the last red cent. She'd won. She'd been panic-stricken.

And yet, it had been worth it—just to see the look of utter disbelief on Jace Tucker's face.

The memory of it could still make her smile. It had been so supremely satisfying, so uplifting, so utterly pleasurable. It was actually addictive, she discovered, the joy of shocking Jace. She'd wanted to do it again.

Of course if Sloan had fallen in love with her, no doubt she would have seen Jace's jaw dragging on the ground. But Sloan hadn't.

And just as well, because while she liked him a lot, she found that she didn't love him.

Certainly not the way her sister Polly loved him. And not the way Sloan loved Polly.

But seeing them, she knew she wanted that kind of love. She didn't want to be alone for the rest of her life, didn't want to be a spinster hairdresser with no one to love but her cats.

So she made up her mind to keep looking.

Going on a singles cruise in April had been a step in that direction. It had been so completely different from her landlocked, down-home existence that it had seemed like the next logical step for a woman who was trying to jump-start her life.

And it had had the added advantage of flabbergasting Jace Tucker once again.

"A *singles* cruise?" He'd stared at her as if she'd announced that she was going to dance naked on the counter in the middle of Gilliam's Hardware Store. As if a singles cruise was out of the question for a woman like her.

As if she wouldn't know what to do there!

Celie had known what to do. And if she had been scared spitless the day she'd boarded that giant ship in Miami, she'd soon discovered that it wasn't as terrifying as she'd imagined. She'd discovered that the skills she'd developed while talking to people when she cut their hair were useful when she wanted to meet new people, when she wanted to meet *men.*

She'd met quite a few men. She was still wary. Still nervous around them. But she was never as nervous with any other man as she was around Jace Tucker. She'd hoped the cruise would cure that.

But it hadn't. She'd hoped he'd go back to the ranch and she wouldn't see him and it wouldn't matter. But he hadn't done that, either.

''Artie wants me to stay,'' he'd said. ''And Ray and Jodie's is a little too small for us all. I'll stay with Artie while I'm building my place.''

His place. He was settling down, just the way Jodie had said. He'd told Celie so himself. He'd even implied he had a particular woman in mind. But he wouldn't tell her who.

And Celie couldn't guess. It seemed to her that every time she saw him he was with someone else—from her niece Sara to the actress Tamara Lynd, who'd been one of the women staying with him during the auction.

Was it Tamara? She refused to ask. But she didn't want to be around to watch, either. And that was when she'd decided that a job on a cruise ship might not be a bad idea. So she'd set about making it happen.

She was thirty. She wanted a life. She wanted a husband. A family. And taking a job on a cruise ship had seemed as good a way as any to make that happen. So she'd applied and crossed her fingers and hoped.

And last night when she'd got back from Sloan and Polly's wedding, there it was—the job offer she'd been waiting for. The very thought of going terrified her.

But more than that it gave her enormous pleasure—especially this morning when she'd told Jace Tucker she was leaving Elmer for good.

Jace should have known better.

By the ripe old age of thirty-three he should have figured out that drinking himself under the table was a less than successful response to almost anything that ailed him—and that included getting Celie O'Meara out of his mind.

She was out of his life. Had been for a month. A month that seemed like a year. Ten years. Forever, when you got right down to it.

He still couldn't believe she'd left! If ever there was a homebody in the world, Celie was it. But twenty-four hours after she'd come home from Polly and Sloan's wedding she'd put a Going Out of Business sign in The Spa window and seven days later she was gone.

"She didn't even say goodbye!" Jace had said, outraged, when he discovered it.

"Because you were still in bed," Artie told him with blunt disapproval, "sleepin' off that bender."

It was true that Jace had been doing his fair share of drinking at the Dew Drop and down at The Barrel in Livingston since Celie's announcement. He'd also been doing his best to find a woman who appealed to him more. He hadn't, but it wasn't for lack of effort.

"You mighta stopped her," Artie had told him reprovingly.

Jace had scowled. "Yeah, right. Begged her not to go."

Artie nodded. "Yep."

But Jace would never have done that. He wouldn't have admitted anything—not when she'd acted like he was lower than dirt. "I'd have looked like a damn fool."

"And now you don't?"

No, damn it, he didn't! He just looked tired.

He still looked tired a month later—because, damn it, he

was tired. It was a lot of work going out every night, carousing, meeting women, trying to be flirtatious and charming, *especially* when he didn't want to bother, especially when it didn't seem to be doing any good!

Artie was disgusted with him, and Jace knew it. The old man didn't say anything, but he didn't have to. He only had to sit there in his damned recliner every evening with that book of zen wisdom Celie's mother had given him in his lap, regarding Jace with sad resignation over the tops of his spectacles as the younger man headed for the door. It was Nickel Nite at the Dew Drop, which meant that women could play pool for a nickel a game. With luck there might be a new one—one single, reasonably attractive, interested female that he hadn't already met.

"What?" Jace demanded, glowering at Artie's pained expression.

But Artie only shook his head. "I'd think you'd get tired of it."

He didn't have to specify what. And Jace was tired of it. But he didn't see any alternatives.

"You got any better ideas?"

"Could be."

Jace stopped, his hand on the doorknob. He gave Artie a hard look. "Which means?"

"Life is what you make it."

He had the blinkin' zen book on his lap again. Jace ground his teeth. "Sure it is," he spat.

Artie nodded, smiling. "You are what you do."

"I'm *doin'* something!"

"Getting drunk. Picking up women. *Trying* to pick up women," Artie corrected himself, infuriating Jace even more.

"I'm not getting drunk. I haven't in weeks."

"And thank God for that," Artie said piously.

"It didn't hurt *you,*" Jace pointed out.

"Didn't help *you,* though, either, did it?"

"Nothin's helping!"

"Seems not," Artie said thoughtfully. He patted the book on his lap. "Maybe you should try somethin' else."

"I've tried."

"Besides other women."

"Like what?" Jace said belligerently. He nodded his head at the zen book. "I suppose that thing has all the answers."

"You could say that."

"Such as?" Jace challenged.

Artie shrugged. "Wherever you go, there you are." At Jace's confused stare, Artie sighed, then amplified. "And if you don't go, well, then you ain't there, are you?"

"I haven't gone anywhere."

"Ain't that the truth," Artie muttered. "Sometimes, I swear," he said with weary resignation, "you are as dumb as you look. You love Celie O'Meara, don't you?"

"Well, I—"

"You love Celie O'Meara." It wasn't a question. "You been tryin' for a month to forget her, to move on, to get her outa your system, outa your mind, outa your life. You tried work, you tried booze, you tried other women. And it ain't done you a damn bit of good. You haven't been able to do it, have you?"

"Well, I—"

"You haven't." Artie answered his own question. "So you gotta do somethin' else. Somethin' to convince her you love her."

Jace opened his mouth to protest, then shut it again. He didn't see how the hell he could convince her—even if he had a mind to—if she wasn't even here. Besides, telling someone you loved her was risky. It meant saying things he'd never said to anyone—least of all the one woman in the world who had every right to hate his guts.

''Course, if you're chicken...'' Artie murmured.

Jace's teeth came together with a snap. ''Fine. By all means, let's hear it. What do you suggest?'' he said. ''What zen proverb is gonna make it all better?''

''Ain't zen,'' Artie said. ''It's just good old-fashioned common sense. If the boat don't come to you, boy, it's time you went to the boat.''

Two

Working on a cruise ship was totally different from *cruising* on a cruise ship. Celie learned that in about ten minutes flat.

It was long hours spent doing exactly what she'd done back in Elmer—cutting, combing, shampooing and coloring, and two afternoons a week giving massages to passengers hungry for a little pampering—and sometimes doing it with the deck swaying under her feet. It was sharing a room barely big enough to get dressed in, a room so deep in the bowels of the ship that she wondered if she ought to decompress on her way up to the salon where she worked. At work it was a supervisor who didn't carry a whip, but who might as well have. She was called Simone.

''Actually Simon,'' Stevie, one of the other hairdressers said. ''As in Simon Legree.''

Celie could believe it. Simone had sacked her first roommate, Tracy, for coming out of a passenger's stateroom one morning wearing the dress she'd worn to dinner the night before.

"You charm the passengers," Simone said. "You don't sleep wiz zem."

Celie took the lesson to heart. Not that she'd had her heart set on sleeping with any of them, anyway. It was enough to be charming. She'd met a lot of people. A lot of men, actually. She'd visited several Caribbean ports on her days off with a few of them. She'd made more memories in the past eight weeks than she'd made in a lifetime in Elmer.

"Aren't you homesick?" Polly had asked her worriedly the first few times she'd called.

And the answer had been yes.

But it was only to be expected, Celie knew. And she told Polly firmly, "I'm fine. I don't have time to be homesick."

It was only the truth.

Besides, even if she did lie awake some nights and think about Elmer and the life she'd left behind, she also knew that staying in Elmer would never have given her what she wanted.

There was no man in Elmer who would love her the way Sloan loved Polly. She knew every man in Elmer, and as far as she was concerned, all the good ones were taken.

She knew there was no hope when she'd called Artie from Kauai to tell him about Sloan and Polly's wedding, about how beautiful it had been, and how wonderfully in love they were. And she'd said, "I hope I find a man like that someday."

And Artie, heaven help her, had said, "What about Jace?"

Jace? She'd practically swallowed her tongue. "Jace?" she'd sputtered. "Me and Jace Tucker?"

"What's wrong with Jace?" Artie had demanded.

Everything, Celie could have told him. Jace was too

handsome, too sexy, too sure of himself, too flirtatious. He also thought she was the dregs of the universe. She was the girl that even a loser like Matt Williams had dumped! She couldn't believe Artie was even suggesting it. Was the old man getting senile at last?

But she couldn't ask that!

''Let's just say it wouldn't work,'' she'd said finally. ''It would be like Little Red Riding Hood and the big bad wolf.''

''Well, now—'' Artie had begun, but Celie had cut him off.

''No, Artie. Forget it. Don't ever think about it again.''

Getting away from Jace's teasing grin and barbed comments had been one of the biggest perks of leaving Elmer. Getting away from Jace was one of her primary reasons for going.

Not that she had been running away! On the contrary, she'd been running toward plenty of wonderful opportunities. She was seeing the world. She was making memories. She was meeting lots of wonderful people. Meeting men.

It was what she'd come for, she told herself. To see the world, to meet new people. To find true love.

Well, she wasn't admitting *that.* Not to anyone else. If the more worldly members of the crew—and virtually everyone on the ship was more worldly than she was—suspected for a moment that Celie had come looking for her one true love, they'd never let her live it down. They already thought her wide-eyed innocence was somewhere between charming and a colossal joke.

Carlos, the debonair, slightly jaded waiter from Barcelona, teased her about it on a daily basis. ''Such big eyes you have,'' he would say, grinning at her amazement at the beauty of places they visited.

''I make her eyes even bigger,'' Yiannis, the wine steward from Greece, promised. He offered to show her around the ''spots the tourists don't visit'' in ports they came to.

But Allison, the hairstylist who became Celie's roommate after Tracy got sacked, wouldn't allow it. ''You're not going anywhere with him! Spots the tourists don't see, my sainted aunt Effie! And what does he mean by that but sleazy hotel rooms!'' She sniffed. ''He'd have you naked in five seconds flat!''

While Celie had no desire to go ashore with Yiannis, she felt compelled to protest that she wasn't so foolish as to be talked into a sleazy hotel room or out of her clothes.

Allison had lifted a brow. ''Oh, yes? And who was it let Armand take her up on the fantail at midnight to watch the neon fish?''

She could still blush just thinking about that. So there weren't neon fish. Live and learn.

And anyway, she'd come to no harm. Armand, who ran the gifts and precious gems shop on board the ship, had turned into a perfect gentleman when Celie, trapped in his passionate embrace, had slid one knee between his and explained the options facing his own family jewels.

''You're learning,'' Allison had admitted later.

Indeed, Celie was learning a lot. And in the past two months she'd met a lot of fascinating people from all over the world. She'd seen amazing sights, had sent home a dozen postcards, had determinedly embraced the life she'd let pass her by for the past ten years.

But she hadn't found true love. Yet.

She would, though. She was determined. After all, she couldn't expect to find her one true love just waiting for her to come along, could she? Of course not. It was bound to take a little effort on her part. So she had enjoyed a few ports of call in the company of the opposite sex. Men Allison approved of. Ones unlikely to drag her off to a sleazy hotel room.

"Gentlemen," Alison had said, giving Armand and Carlos and Yiannis a look that would singe the hair on their heads.

They'd backed away, palms out, muttering, leaving Celie to Allison.

"Carlos is a gentleman," Celie had protested.

"Carlos is a Casanova," Allison said firmly. "Not your type. You need a nice man."

As if she couldn't handle any other kind, Celie thought, a little put out. As if she were a novice, barely out of the cloister. As if she needed training wheels.

"Seen any neon fish lately?" Allison murmured whenever Celie grumbled.

So she'd dated men whom Allison approved of. She'd gone to the straw bazaar in Nassau with a charming Scot called Fergus. She'd water-skied in St. Thomas with an Australian named Jeff and she'd drunk margaritas on the cruise line's private island beach with a Canadian called Jimmy.

They were sweet. They were fun. They were "gentlemen." They were certainly better than staying home in Elmer and letting life go on without her.

But none of them was "the one."

What if she never met "the one"? The thought niggled in her brain sometimes late at night. What if she stayed not just weeks or months, but *years* and never met the man of her dreams? It didn't bear thinking about.

It would happen. Of course it would.

Sometime when she least expected it, she would spot him coming onboard, or she'd catch him watching her during her little spiel during the safety section, or she'd look up from cutting hair, glance in the mirror and their eyes would meet.

Just like that, there he would be—the other half of her heart.

And just like that, they'd fall in love, get engaged and go home to Elmer to get married. And this time the whole valley really would get to celebrate as Celie O'Meara got married at last.

And when she came down the aisle toward the man of her dreams, Celie vowed that she'd stick her tongue out at Jace Tucker!

Artie had had some dumb-ass ideas in ninety years. But Jace doubted the old man had ever had a stupider one than this.

So how stupid did that make him for going along with it?

How big a fool was he that he'd anted up more money than he wanted to think about for "seven fun-filled days *and nights* cruising the Caribbean" on the ship on which Celie O'Meara cut hair?

He had to be out of his mind.

"Of course yer outa yer mind," Artie said cheerfully, bright and early the morning he drove Jace to the airport in Bozeman. "We're all fools when we're in love."

In love. He kept stumbling over the idea every time he thought about it. Love was something that happened to other people. Love was something that made their worlds go around—not his. It was something other guys sweated out—not him.

And now? Now he was an hour from getting on a plane and chasing thousands of miles after Celie O'Meara.

He considered backing out.

Artie wouldn't let him. "No, sir. You do, an' you'll regret it."

Jace thought he might regret it a whole lot more if he went. What if he went and Celie took one look at him and turned up her nose and walked away? What if he went, laid his heart on the line and she told him to go to hell?

Worst of all, what if he went and couldn't open his mouth and say a word?

''You?'' Artie darn near drove off the road, staring at him when he mentioned that. ''Not talk? Huh? Can't imagine it. You ain't exactly no shrinkin' violet, you know.''

''Watch where you're going!'' Jace growled. It was true, ordinarily he didn't find dealing with women any hardship at all. He could talk to women, he could flirt with them, he could charm the pants off them—literally.

Other women.

He'd never got to first base with Celie O'Meara.

''You never did anything this harebrained, I'll bet,'' he muttered as Artie took the turnoff to the airport.

There was a long moment's silence—necessary, Jace figured, when a man had ninety years to think back through—and then Artie sighed. ''Shoulda,'' he said.

Jace's eyebrows lifted. ''Oh, yeah?''

''Mebbe.'' Artie allowed, shrugging bony shoulders. ''Or mebbe not.'' He stared straight ahead again, concentrating on making the turn into the airport.

Jace waited for him to elaborate. He didn't.

''Thanks,'' Jace muttered finally as Artie pulled into a parking space. ''You're real encouraging.''

''Gave you the idea, didn't I?'' Artie said. He cut the engine, grinned and cuffed Jace lightly on the arm. ''Give it a shot, boy. What've you got to lose?''

His hope, Jace thought. As long as he didn't confront Celie, as long as he didn't spell out what he wanted, as long as he didn't tell her he loved her, he could still believe they might have a future together.

''Come on.'' Artie shoved open the truck door. ''Git the lead out. Faint heart ain't never won fair lady.''

''Wish t'hell you'd stop with this zen stuff,'' Jace muttered as he climbed out.

Artie gave him a long-suffering look over the hood of the truck. "Not zen. Romance novels."

Jace stared.

Artie gave another bony shrug. "Joyce gave 'em to me. Feller's gotta do somethin' with his time when it's damn near all he's got left. Besides, I believe in love. I believe in you."

Startled by Artie's uncharacteristic words of approval, Jace blinked. "What do you—"

But Artie wasn't waiting around to repeat them. "C'mon." He jerked his head, then turned and tottered, bowlegged, in the direction of the airport terminal.

Jace stood still. His fingers clenched around the handle of his duffel. The grip felt almost familiar, the way his hand had tightened on the ropes of a thousand bucking horses.

"Ride of your life," one of his old rodeo buddies, Garrett King, used to say.

Back then he'd treated each one that way. He'd seen each ride as a step on his way to winning the world. Back then he'd believed he would. With the confidence of youth, he'd been sure he'd succeed. He had grit, he had try, he had talent, he had stamina. Why shouldn't he win it all?

But grit and try and talent and stamina hadn't been enough. There were things he could control and, Jace had realized this past year, things he couldn't.

When he'd had that wreck in December at the National Finals, he'd been so close…so very close to the top that he'd been almost able to taste it. He'd gone to Vegas, dreaming of the day the gold buckle would be his.

And now it never would be.

As long as he'd had his career, he'd had hope. Now he didn't.

He didn't want to admit what he felt for Celie O'Meara—not to Celie, at any rate. Not the way she felt about him. Not until she changed her mind. If he said, "I love you,'' and Celie said, ''I don't love you and I never ever will,'' that would end it.

He'd have no hopes left at all.

Still, what was he going to do, back out now? Goaded by Artie, he'd already spent the money. And everybody in Elmer knew—again thanks to Artie—that he was takin' a little cruise. Of course Artie had told them all, too, he'd be going on Celie's ship.

If that had earned him more than a few speculative looks from the Elmer gossips, Jace tried not to think about it. But even now he could feel the tide of red creep up his neck just thinking about those two old biddies, Cloris and Alice, clucking and smiling and murmuring about him having ''a thing'' for Celie O'Meara. He'd tried to ignore them. But they weren't alone in their speculation. Even sensible women like Felicity Jones and Tess Tanner had eyed him up and down last time he went out to the Jones place to deliver some lumber. He'd thought he was imagining their interest until he'd been about to leave and Tess had sung out, ''Be sure to get your hair cut while you're there!''

Felicity had even said he might want a massage, too—if Celie were giving them.

Cripes! Just thinking about it made his jeans tight.

But that was sex, not love. This wasn't about sex. Not entirely, at least. What he felt for Celie was more than simple desire. It had to do with things like forever and commitment and waking up together every morning. Still, it was true that he felt plenty of good old-fashioned lust where she was concerned.

Now he thought about getting a massage from Celie onboard ship. Did he dare?

''You comin' or you gonna stand there till you take root?'' Artie was scowling at him over his shoulder.

Jace's fingers gripped his duffel even tighter. *Ride of*

your life, he said to himself just the way Garrett used to say it.

He just hoped it didn't grind him into the dirt.

He flew to Salt Lake City, then to Miami. It was hotter than Hades, flat and smoggy when he arrived. Hardly the paradise he'd been promised. But he grabbed his bag off the luggage carousel, mopped his brow with the bandanna tucked in his back pocket, then caught the shuttle bus to the cruise ship where paradise—and Celie—were waiting.

He tried to imagine what she'd say when she saw him. Then he tried not to.

He tried to soak up a little of the atmosphere, smile at his fellow passengers, feel like he wasn't a fish out of water and about to meet up with the fillet knife.

Almost everyone on the bus was staring at him. At his hat. Most everyone was wearing open-necked shirts and golf slacks. A couple of men had flat caps. There didn't seem to be any other cowboy hats in sight.

Jace took his off and rubbed a self-conscious hand over spiky damp hair. He thought he should feel better now, less self-conscious, more part of the group. The truth was he felt bare and vulnerable without it. He felt naked.

And that was the last thing he needed when he met Celie again. He jammed his hat back onto his head. The hell with it. So what if he looked like a cowboy and they all looked like golf club professionals? He *was* a cowboy, damn it. And he doubted, for all their golf clothes, any of them had ever hit par.

He couldn't afford to buy clothes he'd only wear for a week. Besides his long-sleeved, western-style shirts like the one he was wearing, he had packed a polo shirt and a couple of T-shirts, and the travel agent had told him to take a pair of dark slacks. The only pair he had were the ones he'd worn to his sister, Jodie's, wedding ten years ago, to his father's funeral three years back and to the few rodeo functions where jeans weren't acceptable attire. He figured they'd still look new when it came time to bury him. Not that he wanted to be buried in them! Wherever he spent eternity, Jace wanted to do it in jeans. And boots.

He was wearing boots now. He damned sure wasn't buying any loafers with tassels on them. They'd laugh him out of Elmer if he came home with silly shoes like that!

They'd probably laugh, anyway, if he came home without Celie.

Life without Celie didn't bear thinking about.

He tried not to. He tried to muster up a little interest in the people on the bus. Jace generally liked people. He liked talking to them, learning about them, listening to them. And so he smiled at the lady sitting next to him.

''How you doin'?'' he said, smiling at her. ''This your first cruise? It's mine.''

The lady smiled back, stopped looking askance at his cowboy hat and started telling him that it was her first cruise, too, and she'd been saving for it for years. Then two more women jumped into the conversation, and by the time they got to the ship, they were pretty much one big happy family—him and a bunch of women.

Well, they weren't all women, but most of them were. He discovered pretty quickly that unattached single men of his age—or any age, for that matter—were in short supply on cruise ships. A couple of them even asked him if he was an escort.

''An *escort?*'' Jace was aghast, and he knew his face was bright red.

The woman who had been sitting in the seat in front of him turned around as they got off the bus. ''Not that kind of escort,'' she said kindly. ''But they sometimes recruit gentlemen to come along on cruises for free—as escorts—so we lonely women will have partners to dance with.''

"Oh." Jace ducked his head and scratched the back of his neck. "I didn't know. I thought maybe you reckoned I was..." He didn't finish the sentence.

Several of the women laughed, but it was friendly laughter, and one of them—Jace would have sworn—patted him on the butt!

"I wouldn't mind," one said cheerfully.

"Nor me, sugar," added another.

More laughter, and Jace laughed with them. "Thanks," he said, "I'm flattered. But I came to see a friend."

They were immediately all ears. "A friend? A *girl*-friend," they said.

"We hope," one of them muttered.

"Yes," Jace said at once. "Well, not exactly a *girl*-friend, but—a girl, a woman," he said quickly at a few widened eyes. "Just she's not exactly my girlfriend. Yet."

They were all avid. "Who is she?"

"What's her name?"

"Is she a passenger?"

"No," he said. "She, um, works here."

He didn't want to tell them too much. He didn't want them to know who she was. The last thing he wanted was to conduct his courtship under the watchful eyes of a ship full of eager women. That would be worse than trying to do it back in Elmer!

"Don't press the poor boy," the lady who'd sat next to him said, patting his arm maternally. "You'll make him nervous."

As he moved through the line to get registered and get assigned to his stateroom, Jace was already nervous. The ship was huge. It was like a gigantic, multistory floating hotel. A very ritzy floating hotel. And there were uniformed good-looking guys all over the place, smiling and nodding at the passengers, saying hello in half a dozen foreign languages. They said hello to him, too, even as they blinked at the sight of his cowboy hat.

Not one of them, he noticed, was wearing a wedding ring. They'd probably all come to work here in order to meet women—exactly the way Celie had come to meet men. They probably knew her.

She was probably already in love with one of them!

He tripped over his own boots and almost went sprawling. He would have if three blonde women he'd met on the bus hadn't caught him and hauled him upright.

"You okay, sugar?" one of them asked.

"Fine. Just fine. I—" he fumbled with the map of the ship that the registration clerk had given him, as he tried to get his bearings "—just gotta figure out where I'm going."

One of the blondes peered over his shoulder and studied the map and the room the registration clerk had circled. "Why, you're just down the hall from us." She beamed and took his hand. "I'm Lisa, sugar. Deb and Mary Lou and I will take care of you. Just come along now."

And Jace, feeling as if he'd been tossed from a bronc and landed on his head, gave himself up to the inevitable and did exactly that.

Lisa and Deb and Mary Lou appointed themselves his guardians. They were cousins, all from Alabama, all schoolteachers, all single and in their midthirties. They went on a cruise every summer to spend time together and maybe, just maybe, meet the men of their dreams.

"It hasn't happened yet, of course," Deb said with a fatalistic shrug.

"But we're optimists," Mary Lou said.

"Or masochists," Lisa said wryly.

"Whichever," Deb finished, "we'll keep an eye on you."

"I—" Jace started to protest, because he wasn't the man of their dreams and he needed to be sure they knew it.

Lisa patted him on the cheek as they stopped outside his stateroom. "Don't you fret, now," she told him. "We aren't goin' to poach on some other girl's property. We know you're taken."

"I—"

But Mary Lou nodded in solemn agreement. "Taken. We understand. We're delighted. It's so romantic."

It was?

"Absolutely," Deb agreed and added fervently, "we're just glad to know there are real men like you around."

Jace hoped Celie felt the same way. It still worried him. He'd put it out of his mind as best he could all the way down here. He was committed, he was going on the cruise. But he didn't have a clue as to what to say to Celie when he ran into her.

Hell, the damn ship was so big he reckoned he could go the whole week and never run into her at all. He wondered, for a split second, if he could get away with going home and telling Artie—and the rest of Elmer—that he'd tried to find her, but he'd just never managed it.

Somehow he didn't think it would wash.

He had to figure it out, though, now that he was here. After the Alabama triplets left him, he let himself into his stateroom. It was bigger than he'd imagined, with more closets than his sister's whole house. He set his hat on the desk and surveyed his digs for the week. It wasn't flashy like some of those Las Vegas hotel rooms he'd stayed in. It was more subdued, had more class. The furniture was light oak, the drapes were a soft sky blue. There was a little refrigerator by the desk, thick carpet under his boots, and right in the center, a close to king-size bed.

More than anything else, Jace admired the bed. Used to sleeping on a bunk bed in his nephew, Robby's, room when he was at the ranch or on the hard narrow bed in Artie's spare room when he was in town, he thought the bed alone might be worth the cost of the cruise.

Well, not *alone,* he amended. His mind's eye was already envisioning Celie in it with him. The notion grabbed him, held him. He sank down onto the bed and let the vision play out in his head.

After all, it made sense. If he'd learned one thing in all his years of bronc riding, it was that visualization was a good thing. You'd never get anywhere close to winning the gold if you worried that you weren't going to make the ride. You needed to imagine yourself sticking to the saddle, needed to see yourself doing everything you needed to do to win.

It was way too easy to see himself doing things in bed with Celie O'Meara.

The trouble was that he couldn't quite see all the intermediate steps that he would have to take to get there.

He lay back and folded his hands under his head and tried. He tried to imagine her smiling when she saw him. He'd seen her smile often enough, though rarely at him. He envisioned that smile. He envisioned her saying his name like she was glad to see him. He saw himself reaching for her, drawing her close, wrapping his arms around her. His brain fast-forwarded to them in bed, to him skimming off her clothes, to him shedding his own, to the two of them learning each other's bodies—

A quick staccato tapping on his door made his eyes fly open and his whole body jerk.

He leaped to his feet, heart pounding, mind reeling, body aching. Cripes, if it was Celie— He shut his eyes and prayed for inspiration. Then he ran a hand over his hair, shoved his shirt in his jeans and, wincing, adjusted their very snug fit. It didn't help much. So he grabbed his hat and held it in front of him as he answered the door.

Of course it wasn't Celie. She didn't even know he was here.

The Alabama schoolteachers, all looking cool and fresh in clean, bright dresses, stood beaming at him. ''We're headin' off to the safety demonstration. It starts in five minutes. Y'all wanta come along?''

He had to, of course. The safety demonstration or ''life boat drill'' as one of the crew had called it, was the only mandatory event on the cruise. ''I, er...'' His voice sounded thick and ragged. He cleared his throat desperately. ''Yeah, sure.'' He took a deep shuddering breath and tried to get a grip.

Mary Lou looked at him closely. ''You all right, sugar?'

Feeling like an eighth grader whose brain—and body—were out of control, Jace nodded. ''Yeah. I just... Lemme just...wash up a sec. I just sorta...dozed off.''

He didn't wait to see if they looked as if they believed him. He ducked back inside his room, shut the door and hurried to the bathroom to splash some water on his face. He toweled it dry, then yanked on a clean shirt, buttoned it and jammed it into the waistband of his Wranglers.

They were still annoyingly snug—because he was still annoyingly horny. He hadn't been with a woman since February. Not since the night of the auction, when Celie had won Sloan Gallagher. Not since Tamara Lynd had walked into his bedroom, slid her arms around him and assured him that Celie wasn't the only fish in the sea.

In a fury because Celie had not only bid on but actually won a weekend with Sloan Gallagher, Jace had slaked his need with Tamara that night.

It had been a disaster. At least for him. He hoped Tamara didn't hate him. He'd hated himself enough for both of them. And he hadn't been with a woman since.

No kidding his frustrated body grumbled now.

He grabbed his Stetson again, but he still didn't put it

on. Instead, with determined nonchalance, he clutched it in front of his belt buckle and opened the door again.

Lisa, Deb and Mary Lou were still waiting with identical smiles on their faces and bright-orange life jackets in their arms.

"Hang on." Jace went back and got his, clapped the Stetson on his head and carried the life jacket in his arms. "All set."

Deb looped her arm through his right arm, Mary Lou clutched his left hand, and Lisa led the way. "Y'all follow me. I've been here before."

The lounge was already full of people. A staff member, smiling brightly, ticked off their names when they arrived and directed them into the room. A handsome, uniformed guy greeted them with a cruise-ship trademark smile, told them his name was Gary and proceeded to run through the safety measures. The point was, if any emergency occurred, everyone was supposed to come here and wait for further instructions.

"Now," Gary said, "we'll just make sure you all know how to put on your life jackets, and then you can get on to the fun part of your holiday."

He demonstrated, putting the jacket on over his head, tightening and fastening the straps. "Your turn," he told them. "If anyone has any problem we've got plenty of staff here who can help you."

It was like the first day of football practice in high school when the coach had handed out the shoulder pads. There was lots of bumping and bumbling as too many people in too small an area raised their arms and fumbled as they put on the unaccustomed vests.

Jace fumbled, too, and, now that his arousal had subsided, wished he hadn't brought his hat.

''Hey there, cowboy, let me hold that for you,'' a familiar female voice behind him offered.

He turned and found himself staring into the bright, beautiful eyes of Celie O'Meara—a Celie O'Meara whose cruise-ship smile was fading fast.

Three

"*Jace?*" Celie said his name, disbelieving, her voice soundless in the tumult of the lounge.

She truly didn't believe it. Jace Tucker? *Here?* Celie felt as if she'd been punched in the gut.

She closed her eyes for a moment, certain she had to be hallucinating, certain that the wholly incongruous cowboy hat she'd glimpsed across the room, which had drawn her like a moth to a candle, would vanish and her momentary twinge of homesickness would not have turned into a nightmare.

A cowboy on a cruise? she'd thought, smiling when she'd spotted the Stetson, unable to stop her feet moving in its direction. Seeing it brought so many memories of home.

Home. Not Jace. It couldn't be Jace Tucker! It just couldn't!

Her mouth was dry. Her palms were damp. Her heart

was playing leapfrog with her stomach. Celie squeezed her eyes shut, willing the hallucination to vanish.

But when she opened them again, Jace was still there. And if he'd looked astonished, too, at first, and had blinked and swallowed at the sight of her, now he was grinning. Of course he was grinning—the same crooked, teasing grin with which he'd baited her ever since he'd come back to Elmer.

"Well, Celie O'Meara, fancy meetin' you here," he drawled.

"Ooh, is this your friend, honey?" a soft female voice asked.

And Celie was suddenly aware of a wide-eyed blonde at Jace's right elbow looking at her eagerly. At his left elbow stood another blonde, looking equally interested. And, of course, since this was Jace, who obviously believed The More The Merrier, a third blonde, just fastening her life jacket straps, was looking her way, too.

Trust Jace, Celie thought, jaw tightening, to go on a cruise with *three* women!

Damn it to hell, she didn't see why he had to go on a cruise at all!

Especially *her* cruise!

"What are you doing here?" she demanded furiously.

All the blondes' eyes widened at her tone.

Jace's grin wavered just a little. And his body seemed momentarily to stiffen. But then he flexed broad shoulders, slouched slightly, lifted those shoulders in a negligent shrug and gave her an easy, lazy Jace Tucker smile. "Well, I came to see you, of course."

Celie felt as if steam were coming out of her ears. "Oh, of course you did," she spat.

If he had come intentionally—if his being here wasn't the most awful coincidence in the world—it was because

Jace Tucker was apparently willing to go to the ends of the earth to humiliate her.

He, of all people, knew what a failure she was. He knew Matt had dumped her. He probably even knew why, which was more than she did. Matt had probably spelled out all her failings in great detail.

And if that wasn't enough, he knew she'd spent ten years getting over it, refusing to date anyone else, dreaming about a movie star. He knew she'd bid her life's savings on a date with that star—only to have him turn around and marry her sister! Not that Sloan's marrying Polly had been a bad thing. It hadn't. And it hadn't hurt her, either.

But to anyone else hearing the story, she was sure she would sound like the most pathetic fool in the world. And she was sure Jace Tucker would be only too happy to share it.

Damn Jace Tucker! He knew every terrible secret she had—all the ones she'd put behind her, the ones she'd thought she'd overcome. She had made a new life for herself here. She wasn't The Girl Matt Williams Jilted here. She wasn't even The Woman Who'd Bid Her Life's Savings On Sloan Gallagher And Was Now His Sister-in-law.

No. She was Celie O'Meara, a bit of an innocent, perhaps, but still likable. She was a woman with a life. Not much of one yet, but it was improving. She had made friends. She had met men. Maybe not her perfect man yet…but she had hopes that she would, given time.

She wasn't stuck anymore. She was finding the confidence in herself to believe that she could pursue her dreams.

And now Jace was here—grinning, teasing, infuriating Jace—staring at her, *laughing* at her, undoubtedly finding her pathetic attempts amusing, and capable of ruining everything!

''Is this your girlfriend, Jace?'' one of the blondes asked.

"The girl from back home?" said the second.

"Aren't you goin' to introduce us, honey?" said the third.

At their questions, Jace looked as startled as Celie felt. He also seemed to blush. Jace Tucker? Blush?

From embarrassment, no doubt, Celie thought, at the absurd idea that she could possibly be his girlfriend.

Not hardly.

Celie expected a prompt denial. But he just looked agitated and cleared his throat. "Um, this is, er…Celie," he said quickly.

They all beamed at her. "Hi, Celie!"

She blinked, surprised at their enthusiasm, but before she could ask the names of his harem, another voice cut in.

"You know zis man?" It was her boss, Simone, arching perfectly plucked eyebrows as she appeared next to one of the blondes and looked from Celie to Jace and back again. Her disapproval was obvious.

And there was no way to deny that she knew Jace now.

"He, um, used to work with me," Celie said. "That's all," she added firmly, because she knew how Simone felt about fraternizing between staff and guests.

Simone's brows arched even higher. "Zis man, he cuts ze hair?" She looked at Jace in disbelief from the top of his Stetson to the pointed toes of his cowboy boots. The blondes in Jace's harem looked equally astonished.

"No, he doesn't cut hair," Celie said hastily. "My other job. I worked in a hardware store back home, too." Not something she had put on her résumé. Her job at Artie's was something else she was quite sure Simone would look down her aristocratic nose at.

Simone, who made of point of telling everyone she had been "born in Paree," had very high standards. She believed in Sophistication, with a capital *S* and Elegance, with a capital *E.* She believed all her stylists should look like Paris models.

"You zink ze guests trust you to make zem be-you-ti-ful when you look like ze frump?" she'd demanded when Celie had shown up for work the first week with her hair in a smooth, unsophisticated style.

While Simone wanted her stylists for their skills first and foremost, she wouldn't take anyone who didn't have "ze potential." To look beautiful, too, she meant.

Celie, while always doing her best with what she had, had never considered herself beautiful. What Simone saw she wasn't sure, but from the amount of work Simone and the other stylists had expended on her, she was pretty sure her boss considered her a reclamation project.

The first day she arrived Simone had demanded that Stevie, the top stylist, cut her hair. "We bring out ze cheekbones, yes?" she said, and Stevie, nodding, had cropped Celie's dark hair in a short, feathery cut.

Amazingly it had brought out her cheekbones. Then Birgit, who was the closest thing to a makeup artist Celie had ever met, had been deputized to show her how to "make ze most" of what she had. With the deft use of liner and shadow and just a hint of blush on "ze cheekbones," Birgit had made her look almost elegant.

At least Celie had dared to feel elegant then. Now she felt like nothing so much as a fraud—an imposter—a country bumpkin trying to pass herself off as an urbane sophisticate.

And she was sure Jace Tucker could tell.

There was more than a hint of a blush on Celie's cheekbones now. She would have liked to drop right through the deck.

"Is no time for socializing now," Simone decreed. "You will get back to work." It was an order, and Celie knew it. And even though at the moment her "work" was supposed to be helping the passengers, she knew what Simone meant. Leave. Go up to the salon. Do not flirt with the passengers.

As if! Celie thought.

The last person in the world she would flirt with would be Jace Flaming Tucker. But she wasn't going to say so. And she was going to take advantage of the out Simone had given her.

"Of course," she said brightly to Simone. "I'm on my way."

Then she turned her best, polite-cruise-ship smile on Jace and his harem, trying to mask her panic as she said cheerfully, "Welcome aboard."

So much for inspiration.

So much for seeing Celie again and being the easy, teasing guy he was with every other woman. So much for knowing exactly what to say.

Cripes, he was lucky he'd managed to say anything!

Jace hunched on a bar stool, downing his fourth—or was it fifth?—whiskey of the evening, feeling the burn all the way to his toes and wishing that instead of feeling it, the booze would send him straight to oblivion.

God, what an idiot he was! He'd heard her voice, turned around, and had had his breath taken away.

Far from knowing what to say, he'd simply stood there, like a fence post, staring at Celie as if he'd never seen her before.

Well, he hadn't! Not like that!

He'd expected to see the Celie he knew, the quiet demure wallflower Celie. The sweet, self-effacing Celie. The Celie who had been in the background of life in Elmer as long as he could remember.

Sure, he'd always known she was pretty, but it had been

a quiet sort of pretty, a gentle, soft sort of pretty. It had never called attention to itself before.

Not like this!

This Celie was almost exotic—with huge eyes and sooty dark lashes, a Celie whose soft curly hairstyle had been exchanged for a snazzy funky layered look, a Celie with cheekbones!

Where the hell had she got those cheekbones?

Polly had always been the one with the cheekbones in the family. And you noticed because Polly had always had a thousand freckles which had called attention to them. Celie, on the other hand, had had the peaches-and-cream unblemished look. And damn it, her face had always been *round!*

Now she looked as if she'd been sculpted! As if some hotshot sculptor had taken her and discovered not just the curves, but the bones within.

Jace's mouth had flapped while he'd tried to think of something to say. That had been bad. Worse had been knowing she wasn't at all glad to see him.

He'd been afraid of that. But he'd dared to hope that maybe a little homesickness would have made her look on him as a friendly face.

Fat chance.

He felt—along with the whiskey—a hollow, desperate feeling deep in the pit of his stomach. What the hell was he going to do?

All around him people were having the time of their lives. They were laughing and talking, getting to know each other. They'd just had the first of what promised to be the most incredible bunch of meals he'd ever seen—which everyone else had relished and he'd gagged on.

"Are you feeling a little seasick?" Mary Lou had asked him sympathetically as he'd pushed lobster around his plate.

He'd shaken his head. It wasn't the sea that had made him sick.

''I always feel that way the first night out,'' Lisa confided. ''Getting my sea legs takes me a day or so. You'll feel better tomorrow.''

Jace had nodded and tried to eat. He'd tried to look like he was enjoying himself.

''I think it's his girlfriend,'' Deb said.

He'd been attempting to crack a lobster tail and, not exactly adept, he'd managed to make it skid off his plate.

Deb had just nodded triumphantly. ''I'm right, aren't I?'' she'd queried. ''She's worrying you.''

''She's not worrying me.'' Jace debated going after the lobster on the floor and decided he'd look even worse scrabbling around down there.

''Of course she's not,'' Mary Lou came to his defense like a mother bear whose cub needed protecting. ''She was just surprised. And with her boss looking over her shoulder, I'm sure she had to try to appear indifferent.''

''As long as she wasn't indifferent,'' Deb said with just a hint of ominousness in her tone.

''Of course she wasn't indifferent.'' Mary Lou huffed, looking offended on Jace's behalf. Then she gave him an encouraging smile. ''I'd bet she was thrilled down to her toes. Goodness knows, I would have been. Land sakes, it isn't every day a man goes halfway across the world chasing the girl he loves.''

Which made him feel like an even bigger idiot than ever.

''She'll come around. You'll see,'' Lisa assured him. ''She'll just have to bide her time.''

''Yeah.'' He hadn't thought about that. Just what he needed—another obstacle.

''Cheer up,'' they'd encouraged him. ''Come to the show with us. Enjoy. Have a good time.''

"Maybe when you get to your room tonight she'll be waiting for you," Lisa said brightly.

Maybe she would be.

But Jace didn't think so. And he was in no hurry to get there and find out. He hadn't gone to the show with Lisa, Mary Lou and Deb. He knew he couldn't sit through anything like that. He'd be too antsy. And when he tried sitting still for any length of time every rodeo injury he'd ever had came back to haunt him. He didn't need an evening full of aches and pains to go with the mess that his brain was already working up to.

He'd said thanks, but he thought he'd just hang around the sports bar, maybe watch a baseball game. He wondered if they had a pool table. He could pretend he was back at the Dew Drop in Elmer.

Artie would be rolling his eyes in despair.

Artie and his great ideas. Huh!

"How ya gonna know if ya don't even try?" he'd said again and again when Jace had waffled about going on the cruise. "She might just be bowled right over," Artie had said with a happy anticipatory grin. "Might throw her arms right around you."

Or wrap her fingers right around his neck and squeeze, Jace thought.

He sighed and signaled to the bartender for another whiskey.

Celie *never* called home from the ship.

From the very start she'd told herself she wouldn't do it. It was a matter of maturity. She was a grown-up, an adult. She didn't need hand holding anymore. She could manage on her own.

For thirty years she'd depended on her family—on her mother, but mostly on her oldest sister, Polly, to give her moral support, an arm to lean on, a shoulder to cry on. She'd been determined to stop.

So when Simone had yelled at her, when a passenger got upset with her, when Armand laughed at her and Carlos tried French kissing her and Yiannis's hands had wandered where they definitely should not have been, Celie had solved her own problems. She had coped.

She wasn't coping with this—not with Jace Tucker on her cruise. Her fingers were shaking as she called Polly. She'd punched in the number three times, having made mistakes because she'd had to look up the number since Polly wasn't in Elmer anymore. She and the kids had moved to Sloan's ranch near Sand Gap as soon as school got out.

It was possible that Polly might not even know he was here. But then again she might.

She might even know *why* he was here.

Better yet, she might know what Celie should do about him.

So much for being grown-up. So much for being able to cope.

"Celie? What's wrong?" Polly demanded the moment she heard her sister's voice on the phone.

"Nothing," Celie said quickly, trying to assuage the worry in Polly's voice. "Nothing at all."

"Then why are you calling?"

"Can't I just call to be sociable?" Celie tried to sound casual, cheerful, the "new improved version of Celie O'Meara."

But Polly, of course, knew better. "You could, but you haven't, so why start now?"

Celie sighed. Still, she knew she could hardly blame Polly for her cynicism. She'd always been the one Celie had turned to in moments of disaster. She was the one who had held Celie while she'd wept buckets over Matt. She was the one who'd made the brisk announcement in church that "that skunk Matt Williams" had chickened out. She was also the one who had encouraged Celie to get her cosmetology license and set up her own salon. She was the one who had urged Celie to get on with her life. And when Celie had, years later, finally got up the gumption to do it—and had bid on Sloan—Polly hadn't once said she was in love with him. She'd buried her own desires and had simply cheered Celie on.

Polly was the kindest, wisest, most wonderful sister in the world. But she, too, had a life these days Celie reminded herself. She didn't need to be bothered with her sister's woes.

"No, really," she said. "It's not a big deal." Celie tried backpedaling a bit.

But Polly was having none of it. "What isn't? You might as well tell me."

And Celie knew that was true. Once alerted to a problem, Polly didn't rest until she'd solved it. Celie sighed. "Jace."

"Jace? Something happened to Jace?"

"Nothing's happened to Jace. Yet."

"But..." Polly's voice died out. But before it did, it had sounded mystified.

"He's here!"

"Here? Here where? Where are you? In Elmer?"

"No! He's here on the boat!"

There was a moment's astonished silence. Then an intake and a slow exhalation of breath. And when she did speak it was a soft murmur. "Well, I'll be damned."

"You're not the one who's going to be damned," Celie muttered. "If he says one word about Matt, about Sloan, about the auction, about...*anything,* I'll kill him!"

"He won't," Polly said soothingly.

"How do you know he won't?" Celie was raking one

hand through her hair and strangling the telephone with the other. "What did he come for if not to make trouble?"

Polly started to say something, then hesitated. "Maybe you should ask him."

"I did ask him!"

"And what did he say?"

"He said—" What had he said? Celie tried to remember, but she'd been so aghast at the sight of him it took her a moment to reconstruct the conversation in her mind. And then all she could report was, "He said he'd come to see me!"

"He didn't say I've come to ruin your life?" Polly asked.

"He didn't have to say it," Celie grumbled. "What's he doing here?"

"He came to see you," Polly repeated what Jace had said. "Maybe he missed you."

Celie snorted. "Because there's no one else in Elmer he enjoys annoying half so much?"

"Possibly. Maybe he wondered what you were doing."

"He could have asked Artie."

"Maybe he did. Maybe he got curious and decided to see for himself."

"Maybe, maybe, maybe..."

Polly could go right on spouting maybes forever, Celie thought. They weren't convincing.

"Never mind," Celie said. "The real question is, what am I going to do about him?"

"Well, you could throw your arms around him and kiss him," Polly said dryly, "but somehow I suspect you've already rejected that notion."

Celie shuddered at the very thought. "No way. I want to stay as far away from Jace Tucker as possible."

Again Polly hesitated. Then she ventured, "Didn't you

ever hear the saying about the best defense being a good offense?''

''I never played football,'' Celie reminded her. She had not been the tomboy in the family. But even though she hadn't, she suspected she knew what Polly was getting at. ''You want me to be nice to him.''

''Well, I should think that would go without saying,'' Polly said tartly. ''I was thinking you might go a little further.''

''Throw my arms around him and kiss him?'' Celie could barely get the words out of her mouth.

''It would definitely give him a shock.'' Polly laughed.

But Celie wasn't about to do that. She shouldn't have called Polly, either. Her sister was newly and happily married. She couldn't be expected to come up with ways to deal with a pain in the neck like Jace. ''Forget him. Forget I mentioned him,'' she said firmly. ''Tell me about the kids, about Sloan.''

It was a measure of how happy Polly was that she did precisely that. In the old days, after her husband Lew had been killed and before Sloan had appeared in her life, Polly had never just rattled on cheerfully about her life. She was too busy coping to sit back and reflect on it.

But tonight she did. She told Celie about the kids—about Jack's new puppy and the play that Lizzie was writing and the horse that Sloan was helping Daisy to train. She talked enthusiastically about having Sloan home for another month this summer before he had to go to Mexico to begin making his next film.

She even seemed philosophical about her oldest daughter, Sara. ''She's doing all right,'' Polly said now. ''Coping. Far better than I thought she would.''

Sara, a student at Montana State, had set her sights on medical school at an early age. She'd bought a day planner when she was in sixth grade, and she'd never settled for a

B when an A was a possibility. Her life had always been planned out five years into the future.

Until last February.

In February Sara had met Flynn Murray, a reporter who'd come to cover the auction as a bit of weird western local color for the offbeat New York based magazine, *Incite.* One look at Flynn, and Sara's well-ordered life had gone spinning out of control.

Just how far out of control no one, not even Sara, realized at the time.

Four weeks later with the auction long over and Flynn long gone, she did. Goal-oriented, schedule-bound Sara was pregnant with a child who fitted into neither her schedule or her long-term plans.

It must have devastated her, Celie thought, but she'd never said a word.

Not until May on the eve of their leaving for Hawaii so Polly could marry Sloan, did she end up having to tell. The stress of the past months had taken their toll and she'd nearly lost the baby. She'd lost weight, lost sleep, begun bleeding.

That was when Polly had found out.

It hadn't been an easy time for any of them. Polly had called off the wedding and had taken Sara to the hospital. She'd sat by her daughter's bedside day and night. Sloan had come flying home from Hawaii, worried about Sara but frantic that Polly meant to call the wedding off forever—which she had.

Polly—ever-capable Polly—had finally reached her limit. She'd raised four kids almost single-handedly for the past six years. She'd salvaged Celie from depression after Matt; she'd helped their other sister, Mary Beth, through her pregnancy with triplets; she'd been the tower of strength for her mother when their dad had died. And she hadn't even known her own daughter was pregnant!

She had failed. That's what she'd told Celie in the middle of the night as they'd paced together outside Sara's hospital room.

"No, you haven't!" Celie had argued. "You're always there for everyone. Now it's time to let Sloan be there for you."

But Polly wouldn't do it. She couldn't, she admitted. She was afraid to.

In the end it was Sara who'd made her mother see reason. It was Sara, home from the hospital, pregnant and determined to have this baby and see what life brought her, who took her mother to task.

Polly, her daughter had told her, was the one who had taught them all that life and love were worth taking risks for. That was why she'd loved Flynn, she'd told her mother.

"As if it were my fault she got pregnant," Polly had muttered later to Celie. But there had been color in her cheeks again. She had looked like Polly again, stubborn and determined, as she'd packed her suitcase to go to Hawaii to face Sloan, to tell him she loved him, that she was ready to take a risk.

Between Polly and Sara—not to mention her mother who, marrying Walt Blasingame last month, had taken some risks herself—Celie had had plenty of role models. It was because of their influence that she'd dared take this job in the first place.

And now, as she thought about it, her resolve returned. She stood up straighter. She took a deep breath. "Thanks, Pol'," she said.

"Thanks? For what?"

"For everything," Celie said. "For being there."

"Are you all right, Cel'?" Polly asked worriedly.

"I'm fine. I'll be fine," Celie assured her. She hung up and squared her shoulders.

She could deal with Jace Tucker.

* * *

The phone's shrill ring jarred Jace to semiconsciousness. He groaned, eyes closed and yanked the pillow over his head. Artie could answer it.

It rang again.

C'mon, Artie.

And again.

Annoyed, Jace rolled over and felt as if Noah Tanner had turned out a herd of bucking horses inside his head. "Artie!" He tried yelling, in case the old man didn't hear it, but then he realized the old man wasn't going to hear it—he was a couple of thousand miles away.

And the phone ringing by his bedside was the cell phone he'd agreed to take along so Artie could call him in case of "emergencies," though what emergency he could possibly do anything about from the deck of a ship miles away, Jace had no idea.

Hell's bells, had the old man had another heart attack?

Disregarding the pounding in his head, Jace pried his eyelids open, grimaced at the little light filtering around the heavy drapes into the room, and reached for the phone. *"What?"*

"Took ya long enough," Artie said cheerfully. "Does that mean you ain't alone?"

"Wha-what are you talking about?" Jace tried to sit up, got kicked in the head by all those horses inside and carefully lay back down again. "What's wrong?" he asked, trying not to raise his voice.

"Nothin'. Here." Pause. "How're things there?"

"Things are…all right." That was about the best he could say. And it was the truth, if he lay absolutely still and didn't even move his mouth very much. The horses in his head were just trotting now, but they still made even his teeth hurt. Why the hell had he drunk so much whiskey?

"Seen Celie?"

Oh, yeah. Jace remembered now why he'd drunk so much whiskey. He didn't answer Artie. "What's the emergency?"

"Told ya. Ain't none. 'Cept I ain't slept for worryin' about you."

"Well, stop worrying about me," Jace said through his teeth.

"Can't," Artie said matter-of-factly. "Lessen you can give me a reason to—like you proposed already an' Celie said yes." There was so much hope in his voice that Jace's teeth came together with a snap.

His head very nearly exploded. All the horses bucked at once. And the pain was so fierce it robbed him of breath.

"Ah, well, I figured it'd be too much to hope for," Artie said in the silence that followed. "But ya did see her." It wasn't a question, but it came close.

"I saw her," Jace managed at last.

"She glad to see ya?" Artie asked eagerly.

"Thrilled. Threw her arms right around me. Gave me a great smackin' kiss," Jace said dryly.

"Knew it!" Artie chortled happily, then suddenly stopped. "Yer havin' me on," he accused. "What did she do? Really."

"She looked like she wanted to throw acid in my face. This wasn't a good idea, Artie."

"Huh." The old man snorted. Then he paused. "Don't be a quitter. It's just gonna take some doin' is all."

Jace would have rolled his eyes, but he figured it might set the horses to bucking again. "Uh-huh."

"Don't worry. She's just playin' hard to get."

"That's one way of describin' it."

"So you gotta do the same."

Jace groaned. "Artie, you're nuts. I'm *here,* for cryin' out loud. I'm stuck on this blinkin' ship for a week. How hard to get can I possibly be?"

"Well..." Artie considered that.

Jace regretted once again letting the old man talk him into the cell phone. "Artie, this is not an emergency."

"Sez you." Artie sighed. "So if you ain't gonna sweep her off her feet, and you don't want to play hard to get, what're you gonna do?"

"Enjoy the cruise."

Artie groaned. "You are a quitter."

"I am *not* a quitter! I'm just...bidin' my time."

"Uh-huh." Scepticism dripped from the word.

"Lettin' her get used to me bein' around."

"Right."

"I'm serious. I think she's afraid of me."

"Yup. Terrifyin', that's you."

"C'mon, man, gimme some moral support here!" Agitated, Jace started to sit up. The horses kicked him in the head again. He groaned and lay back down.

There was a long moment's silence. Finally Artie said, "Okay, here's your moral support. I believe you ain't as big an idiot as you're actin'. But goldarnit, Tucker, you're comin' close!"

Celie waited all the next day for the other shoe to drop—for Jace Tucker to show up, for word to drift down about her being jilted, about her bidding on Sloan Gallagher, about what a sorry sad woman she really was.

But she didn't hear a word.

She worked an incredibly long day—starting before eight in the morning and finishing up after eight that night because it was a sea day. The first formal dinner would be held that night, and half the women on the ship wanted their hair fixed. They all talked and chatted and gossiped about everything under the sun.

But she never heard a word about herself.

And she never saw Jace, either.

She could almost have believed she'd dreamed him, but Simone came up to her when she'd been leaving that evening and buttonholed her as she headed for the door. ''Zat man—zat *cowboy*—who come on ze ship, he is your lover?''

''No!''

Simone's very expressive brows did their disbelieving arch. ''No? But he say he comes to see you.''

''To annoy me.'' How could she possibly explain the very antagonistic relationship she had with Jace? ''I'm sure he was as surprised to see me as I was to see him.''

''He did not know you were here?''

Celie wetted her lips. ''I...don't know.''

''Hmm.'' Simone tapped a bloodred fingernail thoughtfully on her chin. ''We shall see,'' she said after a moment's consideration. Her gaze leveled on Celie. ''You know ze rules.''

''Yes.''

Simone nodded. ''We charm ze guests. We have a drink wiz ze guests. We don't sleep wiz ze guests.'' She came down on this last with both feet in hobnailed boots.

''Of course not!''

''And you will remember.'' It wasn't a question. It was an order.

As if she needed one.

Remember not to sleep with Jace Tucker? Celie wouldn't have any trouble at all remembering not to do that!

Four

Jace spent most of the morning in bed, nursing his hangover and resolving, regardless of the provocation, to leave whiskey alone for the rest of the cruise. Hangovers, he discovered, were bad enough on dry land. On a ship, where the floor tipped and swayed, they were close to fatal.

He couldn't manage breakfast. The very thought turned him green. So he turned down Lisa and Deb and Mary Lou's invitation to join them. He didn't even bother to open the door.

''I'm gonna sleep in awhile,'' he told them as loudly as he dared. A certain decibel level caused his head to threaten to fall off.

''You do that, sugar,'' one of them called back cheerfully. ''We'll stop by later.''

Take your time, Jace thought. But he didn't say it. He just carefully—*very* carefully—rolled over and tried to go back to sleep.

He must have done it because the next thing he knew he was awakened by more knocking on the door.

"Jace? You all right, sugar? Feelin' better now?"

"F-fine," he croaked. "'M fine." He winced and slowly levered himself up. His head hurt, but the horses weren't bucking so hard anymore—and the room wasn't spinning quite so fast. In fact, as he got his bearings, it slowed and stopped.

"Great! You can come to lunch, then."

Lunch? It didn't sound as repulsive as breakfast had. He didn't feel nauseated anymore. His stomach actually rumbled. Slowly he hauled himself to his feet. His brain still felt a little too large for his skull.

"It's what comes of picklin' it," Artie would have said.

Jace didn't want to think about Artie.

"If you don't feel well enough," one of the blondes outside his door called, "we could send for the doctor."

"No! I mean, no. I'm…fine. Like I said."

"So you want to come to lunch? We're going swimming this afternoon. You could come along."

"Er," Jace wasn't sure he was up to swimming. But then, he thought, he had to do something. If he didn't, the whole cruise would be over and he'd have nothing to show for it—not even a tan!

"Yeah. Okay. Gimme twenty minutes. I gotta grab a shower."

It took him half an hour. He showered. He shaved. He studied his sunken bloodshot eyes and told himself to get a grip. He wasn't going to let Celie drive him to drink. He wasn't going to let Celie drive him crazy. He was going to act like a sensible, honest-to-goodness adult.

He could just imagine Artie rolling his eyes.

"Yeah," he said to his reflection in the mirror, "but Artie doesn't have any better ideas."

* * *

He went to lunch with Lisa, Mary Lou and Deb. He was a little shaky and a little pasty-faced, and his stomach recoiled at the thought of some of the dishes he was offered. But he did manage to eat a reasonable lunch. And he managed to find his sense of humor and the dregs of his usual charm, and after lunch he went on deck with them to check out the swimming pools, and before long not only were Lisa and Mary Lou and Deb smiling and laughing with him, but half a dozen other women were smiling and laughing and chatting with him, as well.

"We don't often see a cowboy on a cruise," some of them said to him.

And Jace quite frankly said that most cowboys really didn't have time to go on cruises, and when they asked him to explain what it was that cowboys—real cowboys—did all day, he sat down on a deck chair by the pool and held forth.

He talked about rodeo cowboys and then about regular ranch hand cowboys. They listened avidly, as if they were amazed such creatures still existed.

"It's like something out of a movie," one of the women said. "Like Sloan Gallagher's latest."

Jace grinned. "Oh, not really, ma'am. On film Sloan's a little too neat and clean. Not like real life at all."

"You know Sloan in real life?" another woman asked.

And Jace said he did.

"Ohmigod, he knows Sloan Gallagher!"

The cluster of women by then had reached more than a dozen. "Tell us about Sloan," they clamored. "Tell us more about cowboying."

Jace did. He told them his best Sloan Gallagher story—the one where they'd got into a fight as teenagers and he'd broken Sloan's nose. Then, because he played fair, Jace told them about their next battle where Sloan had broken his, as well.

''We sort of declared a truce after that,'' he said. ''An' then he moved away.''

''He's from Montana, though, isn't he?'' a pert redhead asked.

Jace nodded.

''From that funny little town that had the auction last Valentine's day,'' a brunette remembered. ''Wilmer?''

''Elmore?'' a blonde suggested.

''Elmer,'' Jace said.

More women joined the crowd. ''Tell us about Elmer.''

So he told them about Elmer. Most of them knew a little bit. They'd all read articles about it. They had all seen Polly on television.

''The postmistress.'' They all nodded and beamed, remembering Polly's fifteen minutes of fame. ''She was wonderful. So sane. So sensible. So strong. Do you know her?'' they demanded.

Jace said he did.

''What's she like?'' an older woman asked him. ''She married Sloan, didn't she?''

''After her sister won him in the auction!'' the redhead said.

''Talk about sibling rivalry! Wonder what her sister thought of that!'' The women tittered.

Jace didn't say, *You could always ask her.*

Celie obviously hadn't claimed the fame of having spent a weekend with Sloan Gallagher. And she wouldn't thank Jace for mentioning it, either. So he answered their questions about Elmer, about Sloan and Polly in general terms, and he didn't mention Celie by name at all.

''It sounds wonderful.'' Several of them looked dreamy-eyed at the notion of packing up their lives and moving to Elmer.

"Maybe we should have done that instead of having come on the cruise," one mused.

"Maybe you should," Jace said, feeling like a member of the chamber of commerce.

"Maybe we will," said the redhead. "How many unattached cowboys would you say there are?"

Jace's brows lifted. All the women were looking at him expectantly. He scratched his head and tried to tick over all the guys he could think of. If he counted all the ones who came out of the woodwork to attend Noah and Taggart's bronc and bull-riding school there were quite a few.

When he said so, they crowded in closer. "Bull and bronc riders?" they said eagerly.

"Like you?" asked a woman who had just joined the group.

"I was," he said. "Not anymore. I'm done."

"Aw." Several of them looked sad on his behalf.

"Why are you quitting?" the redhead asked.

"Doc said I oughta find another line of work. Got in a pretty bad wreck at the finals last year. Broke my leg in two places. Got concussed."

The women all winced. One patted his jeans-clad leg gently. "Poor Jace."

"I'm all right now." He wasn't interested in sympathy. "I'm ready to move on, do somethin' else." And if he hadn't been sure of it last January, he was now. He liked being back in Elmer. He just wanted Celie there with him. "I'm ready to settle down."

Every pair of female eyes widened. Several women's mouths formed small round *o*'s. There were murmurs and mumbles. The women all looked at each other, then every one of them looked at him.

Cripes, didn't they believe him?

Was the whole world made up of Celie O'Meara clones?

"I am," Jace insisted. "I'm done travelin'. I'm diggin' in back in Elmer, settlin' down, puttin' down roots."

Still they stared. One or two even blinked their disbelief.

"I want to get married," Jace said firmly.

"Just ask me," one of the women in the back said.

They all laughed.

And Jace laughed, too, albeit a little grimly. "I already got the woman picked out," he told them.

"She works here," Lisa said.

"On this ship," chimed in Mary Lou.

"Who is she?" a chorus demanded.

"Yeah, just tell us and we'll knock her off," said the one in the back.

They all laughed again.

Then the older woman patted his hand. "She's a lucky lady, dear."

Jace wondered if she'd like to tell Celie that.

"Have you seen the cowboy?" Celie's first appointment asked her the following morning. It was the second full day of the current cruise and they had docked at Nassau early this morning. Only Celie and Stevie were working in the salon, the rest of the staff taking advantage of a day in port to go ashore, like most of the passengers.

The staff rotated working on-shore days, and since Celie had been in Nassua several times already, she was quite happy to work this shift. She told herself she'd rather be here than out wandering around the straw market or sunning on the beach where she might run into Jace Tucker.

She hadn't seen him since the first night. And even after Simone's little lecture about "not sleeping wiz ze passengers," she had begun to think she'd hallucinated the whole thing.

But now the pixyish redhead whose hair she was shampooing made her stop in her tracks.

"Cowboy?" Celie echoed carefully.

"Mmm." It was a very appreciative mmm. "What a

hunk. I never thought I'd say it...I'm a city girl myself,'' the redhead confided, ''but he can put his boots under my bed anytime.''

''Did he offer?'' Celie asked before she could stop herself. ''I mean...'' she began, but the redhead cut her off.

''Don't I wish.'' The redhead sighed.

Half an hour later Celie's next appointment asked almost the same question. ''Did you meet the cowboy?''

They couldn't all mean the *same* cowboy, could they?

''The cowboy? Is he a stage act?'' There were plenty of entertainers on the ship. They changed periodically and she couldn't keep them all straight. Maybe the cowboy was a new one.

''No.'' This woman was sixty if she was a day, but her eyes lit up when she spoke. ''Not this one. This one is the real thing!''

''The real thing?'' Celie echoed, nerves really tingling now as she clipped away on the woman's hair.

''Oh, my, yes. I met him at the swimming pool yesterday afternoon. He was just the cutest thing in his jeans and his boots. And so polite. 'Yes, ma'am, no, ma'am.' Why, he could give lessons in proper behavior.''

Give lessons on proper behavior? It couldn't have been Jace.

The next woman who came in had been there, too.

''Oh, yes, he's polite,'' she agreed. ''And gorgeous, to boot. Dark-brown hair. Deep-blue eyes. And he said he knew Sloan Gallagher.''

''He did?'' Celie almost dropped the scissors.

The woman nodded. ''Broke his nose, he said, when they were boys. And then—'' she giggled ''—he said Sloan turned right around and broke his!''

''Um,'' Celie said, mind whirling, fingers clenching on the scissors. ''Is that...all he said?''

''He said he was settling down.''

''What?'' The scissors hit the ground with a clatter. ''Oh, dear. I'm sorry. I—'' Celie bent to pick them up and tried to regain her equilibrium at the same time.

After all, it wasn't entirely news. She'd heard that before—from Jace himself. He'd begun building a house on the ranch he owned with his sister and her husband to settle down in—at least that was what he'd told her months ago.

''Settle down? You?'' she'd said snidely. Then she'd asked if he had someone in mind to share it with. She'd been shocked when he'd said yes. But since then he'd shown no signs of settling on one particular woman.

Maybe he wasn't planning on settling down with just one, she thought grimly. Maybe he was planning on settling down with a harem—like the three blondes he'd come to the safety demonstration with!

How very like him, Celie thought later as she scrubbed furiously at the hair of her next client. The woman winced, and Celie, realizing how fiercely her fingers were rubbing, stopped abruptly.

''Sorry,'' she apologized. ''I just...get a little enthusiastic sometimes.'' All she needed was for the woman to complain to Simone.

''Wouldn't mind him settlin' down with me,'' that woman said with a smile, ''but he says he's got someone in mind.''

Celie didn't believe it. Not for a minute. If Jace Tucker had a woman in mind, she'd know it. She'd know *her!* There weren't that many women in Elmer and the surrounding valley.

If a guy was courting seriously, he'd never be able to keep it a secret.

Jace was just telling them a tale about this ''someone'' he was serious about, Celie decided, so they wouldn't any get ideas about roping him and tying him down.

What better way to make sure the women he wanted to

play with didn't take him seriously than to claim he already had a girlfriend?

The man ought to come with a warning label, she thought: Hankering After This Man Can Be Dangerous To Your Emotional Health.

All day long she was treated to the wonders of Jace Tucker. He was handsome, he was sweet, he was drop-dead gorgeous. He could braid horsehair bridles and play the guitar and he could dance the two-step.

The women seemed to be falling all over themselves talking about how great he was. Even Kelly, who ran the fitness center, came in singing his praises.

"Did you meet the cowboy yet?" she asked Celie, eyes shining. "He came in to use the whirlpool last night to help his leg. Poor guy, he got hurt in a rodeo accident."

Celie grunted. She didn't want to talk about Jace. She didn't want to hear about Jace. She didn't want her mind's eye to even attempt to imagine what Jace Tucker would look like sitting in a whirlpool.

She grunted and turned away, going back to the woman whose hair she was coloring. But the woman had been in the whirlpool with Jace.

He was, she said, "edible."

Celie did not want to think about it.

She didn't want to think about him—but she did. And as she did, she figured out finally why he'd come on the cruise.

It was an ideal place—a perfect place—to meet women.

Cruises attracted women, *lots* of women. Some married couples came on them. Relatively few single men did. Mostly there were just lots and lots of unattached women. Women looking for a little excitement, a shipboard romance, a one-week fling.

They were like buckle bunnies without the rodeo. Oh, not all of them, to be sure. But enough to keep Jace plenty busy. No wonder he'd booked a cruise. He couldn't rodeo anymore.

What better place for a babe magnet like Jace to have his pick of eager females, make a little whoopee and ride off into the sunset at the end of the week?

Celie, having listened over the past few weeks to more than one woman whose heart had been broken by just such a bounder, was incensed on behalf of all the foolish women he would be deceiving!

What's more, she felt responsible!

If Simone caught her prowling up here, Celie knew she—and her fledgling career as a shipboard hairstylist—would be toast.

Allison, her roommate, had told her to mind her own business. Stevie and Troy had said there was nothing wrong with having a good time with other passengers, for heaven's sake. They were all adults here, weren't they?

They were. But it didn't matter. Celie didn't know why it didn't matter—other than the fact that everyone knew Jace came from Elmer, which put Elmer's reputation on the line!

"What?" Stevie stared at her, disbelieving, when she said that.

"It's true!" Celie exclaimed. Jace Tucker was sullying Elmer's good name. And she was going to do something about it!

When she finished work, she lurked about waiting for the passengers to come back from Nassau, hoping to catch him then and have a word with him. But when she saw him, he was surrounded by a bevy of females. And when he went to the whirlpool, there were so many following him in he looked like the Pied Piper of Hamlin.

Kelly caught a glimpse of her and waved. "He's here!" she hissed in a loud whisper. "Wanta get a look?"

Celie shook her head fiercely. ''No, I was just looking for, er, Allison.''

She'd ducked back out, fretted and fumed, pacing the halls. Then, when Simone came by and gave her a steely look, she beat a hasty retreat down to the staff quarters. She didn't need Simone getting annoyed with her again.

She went back up at the end of the dinner hours. But Jace hadn't gone to the same place he'd gone last night. He must have gone to one of the buffets. Or maybe, she thought grimly, he was sharing a meal in some woman's room.

She prowled the sports bar and the lounge and didn't find him. She couldn't imagine Jace going to one of the singing and dancing shows that every cruise put on. But, just in case, she checked the crowds pouring out of the theater.

She didn't see him anywhere.

So there was no hope for it.

She just had to hope that Simone, whom she'd seen in one of the lounges with a tall, handsome investment banker from Toronto, would be too busy ''socializing'' to check up on the whereabouts of the junior members of her staff.

Then she would never notice that Celie O'Meara was where she had no business being—about to knock on a passenger's stateroom door.

''You'll be sorry,'' Allison warned. She'd followed Celie, talking furiously all the way, trying to dissuade her from interfering.

But Celie wasn't dissuaded.

And she wasn't going to be sorry. Jace was!

She thumped loudly on the door.

''Heaven help us,'' Allison muttered. ''I'm gone.'' And she went skittering down the hall, leaving Celie by herself.

One second passed. Two. Five.

He wasn't there, Celie thought, unsure whether she was relieved or more annoyed than ever.

Then suddenly the handle rattled. The door opened.

And Jace, barefoot and bare-chested, clad only in faded jeans, braced an arm on the door and said, "Look, I'm really tired. I—*Celie!*" His eyes widened in shock.

It was all Celie needed. "I'm not at all surprised," she said scathingly. "All those women can wear a man out."

His jaw dropped. "What?"

"Women. The blondes. The redhead. The brunette. The girl whose hair I just colored. She's platinum now, by the way, in case you don't recognize her in the morning."

"What the hell are you talking about?"

"I figured out why you're here," she told him icily.

Jace blinked. He looked suddenly nervous. As well he might, Celie thought angrily.

His shoulders hunched. The movement drew her attention to them, and then, because she couldn't seem to help it, she noticed his chest, his abs. A vision of Jace in the whirlpool rippled unbidden to the surface of her mind. Furious at the direction of her thoughts, Celie shut her eyes.

"And I want you to stop."

He went rigid. Nothing moved but his adam's apple. He swallowed once, then again. "Stop?" He ran his tongue over his upper lip. "Stop what?"

"You know very well what! What you came for! Hitting on all these women!"

Jace's eyes widened fractionally. Then it seemed almost as if a small shudder ran through him. He flexed his shoulders, took a breath, then grinned a little. "Yeah, right."

"I mean it," Celie said, refusing to give in to the lethal Tucker charm. "I want you to stop it," she repeated.

"Okay."

"What do you mean, okay?" she asked suspiciously.

He shrugged. "I'll stop."

''Well, good. See that—'' But before she could finish her sentence, she heard voices coming from the stairwell at the far end of the corridor, and a couple came around the corner—a man in a tux and a woman with a tinkling laugh and a French accent.

Oh, dear God! There was no help for it—Celie pushed past Jace straight into his stateroom. ''Shut the door.''

It was his turn to blink. ''What?''

''Shut the door!''

Jace shut the door. Then he turned and leaned back against it, folded his arms across his bare chest and regarded her levelly. ''What a good idea,'' he said.

''It is not. But Simone was coming down the hall. My boss,'' she explained.

A brow lifted. ''Ze French woman?''

Celie made a face and nodded. ''She's...particular.''

''Ah.'' He was still looking at her, his expression unreadable. He was grinning, but there was something in his eyes she couldn't fathom. Nervously Celie moved to the far side of the room so that the bed was between them.

A mistake, she realized at once. They both stood looking at each other—and the bed. And even though Jace hadn't moved, it felt as if he was closing in on her. ''Stop that,'' she commanded.

''Stop what?''

''Looking at me that way.''

''What way?''

''Like you...like you...'' But she couldn't say the words *want me.* It was ridiculous to think such things. It was the way Jace looked at every woman!

''What happened?'' she asked. ''Did you run out of women in Montana?''

''You could say that.''

She snorted. ''I might have known! Well, you needn't think you're going to score here.''

"No?" The word was a soft growl.

"No," Celie said recklessly. "You don't belong here!"

"And you do?"

The quiet challenge made her stop and glare at him. "What do you mean by that?"

"We don't either of us belong here, do we?"

"I have a job here!"

"Only because you ran away."

"I did not!"

"Did so. You had a perfectly good job back in Elmer. You had a perfectly good life back in Elmer!"

"Oh, yes," Celie said scornfully. "Living with my mother and her new husband? Or maybe living with my sister and *her* new husband?"

She supposed she could have stayed in the house she'd shared with Polly's family and her mother after they'd each moved away, but she couldn't imagine it. It was a huge place. She'd have rattled around in it. And she'd have been lonelier than ever.

"You could get your own damn husband!" Jace's eyes flashed.

Stung, Celie retorted, "What do you think I'm trying to do?"

His jaw worked, and he shoved away from the door to pace into the room. "You didn't have to come all this way for that!"

"No? What was I supposed to do in Elmer?" Celie said scornfully. "Put a sign in the window—husband wanted? Or maybe I should have put an ad in the paper?"

Jace was glaring at her. "You could have looked around. Found a local guy."

"Right. Like Logan Reese maybe? Spence Adkins? Lots of temptation there. A convicted felon and a surly cop. No, thank you very much. They're not my type."

"Thank God," Jace growled. His chest was heaving and his eyes glittered fiercely.

Celie folded her arms across her chest and glowered back at him as he came to loom over her. "Who else is there? Artie?"

"Guess," he ground out. And before she could respond—before she could do anything!—Jace reached out and hauled her into his arms and fastened his lips to hers.

In her life Celie had, of course, been kissed. She'd been engaged, after all. She'd experienced the fervor of Matt's youthful fumbling passion. She'd tasted masculine desire.

Even after Matt had jilted her, she'd known it vicariously. She'd dreamed of Sloan Gallagher's kisses. And in the past few months she'd actually had a few brotherly ones from Sloan for real. They'd had potential. But they were nothing like the kisses he'd given Polly. Those had been intense. One of the things that had driven her to take this job was her desire to experience that intensity directed at her.

And now she did. She felt an intensity, a hunger, a need that rocked her. She felt the power of masculine desire, pure and simple. And very definitely directed at her.

By Jace Tucker?

On the verge of melting, instead Celie came to her senses. She jerked back, pressed her hands against his chest and shoved. Hard.

She stared at him, her heart hammering. "'G-guess'?" she gasped, looking around wildly. Her mind buzzed. Her blood roared.

"What on earth do you—" But she couldn't finish, could only stare, transfixed, into his fierce gaze.

"That's what I'm doing here, Celie," he said harshly, and his voice was as fierce and forbidding as his face.

Celie gaped, mind reeling.

Then, desperately she lurched past him and wrenched

open the door. She darted out into the hall and practically knocked down the couple walking by as she flew past them down the hall.

''Mademoiselle O'Meara!'' the woman in the twosome called after her.

Oh, God! But there was no way on earth Celie was stopping now.

Five

He'd blown it. Big time.

Damn it all to hell! He *knew* Celie was skittish. He knew she had to be handled with kid gloves, had to be made to feel warm and loved and secure.

So what had he done?

He'd grabbed her, for heaven's sake! His kiss had been anything but warm and tender. It had been hungry, uncontrolled, desperate.

Like him, Jace thought grimly, wiping a palm down his face. And if that wasn't bad enough, he'd blurted out all that stuff about her finding a local guy for a husband, too, then telling her that's why he'd come!

Nothing like playing all your cards by simply throwing them at her face!

Of course, if she'd gone all starry-eyed and eager and said, ''A local guy? Like you?'' he might have been glad he'd done it.

But she hadn't. She'd been scathing in her dismissal of Spence and Logan—and she hadn't considered *him* a candidate at all. For a single instant while he was kissing her, he thought he'd felt her surrender, he thought she'd begun to kiss him back. And then she'd shoved him away and bolted from the room.

He'd wanted to run after her, to apologize, to take that terrified look off her face. But she'd run desperately down the hall away from him, practically trampling the couple in her way, and before he could move, he'd heard a shocked, "Mademoiselle O'Meara!"

It had stopped him dead.

Her boss, the French dragon, was staring, astonished, after her. And when Celie disappeared around the corner, the dragon turned and fixed him with a hard stare. It centered for a very long moment on his bare chest and then slowly, disconcertingly, traveled up to meet his eyes.

"Ah," she said, ice dripping, "the friend." It was amazing how much doubt and distrust the woman could get into one single word.

Jace bristled, then gathered his wits and forced himself to calm down. It didn't take a psychologist to know that Madame Dragon was ready to fire Celie. And it didn't take a conflict-resolution specialist to know that being the guy who got her fired would rank right up there with being the guy who'd called to tell her Matt wasn't marrying her.

Not in his best interests, to say the least.

He took a slow, careful breath. "That's right," he said. "We go back a long way, Celie and I. We grew up together, and I invited her to come see some pictures from home." He spoke matter-of-factly and hoped the dragon bought it.

"Pictures," she echoed, her gaze sliding down to his bare chest again. "Indeed?"

"Indeed," Jace said firmly. "She's been kind of homesick. Told her sister, and she told the old man I work for…'' He shrugged, as if the conclusion ought to be self-evident. ''Celie's a good kid. Kind of naive. But sweet.'' God, he couldn't believe he was saying this. ''She spent her whole life in Elmer, you know. But she always wanted to see the world. It just took her a while to get up the gumption to do it. We're all real proud of her for goin' out and doin' this.''

He was, in a perverse, annoyed sort of way damned proud of her. Taking this job, bidding on Sloan, going to Hollywood with him—drat her!—had all proved that Celie had more guts and gumption than he'd ever have guessed.

''So you come to check on her?'' Fine dark brows arched skeptically over the dragon's dark eyes.

''Yeah. Her sister thought it would be nice if she saw somebody from home. And I sort of figured it was time for a vacation. So I said I'd come and see her. Kinda let her know we aren't so far away, after all. An' it worked,'' he said brightly. ''She's cured.''

''Cured?'' The dragon brows arched even higher.

''Not lonely anymore,'' Jace said. ''In fact she didn't even stay to see all the pictures. She noticed the time and jumped up just like that an' said she had to go.'' He gave the woman his most charming smile. ''That's why she was runnin' out the door. She knew she had to get up and get to work early tomorrow. Real conscientious, that's our Celie.''

''Mmm.''

Whether the dragon believed a word he was saying he had no idea. But short of calling him a liar—and if staff weren't supposed to fraternize with passengers, they probably weren't supposed to call them liars, either—Jace knew there was little she could do but nod her head and, he hoped, forget whatever notions she had about causing Celie any more grief.

"Ah, yes, Celie is most conscientious." She dredged up a begrudging smile and politely bestowed it on Jace. "A hard worker. But she is, perhaps, as you say, a little too naive...a little too innocent." She fixed Jace was a knowing look. "Is not ze best zing to go to a gentleman's room."

It didn't seem the time to tell her that Celie didn't consider him a gentleman.

"We're friends," Jace said firmly. "Like I said. I came to give her some moral support, see she was okay."

"And now you have seen her. Yes? Then how do you say...mission accomplished? So, enough mission. Now Celie gets her work done."

It wasn't a question. Bright eyes nailed him where he stood.

Jace nodded. "Of course."

The dragon bent her head. "I am glad we agree. Is good for everyone, you understand, that Celie will not be coming to your room again." Her smile blinded him. She gave an encouraging nod.

Jace knew what she wanted him to say. "I understand."

The smile grew several megawatts brighter. "Zen we say good night, monsieur." And, hooking her arm through the crook of the arm of the suit accompanying her, the dragon gave him one last nod, then waltzed away down the corridor.

Jace went back in his room, shut the door and sagged against it. Had he done it? No, better question. *What* had he done?

My God, he'd kissed Celie O'Meara! He'd virtually told her he'd come to marry her. And she'd turned tail and run in the other direction.

The phone rang. He snatched it up.

"So," said Artie. "You makin' any progress?"

* * *

The trouble with being on a boat, Celie thought, pacing the upper deck, whirling at the fantail and pacing back the way she had come, was that wherever you went, there you were.

On the boat.

With your thoughts jumbled, your wits scattered, your mouth still tingling from the hard press of Jace Tucker's lips.

She pressed her fingers against her own lips now and could still feel the sensation that had shocked her to her core. *Jace Tucker had kissed her?*

Jace Tucker didn't even like her!

Did he?

She would have said not. She had always thought not. She had always thought she was beneath his notice. Silly, dull Celie O'Meara was hardly the sort of girl to catch a guy like Jace Tucker's eye.

Or was she?

The thought sent a shiver right down her spine. She and Jace Tucker?

Good God.

She reached the bow end of the deck and stopped, clutching the railing and staring out into the inky velvet sky and tried to arrange her thoughts, tried to make sense of a world turned upside down, tried to think! She tried to be logical like her niece Sara.

Well, like her niece Sara used to be. Before Flynn.

Sara said logic had gone right out the window where Flynn was concerned. Trying to explain how she could have simply tossed her day planner and her common sense right out the window, she'd told Celie, ''I don't know really. I felt some sort of primordial attraction I never even imagined existed until he walked into my life.'' She'd looked dazed. And then she'd said urgently, ''Do you know what I mean?''

Celie hadn't. Now she suspected she did.

She'd felt an urge she'd certainly never experienced before, when Jace's lips had touched hers. She'd felt hot and hungry and eager and desperate. She'd wanted the kiss to go on and on and on. She'd wanted other things to go from there. She'd wanted...Jace!

She gave herself a little shake and began pacing again, mind still spinning, body flushed with desire and barely cooled by the late-night breeze that caressed her skin. She barely felt it. Just as she barely saw the sliver of moon in the black velvet sky or the stars scattered like diamonds across it.

Instead she saw Jace's face. She saw the way his blue eyes had glittered as he'd looked at her, the way his hard mouth had twisted when he'd said those words. *That's what I'm doing here.*

Those words. She ran them over and over in her mind. "You could get your own damn husband! You could have looked around. Found a local guy." And then, when she'd scornfully challenged him to name a local guy, he'd said just one word: "Guess." And then he'd kissed her.

And then she relived the kiss. She'd never been kissed like that. Had never known that hunger, that intensity, had never *responded* with equal need. She still felt weak at the knees and fuzzy between the ears.

"That's what I'm doing here, Celie." She could hear the harsh words now.

That's what I'm doing here.

She stopped pacing and stood absolutely still, letting the late night breeze hit her squarely in the face as she stared into the darkness and considered the meaning of those words.

He'd come to...to *court* her?

It seemed so unlikely she shook her head. It boggled her mind. It was so unlike Jace.

Wasn't it?

She tried to think. Jace Tucker wanted her. She tried out the notion. Bent her mind around it. Said the words.

"Jace Tucker wants me." She rolled his name around in her mouth, tasted it the way she had tasted his lips less than an hour before. Could still taste his lips now.

Jace Tucker wanted her.

No. He didn't simply *want* her. That wasn't what he'd said.

He wanted to *marry* her!

Well, he hadn't said that, either. Not in so many words. But that was what he'd meant, wasn't it? It was her finding a husband that they'd been talking about.

She tried saying, "Jace Tucker wants to marry me," out loud and couldn't. Her tongue seemed welded to the roof of her mouth. She gripped her hands together tightly, as if the pressure from them would push more blood up through her over-heated body into her befuddled brain, as if it would help her make sense of this astonishing notion.

He wanted to *marry* her?

No. He couldn't.

But if she put everything he had said together—and combined it with that kiss!—that was the total she got. She did the addition again—and again. Every time it came out the same way.

And she, ninny that she was, instead of asking him what he was talking about, instead of insisting he spell it out, had panicked and run!

"Jace Tucker wants to marry me?" She got the words out finally, but they came out a question. She couldn't quite say them matter-of-factly. Still she stood staring out into the distance and felt this incredible wave of…what? Peace? Joy? Satisfaction? Inevitability?…wash over her.

Inevitability?

Oh, Celie. She shook her head at her own idiotic notions.

The first gurgle welling up in her chest caught her by surprise, jolted her. But she couldn't swallow it, couldn't make it go away. And it spilled over. She giggled. She gurgled. She laughed. She could feel tears she laughed so hard.

It was preposterous. She and Jace Tucker. And yet...it wasn't.

She didn't believe it. And yet she wanted to.

And that surprised her, too.

She'd dreamed of finding the other half of her soul for as long as she could remember. She'd thought she'd found him with Matt. She'd dreamed foolishly that she'd found him in her fantasies of Sloan. Those, she'd begun to realize recently, had existed merely to keep her hopes alive. They hadn't been real. They hadn't been substantial. They'd simply been there—holding a place for the real man whenever he came along.

And was the real man Jace?

Did he love her?

Did she love him?

God knew she hadn't thought so. She'd hated him for years—even as she'd been fascinated by him.

Watching Jace had always been like staring into the sun—tantalizing and dangerous. His joy of life, his boundless enthusiasm, his easy way with people—especially his ability to charm the opposite sex—had always been a source of fascination. When Matt had gone down the road with him, she remembered listening eagerly to the tales he'd told about Jace. And Celie had been torn between her fascination and her very real fear that emulating Jace's lifestyle would not be conducive to Matt's getting happily married to her.

It turned out that she was right. And that was when her fascination had turned to resentment.

She had been convinced that Jace didn't think much of

her, either. He'd certainly gone out of his way to tease her, to bait her, to get in her way these last few months every time she'd turned around.

She'd thought he had been doing it to annoy her.

Now she didn't know what to think.

But she was intrigued. Astonished. Amazed.

He'd kissed her—very nearly melted her where she'd stood—and instead of seeing where things would lead, she had panicked and run.

She couldn't go back, either, she realized now. Because somewhere down there Simone was lurking—no doubt ready to fire her.

Oddly the possibility didn't make her knees knock. She would have expected to be gibbering with fear that Simone was going to sack her. But she wasn't. She wasn't even thinking about Simone.

She was thinking about Jace.

Something had quickened inside her at his kiss. Something had happened between them. It scared her and attracted her at the same time. The old Celie would have been crawling into a hole right about now. This Celie was intrigued. This Celie wanted to know more.

Tomorrow she would. They would sort it out, she and Jace.

They would talk tomorrow *after* she'd been fired. For the moment she would play it all over and over in her mind. She would taste his kiss and remember his words. *You could get your own damn husband. Find a local guy. That's what I'm doing here.* She knew she wouldn't sleep a wink tonight.

She didn't care.

Celie was up, waiting for Simone to rap on her door before seven. It had happened when she'd sacked Tracy. She'd turned up while Tracy was still in her nightclothes and had sent the other woman packing then and there. Celie expected the same.

"What are you doing?" Allison had squinted at her out of one bleary eye when Celie had got up at six. She hadn't slept at all, so it really hadn't mattered when she got dressed. It had been all she could do not to bounce off the walls. She wanted it over and done with. She wanted to go see Jace.

"I'm...restless," Celie said. She was tempted to tell Allison about last night, about Simone, about Jace. But she didn't want the entire ship gossiping about her. There would be plenty of that after Simone fired her.

So she sat on her bed, fully dressed, and waited. And waited. Allison dragged herself up finally, grumbling. She gave Celie an odd look, went to take a shower. When she came out Celie was still waiting.

"What are you doing?" Allison demanded.

Celie shrugged. She picked up the book she'd been holding in her lap. "It's a thriller."

Allison didn't look impressed. "If it's so thrilling how come you're on the same page you were when I went in to take a shower? Coming to breakfast?"

Celie shook her head. She didn't want to be at breakfast when Simone arrived. She might not care that she was getting sacked, but she didn't relish public dismissal. She nodded at the book. "I want to read this."

Allison shook her head. "Whatever." She waggled her fingers and went off to get a bite to eat.

By ten minutes to eight Simone hadn't come. She was obviously going to force Celie to come to work. So it would be a public dismissal in the salon. Celie squared her shoulders and went.

Simone was already there, picture-perfect in her pencil-thin black skirt and black silk shirt. She was chatting with two of the passengers, but looked up when Celie came in.

''A word wiz you, *s'il vous plaît,* Mademoiselle O'Meara.'' Her mouth, outlined in bloodred lipstick, formed the words as one long finger with an equally blood-red nail beckoned Celie into her office.

So the execution wouldn't be public after all. Celie was grateful.

''Come in. Shut ze door, mademoiselle.''

Celie shut it. She took a deep, careful breath and let it out slowly. She would explain. She would be polite. And then she would be on her way. ''About last night...Ms. Sabot. I went to—''

Simone cut her off. ''I speak, mademoiselle. You listen.''

Celie fell silent. The woman was, after all, still her boss, and Celie was always polite. She had also never been in a situation like this before. This must have been what it was like to be sent to the principal. The very notion of being so bad as to be referred to a higher authority had horrified her as a child. Now she simply waited for the inevitable and didn't really care.

''I speak wiz your friend,'' Simone began.

''My friend?''

''Ze man in ze room,'' Simone said patiently. ''He explain why you were zere. He tells me he invite you to see pictures from home.''

Celie stared, nonplussed. Jace had done what? She didn't speak.

Just as well because Simone went right on. ''Of course, you understand zis is not so good.'' Simone shook her finger under Celie's nose. ''Going to rooms of passengers is not recommended. You remember I say zat?''

''No, ma'am. Yes, ma'am.'' Three bags full, ma'am.

''But I understand homesick. Is a difficult zing to be homesick.''

''Er, yes.''

''You are new, Mademoiselle O'Meara. I understand you

can be homesick when you are new. You will not let zis happen again. Yes?'' Hard eyes bored into hers.

''Um...'' Celie floundered.

''Yes,'' Simone answered her own question for Celie. ''Ze answer is yes. You understand? So, good. Now is time to get to work.'' She gave a brisk nod, turned away and opened the door.

Celie didn't move. She stood stock-still, staring. She wasn't fired? Jace had lied and saved her job for her? And why had he done that? Her mind was doing somersaults again.

''And so, what do you wait for, zen, mademoiselle?'' Simone tapped her pointy-toed shoe impatiently. ''Your first appointment is waiting.''

''Er, right.'' Celie hurried out past the older woman. She still had a job.

But what about Jace?

All day long Celie expected him to come to her.

It was a sea day. And the seas were somewhat rough because the wind had come up and there was a storm brewing. But though the ship rose and swayed, Celie remained steadfast at her post. The weather didn't bother her—and she wanted to be here when Jace came.

As long as she was here, he knew where she'd be.

She cut hair all morning, and though she kept one eye on the mirror as she clipped and snipped and shampooed and styled, Jace never came. In the afternoon she worked in the spa, giving massages. There was no mirror where she worked, and she had to crane her neck to see who came in. So making sure she saw him was a little more difficult.

''You remember my friend,'' she said to Allison and Stevie, ''the guy from home? Well, if he comes in looking for me, let me know.''

''You don't want us to tell him you're not here?'' Allison said.

''No. I...I want to talk to him.''

But the afternoon passed and Jace didn't come.

She didn't understand it. A guy didn't just blurt out things like Jace had and then vanish into thin air.

Except it seemed that Jace had. She worked until six o'clock. But he never came.

Lots of second thoughts did. They made her crazy. They caused her to question what she'd heard last night. Had she misinterpreted it? Misunderstood? She felt hot and then cold and then sick to her stomach.

But regardless of the words, there was no misinterpreting that kiss.

Was there?

Celie didn't see how. But she didn't see Jace, either.

Where was he?

''He never came in?'' she said to Allison when they got off work.

Allison shook her head. ''Never saw him. And—'' she grinned ''—believe me I looked. He's so gorgeous he'd be hard to miss.''

''I know.'' It was one of the things that had always made him seem so daunting. When you got right down to it, he was every bit as good-looking as Sloan Gallagher. Far more gorgeous than she was, that was for sure.

Jace Tucker could have any woman he wanted. He couldn't really want her!

But every time she thought that, she thought about the kiss. She thought about his words. And she thought she had to know.

She would have to go to his room.

Simone breezed past on her way out the door and gave Celie an arch look, as if she had been reading her mind.

Celie took a deep, desperate breath and smiled brightly.

"Want to catch the film after dinner?" Allison asked as they left the salon.

"Not tonight. I need to...to do something."

"Oh, yes?" Allison slanted her a glance. "Going to read some more of that thriller?"

"What?"

Allison just laughed. "I thought so."

She didn't push any further, just grinned and said, "Good luck."

Celie figured she needed it. She felt wobbly and uncertain. All her insecurities came clamoring back. Maybe she should just forget the whole thing, pretend it hadn't happened.

Impossible. She couldn't.

She hadn't come this far to turn and run now. So what if she was mistaken? So what if she'd misinterpreted? She had to go see him, anyway, didn't she, to thank him for saving her job?

Yes, definitely. She had to do that.

She showered and changed her clothes, tossing the polo shirt and white denims that were her work uniform into her laundry bag and putting on a pair of dressy black slacks and a red silk shirt. It had been one of her first purchases after her first week's work, a bit of casual sophistication. Whenever she wore it she felt braver.

She needed to feel brave tonight.

Then she did her makeup, using every trick of the trade that Simone and Stevie and Birgit had taught her. War paint, Allison had called it once laughingly before she'd headed out on a date. Celie needed that tonight, too.

It was hard to do it well because the stormy weather was still rocking the boat, making her attempts at mascara and eyeshadow difficult. And she smeared her lipstick on the first attempt and had to scrub it off and start over. But finally she was ready.

Or not.

"Ready," she told herself firmly. She could do this.

But why hadn't he come? The thought niggled at her all the way to his room. It taunted her, worried her. It was making her crazy. Jace had always made her crazy.

Was it only twenty-four hours since she'd come to take him to task for attempting to seduce every woman on the ship? Oh, God. She stopped stock-still in the hallway, feeling equal parts panicky and foolish.

There was still time. She could turn around and go back to her room.

No, she couldn't.

At Sloan and Polly's reception she had danced one slow dance with Sloan. Once upon a time that would have been the stuff of dreams. It was very special even when he was Polly's husband.

But what made it most special of all was right at the end, when he had stopped and looked down into her eyes, his own gentle as he'd said, "It will happen to you, Celie. Believe it."

She knocked on Jace's door.

He didn't answer.

She shifted from one foot to the other, hyperventilating—her nerves jangling and fingers clenching as she waited. Far down the hall a couple came around the corner. *Please God, don't let it be Simone.*

It wasn't. The couple approached. Celie knocked again. They smiled at her as they passed. She jigged from one foot to the other and told herself she might as well leave, he wasn't there.

Of course he wasn't there. It was just past dinnertime. He was probably in one of the dining areas with the blondes. He was probably at the captain's table—he and the captain and eight of the ship's most gorgeous women.

He was probably in some woman's room right now—in bed. He was…

The door opened a crack, and Jace's unshaven face peered out. He took one look at her and groaned. "Oh, hell."

"What's wrong?" Celie demanded.

He looked awful. His dark hair was spiky and uncombed. His face was pale beneath his normal dark tan. He was wearing a T-shirt and a pair of jeans. It looked as if he'd dragged them on as they hung low on his hips and didn't seem to be completely zipped.

"Jace?"

"Go away." He started to shut the door.

She stuck her foot in.

"Damn it, Celie!" He pushed again, but she pushed against it and practically knocked him down as she went in.

"What's the matter with you?" she demanded as he glowered at her.

He looked around desperately, helplessly, then shrugged, took half a dozen steps and crashed facedown on his unmade bed again. "I'm seasick."

It was, Jace was sure, worse than being dead.

Dead sounded great. If he were dead, it would be over. He wouldn't be spending hour after hour enduring the most gut-wrenching, sweat-inducing, head-pounding experience of his life.

Boats! Cripes! Why had anyone ever invented them? If God had wanted men to float He would have made the sea flat. How the hell did people live like this?

Why had he come?

Celie. He'd come to win Celie. Artie had thought it would be a good idea. Jace wanted to kill Artie. Drowning would be too good for him.

He'd been moaning and tossing and turning for hours. He hadn't had a rational thought since sometime in the middle of last night. He'd lain awake most of it, worrying about what Celie must be thinking.

He'd known he would have to track her down first thing in the morning and tell her what he'd told her boss about her coming to see pictures in his room. She had to know he hadn't tried to get her fired.

And she had to know he wasn't trying to seduce her, either. Or take advantage of her. Which heaven only knew that kiss certainly could have implied.

That kiss. He'd tried to regret that kiss. He couldn't. He'd savored it.

But he knew he'd have to explain it, too—if she'd let him. He'd tried to figure out what he'd say. He'd muttered and paced and raked his fingers through his hair for hours. His head had begun to pound, his mind to reel.

He wasn't exactly sure when it was that he'd started feeling sick. Maybe it was when the floor began to shift sideways as he walked. Maybe it was when the lights seemed to sway. He got dizzy watching them and lay down so it would wear off.

It hadn't. And when he'd tried to get up again he could barely make it to the bathroom without losing his dinner. He made it. He lost his dinner. Things had gone downhill from there.

"Bit of a storm," the steward had said when he'd come to make up the room. He'd been smiling brightly. Jace had groaned and told him to go away.

The man had offered to bring him something to make him feel better. "Perk you right up," he said with considerable relish.

Jace had declined. The very thought of putting anything in his stomach had sent him staggering toward the bathroom again.

The steward had straightened up while he'd been in there. ''You call when you want something,'' he'd said as he was leaving.

How about a funeral? Jace thought. It was the only thing that appealed.

He didn't get out of bed all day. The ship continued to rock. The lights continued to sway.

The blondes stopped to see if he wanted to come to lunch and dinner. He didn't. The understatement of the year.

''Want us to bring something back for you?'' Deb asked, looking at him sympathetically as he clutched the door and tried to remain upright until they left. ''There's something you can drink that's supposed to help.''

''No.'' Jace didn't think he'd ever drink anything again, and he said so. They left with Deb muttering that he really should try. He stumbled back to bed again and wanted to die.

An hour later he heard knocking again. He didn't want to answer it. It would be Deb, undoubtedly, determined to force some awful medicine down his throat. He ignored the knocking. But it continued. She didn't go away.

He groaned. Damn it. Every knock pounded not just on the door, but in his head. ''Okay, all right. I'm coming.'' Anything to get her to quit. He staggered up, stumbled across the room and wrenched open the door.

''Oh, hell.''

He'd been horrified to see Celie standing there. God, no. He couldn't deal with her tonight. But he hadn't been quick enough to shut her out. And now he was lying facedown on the bed and she was standing over him.

''How long have you been like this?''

''Forever,'' he muttered into the sheet.

''Did you take anything for it?''

''No.''

"You should. You'll be sicker if you don't. I'll go get something."

He tried to shake his head. A serious mistake. He hauled himself up and bolted for the bathroom, slamming the door behind him. A man needed a shred of dignity. He'd be damned if he'd let her in to play Florence Nightingale and hold his head for him.

Beyond the door Celie said, "I'll be right back."

He sank down and slumped against the wall of the bathroom and tried to muster the willpower to get up and go lock the door so she couldn't come right back.

He didn't make it.

"Drink this."

"No." Muffled into the sheet.

"Yes." She prodded his ribs.

Jace groaned. "Go away."

"No. I'm trying to help you."

"Shoot me."

"Sorry," she said with disgusting cheer. "No gun. Come on, Jace. I promise this will help. Truly. The bartender swears by it."

"The bartender?" He shuddered, remembering his hangover. He did not want to think about alcohol at a time like this. Bile rose in his throat.

"Nonalcoholic," Celie said, apparently able to read minds now. "Come on." She nudged him again.

Jace groaned and turned his head to eye her blearily. "If I drink it will you go away?"

She was looking down at him with those beautiful deep-blue eyes of hers and she shook her head solemnly. "Not a chance."

He shut his own eyes.

"We have to talk, Jace." Her voice was soft, tender, concerned, edged with worry. "About last night."

"I don't...didn't—" But he couldn't explain. Not now. Probably not ever.

He heard her swallow. She hesitated, then said quietly, "Didn't mean it?"

Something in her voice got to him. She sounded nervous, apprehensive. Doubtful. He opened his eyes and looked at her. The beautiful eyes were dark and serious, taking everything to heart. Jace pressed his mouth together in a thin line, drew a breath and nodded just slightly. "Meant it," he admitted.

Celie smiled then. It was like the sun coming out. It was her angel's smile. Sweet and pure and joyous. He'd seen it before—when she'd held a baby, when she'd come to see Artie at the hospital, when she'd kissed her mother and Walt at their wedding. He'd never seen it directed at him.

Her hand brushed lightly over his hair, and then cool fingers stroked his hot cheek. He very nearly moaned.

"Come on, Jace. Drink. You'll feel better." She held out the glass to him.

He struggled up and drank. It was vile. He gagged it down. Then he sank back against the pillows, spent.

"Satisfied?" he muttered when he could manage it.

Celie smiled and sat on the bed beside him, shaking her head as she did so. "Satisfied?" she echoed. "No, not quite yet."

Six

It was the weirdest dream he'd ever had.

He and Celie had been together in bed, their arms around each other. They were touching. Her hand had been stroking his hair. He thought she'd kissed him…before they'd slept.

He awoke dazed and disoriented, tangled in the bedclothes, straining to remember, to bring the dream back, to hang on to it for a few more minutes.

And then, slowly, as he looked around the room, he noticed that his head wasn't pounding anymore, that lights weren't swaying anymore and that there was an empty glass on the bedside table. And he realized that it might not have been a dream at all.

Celie had been here.

He rolled over, reached out. The other side of the bed was empty. But the pillow was crushed against the headboard, the blanket was rumpled. He rolled over and pressed his face to the pillow, inhaling deeply and groaning as he savored the soft fresh scent that was Celie.

Celie had been here.

And now she wasn't.

Why? He vaguely remembered her touching his cheek, smiling, saying. ''Going to check in with Simone,'' she'd said. ''Be right back.''

How long ago had that been? He had no idea of the time, but beyond the drapes the sun looked high in the sky. It had to be late. And she wasn't back?

Why hadn't she come back?

Second thoughts? Had he done something unforgivable while he was asleep? He tried to think back, to dredge up more memories. The ones he did remember were embarrassing for the most part. He'd been sick as a dog all night, barely coherent, hardly in control. Pretty unforgivable. But she had stayed then. She'd stayed through it all.

She could have vanished right after she'd brought him that ghastly stuff to drink. She hadn't. Instead she'd climbed right onto the bed with him and let him put his head in her lap. And later, if he remembered right, he'd awakened once to find that she had slid down to lie beside him and they were wrapped in each other's arms.

He'd spent ten years imagining what it would be like to go to bed with Celie O'Meara. It had never been like that! Thank God.

And yet…

There had been something right about just lying with her, being with her. Something honest. Something real. Something he'd never experienced with any other woman.

''No kidding,'' he muttered gruffly. Celie was the first woman he'd ever only slept with—in the literal sense of the word.

Now he slowly eased himself to a sitting position and waited for disaster. But it didn't come. The room didn't rock. His stomach didn't roll. His mouth tasted foul, but he could solve that. He could brush his teeth, take a shower, clean up, get dressed.

And then he would go find Celie O'Meara—and they would talk.

"What do you mean I have to work?" Celie demanded.

Simone smiled unflappably and unrepentantly. "I'm so sorry," she said. "Stevie is sick. He cannot come in and of course Allison cannot do it all herself. Her schedule is full. Stevie has haircuts all morning and he was to do massage this afternoon. It's is a very good thing you, too, are qualified."

"But—"

But there was no *but*—and Celie knew it. There was only her job. And filling in when someone was sick was part of it.

Shore days were just like any other day if you were needed. Only today Celie hadn't intended to go ashore. She'd left Jace at the last possible minute, run back to her room, changed into the polo shirt and white jeans she wore when she was on duty and then run down to the salon. She expected to check in with Simone, grab a quick shower and run right back to Jace again.

"So you will start, now, yes." It wasn't a question. Simone was looking at her expectantly. She nodded at the woman who had just come into the salon. "Your first appointment is here."

Celie sighed. She took a deep breath. She hoped Jace understood. Then she pasted on her cruise-ship smile and beckoned the woman to her chair.

Allison was looking at her speculatively. "Missed you last night," she said. What she meant was *Where were you?*

Celie smiled. "Yes."

Allison's gaze narrowed. "What have you been up to?"

''Nothing,'' Celie said, still smiling. It was nothing but the truth. She had spent the night in a man's bed—in *Jace Tucker's* bed!—but she hadn't done a thing.

Yet.

Thinking about what she might do had her going hot and cold by turns. Just lying there watching Jace sleep, stroking his hair, holding him in her arms had made last night the most memorable of her life.

Which just, she thought with a certain amount of ironic self-awareness, went to show what a pitiful life she'd led so far.

Allison was still looking at her carefully, but Celie didn't say any more. She set to work shampooing her first customer, listening to the woman talk about how she was going to spend the day ashore on the private island that the cruise line leased.

It was billed as ''the island idyll of your dreams,'' and it had everything—a beautiful pink sand beach for swimming, a reef for snorkeling, glass-bottom boats for those who weren't into getting wet, and Para-Sails, Jet Skis and Boogie Boards for those who were. There were volleyball and Frisbee for the sports aficionados, sand castle building contests for the artistically minded, a straw market for those who could never get enough of shopping, limbo dancing for the exhibitionists and, to top it off, a sort of Caribbean-island-barbecue-luau which pulled out all the gourmet stops.

It was a lot of fun. Celie had been there several times and she replied enthusiastically to the woman's questions and comments without even having to think about it. Instead she thought about Jace.

Was he still asleep? What would he think when he woke up? Would he even remember that she had been there? *She* would never forget.

The salon was reasonably busy. She and Allison had a

steady stream of people all morning. Marguerite, the receptionist, was on the phone taking appointments, and Simone, who disdained "island idylls" in favor of trips to the casinos of Paradise Island when they were in Nassau or night clubs in St. Maarten, was on hand, too, doing paperwork in the office and keeping an eye on things.

Once or twice Allison tried to get her to talk about where she'd been last night. But Celie wasn't doing that. She simply smiled and brushed the questions off—and drifted right back to thinking about Jace.

She hadn't wanted to leave him this morning. Nothing was settled. Nothing had been said. They hadn't talked. They'd only touched. Which was maybe just as well, she thought. She and Jace had never done very well with words.

It was still hard to imagine they were doing well at all. It was even hard to imagine a "they" that included just the two of them—as if they were a couple. How could they be a couple when they'd fought like cats and dogs or ignored each other for half her life?

What if she was completely wrong?

So she replayed it all again and again—from his fierce words last night to his kiss to his head in her lap as he slept only hours ago .

"I said a trim, my dear! A *trim!*" the woman in the chair said irritably and Celie jolted back to the present to discover she'd taken the woman's pageboy style to the bottom of her ear.

"Oh! Er, right. I…um…just wanted to even this out a little." Celie blushed, took a deep breath, and forced herself to concentrate on the business at hand. It wouldn't do to scalp the passengers just because she was shell-shocked. She could see Simone look at her through the glass that separated the salon from the office. She gave Celie a severe look.

Celie gave herself a little shake and studied the passenger's face. "Have you considered trying something a little shorter and layered? Like this?" She drew the woman's hair back, then fluffed it lightly out on the sides. It was less harsh. It softened her features, and the woman who had looked about to snap at her, blinked and reconsidered.

"Oh!" She turned her head to get another angle. Celie demonstrated what she had in mind. "Well," the woman said. "That might be interesting."

"It could be very flattering," Celie said. "It brings out your bone structure. Shall I?" She cocked her head and looked at the woman in the mirror.

The woman nodded. "Go ahead."

Celie smiled and began to snip, determined not to think about Jace for the moment. No sooner had she made the resolution than she almost took off the poor woman's ear when she looked up into the mirror to see Jace himself standing right behind her.

"Oh!" She jumped and snipped and—fortunately—did not draw blood. "I'm sorry," she babbled to the startled woman, but then she spun around, turning her attention wholly to Jace. "What are you doing here?"

Memories which had kept her entertained all morning—and which she had thought were vivid in the extreme—paled compared to the real man.

Jace stood, shaved and combed, lean and handsome, directly in front of her. He wore a pair of soft, faded Wranglers and a hunter-green polo shirt, and Celie had to admit that, as her dad used to say, he "cleaned up good."

Though his face was still a little pale, his color was coming back. His eyes were bright. He didn't look like death on the hoof any longer. On the contrary, he looked more drop-dead gorgeous than ever.

And judging from the look on her customer's face, she wasn't the only one to think so. The woman stared at him, openmouthed. So did the two ladies who were waiting. So did Allison. So did Marguerite. So did Simone.

Oh, dear.

''You said you were coming back.'' He looked at her intently.

''I was. But I got shanghaied into working. Stevie got sick.''

''We need to talk.'' He didn't even seem to notice the attention he was attracting. He didn't seem to notice anything—or anyone—but her. And Celie barely saw anyone but him.

And then, out of the corner of her eye through the glass, she saw Simone get up out of her chair in the office. ''We can't talk now,'' she said quickly, nodding toward the woman coming their way.

Jace didn't even glance at her. His eyes bored into Celie's. ''Why not?''

''My boss,'' Celie began.

''Ah, the friend.'' Simone's voice cut in. She gave Jace a glacial smile and arched her perfect brows. ''I thought we spoke before.''

''We did.'' Jace brushed her off. ''Now I need to talk to Celie.''

''Celie is working. Do you wish an appointment, monsieur?''

''No, he just—'' Celie began.

''Yes, I do,'' Jace said firmly. ''I want an appointment with Celie.''

Simone blinked. Her gaze narrowed momentarily, but when Jace stood his ground, she nodded and opened the schedule book and scanned the day. ''Ah, too bad. I am afraid we are full,'' she said with evident satisfaction after a few moments' perusal. ''No haircuts or massages from Mademoiselle O'Meara. What a pity.'' A saccharine smile appeared.

But Jace's attention was caught by something else. "Massages?" His brows lifted a mile.

"Therapeutic massage," Simone said flatly, "for neuromuscular rehabilitation and relaxation. You understand?"

"Oh, yeah," Jace grinned. "I understand." But there was such obvious devilment in his tone that Celie was sure Simone knew she was being deliberately misunderstood. She winced as she considered how Simone would take that.

Simone evidently had no intention of taking it. She gave an audible sniff. "If you wish an appointment with Allison..." She nodded toward Celie's friend.

"No."

"Well, then, I am sorry. If you will excuse us..." Simone started to herd Jace toward the door the way Celie's dad had herded balky steers toward the corral.

Jace stiffened and remained unmoving. Anticipating disaster, Celie sucked in a quick breath. So did Allison. So did Marguerite. So did both the customers.

But after a long moment of collectively held breath, Jace shrugged. With one unreadable look at her, he nodded.

"Sure," he said, and turned on his heel to head for the door. When he got there, he stopped and looked back at Celie. "I'll be back."

She wondered if he would storm the salon. It didn't seem likely, but with Jace Tucker you never knew.

She worked until two cutting hair under Simone's unrelenting eagle eye. Then she moved to the relative peace of the spa where she took over Stevie's massage clients.

It was easier to think there with the soft Celtic music playing in the background and the scent of almond oil in the air. Easier, too, to dream of Jace.

Not to mention safer. No matter how much detail her mind indulged in as she replayed those hours she'd lain in bed with Jace, when she was giving a massage, Celie wasn't in danger of amputating anyone's ear.

It was therapeutic for her, too, in a way, she thought as she changed the sheets on the massage table in preparation for the last client of the day. She had spent the afternoon channeling all her longings into her work, into easing the stress and loosening the muscles in her clients.

One more and she would be finished. She buzzed Marguerite to send in her next appointment.

"Saving the best for last," she muttered when she looked at her list and saw who it was.

Gloria Campanella was what Armand had called "the first lady of the ship," a healthy, wealthy eighty-five-year-old widow who spent a good part of the year cruising from one port to another in search of heaven knew what.

"The cure for loneliness," Armand claimed. "The perfect mate."

Mrs. Campanella had been on three cruises since Celie had come aboard. She was always dressed to the nines, always had a martini in her hand, always had Stevie do her hair and give her a massage. He was her favorite, the only one who could soothe and charm her at the same time. Everyone else got the sharp side of her tongue. They all knew her—and knew not to cross her.

Then the door opened—and Jace walked in.

Celie stared. "What are you—?"

"I couldn't wait."

"But—Mrs. Campanella! You've got to get out of here! Mrs. Campanella will have a fit. She'll raise a stink. Simone will be furious!"

"Simone doesn't need to know."

But she would know. "Mrs. Campanella—"

"Mrs. Campanella changed her mind."

"What! She never!"

Jace nodded. "She did." He paused. "I bribed her."

"You never!" Celie was gaping at him.

But Jace nodded, perfectly serious. "She wasn't all that keen on getting a massage from you," he said cheerfully. "She prefers the guy."

"Yes, but—"

"I bought her a martini and listened to her life's story. She's a lonely old lady and she likes men. She especially—" he grinned "—likes cowboys."

Hard to imagine. But then, what he'd said was true. Mrs. Campanella did like men. Celie tried to envision tiny, immaculate Mrs. Campanella, who always reminded Celie of a well-dressed paperclip in her Felix Diamante designer originals, with Jace, in his jeans and shirt. It boggled the mind.

"She's not..." Celie waved a hand toward the waiting room, still expecting to hear Mrs. Campanella's strident tones demanding to know why she was being kept waiting.

"She's busy planning a trip to Elmer," Jace said. "I told her if she'd let me have her spot I'd get her a date with a ninety-year-old cowboy."

Celie's jaw dropped. "Artie?" *And Gloria Campanella?* Good God.

Jace grunted. "Figured it was the least he could do for the cause."

"What cause?"

"Us."

And there it was. There *they* were. Face-to-face at last.

Us. Celie O'Meara and Jace Tucker. Hardly stranger than Artie Gilliam and Gloria Campanella.

Their gazes met. Locked. Jace's eyes were bluer than the sea and even more unfathomable.

Celie wetted her lips nervously and cleared her throat. Us. He wasn't looking away.

"Did you..." she faltered, then tried again. "Did you really come on the cruise because...because of...me?"

In the background the Celtic tune wove its mysterious pattern. Outside Celie could hear the muffled calls of the exercise girl leading a group in calesthenics.

"Yeah," Jace said, his voice sounding as rusty as hers. "I did."

"But I thought—" She stopped and rethought, going over once more what she'd believed all these years. Then she shook her head. "I thought...you couldn't stand me," she told him.

Jace looked perplexed. "What? Why?"

"When Matt...when Matt brought you over that day, when he was going down the road with you...you barely even looked at me. You wanted nothing to do with me."

Jace looked away now. "Couldn't." He jammed his hands in his pockets and stared out the window at the sea.

"Couldn't?" Celie echoed. "Couldn't what?"

"Look at you! Want anything to do with you!"

She stared at him, mystified. "Why not?"

Jace rocked on his boot heels. A muscle ticked in his jaw. She thought for a long moment that he wasn't going to answer her. But then the words burst from him as he turned and glared at her. "Because, damn it, you were Matt's girl!"

"What!"

Jace hunched his shoulders, took a couple of steps away, but there was nowhere to go in the small room, so he turned and scowled straight at her. "You heard me."

She was Matt's girl.

"It mattered?" Celie asked, trying to work this out. It didn't fit with anything she had thought and was wholly new and surprising to her.

"A guy isn't supposed to want his buddy's girl." Jace growled.

Her mouth opened and closed silently as the implications

hit. He'd *wanted* her? All those years ago Jace Tucker had *wanted* her? The notion was absurd. And yet…

He was still glaring at her as if it were somehow her fault.

Finally she managed one tiny sound. ''Oh.''

Jace's mouth twisted. ''Yeah. Oh.'' He raked a hand through his hair. ''It seemed better not to have anything to do with you,'' he said.

She didn't know what to say. Her mind was whirling as she tried to put an entirely new interpretation on so many different events.

''You and Matt…'' she began, trying to sort that out. ''Did you…''

Jace ground his teeth. ''I did not deliberately lead him astray.'' He bit out the words harshly. ''Is that what you want to know?''

Numbly Celie nodded.

He shook his head. ''I didn't,'' he swore. ''Maybe I was a bad example—all right, I *was* a bad example. I did a lot of racketin' around in those days. But what he did, he did on his own.''

''He wanted to be like you.''

''The more fool he.'' Jace paced a couple more steps, did a little hop which, Celie suspected, had to do with nervous energy, then turned and confronted her again. ''Look, I'm sorry it turned out the way it did—for you. You got hurt. He should've told you he wasn't ready. But really, Cel', you're better off without him.''

''I know that,'' Celie said quietly.

Her agreement seemed to surprise him. ''You do?''

She nodded. ''In retrospect I could see he had been trying to tell me by leaving. Running off to the rodeo is not the sign of a man who wants to settle down.'' She smiled faintly. ''I just didn't want to see it. I had my dreams.''

The fault, she realized, had been at least half hers. She'd

been more in love with her dreams than she had been with Matt. He'd merely been the means to accomplishing them.

"It was just as well it happened," she said softly now.

"Yeah." Jace raked his fingers through his hair. "Well, you didn't exactly think so at the time." He took a deep breath. "You hated my guts."

"Yes."

"For a long time you hated my guts," he persisted.

Celie nodded. He was shaking his head, not understanding, and she knew she had to explain. "You knew I was a failure."

He stared at her. "Huh?"

"Matt dumped me!"

"Matt was an idiot. I thought we'd established that."

"No. He had his…oats…to sow," Celie said. "But I thought…I thought that—" her mouth seemed suddenly dry. She swallowed desperately. "Another woman might have been enough for him. Just…not me." She turned away, wouldn't look at Jace then. Couldn't believe she was having this conversation with him. She burned—her face, her neck, all of her.

"No," Jace sounded shocked. "Oh, no."

He took a step and reached out to catch her hand and draw her into his arms. Celie, for a moment, held back. But he persisted. He held her close, whispered her name against her lips. And then he kissed her.

This kiss was as deep and hungry and intense as the one he'd given her in his room two days ago. It spoke of longing and need and desire. And Celie was no proof against it. She stopped resisting and began to respond, to say with her kiss all the things she didn't think she would ever be able to put into words—things about pain and loss and anguish, about years of loneliness and emptiness, about hopes and dreams born anew.

It was Jace who finally broke it off, who stepped back,

shaken and flushed and breathing hard. ''Whoa,'' he muttered, ''unless you want to scandalize that dragon of a boss of yours.''

Celie giggled. ''She would be shocked!''

''Well, we wouldn't want to do that,'' Jace said with a lopsided grin. ''Come on. Let's go finish this where we won't be disturbed.''

''I can't.''

He stared at her. ''What? Why the hell not?''

''I can't leave. Not now. Not until six. She'll be checking.''

Jace looked poleaxed. ''Who cares?''

''It's my job!''

He started to say something, then closed his mouth again and nodded. ''Okay. Fine. Let's get on with it then.''

Celie blinked. ''Get on with what?''

The lopsided grin was back. ''My massage.''

''You want a massage?'' Celie said with a smile after looking momentarily startled.

''Unless you're chicken?'' Jace teased recklessly.

She smiled. ''We'll see who's chicken.''

Jace had a feeling it was going to be him.

''Strip down to your shorts,'' Celie said briskly. ''I'll give you a few minutes.''

''You don't have to leave—'' he began to protest, but she was already out the door.

Grinning, anticipating, he stripped down to his shorts, then boosted himself up onto the massage table, relishing the thought of her hands on him for an hour.

When she came back, she turned on a CD of some sort of soft lilting Celtic tune that reminded him of a movie he'd seen.

Jace's mouth quirked into a grin. ''Music to sink a ship by?''

Celie ignored him. "Lie on your stomach and put your face in the face cradle. Let your arms go loose."

Jace did as she instructed, settling on the sheet she had warmed with a heating pad. She folded another sheet over him, baring only his back and shoulders. He heard her rub her hands together and felt his anticipation grow. That wasn't the only thing that was growing.

Cool it, buddy, he advised himself. If he was going to last the hour, he was going to have to think pure thoughts and multiplication tables. Indeed the first touch of her hands sent a jolt right through him. She'd only touched his back, between his shoulders, but his mind sent impulses zinging from his back to his brain to his groin like lightning strikes.

Celie paused, her hands resting lightly on his back. "You're very tense."

"I'm very horny," Jace corrected.

"We'll take care of that," she promised.

That startled him. "Here?" he said, aghast.

"Oh, yes," Celie said, stunning him.

But it wasn't long before he realized that she didn't mean what he thought she'd meant.

He'd expected to lie there and allow Celie to work her magic on him, seducing him with her hands. Instead she found every injury he'd ever had and ferreted out every single protesting muscle and bit of scar tissue.

He was lulled at first by the strong smooth strokes on his back and shoulders, and he gave himself up to it until her fingers slowed and she traced old scars and sore spots and probed lightly.

"Does this hurt?"

"No," he lied, wanting her to move on.

But she kneaded some more, deepening the massage. "How about this?"

"What are you, a sadist?"

"No. But it's tight. I can feel it knotted up there. Let me

see if we can't work it out. I do a terrific neuro-muscular massage.''

So much for seduction.

''It will feel better when I'm done,'' she promised.

''Like it feels so much better to stop banging your head against the wall?''

Celie laughed. ''You could say that.''

She worked over each and every tender spot he'd ever had in his life—in his neck, on his back, on the shoulder of his riding arm. She found the spots where he'd broken ribs, the vertebrae he'd cracked in his back. With her thumbs and fingers she rubbed them gently, then more deeply, and finally began digging her fingers down to lift and roll the muscle.

''Jeez!'' The word whistled through Jace's teeth, arousal fading fast.

''Too much?'' Celie asked, her voice concerned. ''If it is, say so. I tend to get a little carried away trying to work out these spasms.''

''It's okay,'' Jace said gruffly.

Her thumbs kneaded the cords of his neck, pressing up into his scalp, sending goose bumps down across his shoulders and back. Then she worked over his neck and shoulders and down his back, her fingers and thumbs walking up and down his spine, stopping to find the bunched muscles, kneading them, working the spasms out.

It wasn't seductive—not the way Jace had imagined it. But like the time they'd spent together in bed last night, it felt good. It felt...right.

She moved on to his legs.

''Ah,'' she said softly as he tensed when she touched the one he'd broken at the finals last December. ''That still hurts, does it?''

''It's...a little tender.''

''I'll take care of it.''

She did his other leg first, rubbing and kneading, warming it and stretching it, before she left it tingling and moved on to the one he had broken.

She bent his knee, testing his range of motion first. Then starting from his heel, she began working her way up the muscles in his calf. At first it hurt a lot. His leg always hurt a lot. He'd got used to it, had tried to learn to live with it. Had never really considered that it wouldn't. But now, as Celie worked on him, gradually the hard tight spots seemed to soften and relax.

"Ah." He couldn't help the sound escaping. He leg felt so much better, looser, less tense.

"Better?" Celie asked.

He nodded. "Yeah. Oh, yeah."

"Good." She moved up above his knee and began working on the hamstring, easing the tension there, as well. And it worked.

"Great," he murmured. "Thanks."

"Still horny?" she asked lightly.

Jace grimaced, realizing he was not. "I could be again in a few minutes," he said hopefully.

Silently Celie ran her hands up the backs of his legs. Her fingers felt very different all of a sudden. Intimate. Personal. Very personal.

Jace's body went on alert as the fingers moved up over his butt and traced the waistband of his shorts. It didn't take him a few minutes to get horny again. A few seconds, more like.

He turned his head to look back over his shoulder at her. "Celie?"

She gave him a smile, then consulted her watch. "Oh, gee," she said with a grin now wholly unrepentant. Her eyes danced. "Time's up."

Seven

It wasn't the devil who made her do it, but there was definitely an impish rogue hidden somewhere inside Celie's head who dared her to dare Jace.

Because that's what it was—those fingers, there at the end of a perfectly legitimate massage, dancing up the back of his thighs—a dare. They'd gone from skilled professionalism to tempting teasing in seconds. They wanted what Celie had wanted all along.

She'd wanted it at the very beginning. She could have turned the massage into a seduction at any point. She hadn't because she was at work. She had standards to uphold, and she intended to uphold them.

Even with Jace.

Besides, it had been quickly apparent that Jace needed something she had it in her power to give. He was a rodeo cowboy. Rodeo cowboys, by definition, hurt. It was the name of the game. And old rodeo cowboys went on hurting even after they'd given up the game.

They were walking masses of scar tissue, muscle spasms and various and sundry contusions and adhesions. Jace was no exception.

Last night in bed she'd seen old scars. She'd touched them lightly as he slept. She'd wondered how he'd got each one and thought someday, perhaps, he'd tell her.

In the meantime, though, today for an hour, she'd done her best to ease those pains.

If Simone had got wind of his deal with Mrs. Campanella and come to see exactly what was going on, she'd have seen exactly what she was supposed to see—Celie acting like what she was: a professional massage therapist.

Until the last few seconds, when she'd turned into the woman who wanted to make love with Jace.

"You," he told her, rolling over so fast she thought he might flip right off the table, "are asking for it, Celie O'Meara."

She fluttered her eyelashes at him. "I am?"

He leaped off the table like a man who had no aches and pains at all, grabbing her around the waist and hauling her into his arms. It took no imagination at all to figure out how aroused he was.

"Jace!"

"Don't start something you don't intend to finish," he muttered against her lips.

"I intend to finish it," Celie said. "I *want* to finish it. But not here."

"Then let's get out of here. I presume you're finished now? Do you have to sign out with the dragon?"

Celie shook her head. "No. I just have a few things to take care of. Quick things," she promised when he glared at her.

"Damn quick," Jace insisted.

"Yes. You get dressed. I'll finish up." She stripped the

bed linens off the massage table and started toward the door.

Jace caught her by the hand and tugged her around. ''You're not going to disappear.''

Celie smiled. ''I'm not going to disappear.''

He felt like a teenager. Gauche and awkward. Eager, yet desperate.

For a guy who'd relished—and deserved—his reputation as a ladies' man, Jace felt like a dumb kid now.

He'd practically dragged her to his stateroom. But the minute he got her there and shut the door, everything changed. He leaned against the door, his palms sweating, his breathing shallow. And not from arousal. From nerves.

He was going to make love with Celie O'Meara.

And his stomach was clenching and his body was quivering, and if he didn't get his act together, he was going to make a complete mess of it. If it hadn't mattered so much, he'd have laughed at himself.

Jace Tucker, panic-stricken at the thought of taking a woman to bed?

No, not *a* woman. She wasn't just any woman.

She was the only woman who'd really ever mattered—and that made all the difference.

Every other time Jace had gone to bed with a woman, it had been to have a good time then and there. He'd always been a generous bed partner, always happy to make sure his companion enjoyed it as much as he did. But the act itself had never had a deeper meaning, had never gone beyond the physical. It had been fun. It had provided a release. And always he'd been able to walk away without looking back.

No more.

He couldn't walk away from Celie. And it wasn't just *his* body, *his* mind, *his* heart and *his* soul that were involved. It was *Celie's,* too. He had to make it right for her. Had to make it beautiful for her. Had to show her how much he loved her.

For a guy who wrote the book on lack of commitment, this was pretty scary stuff. In fact, it was damn near paralyzing.

"Is something wrong?" Celie asked. She was looking at him curiously as she stood by his bed, apparently without a qualm in the world, already unbuttoning her shirt. She smiled and peeled it off her shoulders, baring a tanned midriff and full breasts covered by the peach-colored lace of her bra. Her hands went to unfasten the front-clasped bra.

Cripes, she was going to be naked before he got his boots unnailed from the floor. "Stop!"

At his exclamation, Celie stopped. She stared, her fingers stilled on the clasp of her bra. "What?"

"I want..." He swallowed. His mouth felt like the Sahara. He cleared his throat desperately and tried again. "I want to do that."

Celie's hands dropped to her sides. She nodded—and stood waiting for him.

He almost tripped over his boots, crossing the few feet of carpet between them, until he was standing right in front of her, looking down on the rise and fall of her breasts beneath the lace. He took a breath and put his fingers to work on the clasp. They were like thumbs—a tenth-grader's thumbs! He was mortified watching them tremble.

He flicked his eyelids up to see if she was laughing at him. He wouldn't have been surprised. But she wasn't laughing at all. Her lower lip was caught in her teeth and she was trembling, too.

It made him feel better. He got her bra undone. Opened it. Feasted his gaze on full, creamy breasts. He smiled. "Ah."

He caressed them with his thumbs and fingers, his palms

brushing her nipples. He saw her suck in her breath and felt her shudder. She didn't move, though, just clenched her fists at her sides and remained absolutely still as his hands stroked her. Beneath his fingers he could feel her shallow, unsteady breathing. He could hear the faint gasp of her breath as he explored her further, letting his hands mould the shape of her rib cage, then settle at her waist, then slide a finger inside the waistband of her jeans.

Her stomach muscles clenched. "Jace!"

"Mmm?" He bent his head, dropped kisses along one shoulder, then across her jaw and neck and across the other shoulder. With his tongue he touched her heated flesh. He nipped and tasted, and she shuddered, and suddenly her arms wrapped hard around his waist.

She pulled his shirt out of his jeans and slid her hands up underneath it to caress his back. There was nothing professional about her touch now. Her caresses were as heated and hungry as his. She grasped the hem of his shirt and drew it up and over his head, then tossed it aside and pressed her palms against his chest.

Her thumbs rubbed over his nipples and were immediately followed by her tongue. Jace sucked air. His fingers tightened on her buttocks and pulled her hard against him, letting her feel his urgency. "Careful," he muttered.

But Celie shook her head and continued the hot wet kisses. "I've been careful way too long already." And her fingers began to work on the buckle of his belt.

Telling him she'd had enough of being careful was like throwing kerosene on a roaring fire. It did no good to bank the flames now. There was no chance to slow things down, to throw a little water on their passion. All Jace's worries were overtaken by desire. All of his panic was swallowed by need.

He'd waited forever. At least it seemed that way. "You're sure?" he rasped.

But she'd got his belt undone by then, and when her fingers slid down the zipper of his jeans, Jace had all the answer he needed.

As she freed him and he felt the cool air hit his heated, hungry flesh, he was tearing at Celie's jeans, making quick work of them, unfastening, unzipping, peeling them and her panties, in one deft movement, over her hips and down her legs.

She kicked them aside and pushed his down as well. They tangled around his boots and he stumbled and muttered a curse as they tumbled together onto the bed.

"Sorry," he mumbled, then swallowed the word in a gasp as her fingers traced the burning length of him.

"I'm not." Celie wriggled beneath him, making him crazy, bringing him to the verge of forgetting every sane, sensible thought he'd had about going slow and taking time and making it perfect for her.

"Cel'! Wait! Slow down! I—"

"Can't keep up?" she whispered against his lips, smiling at him while her hands drove him to distraction.

He grabbed them and held them, pinned her to the bed with the weight of him and took a shuddering breath as he looked down into her eyes. "I want," he said with difficulty, "for it to be good for you. I want it to be perfect for you. I don't want to…to take—" He stumbled over this last as she moved beneath him and the feel of her made him catch his breath. "I want it to be right."

Celie lifted her head to bring her lips to his. She kissed him softly, lingeringly. "It *is* right, Jace." She kissed him again, traced his lips with her tongue, raised her hips against his, rocking them together. "Take me."

He did.

He couldn't wait any longer. He'd waited forever. He needed her now.

And from the way she clutched at him, opened for him

and drew him in, Celie seemed to need him, too. Her fingers dug into his back, her head tossed, and once more her hips lifted to welcome his thrust. "Come to me, Jace."

"Yesss." The word whistled through his teeth. He had Celie beneath him, Celie surrounding him, Celie loving him. At last.

At last, Celie thought.

It was the stuff of dreams. Of fantasies. Of thousands of nights of loneliness finally filled. It was Jace Tucker doing the most wonderful things to her, stroking her, touching her, kissing her, wanting it to be right for her.

It *was* right for her. It was the most right thing she'd ever done—welcoming him into her body as well as into her heart. Loving Jace was finding the other half of her soul.

And when he filled her, stroked her, shattered her—and himself—he took the pieces of all her broken dreams and once again made them whole.

He lay, spent, still shuddering on top of her, knowing he should move, that his weight had to be too much for her. And yet when he tried to, she held him fast.

"No," she whispered, hands clasped against the small of his back.

He lifted his head to look down at her, and the sight that met his eyes stabbed him to the core. "Oh, God. Did I hurt you?"

He'd never made a woman cry before!

But Celie shook her head and smiled through her tears. "You didn't hurt me at all. It was wonderful. Marvelous. *You're* wonderful. Marvelous."

Jace blinked. He was? "Then why—"

She shook her head again and swiped at her eyes. "I always cry when I'm happy."

She was happy. She was in his arms, and she was happy.

Jace grinned, happy, too. Happier than he'd ever been in his life.

He laughed out loud and rolled over, hauling her on top of him. Her legs tangled with his, caught in the jeans and boots he'd never managed to shed. She sat up and began to extricate herself—and stripped off his boots and jeans, as well.

She ran her hands over him. Intimately. Possessively.

His breathing quickened. His own desire was immediately rekindled. And he reached for her, drew her back into his arms and began to love her again. Slowly this time. Tenderly. With all the finesse he'd lacked before. And she watched him, touched him, smiled at him.

The phone rang.

Jace jerked, biting off a curse as he reached over and grabbed it. "What?" he barked.

"Just wonderin' if you been makin' any progress," Artie said cheerfully.

"Yes," Jace said. "Go away."

As a girl Celie had imagined more romantic interludes than she could remember. She'd dreamed of mountain idylls, walks on a moonlit beach, dinners for two on a cozy terrace, and a hundred other incredible settings where she and the man of her dreams would commit themselves to each other forever.

But even Celie didn't believe it would happen just that way.

The next day they sailed all day—and Celie, of course, worked while Jace stayed out of Simone's way.

"I don't even want her to see you," Celie said. "I don't want her to think anything happened."

Jace just grinned. "She's only got to look at you to know something happened," he said with considerable satisfaction.

Celie felt herself turn red, and one look in the mirror in Jace's stateroom told her he was speaking the truth. Her eyes were sparkling, her mouth looked well kissed, and she actually seemed to glow.

It was embarrassing. It was wonderful.

"I don't want you coming there," she said severely.

Jace's grin grew even more wicked. "I don't want to come there, either," he said, deadpan. He wrapped her in his arms and pulled her hard against him, so that even after a night of loving she could feel his growing arousal. "I want to come here. With you."

"Stop that! Behave." She pulled back and shook her finger at him.

He caught it and nibbled the end of it, sending a shaft of longing streaking through her, too. "You don't want me to behave," he said gruffly, and his eyes dared her to deny him.

"What I want has nothing to do with it," Celie said firmly. "I work here. I have to do my job."

"Tomorrow you're off, though? When we get to St. Maarten?"

"Unless Stevie is still sick," Celie agreed, "and I have to cover for him again, yes. I should be able to go ashore."

"Stevie won't be sick."

"You know that, do you?"

"He won't dare."

And he didn't. He was there bright and early when Celie went to check in. She half expected Simone, who obviously knew something was going on, to come up with some other way of preventing her from spending the day with Jace. But Simone was busy when Celie breezed in, and she didn't even look up.

"Have fun," Stevie called after her, grinning.

"I will," Celie said as she hurried to join Jace to go ashore.

It was the day she'd always dreamed of. The streets of Philipsburg, the port city on the Dutch side of St. Maarten, were crowded with tourists from ships as well as with other vacationers. It was hot and, away from the beach, there was little breeze.

But it didn't matter. They were together, hand in hand, hips and shoulders brushing as they prowled the narrow streets. Jace bought her a straw hat to keep the sun off, and Celie insisted that she get him a pair of shorts and a pair sandals so he wouldn't have to spend the day in jeans and boots.

''Nothin' wrong with jeans and boots,'' Jace protested when she dragged him into one of the *steegjes,* the little lanes between Front Street and Back Street where she found a casual-clothing store.

''Nothing at all,'' she said. ''Jeans and boots are fine for Montana. Not for here. You'll be too hot. Besides,'' she grinned, when he came back out of the dressing room wearing a pair of shorts and looking self-conscious, ''I like looking at your legs.''

A flush crept up Jace's neck. ''Celie! You're not supposed to say things like that,'' he growled, clearly embarrassed, as the clerk smiled.

Celie, unrepentant, just laughed. It was true—she did like looking at his legs. And, freed from constraints at last, she was going to enjoy every minute of it. For years she had tried not to look at him at all. Now she couldn't seem to stop.

She'd awakened early this morning and had resisted going back to sleep even though they'd been awake most of the night. Instead she'd simply lain there and feasted her eyes on Jace. She had traced the hard good looks, tough sinewy muscles, and the myriad nicks and scars on his taut, tanned skin that made him Jace. He was beautiful, she'd thought.

Though she knew if she ever told him that, he'd blush even more deeply than he was right now as the clerk handed him a carrier bag with his jeans and boots. He stood staring in dismay down at his bare, hair-roughened legs.

"I feel naked," he complained.

"Not even close," Celie said. "But if you want to really feel naked, we could go to the beach."

"A nude beach?" Jace said mockingly.

"If you want."

He gave her a hard look, decided she was joking and said, "Right. Let's go."

She took him by the hand and said, "Follow me."

Armand had been only too happy to see to her "education" the first time she'd come to St. Maarten. He'd blithely suggested they go to the beach, and she had agreed, only discovering after they arrived that clothing was optional. To his dismay she'd opted for it, insisting on wearing her bathing suit, as she had the two subsequent times she'd come.

She didn't know what she would do if Jace willingly doffed his clothes. But she didn't need to worry. He took one look, his jaw dropped, and he began hauling her in the other direction.

"No way," he said. "No blinkin' way!"

Celie grinned at him. "You don't want to strip off?"

"Me?" He shrugged as if that hadn't even occurred to him. "Hell, nobody's gonna look at me. I don't want a bunch of guys gawking at you!"

They went to another beach a distance away where they both wore bathing suits, and Celie got to put lotion on Jace and he got to put lotion on her, and afterward he muttered thickly that maybe they should just forget the beach and get a launch back to the ship.

But Celie said no. "You'll love the water. Come on!" And she jumped up and took off running toward the water.

Cursing, Jace levered himself up and chased her into the surf. And he did love it. They swam and played in the clear blue water and then lay side by side on the beach to dry off before heading off to have lunch.

There was no shortage of options for the meal—everything from gourmet French restaurants in Grand Case to you'd-think-you-were-in-the-states hamburger joints. They opted for conch fritters and cold beer at a sidewalk café where they could sit and watch the people passing by.

Except, Celie realized, they only seemed to have eyes for each other. Jace fed her a conch fritter dipped in saffron sauce, and she nibbled it all the way down till she was nibbling his thumb.

"You don't maybe want to go back to the ship?" he said plaintively.

But Celie just grinned and shook her head. "Not yet." The day was too perfect, too beautiful. She would savor it for a lifetime.

After they'd eaten, they walked around some more, looking in shops. There were a thousand of them, selling everything from diamonds and Rolex watches to seashells and silly T-shirts. Celie wanted to find presents for her mother and Walt, for Sara's soon-to-be-born baby and for Artie.

"I owe him," she said. "We both do. We need to find the perfect gift."

Jace groaned. "You look. I'll have another beer." He nodded hopefully toward a bar across the street where reggae music was pouring out. There were some lengths, Celie realized, to which even fairy-tale days didn't extend. Expecting Jace to enjoy shopping was one of them.

"All right. I'll meet you at the bar in an hour."

"Sure." He headed across the street eagerly. Celie, watching him go, thought he looked almost as good in shorts as he did in Wranglers.

He looked best of all, though, in absolutely nothing. Her

cheeks warmed at the thought—and at the memory of his lean, hard, bare body. She giggled, amazed at how free and comfortable she felt thinking that way about him. It was as if all the desire and need and dreams that she'd held pent-up inside for years had suddenly found their focus and come pouring out. Which was pretty much the truth.

She was half tempted to run after him and agree to go back to the ship right now. But she did want to get something for Artie.

They really did owe Artie. A lot.

She got her mother and Walt a photo album for the pictures of their own travels. They had gone to Vietnam this summer to meet Walt's daughter. She was sure there would be plenty of photos to fill the album. She got Sara's baby a romper set with pineapples and palm trees on it and a CD of nursery songs set in reggae style.

Artie was harder to buy for.

What did you get a ninety-year-old man who might not have everything, but who certainly had virtually everything he needed or might want?

What he would want, Celie decided, was to share a part of the cruise. So she ended up buying him a photo album, too. Then she got a couple of disposable cameras so she could take pictures of all the places she and Jace went. That way he could see where they had been. It had, after all, been his determination that had finally got them together. They might have gone on forever at cross purposes if he hadn't insisted on Jace coming on the cruise.

She'd walked halfway down Front Street before she found everything she wanted. But finally, clutching her purchases, she hurried back to the bar. Jace was there, drinking a beer with the three blondes from the ship.

Seeing him surrounded by women, Celie felt momentarily awkward. But as soon as he saw her, a grin lit his face.

''Ah, good. Gotta go,'' he said to the blondes. He left them and his beer to join her.

''You didn't have to leave,'' Celie said quickly.

But he took her hand and walked her back out into the street. ''Yes, I did. Where do you want to go now?''

It was getting on toward evening. They would have to be back at the launch in an hour or so. ''How about just walking on the cliffs overlooking the beach?'' Celie suggested.

Armand had shown her the cliffs above Cupecoy Beach. In her most recent romantic dreams, she'd imagined meeting her perfect man and walking there hand in hand with him.

Jace smiled. ''Sounds good.''

Celie took a picture of Jace in front of the bar, and then he took one of her. And then they got a passerby to take one of them together. ''For Artie,'' she said. ''We're taking pictures for him to share our trip.''

''Of some things,'' Jace agreed. ''Not everything.''

Celie smiled. ''No, not everything.''

But on their way to the cliffs they stopped and took photos of the other places they'd been in St. Maarten. Then they took a taxi up to the cliffs. ''Half an hour,'' Jace told the driver.

It was every bit as beautiful as she'd dreamed it would be, with the sun going down and the sky turning pink and orange and purple. The breeze ruffled her hair and touched her sunburned cheeks, and she turned and smiled at Jace.

''Isn't it beautiful?'' she said.

''Mmm,'' he murmured. But he wasn't looking at the view at all. He was looking at her. He had hold of one of her hands and he drew her close and lifted his other hand to cup the back of her neck and tilt her face up to meet his.

And then he kissed her.

He tasted of the sea and the sun and the spicy saffron dip from the conch fritters. His mouth was hard and warm and persuasive against hers, and Celie responded, fulfilling her dream, kissing him in return, loving him, wanting this moment to go on forever.

And then Jace broke off the kiss and stepped back.

Bereft, Celie opened her eyes to see what was wrong. "Jace?"

His face was inches from hers, his eyes dark and intent. "I love you," he said, his voice ragged. "Marry me."

And Celie knew only one answer to that.

"Yes," she whispered, and wrapped her arms around him to kiss him again. "Oh, yes."

Eight

"It is a shipboard romance," Simone said firmly, fixing Celie with a hard stare. "Zat is all."

"It's *not* all," Celie protested. "Besides, I didn't meet him on the ship. I've known him for years."

"Humph." Simone shook her head disapprovingly. "Even so. Everyone knows ze shipboard romances, zey don't last."

"Ours will," Celie insisted. "We're getting married! We've set the date." Celie waved her left hand in front of Simone's doubting gaze. On her ring finger was the solitaire diamond ring that Jace had given her last night when he'd asked her to marry him.

She'd been astonished to see the tiny black-velvet-covered box he'd pulled out of his pocket. "Wherever did you—" She'd stared at it, and then at him, amazed.

Jace had simply grinned. "You weren't the only one who went shopping."

While she had been out buying photo albums and cameras and rompers with pineapples on them for her family and Artie, it seemed that Jace had been buying her a diamond!

"He said I could bring it back," he'd told her almost diffidently, "if you don't like it. Or if—" he grimaced "—if you'd said no."

"I love it," Celie had said. And she certainly hadn't said no. It was the stuff of dreams. She might not even believe it now if she couldn't look at the ring on her finger. It was a simple, elegant solitaire with a white-gold band. Very traditional. Absolutely perfect.

Simone looked at it and sighed mightily. "Shipboard romance! It doesn't last," she repeated. "And if you quit before your six-monz commitment is over, Celie, you will not be able to come back."

"I don't want to come back," Celie said stubbornly. "I never wanted to do this forever. I only wanted to travel, to see the world, to meet people—"

"To meet a man," Simone said.

Celie flushed. "Well, yes," she admitted. "But I certainly never thought it would be Jace."

But it was Jace—and she had the ring and the man to prove it. "We're getting married on October third," she told Simone.

Jace had suggested they get married right away. "We can get married on the ship," he'd argued. "People do."

But Celie had shaken her head. "I don't want to get married on the ship. I want to get married at home. In Elmer." It would make up for the last time, for Matt's defection, for having to call everything off.

Jace hadn't been thrilled. "Are you sure?"

"Yes." Celie had been adamant. "I want to get married at home."

She was just as adamant now with Simone. "I'm going

home. I'm handing in my notice. I don't care if I can't come back. I don't *want* to come back!''

''Zey all say zat.'' Simone sighed wearily. ''And zen, two months later...'' She gave a mournful shake of her head.

Celie ignored her. Undoubtedly Simone had dealt with plenty of starry-eyed young women over the years, women who'd thought they'd met the man of their dreams—only to discover they were wrong, that the men were nightmares.

But she was not one of those women.

And Jace was not one of those men.

It wasn't the same. It wasn't the same at all.

''You are going home? Getting married?'' Armand's eyebrows lifted in surprise at the sight of the ring on Celie's finger.

She had spotted him in the staff lounge and had gone over to say goodbye and, maybe if she was honest, to prove that there was another man in the world who didn't think she was naive and basically hopeless.

''Tomorrow's my last day,'' she told him.

''So soon you quit? Must be very persuasive.'' He waggled dark eyebrows. ''And who is the lucky man?''

''A man I knew at home.''

''Ah, yes. Of course.'' Armand nodded understandingly

''What do you mean, of course?'' Celie demanded.

Armand gave a negligent shrug. ''Just that he is, how do you say...? A homebody, too.''

''He's hardly a homebody.'' It was hard to imagine anyone describing Jace that way. As long as she'd known him he'd always been a moving-on, show-me-the-bright-lights sort of guy. But Armand didn't know that.

''Is better for you to be there,'' he approved. ''Is where you belong...in the home with children and puppies, yes?''

He looked her up and down critically, then nodded in satisfaction. "I always think you look like a wife."

Coming from Armand, that was not necessarily a compliment. But Celie couldn't really argue with him. Nor did she want to. After all, a wife was exactly what she had always wanted to be.

She smiled. "Thank you. I just came to say goodbye," she told him. "And, thank you for the…um, education, too." She smiled a little wryly. "It was…interesting."

Armand grinned and winked at her. Then he kissed her lightly on both cheeks. "Always I am happy to educate. Be happy, *ma petite.*"

Artie and her mother were at the airport to meet them.

"Is it true?" Joyce demanded, hurrying toward them, eager eyes going from Celie to Jace and back again. "Artie says you're getting married?" She sounded as if she didn't trust Artie not to be pulling her leg.

But Celie, beaming, held out her hand for her mother to inspect the ring, and Joyce gave a little cry of delight. "Oh, darling, how wonderful." She wrapped Celie in a fierce hug, then reached out and dragged Jace into a three-way embrace.

Then she gave him a smacking kiss. "You dark horse, you," she chided him. "I had no idea."

Artie huffed. "Tol' her, didn't I? An' they say women are the romantics." He shook his head in dismay. Then he winked at Jace. "Told ya so."

Jace grinned, looking both embarrassed and pleased. But then he protested, "I coulda done it myself."

"Yeah, right." Artie snorted. "In which century? Hell's bells, boy, I ain't gonna live forever, an' the rate you two were goin', I'd'a had to. If I wanted to see the two of you hitched, I reckoned it was up to me to kick you in the tail and get you movin'."

"Right," Jace said dryly. "It was all your idea."

"Mebbe not all," Artie allowed as they moved toward the baggage claim. "I can't say I would a picked out such a purty engagement ring." He put an arm around Celie's shoulder and gave her a squeeze. "Sure am glad you're home, missy."

Celie looped an arm around his narrow waist. "Me, too."

"I've got a stew simmering." Joyce herded them down the stairs. "You'll all come and eat with us, of course. And you can stay with us, if you want," she said to her daughter.

In their new home, Joyce meant. The one Walt had just finished building on his ranch. Last year he'd turned the old house over to his daughter, Cait, and her new husband, Charlie.

"Thanks, but I think I'll stay in town," Celie said. "At the house—if you don't think Polly will mind." The huge, rambling two-story Victorian just off the main street of Elmer where they had all lived until this spring still belonged to Polly, after all, even though she and the kids had moved to Sloan's ranch as soon as school was out.

"I'm sure Polly won't care at all," Joyce said. "She'll probably be glad to have someone in there instead of leaving it empty. Now that she and the kids are up at Sloan's place, I think she's planning to sell it."

"She is?" Celie didn't like the thought of that. There were so many memories associated with that house. "Maybe we could buy it," she said to Jace. "It would be close to the store if you're going to stay at Artie's. And I could reopen The Spa," she added eagerly.

"I was thinkin' of building a place out by Ray and Jodie," Jace said as he grabbed their bags off the luggage carousel and led the way toward the parking area. "I'm gonna be training horses out there."

"Whichever," Celie said happily. "We can discuss it later. We have other things to think about now." She grinned. "Like the wedding."

"About the wedding..." Joyce looked at her daughter a little worriedly, and Celie knew she was remembering the last wedding.

"Thought mebbe you'd a got married on the ship," Artie said.

"No." Celie shook her head. "I wanted to get married here. This time it will be perfect," she said, looping her arm through Jace's and smiling up at him.

"Yep," he said equably. He glanced back at her mother and Artie. "Told her I'd get married anytime, anywhere."

"But we had to come back here. We couldn't get married without Artie," Celie said. "Or the family."

"I could have." Jace tossed the bags in the back of Walt's crew-cab truck that Joyce had driven over. "Don't matter to me."

"Well, it matters to me," Celie said.

She had been dreaming about this wedding for years.

Artie was stretched out in his easy chair, his feet stuck up on the hassock, as he regarded Jace over the top of a glass of Jack Daniel's. In his lap was the photo album Celie had given him. He had studied it with considerable satisfaction, nodding and smiling while Celie had been there. But now she was gone and he was looking at it again and still nodding.

"See, what'd I tell you?" He said to Jace. "Worked like a charm."

"Not exactly a charm," Jace countered mildly. He wasn't telling Artie about all the bad times. It was enough to remember them himself. He settled into the sofa, balancing his own glass of Jack Daniel's on his belt buckle. The Jack Daniel's had been his gift to Artie.

He figured they'd need a damn sight more of it before this wedding was done. After two weeks at home, he'd barely had a chance to sit down and take a deep breath. He worked, of course, for Artie and on the ranch, and he trained horses every morning for Taggart Jones. But every second he wasn't working, his presence had been demanded by Celie, and he'd been presented with a thousand options for wedding plans.

"Why the heck should I care whether we have a sit-down dinner or a stand-up buffet?" he groused. "And what difference does it make what kind of paper the invitations are on? Why can't we just call people up and invite 'em to come?"

Artie sipped the Jack Daniel's and gave an appreciative sigh. "She's gonna marry you, ain't she? Well, then, quitcher fussin'. Everything's hunky-dory."

"And I gotta wear a tux," Jace went on, aggrieved.

Clothing had already been discussed. It wasn't, to Jace's dismay, "optional." Celie was going to do things right and proper, and that, she told him, meant a floor-length gown for her and her bridesmaids and tuxes for him and his best man.

Artie was going to be the best man.

That was the only thing Jace had insisted on when Celie had gone into wedding-planning mode. He owed the old man—and he couldn't think of a better way of paying him back. The fact that Artie would have to wear a tux, too, made it a little bit sweeter.

Jace had wondered if Celie would argue that having a ninety-year-old best man would upset her "perfect" wedding pictures. But she hadn't argued at all. In fact, she'd been delighted at the idea.

She'd only frowned for a moment as she'd wondered: if Artie was the best man, who was going to give her away.

"Walt," Jace had suggested. He was, after all, Celie's mother's husband.

"He could," Celie agreed. "Or Jack." Her ten-year-old nephew. Then she'd brightened. "I know! I'll get Sloan to do it!"

"Don't you dare! He'll turn our wedding into some media circus!" He remembered all too well what a colossal to-do Sloan's presence had made of the Great Montana Cowboy Auction.

"No media circus," Celie had promised. "Very low-key. We won't tell anyone."

"This is Elmer. Everyone will know."

"But everyone knows Sloan, too, so it won't be a big deal. And we'll keep the media out."

"We're definitely keeping the media out." There was no question about that. Not, Jace was sure, that the media would even care that he was marrying Celie O'Meara.

The only person who cared was him. He cared desperately. He loved her desperately. He wanted her to be happy. That was the only reason he was putting up with all of this.

The past two weeks had been insane. Celie had been glued to her wedding planner. She'd been talking nonstop to her mother, to Poppy Nichols, who ran a florist shop down in Livingston, to Milly Callahan, whose dad, John, was a grocer who knew a caterer, to the caterer, to the stationer, to the minister at the local church, to Polly to arrange for renting the town hall.

Jace had wanted to celebrate their engagement by going home, locking the doors and taking Celie to bed.

"We can't do that," Celie had said, horrified.

"We can't? Why not?"

"Because this is Elmer! Everyone will know!"

"They know, anyway," Jace had argued.

But Celie had been firm. She wasn't having Alice Benn or Cloris Stedman or any of the other moral citizens of

Elmer scandalized by their behavior. "What would Artie think?" she'd demanded.

"Artie," Jace had said with absolute conviction, "will be all for it."

Now Artie stretched, sipped his Jack Daniel's and said, "Dunno what yer doin' here. How come you ain't over at Celie's?"

"Because," Jace said, "that is Command Central, and if I go over there she will give me a list of things to do."

"Beginnin' as she means to go on, is she?" Artie chuckled.

"I damned well hope not," Jace said. "I hope she comes to her senses. Soon."

He reckoned he could have put together half a dozen perfectly legal weddings and had time left over to brand a herd of cattle in the past two weeks.

"This thing is turnin' into the wedding that ate Montana," he grumbled now, shuddering again at the thought of tuxedos. "What's wrong with boots and jeans?"

"Beats me." Artie yawned. "Shoulda married her 'fore you left the ship."

"I suggested it. She said no."

"Should've grabbed her by the hair and yanked her right up b'fore the captain."

"Now you tell me."

"Well, hell's bells, boy," Artie replied. "An old man can't be expected to think of everything!"

Celie had a list as long as her arm.

Church: *check.* Minister: *check.* Reception hall: *check.* Invitations: *check.* Flowers: *check.* Cake: *check.* Wedding dress: *check.* Bridesmaids' dresses: *check.*

Maybe it was as long as both her arms.

She had memorized the wedding planner. She knew the symbolic meaning of every flower, of the candles, of the wedding rings. She knew type fonts and alternate wordings and parchment colors.

Sometimes she wished she hadn't bothered. It had been important before—the first time. With Matt. In fact, the wedding had mattered more than Matt.

Nothing mattered more than Jace.

But it was too late to back out now. Everything was rolling. They'd been home a month. She'd set the ball in motion immediately. She had her dress. She'd ordered her bouquet. She'd bought her veil. She'd chosen the bridesmaids' dresses. She arranged for the flowers. She'd picked out a cake. Just this morning she'd addressed the last of the invitations, and half an hour ago she'd stuck them in the mail.

She could hardly say, "Let's just elope, shall we?"

Though if she did, she had no doubt that Jace would instantly say, "Yes!"

Jace was no fan of big weddings. That was evident. He'd steered clear of all the planning. He'd said, "Whatever you want." He'd only asked that Artie be his best man. The rest, he'd said was up to her.

He had put up with a lot, and Celie knew it. Not just the wedding plans, but her insistence that he go back to Artie's every night, too.

"We've already slept together," he'd reminded her.

"Yes," she'd agreed. "But that was there. On the ship. It wasn't Elmer." It mattered somehow that they didn't scandalize Elmer. "You know Alice and Cloris... And what would Artie think?"

Artie, Jace had assured her, would think he was insane to be spending every night at his place.

But he did it. Every night for the past month he'd trekked back up the hill to sleep at Artie's. Celie had watched him make a point of waving to Alice and Cloris on his way.

"Reckon I'll get to wear white at the wedding?" he'd said last night on his way out the door.

Celie had laughed and kissed him. "Absolutely. And a halo, too."

"God knows I deserve it."

Celie thought he did, too.

The wedding was two weeks away when Polly called and asked them to come up to the ranch for the weekend.

"Sloan will be home," Celie said as she put a salad on the table for dinner. "He's coming back from Hong Kong tonight. And then sometime next week he's going to begin shooting his next film in Mexico."

"And you want to go see Sloan?" Jace said just a little warily.

But Celie shook her head. "I want to see them all. And *Polly* wants to see you. I don't think she still believes we're going to get married."

Jace, who had been counting the hours for what seemed like forever, sometimes didn't believe it, either. But there were under four hundred hours left now—and it was beginning to feel more believable.

"She would have come down to visit before now," Celie went on, "but she's been on her own up there with the kids while Sloan has been gone, and she hasn't had time. So, what do you say? Do you want to go?"

"A better question is—can you tear yourself away from preparations?"

"For a weekend," Celie said, "yes, I think so. There are several last-minute things to do. But we still have time."

"Too much time," Jace muttered. But maybe going up to Polly and Sloan's would make the hours pass faster. He hoped.

He picked Celie up bright and early Saturday morning. He had no reason to stay in bed, after all.

"Not for another 335 hours or so. Unless—" he looked hopefully at her "—we're sharing a room at Polly's?"

Celie shrugged. "It's up to Polly."

Jace understood that. He hoped his future sister-in-law felt kindly toward him. She had, he reminded Celie, let Sloan spend the night in her house in Elmer. She hadn't sent him up the hill to sleep at Artie's.

"No, he slept in the Jack's bottom bunk," Celie informed him.

Oh.

Jace tried not to think about it. He tried not to think about Celie sitting so close to him. Tried not to remember how good she'd felt in his arms. How good she'd felt naked.

"Tell me about these wedding plans," he said desperately. That had to be as deadly as naming presidents or reciting multiplication tables.

Celie told him about the reception. She detailed the menu. She talked about the music. She told him about the flowers, about the symbolic meaning of each one. She talked about the wedding cake, about the bridesmaids' dresses, about her own.

"It's gorgeous." She turned shining eyes on him. "You're going to love it."

Jace nodded. She could wear a sack as far as he was concerned. In fact he thought he'd prefer a sack. "I'll love it," he assured her, "only if it doesn't have a lot of little buttons."

Celie laughed. "It doesn't. Well, only forty or fifty or so."

Jace groaned.

She told him he still needed to go to Bozeman to be fitted for his tux. She hadn't given up on the tux idea, no matter how long he'd put it off.

"You need to take Artie, too," she told him. "And the rest of the men. You'll need five."

"Five? What for?"

"Ushers. Groomsmen."

Jace could just see himself talking five of his buddies into wearing tuxes. It didn't bear thinking about.

"The only one you don't have to worry about is Sloan," Celie told him.

That was news to him. Sloan was the only one he'd ever worried about.

"Why not?"

"He has a tux of his own."

Oh. Right. They were talking about tuxes. And Celie would know that Sloan had one, too, because she'd been to a Hollywood premiere with him.

Far from not worrying about Sloan Gallagher, Jace felt suddenly like punching his soon-to-be brother-in-law in the nose.

The feeling lasted until they got to the ranch.

But there, once Sloan and Polly came out to meet them, the feeling evaporated. He could see how happy Sloan had made Polly—and how happy Polly had made Sloan. He could also see that Celie was equally happy for both of them.

Given that, he couldn't really resent Sloan's single weekend in Celie's life. But he couldn't quite forgive the man for having his own tux.

"Oh, I can't believe it! You're getting married!" Polly swooped down the steps and ran toward them, then enveloped them both in a fierce hug.

Jace thought his ribs might crack.

Then Polly stood back and looked them up and down, still beaming. "Look at you! You both look so happy!" She shook her head as if it amazed her.

As well it might, considering the way Celie used to snarl at him and he used to tease her. Now he just grinned and Celie did, too.

''They are happy, Pol','' Sloan said, looping his arm over his wife's shoulders. ''Almost as happy as we are.''

''Impossible,'' Polly said. Then she said, ''Come see the house and meet our guests. Sloan brought his work home with him.'' She slipped out from under Sloan's arm and grabbed Celie's hand and led her toward the house, leaving Sloan with Jace.

Once upon a time as hot-headed teenagers, the two of them had battered each other into the dirt. Jace had broken Sloan's nose. A week later Sloan had returned the favor.

Jace couldn't even remember why they'd been at odds then. Six months ago he had been flat out jealous.

He'd done everything wrong—from teasing her about her crush on a movie star to trying to make her jealous in return by flirting with every girl who came in the hardware store to inviting three of them, including starlet Tamara Lynd, to staying at Artie's with him to goading Celie into bidding on ''the man of her dreams'' at the auction.

Of course he'd hoped she'd see the folly of her ways. He'd never expected her to actually bid enough to win Sloan! He'd been floored—and furious—when she had. And he'd done something even stupider afterward.

Not that she'd noticed what he was doing. She'd only had eyes for Sloan. She'd come home from Hollywood after her weekend there and had let him think she was still madly in love with Sloan.

Thinking about it could still make him simmer.

Now he looked at Sloan and wondered what the other man was thinking.

Then Sloan drawled, ''So I guess congratulations are in order.'' A wry grin touched his face. He stuck out his hand for Jace to shake.

For just a moment Jace hesitated, feeling awkward even though he knew he had no reason. Polly and Sloan were happy. They were in love.

In fact, Celie said, he'd been in love with Polly for years. And she'd said it without any kind of sadness, just very matter-of-fact, as if she really was over Sloan. She certainly hadn't hung around looking goopy-eyed at him. She'd gone off with Polly quite happily.

"You're not sure?" Sloan's grin faded as he misinterpreted Jace's hesitation.

"I'm sure," Jace said flatly. He gripped Sloan's hand and shook it. Hard. Their eyes met.

"You do love her," Sloan said quietly.

It wasn't a question, but Jace answered it anyway. "Yes."

The grin tipped the corner of Sloan's mouth again. "Good. She deserves that. She's had a rough time," he reflected after a moment.

Jace supposed that Polly had probably told him about Matt. Jace didn't think Celie had.

He nodded. "Yes."

"She blamed you."

Jace sighed. "Yes."

Sloan's hard blue gaze bored into him. "Did she have a right to?"

For years Jace would have said no. He'd have said he'd done her a favor, that if Matt Williams wasn't ready to settle down it was better to know before the wedding than after. And that was true. But…

Now he shifted from one foot to the other. His gaze wavered a moment, then came back to meet Sloan's. "I'd like to say no."

But he couldn't. Not honestly. He could have behaved better. He could have been a better example. He could have acted more grown-up and responsible himself.

Sloan's mouth twisted wryly. His gaze dropped for a moment, too. Then he looked up again and nodded. "We should all have no regrets."

Jace knew they were both remembering the foolish fight they'd had. The broken noses and battle scars were probably only small regrets compared to some of the stupid things they'd done over the past twenty years.

"I'm a better man now," Jace vowed, and hoped it was true.

Sloan looked toward the ranch house that his wife and her sister had just entered. "For their sakes," he said, still smiling, though his eyes were serious, "let's hope we both are."

"Jace, I'd like you to meet Gavin McConnell." Polly drew Jace into the wood-paneled living room of the Gallagher ranch house, which was crawling with people. Four of them were Polly's kids. He barely had time to get a look at the others as she turned to the lean, dark-haired man standing by the fireplace who had his arm looped over Celie's shoulders.

"Gavin, this is Jace Tucker. Gavin's an actor," Polly said to Jace. And to Gavin, she said, "Jace is a horse trainer. And Celie's fiancé," she announced proudly.

Calling Gavin McConnell "an actor" was like calling Babe Ruth a baseball player. Even Jace, who was by no means a movie buff, knew his name and the rugged, hard, handsome face that went with it. Gavin McConnell was famous. The characters he played were always memorable, and his films were guaranteed smash hits. He had won two Academy Awards and had at least two more nominations.

He was, according to the Sunday supplements and popular press, a "man's man," an "actor's actor" and "every woman's dream."

And right now he had his arm around Celie.

He was also sticking out his other hand to Jace and saying, "Congratulations! That's great. Celie's a great gal."

"Yeah," Jace said, suppressing the instinct to add, *my*

gal. He was fairly sure Celie wouldn't be impressed by his caveman instincts. He shook McConnell's hand and did his best to behave in a way that would reflect well on the Tucker name. "Pleased to meet you. Heard a lot about you."

"I hope not." Gavin McConnell grimaced. And Jace remembered that besides being all those other things, McConnell was reputed to be something of a recluse, as well; at least, he didn't give many interviews gladly. He seemed to be willing to spend time with friends, though.

"You're workin' on a new film with Sloan?" Jace asked, remembering that Celie had said something about a couple of Sloan's fellow actors coming for the weekend to go over material before they started shooting down in Mexico.

"Yeah. It's my baby." Gavin grinned. "Sloan's starring. I'm directing."

"And I'm costarring," a bright, oddly familiar female voice cut in.

Jace turned around and blinked as a woman with long, dark hair crossed the room toward him, a wide happy smile on her face. It took him a moment to realize why the voice was so familiar. Her hair hadn't been long when he'd last seen her. It hadn't been dark, either.

"Oh, Jace," Polly said, "you remember Tamara Lynd, don't you?"

He hid out with Polly's kids.

He had no other alternative. Polly and Celie were immersed in wedding discussions that Jace wanted no part of. The words "formal attire" and "rehearsal dinner" made him shudder and head for the hills.

But he couldn't hang around with Sloan and Gavin and Tamara, either. And not just because they were "talking shop." They were going over the script, working out motivations, Gavin told him. Discussing their characters, talking about interaction, going on about the impact of past history. They all said he was welcome to listen in if he wanted.

He didn't—because he had no desire to dredge up past history.

Even more than *morning suit* and *tuxedo,* the words *past history* sent a nervous shiver up Jace's spine.

He had a bit of "past history" with Tamara Lynd. Meaningless history as far as he was concerned. Stupid history. History he very much wanted to forget.

He didn't know what Tamara thought about it—or what she might be inclined to do. She had a history of chasing men. She'd chased him.

And caught him—once—in a weak moment.

He wasn't weak right now. He wasn't susceptible anymore. But even so, the last thing he needed was Tamara hitting on him now.

So he kept his distance. He would have trailed Celie around like a sheepdog, but all those wedding plans drove him crazy. So he took refuge with the kids, spending hours in the corral with fourteen-year-old Daisy, helping her work out some kinks in the horse she was training and giving young Jack pointers on his riding so the boy could beat Eric, Sloan's foreman's grandson, when they raced.

He borrowed one of Sloan's horses and raced Jack a few times himself. It felt good to be back in the saddle. It felt right. It felt safe.

And then he turned around and saw Tamara and Gavin and Polly's very pregnant daughter, Sara, standing by the fence watching as he and Jack came back.

"You were wonderful!" Tamara exclaimed. She looked at Jace with shining eyes. "Wasn't he wonderful?" she demanded of the other two.

"You don't mean me, I s'pose?" Jack said.

Tamara grinned up at him. "You were wonderful, too,"

she told him. "You both were. It's just so...exciting... watching men ride. Isn't it?" She turned eagerly to Gavin and Sara.

"I'd rather watch women ride," Gavin said with a grin.

"I'd rather ride than watch," Sara said a little wistfully.

Another time Jace would have seized on that and offered to take her. It would have got him away from Tamara. But Sara was very pregnant—almost eight months—and Jace wasn't quite the rip-roaring cowboy who didn't think ahead that he used to be.

"I'll take you after the baby's born," he offered. "Come on out to the barn while I cool this horse down, and tell me what's been goin' on in your life."

If Sara was surprised at the invitation, she didn't say so. Instead she willingly waddled along with him toward the barn, talking about her pregnancy, about the college courses she was going to take in the spring if she could find the time, about not having given up her hope of going to medical school.

Jace listened. He admired Sara's fortitude, her commitment, her determination. He didn't know or care if Tamara was watching him. He didn't look back.

He couldn't avoid her entirely, though. They all ate together in the evening around the huge oak table in the dining room. Polly, aided by Celie when she could tear herself away from her plans and her lists, cooked enormous, wonderful meals. And afterwards, they all sat around the living room and told stories—about movies, about cowboying, about places they'd been and things they'd done.

Jace held back at first, standing in the doorway listening to the tales, worried that if he went in and sat down, Tamara might decide to come sit beside him. Celie had gone back to her lists and he was on his own. But Tamara barely gave him more than a grin and a glance as he stood there. She was regaling them all with a very funny story about a Paris fashion show she'd been in during the earliest days of her career.

"I didn't know you'd been a model." Gavin looked surprised.

"I was a terrible one. I wanted to be in show business, so I had to get noticed, be a star. And I had good bones—" she shrugged "—so I tried. But I also had two left feet. You need to be able to walk without looking down to be a runway model. They fired me after I fell off the runway!" She laughed and shook her head. "But it was a start. And I'd have done anything then to get my career going. A girl's gotta do what a girl's gotta do."

Even buy Sloan Gallagher, Jace thought. Her career had been stalled in the supporting-role stage last winter. She'd been doing backup roles—nasty other women, girls who died halfway through—for the past five years. She wasn't getting any younger, and she still had the dream. She'd been desperate for a boost. So she'd come to Elmer last winter to be noticed—to get media attention by winning Sloan Gallagher.

But she hadn't won. Celie had.

She'd been upset that day. Disgruntled. Annoyed. But philosophical. A girl did what a girl had to do, but she didn't win 'em all. Tamara knew that.

So she'd moved on that very night—to Jace.

That hadn't been to benefit her career, of course. That had been to assuage her pride. But in an odd twist of fate and serendipity, exactly what she'd hoped for had come to pass, anyway.

Indy film director John Cunningham had seen her in a news feature on Elmer. He'd said she looked haggard and desperate, not at all the way she'd come across in her films. He'd called her in Los Angeles three days later to see if she would be interested in playing the brittle spinster sister in his new film.

''And much to his surprise,'' Tamara said now, finishing the story, ''he discovered I could act.''

''Amen to that.'' Gavin said fervently. ''I tapped her for Sloan's costar as soon as I saw some film.''

Tamara beamed, first at Sloan and then at Celie, who had just come into the room. ''Moral of the story—sometimes losing is winning.'' Then her gaze went from Celie to Jace and she gave him a broad wink. ''Looks like it happened to you, too.''

Celie looked at him a little curiously, but Jace breathed a little easier after that.

Tamara didn't have designs on him. She knew he was in love with Celie. She was happy for them both. She understood. She even spent time with Celie and Polly whenever Gavin gave her and Sloan a break, offering her opinion on wedding plans, saying how handsome Jace would look in a tux, and hoping out loud that she'd get invited to the wedding.

Jace didn't say anything to that.

Celie said, ''Well, of course you will.''

Later that night in bed—they actually had a room together because Gavin was sleeping in the bottom bunk in Jack's—Celie said, ''Tamara's different than I thought she'd be. I mean, she's beautiful and opinionated and, I suppose you'd say…sexy…but she's real. I like Tamara. Don't you?''

''Sure,'' Jace said. ''She's okay.''

He didn't care one way or another about Tamara. He had other things on his mind—another *woman* on his mind.

''Come here,'' he muttered, hauling Celie close. ''I need to love you.''

They had a cookout Sunday afternoon. Afterward Celie and Jace packed up the truck and got ready to drive back to Elmer. In the morning a private plane would come to take Gavin and Sloan and Tamara to Mexico.

"Everybody's leavin'," Jack grumbled. "Don't see why we can't go, too."

"School," Polly said.

Jack wasn't impressed. "Who needs school?"

"You," Sloan told his stepson. "So you can grow up to be smart like me and your uncle Jace."

"Oh, yes," Polly said, rolling her eyes. "You two are such sterling examples of the well-educated man."

"They are good men," Tamara said with broad smile at both Sloan and Jace. Then she leaned up to give Jace a kiss goodbye. "They are wonderful men." Then she lowered her voice so the children wouldn't hear and added with a wicked grin, "And excellent lovers."

"Tam!" Sloan looked apoplectic.

Jace stood stock-still, too stunned to say a word.

"It's true," Tamara defended herself. "I was only saying. And I am speaking in past tense, of course." She patted Sloan's arm as if to reassure him, then turned her gaze on Polly and Celie.

"I never sleep with married men," she informed them cheerfully. "I never even tempt them," she added with a note of regret. "Not even really scrumptious men like these two."

Nine

It was like waiting for the other shoe to drop.

Jace told himself it could have been worse.

Tamara could have said he was a lousy lover. She could have tried to insinuate herself into his life again. She could have wrapped herself around him and declared he was hers, all hers. But clearly she wasn't any more interested in that than he was.

He just hoped Celie understood that.

He wished she would say something.

They'd driven miles—they were almost back in Elmer, for heaven's sake—and she hadn't said a word.

Well, no, that wasn't quite true. She'd said a few words. Whenever he'd asked a direct question, like, ''Do you want to stop and get a cup of coffee?'' or ''Do you want to play a tape?'' she'd said, ''No, thanks,'' politely, even pleasantly. But her words had been distant, almost absent-minded, as if she wasn't really there.

So where was she?

And what was she thinking?

He wondered if he should try to explain. But how did you go about telling the woman you loved about a night you'd spent with another woman?

How could he explain that Tamara meant nothing to him, that in fact, the night he'd slept with her it had been because Celie had spent her life's savings on a date with another man? A man who had a damn sight more to recommend him than Jace did in every way.

He spent miles trying to find the right words, rehearsing them in his mind. But every time he did, the words stuck in his throat.

Sleeping with Tamara Lynd had been immature, stupid and consummate bad sportsmanship. If everything else Celie had ever thought about him over the past ten years had painted him in a bad light, telling her this wasn't going to help matters. It would be like giving her evidence to hang him.

So he kept his mouth shut. About that.

He talked heartily, almost frantically, about what a good time he'd had over the weekend, about what a good guy Sloan had turned out to be and what a nice, down-to-earth guy Gavin McConnell was. And because naturally he had to say something about Tamara, too, or Celie would have known he was avoiding talking about her, he said he thought she'd put on a little weight.

"You'd know," Celie said.

Damn. He should have kept his big mouth shut. Quickly, desperately, he changed the subject to Sara. "Speaking of people who've gained weight..."

Jace always talked fast when he was nervous. He talked a lot when he was nervous. He babbled about how impressed he was with Sara's determination to keep on with her studies, about how smart she was, about how she was making the best of a difficult situation. "She's a good kid," he said when he finally had to pause for breath.

"Yes." Celie stared at the mountains out the side window of his pickup. She didn't say anything else.

Jace drummed his fingers on the steering wheel. He cracked his knuckles. He fidgeted and shot sidelong glances at Celie. She didn't look his way. She didn't say a word.

Say something, he begged her silently. *Ask me what happened!*

Hell, she could even yell at him, if she wanted to. It would be better than this.

But the silence continued.

"So," he said finally as they were approaching Elmer, "did you and Polly get all the wedding plans sorted out? Is everything set?"

"Hmm? Oh, I guess."

"Great. I can hardly wait to drag Artie in to try on a tux." Jace grinned as he pulled up in front of Polly's old house.

Celie smiled faintly. Jace cut the engine and jumped out. Celie was already getting out by the time he came around to her side of the truck. He grabbed her bag out of the topper and followed her up the steps.

She opened the door and took the bag from him. "Thanks. Bye."

"It's not late. Cloris and Alice would let me come in."

"We've been gone two days. You better go check on Artie." She didn't meet his eyes.

Jace felt anxiety swirling through him. "Artie's fine."

She was shutting him out and he had to do something, even the last thing he wanted to do. "Celie, look," he said desperately, "we need to talk."

"I need to think."

"No. You don't! Not about what Tamara said, I mean. We're not—we haven't— Well, once we did,' he admitted.

"But it didn't mean anything. It's over. It isn't ever going to happen again! I swear."

Celie nodded. "I believe you."

"You do?" He stared at her. He gulped. "I mean, of course you do! Good! Great. Thank God!"

A huge wave of relief swamped him. He grinned, though his heart was still slamming and his knees were still wobbling. "So you...understand? She doesn't mean anything to me. It was a one-off. One night. One stupid night."

She nodded again, but she wasn't smiling. She was looking thoughtful.

"Celie?"

She smiled and patted his hand. "I understand," she said.

Did she? Oh, God, he hoped.

Celie understood perfectly.

She'd been a fool. It had just taken Tamara Lynd to open her eyes.

She thought about it all night. She paced the house, twisting Jace's ring on her finger, pressing the diamond between her tight lips and feeling sick.

And in the morning she got up and went to the hardware store before it opened. She wanted to see Jace alone before Artie got there.

He was stacking boxes. And when she opened the door, he turned around and, at the sight of her, a grin lit his face.

Celie steeled her heart against it. She couldn't do this if she let herself fall under his spell.

He hurried toward her. "Hey! You're out early."

She smiled, knowing it didn't reach her eyes. She held out her hand. "I came to give you something. Here."

He stared at her clenched bare, ringless fingers, and then at her face. He shoved his hands in his pockets and shook his head. "No."

"What do you mean, no? Go on, Jace, take it." She thrust it at him again. Her gaze met his for only an instant, then shied away. "It's yours. I'm giving it back."

But he kept his hands right where they were and shook his head. "Why? You said you believed me!" Fierce blue eyes challenged her.

"I do believe you," Celie told him. She kept trying to push the ring at him.

But Jace backed away. "Then why are you doing this?"

"Because I can't...I can't marry you!"

He shook his head. "Why not? She doesn't mean anything to me. It was past. You said you understood. Celie, come on. It doesn't make any sense!"

"It does to me." She wrapped her arms across her chest. She rocked back and forth, the pain of her realization emanating from the very depths of her soul.

"Then explain it to me."

She wet her lips, took a breath, held it, then exhaled with a shudder. "It won't work," she said finally.

Jace's brows drew down. "What do you mean, it won't work? What won't work?"

"Our marriage. You and me!" The pain was welling up now, tearing at her. "It won't work. How can it? I wasn't even enough for Matt!" she said, anguished, and turned away.

"What?" Jace stared at her, poleaxed. He came after her, grabbed her arms and turned her to face him. "Matt? What the hell does Matt have to do with this?"

"You slept with Tamara!"

"The more fool me," Jace said bitterly. "Yeah, I did. One time. The night you bought Sloan at the auction. I was a wreck. I was angry. I was bitter. I wanted—hell, I don't know what I wanted!" He raked a hand through his hair. "I was starin' out the window, lookin' down at your place and wonderin' what the hell had possessed you. And Tamara came to my room and said there were more fish in the sea. So I had sex with her. It wasn't exactly memorable. In fact, it was lousy!''

Celie stared at him. She tried to digest that, to see it as Jace had seen it. But when she had, it made no difference.

''Exactly,'' she said softly.

Jace looked at her, uncomprehending. ''Huh?''

''It was lousy, you said.''

''What?''

''You knew!''

He looked baffled. ''Knew what?''

''That it was lousy! You had comparisons. You could judge. You could tell the difference. And you'll...you'll be able to tell about me!'' Celie pulled out of his grasp and walked away, then turned to face him. ''It's not about Tamara, Jace,'' she admitted in a low voice. ''It's about me. I wasn't enough even for Matt who didn't know anything. You've been with lots of women. You've slept with Tamara Lynd. I can't compete with that.''

''I love you, damn it!''

Celie swallowed. ''Now,'' she said. ''Now you think you do.''

''I do,'' Jace said just as stubbornly.

But she didn't accept that. ''It's not real. It was, like Simone said, a shipboard romance. It won't last.''

''Of course it will last.''

''No. It won't. You thought you had this thing for me for a long time. It's just a matter of pursuit. The thrill of the hunt, the joy of the chase.'' She'd thought about it all night. ''I was like the fish in the lake that you couldn't catch, so you kept coming back until you did.''

Jace was shaking his head, staring at her, a dazed look on his face.

''But then you caught me. And you're happy. You think

you've got what you want. And you do. For now. But it's not enough for fifty years."

Jace said something very rude that made Celie blink. Then he said, "I don't believe I'm hearing this."

"It's true, Jace. Once you've had me, you'll be ready to move on. You've had other women. You've had Tamara—"

"I never loved any other woman!"

"I won't be enough for you. I can't be," she said. And as much as she hated to admit it, that was the bottom-line truth. She couldn't marry him and then fail him. It would be worse than not marrying him at all.

For a long minute Jace didn't speak. He stared at her, at his feet, at the ceiling, then back at her again.

"So it all comes back to Matt, does it?" he said quietly. "You loved him that much?"

"No," Celie said. "I didn't! I don't! I thought I loved him. But I loved the idea of getting married. He was just…just the reason."

"And me? Was I just another reason?" Jace said bitterly.

"Of course not!"

Fierce eyes bored into her. "So you love me?"

"It's not about love, " Celie argued, avoiding his question.

"Yes, it is," Jace insisted. "It's only about love. I love you, damn it, Celie O'Meara. And I'm not going to get tired of you in fifty years or even a hundred and fifty, if we have that long."

"We won't," Celie said.

"We might."

"Stop it, Jace!" She thrust the ring at him again. "Here. Take it."

He pulled his hands out of his pockets, but he didn't reach out and take the ring. Instead he folded his arms across his chest. "No. I'm not going to take it. I asked you to marry me and you said yes."

"And now I'm saying no."

"Too bad."

She frowned. "What do you mean, too bad?"

"The wedding is scheduled."

"We'll call it off."

"No, I won't."

"Then I will."

"You made a promise. You promised to marry me."

"I'll fail you!" There! She'd said it.

But Jace just shook his head. "No. You won't. I believe in you. I believe in our commitment. Don't you?"

"I'm a realist, Jace."

"You're a coward."

Her lips pressed tightly together as she absorbed the blow. "Maybe I am," she allowed. "So take back the ring. You don't want to marry a coward."

"I want to marry you, Celie. And I'm not taking back the ring. I gave it to you in good faith. You accepted it. I'm going ahead with the wedding. And if you don't want to get married, you know what you'll have to do—jilt me."

It was the most ridiculous thing she'd ever heard.

Who insisted on going ahead with a wedding if the bride said she wasn't going to show up?

Jace Tucker, that was who.

Stubborn, bullheaded trouble-making Jace!

Celie despaired of him. She was sorry—God only knew *how* sorry. But she knew, sorry or not, that she was right. She had been living in a dream world, believing that she would be able to keep up with Jace, satisfy Jace.

But it wasn't true.

How could she possibly keep a man like that interested in her? She hadn't even been able to hang on to Matt! And

Sloan! Sloan thought she was a nice girl, but he'd never been interested in her—only in Polly.

She'd gained some self-confidence over the past few months, but after she'd heard Tamara's words, her fledgling confidence had been dealt a death blow.

She was being sensible, practical, smart. She was saving them both a lifetime of misery, because there was no way on earth he could possibly be content with her for the rest of his life.

He'd gone to bed with Tamara Lynd, for heaven's sake!

And while she absolutely believed him when he said it had been a one-off and that he wasn't about to go to bed with Tamara again, that didn't mean he wouldn't be tempted by some other woman.

Of course he would be tempted, because there was nothing special or wonderful or astonishing about Celie O'Meara that would keep him home and content for the rest of his life.

He would get bored. He would want greener pastures. The fault wasn't his; it was hers. In the long run Celie didn't have the confidence in herself that she had what it took.

Jace was just too stubborn to see it. Yet.

He would, though. When she refused to see him, refused to talk to him, called the caterer and the florist and the minister, he'd realize she meant what she said.

And that would be the end of it.

''A tux?'' Artie said doubtfully. He looked at Jace over the baling wire and shook his head. ''I don't believe I've ever worn a tux.''

''Me, neither,'' Jace said. ''But it's what Celie wants. So we're going after work this afternoon to get fitted.''

He'd called the place in Bozeman Celie had mentioned and told them he'd be in. He'd called Noah and Taggart and Gus, too, and told them to get over there and get fitted. He didn't put up with any arguments. He'd moaned and groaned himself. Now he was just going for it.

"Got a suit," Artie went on. "Navy blue serge. Bought it when me an' Maudie got married."

Which would make it sixty-odd years old, Jace thought. "We'll bury you in it, Artie. You're wearing a tux for the wedding."

Artie looked at him with surprise. "Gettin' mighty bossy, ain't you?"

Getting mighty desperate, that was the truth of the matter.

He'd called the minister this morning to make sure everything was set for a week from Saturday.

"Who is this?" the minister sounded surprised. "Jace Tucker? But I thought—Celie said—"

"Celie's just panickin' a little," Jace said. "Hold the date. Hold the time. We'll be there."

He ended up having to do the same with Poppy about the flowers, with Denise, the caterer, with Julie Ann, who was making the cake.

"Celie canceled," Poppy told him about the flowers, Denise told him about the meal, Julie Ann told him about the cake.

And to every one of them Jace said, "No. It's on. We'll be there." And when Julie Ann had sounded doubtful, he'd promised her a check.

"You'll make the cake if you get paid, right?"

"Yes, but—"

"Fine. I'll bring you a check."

Just to make sure, he paid the caterer, too. And the organist for the church. He also sent Polly a check payable to the Elmer Town Fund for rent of the town hall.

She called him when she got it. "What are you doing? Celie said the wedding is off."

"It's not off," Jace said firmly.

"Oh? Well, good. I wondered if the Tamara thing would give her cold feet."

"She, um, got a little nervous," Jace said.

"Well, it was in the past." Polly gave him the benefit of the doubt. "Just like Sloan's experience with her. And I can tell you *that* won't happen again!"

Jace believed her. There was no way Sloan was going to stray from a woman like Polly. There was no way he'd ever stray from Celie.

He loved her and he always would.

He just hoped that by October third at 3:00 p.m., Celie believed it, too.

It was the most bizarre thing in the world.

Celie had called off the wedding—and no one believed her.

She'd phoned the caterer, the florist, the minister, the organist, the baker—everyone who had anything to do with the plans she'd made. She'd told them it was off. And they'd all said they were very sorry to hear it.

And the next day the baker had called and asked if she wanted raspberries on the cake.

"There is no cake," Celie said. "There isn't going to be a wedding."

"Right, Jace said you'd say that," Julie Ann said soothingly. "Don't worry, it's just nerves."

"It's *not* nerves!" Celie insisted.

"Fine. Do you want raspberries or not?" Julie Ann persisted.

"If Jace arranged this," Celie practically shouted, "ask Jace!"

She did the same thing when the caterer called and asked whether to serve baby carrots or green beans. She did the same when the organist wanted her to narrow down the music choices for the wedding.

"Ask Jace," she said, ready to pull out her hair. "Just ask Jace!"

The banging on the door startled Artie. He frowned and dropped his fork. "What in tarnation...?"

Jace, who had a fairly good idea who was doing the banging, pushed himself away from the table and stood up. "I'll take care of it."

It was, just as he'd thought, Celie fuming and pacing on the porch. She rounded on him when he opened the door. "Exactly what do you think you're doing?" she demanded.

He dabbed at his lips with his napkin. "Eatin' dinner?"

She made a furious explosive sound. "With Poppy! With Julie Ann! With the minister!"

"Just firmin' things up," Jace said easily, admiring the high color in her cheeks. "I told Julie Ann yes to the raspberries. I always liked raspberries. I said green beans rather than carrots, but if you want—"

"I don't want! I don't care! I'm *not* marrying you!"

"Sure you are, Cel'. You got to. You love me."

But she wished she didn't. Oh, God, how she wished!

It was because she loved him that she wouldn't marry him, damn it. It was because she didn't want to fail him, to hurt him, to *bore* him for the rest of his life, for goodness' sakes!

He didn't realize how boring she was. She hadn't really realized it until she'd compared herself with Tamara. That had been a wake-up call, all right.

It had awakened every dormant insecurity Celie had ever known.

She had bid on Sloan, yes. And that had been a brave, daring—let's face it, desperate—thing to do. But all her weekend with Sloan had done was prove that she had good taste in men. It hadn't proved that a man like Sloan could love her.

On the contrary, he loved Polly, who was everything she was not. Polly was tough and clever and capable. Polly had always faced the world head-on, had dared to do things that Celie wouldn't dare in a million lifetimes.

She was the right sort of woman for Sloan. She—or Tamara or some other woman—was undoubtedly the right woman for Jace.

But Jace—stupid Jace!—didn't believe that!

He thought she was some daring, adventurous woman who went sailing off into the sunset. In fact, nothing was further from the truth.

She might have sailed off into a few sunsets just recently, but she'd had to make herself do it. They'd been memorable, but no more memorable than the sunsets she'd seen on Jace and his sister's ranch when they'd come home. She'd visited half a dozen foreign ports, too, and she was glad she had. But they hadn't captivated her, either. No more than life in Elmer did. She was every bit the boring provincial girl Armand had always believed she was.

How could Jace Tucker, who had been to bed with Tamara Lynd and heaven knew how many other enticing women, possibly want to spend the rest of his life with the most boring woman on earth?

He could get a job as a wedding consultant, Jace figured, by the time this was all over. And he might have to if he had to get out of town because he'd become the laughingstock of the entire Shields Valley.

It was a possibility—because as time went on, he found that Celie was being just as stubborn as he was.

After their battle on Artie's front porch, from which

she'd stomped away, furious, she had avoided him everywhere.

He'd gone into the grocery store the following day as she was checking out. She had turned her back on him and kept right on talking to Carol Ferguson.

"Hey, Cel'," he'd said. "How ya doin', Carol?"

Carol had talked to him, had chatted a bit. Celie had pretended he wasn't even there.

The next day Julie Ann had called him to ask about the cake topper.

"The what?" Jace was mystified.

"The bit that sits on top," Julie Ann explained. "Celie didn't know what she wanted before. And she won't say now. She says it's your wedding, ask you." Julie Ann seemed to think this was very odd behavior, but dutifully she asked, "So take your pick. You can have a bride and groom, a dove of peace or wedding bells."

He should probably pick the dove of peace, Jace thought. It was clearly what they needed. But even more than that he needed a bride. "The bride and groom," he told Julie Ann.

At least that way one would be there.

"Celie ticked at you?" Artie asked him the Wednesday before the wedding when Jace came home for lunch.

Jace had deliberately not said anything to Artie about Celie's change of heart. He knew Artie. Artie would have a solution. And the last thing he needed right now was a ninety-year-old know-it-all telling him what to do.

"She's just gettin' nervous," Jace answered.

Artie nodded as he slapped ham on bread and slathered mustard on top. "I'll say," he agreed. "Told me she wasn't marryin' you."

So much for circumspection. "What'd I tell you? Nerves," Jace said, trying to sound calm.

Artie stuck another piece of bread on top of the ham,

whacked through it with the butcher knife and handed Jace the sandwich. "You sure it's just nerves?"

"Of course I'm sure."

"So we're still gonna wear them tuxes?" Artie, for all his grousing, seemed to be looking forward to his tux.

"We're going to wear the tuxes," Jace said firmly.

"That's what I told her."

Ho, boy. Jace raised his brows, imagining Celie's reaction to that. "And she said?"

"Didn't say nothin'. Just got all red in the face and sort of steamy lookin'. That's what made me think she was ticked at you."

"How can you lie to that defenseless old man?" Celie's voice was shrill on the phone against his ear.

"Huh?" Jace had been expecting Taggart to call back about some lumber. He straightened up now, hearing Celie instead. His heart began beating double time. "Hey, Cel'. How are you?"

"Don't you 'Hey, Cel' me! Why haven't you told Artie?"

"Told him what?"

"You know very well what! He still thinks the wedding is on."

"It is."

"It's not! You know it's not. You're going to look like a fool."

Jace paused. "Maybe I will," he said slowly. "I guess that's up to you."

Celie was sitting by herself in the kitchen listening to the clock tick and scratching Sid the cat's ears when she heard footsteps on the porch.

Whoever was at the door, she wasn't answering it.

She didn't want to see anyone, didn't want to talk to

anyone. Didn't want to tell one more person that no, she wasn't going to marry Jace Tucker tomorrow even though he was telling everyone she was!

"They can just go away," she told Sid, who scraped his jaw against her ankle and butted her calf with his head. "We don't need anyone, do we?"

But before Sid could respond, the door opened and Polly, Sara, Lizzie, Daisy and Jack all poured into the room, banging and talking and jostling.

"Hey, Aunt Celie!" Jack beamed at her.

"Hi, Aunt Celie!" Daisy and Lizzie chimed.

"Hi, Cel'," Polly said, "Got your dancin' shoes on?"

Celie just stared at them all. "What on earth are you doing here?"

"We came for the wedding," Sara said. The rest of them nodded.

"And tonight we're going to The Barrel," Polly said cheerfully.

"What?"

An evening spent at The Barrel bar down in Livingston near the date of a wedding was a tradition among local women and had been since World War II when a rancher's daughter, set to marry in the morning, had met a visiting sailor there and had run off with him instead.

"Tempting fate," they had called it ever after. Women who did it and went on to marry their chosen man had good marriages—or so the story went.

"I'm not getting married," Celie insisted.

The girls looked scandalized, Jack looked stunned.

Polly rolled her eyes. "You do whatever you want tomorrow, but I'm not missing a night at The Barrel. Get dressed. Let's go pick up Mom and Cait. Get those dancing shoes on!"

It was crazy, Celie thought. Insane. Ridiculous. How

could you go out to test fate against a man you were determined you weren't marrying?

But they went. The Barrel was loud, rocking, riotous and crowded as The Barrel usually was on Friday night. Not Celie's sort of place at all.

Jace had been here, though. Celie remembered that he'd rescued Sara last winter when she'd come here looking for a ride home. There were a hundred girls here more suited to Jace than she was. She wanted to go home.

"How about him?" Cait, her best friend from high school and now her stepsister, poked her in the ribs.

"What? Who?" Celie turned, baffled, "What are you talking about?"

"Him." Cait pointed to a hunky young cowboy wearing skin-tight stacked Wranglers and a hot-pink shirt. He was playing pool, bending over the table, giving them a very nice view. "We're supposed to be offering you alternatives to Jace," Cait reminded her.

"I don't need alternatives," Celie said. "I'm not marrying Jace."

"Or him." Felicity Jones nodded her head in the direction of another handsome man dancing with a hungry-looking female.

Celie shook her head and looked away. "Not interested."

They offered up half a dozen more—a stud playing Keno, two rodeo cowboys clearly just passing through, a dapper-looking gent with a handlebar mustache.

"There are some interesting specimens here," Polly said finally after she'd looked over the crowd. Then she looked at her sister. "But none quite as interesting as Jace."

Celie, whose traitorous mind had been thinking along the same lines, deliberately turned away.

She didn't want to compare Jace to the rest of Livingston's manhood. She already knew the verdict. He was better than all of them. Handsomer than all of them. More wonderful than all of them.

The problem wasn't what Jace was lacking, damn it!

The problem was her!

She felt like curling into a tiny ball of misery.

Polly touched her shoulder. ''Come on. I think it's time we went home.''

Jace had been to his fair share of stag nights.

He'd always laughed and joked and commiserated with the poor son of a gun who, in scant hours, would be relinquishing his freedom, trading his free rein for a double yoke.

Now on Friday night at the Dew Drop, his buddies held a stag night for him—and he could only hope that the woman he loved would be at his wedding.

''You sure you're ready for this?'' Taggart teased him after he'd raised his glass in a toast. ''Celie doesn't seem to be too thrilled.''

''Celie's nervous,'' Jace said. ''She got jilted once, remember.''

Everyone remembered. There was a moment of silence as they stared into their beer and thought about that jerk Matt Williams.

Then Taggart shrugged. ''Well, hell, man, you're not Matt. She oughta know you won't do that to her!''

''Right,'' Shane Nichols seconded it. And half a dozen local cowboys agreed.

And they were right. Jace wouldn't. Ever.

But it was looking very much like she was going to do it to him. She hadn't come around as he had hoped. She hadn't been bowled over by his determination. She hadn't come to tell him she was sorry, that he was right. She hadn't said she loved him.

He wasn't even sure now that she did.

Maybe for her it *had* been a shipboard romance.

Maybe he had swept her off her feet, made her giddy, caused her to dream—but only briefly. Maybe now that she was back in Elmer, her memories of the pain of the past meant more to her than he did.

She was still saying she wasn't going to marry him.

He was still insisting she was. It was just nerves, he'd told everyone. Celie was just remembering the past, remembering what had happened to her last time. And who could blame her? he'd said. But this time wasn't going to be like last time. Of course the wedding was still on. He'd see them at the church at three o'clock on Saturday.

''Here now. Time for a toast by the best man,'' Jace heard Artie say, and he turned to see the old man raise his glass. ''To the best doggone feller I ever known,'' Artie said, ''and to the gal I love like—'' he faltered momentarily and cleared his throat ''—like a granddaughter. I'm so glad they're gonna spend the rest of their lives makin' each other happy!''

Ten

"She's not gonna do it, you know." Jace came and stood in the doorway to Artie's bedroom as the old man was just climbing into bed.

He had to say something, had to prepare Artie. He couldn't let him get all dressed up tomorrow and stand there at the front of the church next to Jace, expecting to see Celie walk down the aisle to meet them when she wasn't going to.

Jace swallowed past the hard lump in his throat and pressed on. "She isn't gonna marry me, Artie."

Artie turned from the bed slowly and straightened up again. "No?"

Jace shook his head. "'Fraid not." He mustered up a wan smile.

Artie wasn't fooled. "You love her."

Jace swallowed again. "Always. I'll always love her. But she—I don't know anymore. Maybe she doesn't really love me.'' It was hard to get the words out. He hunched his shoulders and bent his head.

''So what're you gonna do?'' Artie asked.

Jace's faint smile turned wry. ''You mean you're not going to tell me?''

Artie grinned just a little at the hit. ''A feller doesn't live ninety years without learning a few things,'' he said. ''Don't mean to boss you. I guess I just reckoned you could use a little hard-won wisdom.''

''I still could,'' Jace admitted. ''If I go there tomorrow and she doesn't come—''

It didn't bear thinking about. Yet maybe it was exactly what he deserved—a just revenge for whatever part he'd played in Matt's jilting her all those years ago. Was the world really that fair?

''Well now,'' Artie said. ''Lemme tell you a little story.'' He sat on the bed and nodded toward the rocking chair.

Jace, knotting his fingers together, obediently sat down. Would it be zen this time? he wondered. Or some other self-help guru Artie had stumbled upon. It didn't matter, Jace decided. He just needed help.

''Long time ago,'' Artie said, ''when I was younger than you are now, I met the girl of my dreams...'' He leaned forward, rested his forearms on his knees and stared down at the braid rug beneath his feet.

So it wasn't going to be zen? It was going to be personal? The story of Artie's courtship of Maudie? Jace leaned forward, too.

''I was cowboyin' out in Washington State,'' Artie went on. ''Big spread owned by a feller named Jack Carew. He had a couple a thousand head of Herefords, a ranch that run for miles into the sweetest country you can imagine, and the prettiest daughter you ever did see.''

''Maudie?''

But Artie didn't reply. He went right on. ''I fancied the

daughter somethin' fierce. But I was just a broke cowpoke workin' on her daddy's ranch. Didn't have nothin' to recommend me, that's for sure.''

''Except your charming personality,'' Jace said dryly.

Artie lifted his head. ''Well, sure. 'Cept that.'' He gave Jace a faint grin and flexed his bony shoulders. ''Turned out to be enough. Turned out she fancied me, too.'' The old man flushed slightly. ''We had a, um...bit of a fling. Well, it wasn't a fling really. We was serious. And I asked her to marry me.''

Jace nodded. And they'd lived happily ever after for fifty-odd years. So what did this have to do with him and Celie?

''She said yes. But her daddy said no. Said I couldn't support her the way she ought to be.''

''I hope you told him to go to hell,'' Jace said.

Artie's mouth twisted. ''Couldn't. He was right.''

''But—''

The old man shrugged and bent his head again. ''He was. She'd had pert much ever'thing she could want, includin' a college education. Her ol' man was right when he said she was wastin' her time on me.''

''I didn't know Maudie had a college education.''

Artie's head snapped up. ''Will you stop talkin' an' start *listenin'* fer a change? I ain't talkin' about Maudie!''

Jace's mouth opened. And shut. He stared at Artie as if he'd never seen the old man before. Not Maudie? Then who—?

''She didn't care what I had,'' Artie went on, a faraway expression on his face. ''Told me so. Told me she loved me an' all that didn't matter to her, that I just had to believe her.'' He sighed. ''But I didn't.''

He sat up straight and threw his shoulders back and stared straight ahead. ''I was too worried her old man was right. Figured he had to be, him bein' so smart an' so successful an' all. She wanted me to run away with her. Told me we didn't need him. Didn't need anybody but each other. But I didn't believe her. I didn't want to get hurt. Didn't want to hurt her. So I played it safe,'' he said bitterly. ''I quit an' I came back to Elmer. Didn't even tell her where I was goin'.'' He let out a sigh, then added almost as an afterthought, ''Couple a years later I married Maudie.''

And?

Jace just looked at him, trying to make the connections Artie expected him to make. Hell, this was harder than zen. He didn't say anything, just sat there trying to figure it out.

''I loved her,'' Artie said. ''She loved me. I shoulda taken the risk.''

''You don't know that,'' Jace said. ''It might not have lasted.''

Artie met his gaze. ''It lasted,'' he said simply.

Jace shook his head, disbelieving. ''But...but Maudie...you and Maudie...''

Artie sighed and rubbed a hand over the wisps of white hair on his head. ''I loved Maudie. I was faithful to Maudie. Always. Even after Anna came...''

''Anna? That was her name? She came? To Elmer?''

''Tracked me down,'' Artie said, his gaze still faraway. ''Took her three years. Daddy wasn't inclined to tell her where I'd come from, and I never had. But she was stubborn and determined. She still loved me,'' he said wistfully. ''An' she brung somethin' to show me.'' His gaze came back to meet Jace's. ''Our daughter.''

''Daughter? You had a—'' Jace felt as if he'd been punched.

''Have,'' Artie corrected. He smiled faintly. ''Still have. She doesn't know.''

''But you do? You keep track—'' Jace was floundering. ''Where—?''

"Here. She's here," Artie replied. "Always has been... ever since. It's Joyce."

Jace stared. *Joyce?* Celie's *mother?*

"Then you...you're...you're Celie's *grandfather?* For real?"

The old man's eyes shimmered. He nodded. "Yep."

"Good God." A thousand questions swirled in Jace's mind. "But what—how?"

Artie shrugged. "I was married to Maudie. Anna understood. She didn't want to hurt her. Neither did I. Anna stayed because she and her father didn't agree about the baby. She needed a friend. And that was me. I couldn't marry her, but I could be there for Joyce, be her stand-in father. So that's what I was."

Jace tried to bend his mind around that. He remembered Joyce's mother. She'd been a teacher in the Elmer school. A widow, he'd always thought. Now he looked at Artie, feeling dazed.

Artie shook his head. "It coulda been different," he said. "I shoulda believed in her love. That's all I'm sayin'." He leaned forward again and fixed Jace with a steady stare. "You don't need my advice. When you find a love like that, you do exactly what you're doin', boy. You believe."

After the night at The Barrel, Celie didn't go home.

The house was full. Besides Polly and the kids, her other sister, Mary Beth, and her husband and their triplet daughters were coming up for the wedding.

"There's not going to be a wedding," Celie had insisted.

But Polly said, "When you mobilize triplets, you don't change your plans. Wedding or not, they're coming."

And, even later, a plane from Mexico would be bringing Sloan.

They could all visit. The triplets could play with Jack. Mary Beth and Polly would be glad to get together. They didn't see each other all that often. Tomorrow they could all go out and visit Joyce and Walt. A good time would be had by all.

They'd never miss the wedding that wasn't going to happen.

At least that's what Celie told herself late that night when everyone else had gone home and she checked herself into a motel room in Livingston.

It was a cold room with thin walls and even thinner carpet. Depressing. Grim. Looking exactly the way she felt, which was awful.

Why did she feel so bad? She was doing the right thing.

But Jace was going to be hurt.

He was going to show up for the wedding. He was going to stand up there in front of all those people and wait for her. It was going to be worse for him than it had been for her with Matt. She hadn't marched up the aisle. She'd taken his call privately. She hadn't had to make the announcement, face the crowd, see the pity, hear the snickers.

Not then.

Later, of course, she had. And she couldn't deny that it had hurt.

She didn't want Jace to be hurt. She loved him. That was the whole point of not marrying him.

Wasn't it?

Celie flung herself down on the bed. Oh, God. She didn't know anymore.

Was it Jace she was protecting? Or was it herself?

For years she would have loved to have made a fool of Jace. And he knew it. If he was everything she'd once thought he was, he would never make himself this vulnerable. He would never give her the chance. He'd be laughing at her—not giving her the chance to let the world laugh at him.

So why was he doing it?

Because he loved her. Really.

Celie rolled over and stared at the ceiling, letting the words enter her mind—and finally, enter her heart. She'd heard them; he'd said them.

But she hadn't really believed them before. Hadn't really understood them. Hadn't known how vulnerable they made him, hadn't realized the depth of his faith.

He loved her.

That meant he trusted her—not just for a week on a ship or the month of a fling—but forever. It meant Jace saw something in her, believed in something in her beyond even what she was capable of seeing.

He was right. It had nothing to do with Tamara. It was only about the two of them. About their faith in each other. Their trust in each other.

Celie knew that Jace believed.

The question was: did she?

"We look mighty handsome in these here tuxes," Artie said, studying Jace's white face and his own ruddy one in the mirror as they waited, resplendent in their formal finery in the room just behind the church.

They were all dressed up with just minutes to go—and Jace was feeling sicker by the second. He shouldn't have pushed her. He should have waited. Let her give him the ring back, courted her some more. Been persuasive. But he hadn't. He'd been his usual stubborn self—he'd pushed too hard, trusted too much and dared her when he never should have dared.

And now it was too late. He was committed. He had to go out there now and make an ass of himself. And Celie wasn't going to show up.

He'd seen Polly minutes before and she'd said she hadn't seen Celie since last night.

"What the hell do you mean you haven't seen her since last night? She lives with you!"

"She didn't come home after we went to The Barrel. Too many people," Polly apologized. "Said she wanted some space. A motel room, I think. And no, not with another man," she said, grinning at his look of horror. "It's just nerves, Jace."

But it wasn't. It was more than nerves. Jace knew that now. Oh, God, oh, God, oh, God.

The organ music started. Jace, who had been counting hours up until last night, now wished he had a few hundred more.

"That's our cue." Artie poked him in the ribs.

Jace thought he might throw up. "Artie, I—"

"Celie's a good gal," Artie said firmly. "The best. Let's go. Sooner we go, sooner we can get you hitched. Sooner we get you hitched, sooner I can loosen my collar. I know I said I liked this tux, but goldarn it, boy, this necktie's durned near killin' me."

With Artie at his side, Jace went to stand at the front of the church. It was full to bursting. Everyone who knew him, everyone who knew Celie was there. Alice and Cloris were right up front next to his sister's family. On the other side were Walt and Joyce; Walt's daughter, An, and her two children; Mary Beth and her husband, Jack, and the triplets. Taggart and Felicity Jones and their kids were there, as were the Tanners and McCalls, both the Nichols brothers and their families, plus Gus and Mary Holt. With them was Walt's younger daughter, Cait, holding her brand-new son, Andrew.

Jace didn't see Cait's husband, Charlie, until a flash went off. And he realized that he'd forgotten to contact a photographer. Or maybe he hadn't forgotten. Maybe it had been Freudian—not wanting the fiasco immortalized on film.

But whether he wanted it or not, Charlie was busy taking lots of photos of everyone who'd come to witness his marriage to Celie. Or not.

Oh, God. He didn't believe it. There, halfway back, was Tamara on Gavin's arm. She beamed at him and waggled her fingers. Jace shut his eyes. When he opened them again he spotted Celie's ship roommate, Allison, and that oily Armand and—good grief—Gloria Campanella!

And then the organ stopped. There was an intake of breath, a hush fell over everything—and then the minister appeared. The organist began ''Here Comes the Bride,'' and Jace wanted to go through the floor.

Daisy was the first to come up the aisle, She wore a deep blue, floor-length gown, and she moved with careful, measured steps, at the speed of a snail. She was trying not to smile—or to frown—Jace wasn't sure which. She was managing to look worried all the same. After her came Lizzie, equally slowly, equally worried.

Jace felt ill.

Why the hell didn't they stop the wedding? If she wasn't there, why were they making him go through with this? They could say something, couldn't they?

Or was it up to him?

Sara was next. Her dress was like the others, but fuller to accommodate the burgeoning child. She looked beautiful, so like Celie that it hurt almost to look at her. She came down the aisle like a ship under full sail. Only when she got to the front did she look at Jace. She smiled at him, looking nervous. Looking worried.

And then came Polly, the matron of honor. Her riot of reddish-brown hair had been severely tamed and knotted elegantly on top of her head. She moved slowly, too, staring straight ahead, chin high.

Jace looked around her, trying to see behind her, daring to hope. But he didn't see Sloan. And he didn't see Celie.

Polly reached the front of the church. Her eyes met his, and he thought he saw sadness in them. But her chin stayed up, as if she were willing his to.

The organist played gamely on. And on. The congregation looked at Jace and everyone assembled at the front of the church, and then they looked toward the back. They began to murmur, to wonder…

And then…omigod…there she was!

Her hair was flying all over the place, her cheeks were bright red, and she was wearing jeans and a sweatshirt. But she was hanging on to a grinning Sloan's tux-clad arm and she was walking—not slowly at all—down the aisle to meet him!

The murmurs grew louder. The minister coughed. Artie cleared his throat. Polly and her daughters were caught between laughing and gaping. Charlie Seeks Elk was shooting a ton of pictures.

''I had a flat tire,'' Celie said for Jace's ears only, ''after I got over my crisis of faith. But I'm here now and I'm ready if you are.''

''I'm ready,'' Jace said, and took her hand in his.

The minister nodded. He smiled and gave a little shake of his head. ''Dearly beloved, we are gathered here together…''

It was, in all, a wedding to remember.

They'd forgotten to plan a honeymoon.

''A guy can only think of so much,'' Jace explained as they stood in the kitchen of Polly's house late in the evening of their wedding day. The reception was over. The crowds had dispersed. Sloan and Polly and their bunch had gone one way, Mary Beth and her family had gone another. It was just the two of them. ''Planning a wedding takes a lot out of a fellow.''

''I did most of the work,'' Celie reminded him.

''Well, yeah,'' Jace agreed. ''But only before you got cold feet.''

''They're warm now,'' Celie assured him, waggling her toes.

Jace just grinned. ''Prove it.''

''I will,'' Celie promised. ''As soon as we get to the cabin.''

When the honeymoon lapse had been discovered, Taggart Jones had offered his cabin. ''It's quiet. Isolated. Private.''

''A perfect place for a honeymoon,'' Shane Nichols had said cheerfully with a wink at his wife, Poppy.

Celie hadn't understood that. ''I thought he and Poppy went to Reno for theirs.''

Jace didn't know. He didn't care. ''Come on, then, let's go.''

''I have to get packed and get changed.''

''You look fine.'' She was wearing the jeans and sweatshirt she'd got married in. He, thank God, had changed out of his tux long ago.

''I'll be just a minute,'' Celie promised. She hurried upstairs.

Jace cooled his heels in the kitchen. In his mind he replayed the wedding. He saw Celie again in his mind's eye as he had seen her coming down the aisle. It was a vision he'd never forget. And it meant more to him than he could ever say.

She'd come to him as she was—because she loved him. The dress hadn't mattered. Perfection hadn't mattered. It was their love that had mattered.

Artie, the old son of a gun, had been right again—you just had to believe.

The sound of footsteps on the stairs caused him to turn around. His jaw dropped. He stared.

Celie was coming down the stairs in her wedding dress.

All of it. Yards and yards and yards of it. She looked ravishing, astonishing, utterly beautiful. And wholly inappropriate.

Jace, grinning, said, ''What the hell are you doin'? We're goin' up to the back of the beyond!''

But Celie shrugged happily. ''Well, I couldn't not wear it, could I? Besides, I couldn't let you off the hook completely.''

''Huh?''

''Every man needs a challenge,'' Celie told him, sliding her arms around him, kissing him and fanning the flames of desire.

''Challenge?'' Jace said warily.

Celie grinned. ''Only forty or fifty buttons or so.''

* * * * *

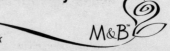

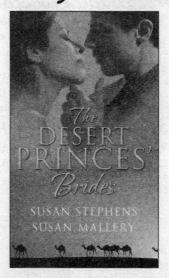

***A mistress should be at his command…
At his pleasure…
And in his bed!***

But these tempting beauties will make these three tycoons break *all* their rules!

**Available
19th December 2008**

***Wedded at his decree…
Pleasured in his bed…
Taken for his revenge!***

But these three commanding Mediterranean billionaires may just have met their match!

**Available
2nd January 2009**

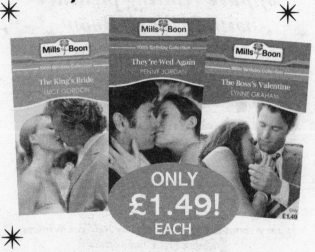

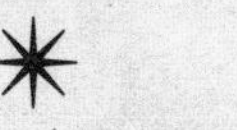

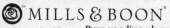